PEACEKE

Mischa Berlinski is the author of the novel *Fieldwork*, a finalist for the National Book Award. He is the recipient of a Whiting Writers' Award and the American Academy of Arts and Letters' Addison M. Metcalf Award.

ALSO BY MISCHA BERLINSKI

Fieldwork

PEACEKEEPING

Mischa Berlinski

Atlantic Books
London

First published in the United States in 2016 by Sarah Crichton Books, an imprint of Farrar, Straus and Giroux, a division of Macmillan, New York.

Published in trade paperback in Great Britain in 2016 by Atlantic Books, an imprint of Atlantic Books Ltd.

10 9 8 7 6 5 4 3 2 1

A CIP catalogue record for this book is available from the British Library.

Trade paperback ISBN: 978 1 84887 138 0
E-book ISBN: 978 1 78649 045 2

Printed and bound in Great Britain by TJ International Ltd, Padstow

Atlantic Books
An Imprint of Atlantic Books Ltd
Ormond House
26–27 Boswell Street
London
WC1N 3JZ

www.atlantic-books.co.uk

In memory of my mother, Toby Saks (1942–2013)

Degagé pa peché.
Getting by isn't a sin.
—CREOLE PROVERB

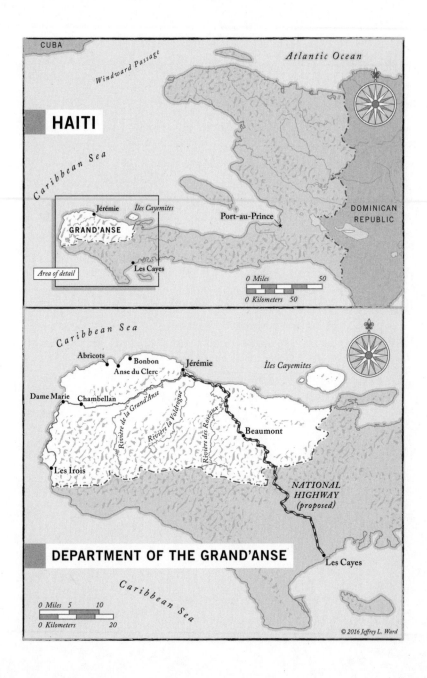

CUBA

Windward Passage

Atlantic Ocean

HAITI

Caribbean Sea

Jérémie   Îles Cayemites

GRAND'ANSE

Port-au-Prince

DOMINICAN REPUBLIC

Area of detail

Les Cayes

0 Miles   50
0 Kilometers   50

Caribbean Sea

Abricots   Bonbon
Anse du Clerc   Jérémie

Îles Cayemites

Dame Marie   Chambellan

Rivière de la Grand'Anse

Rivière la Voldrogue

Rivière des Roseaux

Beaumont

Les Irois

NATIONAL
HIGHWAY
(proposed)

DEPARTMENT OF THE GRAND'ANSE

Caribbean Sea

Les Cayes

0 Miles   5   10
0 Kilometers   20

© 2016 Jeffrey L. Ward

PEACEKEEPING

What you have to understand is that a professionally conducted interrogation is not fair. For my part, I have almost two decades' experience conducting interrogations such as this one each and every day; most of the time, the suspect has never before been interrogated. I am certified in the Reid technique, both Level One and the Advanced Course; the suspect has not flown to Charlotte for the five-day seminar at the Airport Marriott in Advanced Tactics of Criminal Evasion. He does not know the rules in the way I do. He has come to my territory, my office, at the moment of my choosing. I am dressed in a suit and tie. I have my diplomas on the wall, and the shoulder holster of my firearm is visible. I have drunk my coffee, moved my bowels, taken a shower. I am not in a fine sweat and my heart is not beating like a bongo. And of course, the stakes are so much higher for him than for me: should I make a mistake, a criminal will go free, but I will still go home to my wife. Should he make a mistake, he will go to prison. Under these conditions, the moment a suspect sits in my office, naturally he is nervous.

That is always the first thing I say.

"You seem nervous." I try to say this with as much compassion as I can. "Is something bothering you?"

I have had many suspects simply collapse at this point. Almost every criminal—indeed, almost everyone, innocent or guilty—has an urge to confess; later, they will wonder why they didn't just stay quiet. Nobody who works in criminal justice doubts that we are born with sin on our hands.

"We need to clear a few things up," I say. "The sooner we clear things up, the sooner this will be over."

Now I'm required by law to add, "You don't need to stay here and talk to me. You can leave at any time, but I'd very much appreciate your assistance in getting this settled out, so you can get back to your business. You can also have a lawyer with you here if you like. Do you understand?"

In fifteen years, only a handful of suspects have availed themselves of their legal opportunity to stand up and walk out of my office. Only a handful. One was a seventeen-year-old boy named Antwan. He was accused of stealing a Corvette. The victim was the suspect's neighbor, and the victim was sure that Antwan was the culprit. The boy had apparently ogled the car just a little too long. The car was found smashed up in the bottom of a ravine a few days later.

Antwan said, "I don't got to be here, I'm out of here."

"That's no problem," I said. "We've got your endotriglyceride levels from that doorknob you're touching. We'll match those up against the steering wheel, and that'll tell us the whole story right there."

Antwan pulled down the sleeve of his hoodie and began wiping at the doorknob.

I said, "Son, why on earth wouldn't you want us to match up those endo-triglyceride levels if you're not involved in this? If you're afraid of what those endotriglyceride levels will tell me, you should sit right back down. If the truth comes out later and you been wasting my time, I won't be able to help you."

I was right. It was the moment. The endotriglyceride levels never lie. Antwan sat back down.

Then I tell the suspect that he is guilty. Full stop. He is guilty, and I know he is guilty. I tell him all the evidence we have against him, piling it up layer after layer until he feels entombed by his misdeeds, until the suspect is well-nigh positive he cannot escape. If I do not have solid evidence, I invent it.

Sometimes I will tell the suspect that he was caught on a hidden surveillance camera.

Sometimes I will tell him that we have an eyewitness against him.

Once, I told a suspect that Madame Roccaforte, a very well known psychic here in Watsonville County, had given me his name. She had seen him burning in a lake of fire.

The suspect will start to open his mouth, and I shush him quick. If he were to speak, we might start to argue. An interrogation is not a debate. Once he says, "I didn't do it!" it's that much easier to stare me in the eye and say it a second time. Or he might ask for a lawyer. So I say, "Now is the time for me to talk. Your time to talk will come later. For now, you just listen to me."

I do not want information from the suspect: I want a confession.

I say, "Antwan, all your friends tell me you're a pretty good kid, do all right in school, respect your mamma."

"Yes sir."

But his voice is wavering, and he doesn't make eye contact. He is biting his lip. He is staring at my Florsheims.

"But Antwan, I know you stole that vehicle. There is no doubt in my mind. Even if I didn't have the endotriglyceride levels to back me up in a court of law, I can see it right in your eyes. So we need to work together on this."

I let this sink in. And here, so much depends on my professionalism.

"Let me tell you what I know. They say you had that new job down at Arby's after school. They say you were even giving some money to your mom. That's good. They say you were running late all the time, having to take the bus down there every day, I could see that. And I know Lou Wendell. Oh boy!"

All of this has come out of my pre-interrogation interviews. Lou Wendell is the manager over at Arby's. You don't manage a successful franchise like Arby's for eight years without being a prick. Antwan nods up and down slowly, but his foot is jiggling, up-down-left-right, over and over again.

"If it was something like that—you taking that car because you were running late, thinking you'd lose your job, and getting in an accident—I think everyone understands, a good kid like you making a mistake. On the other hand, if it was just that you wanted to go for a joyride, well, that's another thing. Just take a man's car, drive it around for pleasure, ditch it in a gulley . . ."

I shake my head once or twice.

"You see, Antwan, the law makes a distinction between what we call crimes of necessity and crimes of malice, between what we need to do and what we just do because we feel like it. So if you were feeling rushed that afternoon because you can't afford to lose that job, and the keys were right there, and you thought you'd get that car back to him before he even notices it's gone, and you needed that vehicle—that's not the worst thing in the world."

Now Antwan is bobbing his head more than slightly, if I'm telling the story right. He doesn't even know he's doing it. He doesn't know that I've given him the choice between two stories. In one story, he can hold his head upright; in the other, he must live with his shame. Innocence is never an option.

You and the girl were just messing around; she was doing all sorts of crazy things; things just got out of control; you're not the kind of man to hurt a woman. Or: you are a predator. Violent. A threat to society.

A newborn baby in the house? Family comes before anything else. Who can blame a man for looking out for his own? Or: you kited those checks to buy meth, smoked the dope in your own house in front of your own baby.

Which would you choose?

Now Antwan might say, "I've never done something wrong before, you can ask—"

And I'll say, "See? That's good. That's real good. We can work with that. That shows this here was a misjudgment. That matters. I know what happened. I know this was an error in judgment, owing to the stress."

Antwan will be silent a long time. Maybe there are tears in his eyes.

All he wants is for this moment to be over.

So I say, "Antwan, my wife and I been planning a trip to the Keys since last November. We're supposed to be leaving tomorrow. I disappoint my wife and tell her our trip is over because I have to stay here working this case, getting you to tell me the truth that we both know about that car, waiting for your endotriglycerides to come back from the lab—believe you me, when I have to talk to the district attorney, you will feel my wife's pain. She's been dieting three weeks now, feeding me nothing but carrots. The first thing that district attorney is going to ask me when we decide how to proceed is whether you were a man. If I tell him how things really went down, about your error in judgment, about your stress—Christ alive, we all were young once. I can help you. But I need to know from you, right now, what happened."

I look at him a long time, not blinking. The very second he looks away, I say, "Now tell me all about it."

Most times it's just as easy as that.

Sometimes the crime is of greater gravity—a murder or a rape. These confessions, contrary to expectations, are often easier to produce, despite the greater punishment the criminal will incur. For in these cases the criminal's tension is also that much greater, as is his desire to tell his side of the story. He has been telling himself the story of his crime since the moment he pulled the trigger. This is certain: he has done nothing else but think about his crime. He wants to talk *about the most significant thing he has done in his life. A car thief, a vandal, a petty drug dealer will not always understand the gravity of his situation, the consequences of his actions. It will not seem serious to him. Never so a murderer.*

Immediately after the confession—and this is a moment of very great intimacy between myself and the suspect—the suspect will almost always offer a second justification of his crimes, an honest justification. It will come out as an afterthought. This is something he wants me to hear, and no matter what he says, it will remain between us. I already have what the law requires. Sometimes the justification is as simple as "I was bored and wanted to go for a ride," and sometimes as heartbreaking as "I needed the money to buy my daddy's heart medicine."

No matter what the crime, I always say, "I understand."

That's what I hope you'll say too.

PART ONE

1   There wasn't much to the town, really—a triangular spit of land between a river and the sea, and shaped like the bowl of a natural amphitheater, most every street sloping down sooner or later to the azure stage of the Caribbean or guttering out inconclusively into twisting warrens of dirt paths, the houses degenerating to huts, then hovels. In the city center, old wooden houses listed at improbable angles. Energetic, prosperous people had built these houses and carefully painted them, but the salt air had long ago stripped away the color, leaving them a uniform grayish brown. There was a small town square, the Place Dumas, around which a flock of motorcycle taxi drivers circumnavigated in the course of every sunny day, maneuvering always to stay in the shade, and a filthy market where the *marchandes* hacked up and sold goat cadavers under a nimbus of flies. On the Grand Rue, merchants in old-fashioned shophouses with imposing wrought iron balconies sold sacks of cement or PVC pipes, or bought coffee. Jérémie had more coffin makers than restaurants. There were fewer cars on the streets than donkeys. The Hotel Patience down on the Grand Rue was said to be a bordello; word was that the ladies of the night were fat. Several little shops, all identical, featured row upon row of gallon-size vats of mayonnaise, which fact I could not reconcile with the lack of ready refrigeration, and bottles of Night Train and Manischewitz—local belief held the latter was a powerful aphrodisiac. You could buy cans of Dole Tropical

Fruit mix, but you could not obtain a fresh vegetable; Jérémie was on the sea, but fresh fish was a rarity.

At midday, the dogs lay in the dusty streets panting, which is more or less what they did evening, morning, and night also, except when they copulated.

Whole days would pass discussing when the big boat from Port-au-Prince would arrive, staring out at the multicolored sea to register its earliest presence. The boat's arrival brought a momentary flurry of excitement as the cargo was unloaded and barefoot men, muscles straining, eyeballs bulging, dragged thousand-pound chariots of rice, Coca-Cola, or cement through the dusty streets.

My wife and I lived in a tumbledown gingerbread, at least a century old and shaded by a quartet of sprawling mango trees. It was one of the most beautiful houses in all of Haiti. A cool terrace ran around the house, where we ate our meals and dozed away the hot afternoons in the shade. In the evenings it was (mildly) exciting to sit outside in the rocking chair and watch thick purple strokes of lightning light up cloud mountains out over the Îles Cayemites. It was the kind of house in which one might have found behind the *acajou* armoire a map indicating the location in the untended garden of hidden treasure.

The windows of the house had no glass, just hurricane shutters, and very late at night I sometimes heard coming up from Basse-Ville the manic beating of drums and women's voices singing spooky songs with no melody. This was the only time Jérémie really came alive. My whole body would grow tense as I strained to hear more clearly this strange music, which would endure all through the night and well into sunrise. I had never before heard music like that. It was the music of a people laboring to communicate with unseen forces; it was the music of a people dancing wildly around a fire until seized up by some mighty unknown thing.

Only in these midnight dances would the languid tenor of the town change, revealing its frantic, urgent heart.

Our *chef d'administration* was a Trinidadian named Slim. His Sunday barbecues were animated by his personal vision of the United Nations as a brotherhood of man—Asian, African, and Occidental all seated together at plastic tables under big umbrellas eating hunks of jerk chicken. There were maybe a dozen of us there, in the dusty courtyard of his little concrete house.

I was talking to the *chef de transport*, Balu, from Tanzania—his long, glum face reminded me of Eeyore. Balu was unique in that in all his time in Haiti he never sought housing of his own. He kept a bedroll in the corner of his office and unrolled it at night. He had been living there for a year now.

I asked him once if this was difficult.

"I am come from African village!" he said. "This is everything good. I have electricity"—he was referring to the generators, which at Mission HQ went 24/7—"I have water. Maybe I am not even finding a house as good as this. Why should I be paying for anything more?"

Balu had been hired as local staff in Tanzania, supporting the UN Mission to Congo. He had done a good job and won himself a place in Haiti.

"I am not even number one in my village, or number two—I am number twelve!" he said. "If you ask anyone in village when I am boy where Balu will go one day, nobody will say, 'Balu is going one day to United Nations.' They will say, 'Balu, he is going straight to Hell!'"

Balu showed me photos of the house that he built for his family. The house was large and concrete, surrounded by a low wall. It was the Africa the Discovery Channel never shows: Balu had a subcompact car in the driveway, and there was a flowery little garden. Mrs. Balu was a pretty lady of substantial girth in a magnolia-printed dress, and the little Balus were obviously having some trouble sitting still for the photo, all smiles and teeth and elbows. Then there were Balu's eight brothers and sisters and their wives and their children and a congress of cousins and the elderly Mama Balu, Papa Balu having gone to his sweet reward.

I asked everyone I met on Mission to show me their families, and all the photos always looked like Balu's: the concrete houses, the fat wives, the children, the new car, the flat-screen television. There was something reassuring and wonderful about those photos. If you understand those pictures, you'll understand something about the world we live in.

When Balu gets back home to Tanzania, he'll be showing Lady Balu and the Baluettes photos of his life on Mission. Somewhere in those photos there'll be a photo of me and a man named Terry White. For reasons known only to himself, Balu insisted on taking a picture of me with Terry—he seemed to think, because we were both Caucasian American males, that we formed a natural set, like unicorns. He got the two of us lined up in a row and said, "Now you make smiles! You are beautiful man!"

Terry White! Who would believe such a name if it wasn't his? No novelist would dare choose such a name in the context of Haiti. If you are white and walk down a Haitian street, someone will shout *"blan!"* at you within a minute; and if you walk for sixty minutes, you will hear sixty voices shouting *"blan!"* It meant "white!" and it meant "whitey!" and it meant "foreigner!" It meant "Hey you!" Sometimes it meant "Gimme money." Sometimes it meant "Go home," and sometimes, it just meant "Welcome to my most beautiful country!"

In the photo Balu took that afternoon, Terry the White and I are standing in a dirt field with some banana trees behind us. Terry W. had been deputy sheriff in the Watsonville County Sheriff's Office in northern Florida, not far from the Georgia border, and nothing in his appearance ran contrary to stereotype of the southern lawman: he stood about six feet tall, with broad shoulders and a thick waist, heavy legs, and a pair of solid boxer's hands. I later learned that he had been on the offensive line in high school, and you could see it in his chest and feel it in his calluses. In Balu's photo, he has his arm draped over my shoulder: I remember its weight, like a sack of sand. His face was square, not handsome, but not ugly, the kind of mug that you would be unhappy to see asking for your license and registration, but would find reassuring when he pulled up beside your stalled Subaru on a dark night on a lonely road. His short dark hair was interwoven with a subtle streak of gray. He was wearing military-style boots, cargo pants, a gray T-shirt tight across his broad chest, and a khaki overshirt to conceal his sidearm. He gave the impression of brooding, powerful strength; a short, restless temper; and sly intelligence.

Terry was in Haiti as a so-called UNPOL, or United Nations Police, assigned to monitor, mentor, and support the fledgling national police force. The Mission was established in 2004, when the former president, Jean-Bertrand Aristide, fled the country in the face of a violent rebellion spreading down from the north. In his absence, the new government of Haiti, lacking legitimacy, popularity, and power, and confronted with a nation in chaos, requested the assistance of the United Nations Security Council, which responded by creating this vigorous, well-funded multinational peacekeeping mission.

The theory behind the Mission was this: In his time in power, Aristide had dismantled the military and neutered the police force, fearing, not without good reason, a coup d'état from one or the other. The coup came nevertheless; and now the future of the country and the eventual guarantor of security and domestic tranquillity would be a new police force, the Police Nationale d'Haïti (usually referred to by its acronym, the PNH), which the United Nations would train and equip. For this purpose there were about two thousand UNPOLs in Haiti, distributed about the country, of whom there were about twenty-five in Jérémie: a dozen francophone West Africans; a pair of former antiterrorist commandos from the Philippines; four or five French Canadians; a couple of Sri Lankans; a Romanian woman; two Turks, both named Ahmet, hence Ahmet the Great and Ahmet the Lesser; a Jordanian; and one American—Terry White.

Now, I should say straightaway that people either liked Terry very much or could not stand him; and when people said they couldn't take him, I understood. He was a know-it-all: "What you gotta understand about voodoo . . . ," he said when I mentioned that I had been visiting local *hougans*. "What you gotta understand about the African law enforcement official . . . ," he said when I mentioned one of his colleagues. He wanted to argue politics: "What liberals don't understand . . . ," he said. He didn't let the argument drop: "So you really think . . ." He told me how many people he had tased, and he offered to tase me to show me how it feels. He called Haiti "Hades," which was amusing the first time, but not subsequently. He called his wife his Lady. He was vain: I told him I got caught in a current down at the beach and came back to the shore breathless; he told me that his boat once capsized in the Florida Keys, leaving him surrounded by sharks. Even Terry White's kindnesses had about them some trace of superiority: "If you ever hear a noise outside the house at night, just give me a call," he said. "You stay inside. I'll come down and check it out." Between men, those kinds of declarations have meaning.

All that said—I liked him. He was, for one thing, a good storyteller and an effective, if cruel, mimic. When you talked to Terry, time passed very quickly. This was a kind of charisma. So when he told me about an argument he'd had with a colleague a couple of days before, I was all ears.

They'd been headed up to Beaumont, Terry said, and the whole way out, Ahmet the Great was talking about some lady they saw lifting her skirt and taking a leak on the side of the road. She was balancing this big basket on her head at the same time. There was a decapitated goat's head covered in flies visible in the basket. "You gotta figure the rest of the goat was in the basket, too," Terry said. Granted, maybe it wasn't the prettiest spectacle in the world, this lady dropping to her haunches—"You probably wouldn't paint the scene with oils and hang it on the living room wall"—but she did what she was doing with a heck of a lot of grace, for a big lady.

"What you got to realize is that those animals weigh upward of forty pounds," Terry said. "Just try it, peeing like a woman with a goat on your head."

In any case, it was Ahmet the Great who opened the discussion that day on the way to Beaumont.

"In my country, is big shame for lady pee," Ahmet said. "Is never something lady do."

Terry said, "In your country the ladies don't pee? I can't believe that."

"In my country, is big shame lady pee like animal in streets. In my country, lady pee like lady."

"And how does a lady pee, Ahmet? Riddle me that, my brother."

"Not like cow or animal in street."

This argument went round and round, up into the mountains and down, past seaside Gommier and pretty Roseaux and muddy Chardonette, one of those arguments that start out as banter but before long start to rankle, just two guys in a car, each thinking the other's an asshole.

"So just where is this lady *supposed* to pee?" Terry said. "Just stop in the nearest Starbucks?"

"In my place, lady not make pee in side of road like animal or dog."

"Are we in your place?"

"In my place, we have no United Nations. No peacekeepers. Lady not big shame, like here. My place is no-problem place."

Terry looked at me. The incident had been weighing on him. There was hardly a tree in sight, a lady's been walking since before dawn with a goddamn goat on her head, she feels the need—who the hell was Ahmet to judge her? People here gotta live in poverty, suffer from dawn to dusk, sweat rivers, and die young—and Ahmet, with his pompadour and mother-of-pearl–handled revolver and three-bedroom apartment in Ankara, is going to tell them in their own country where they can and cannot pee? What you got to understand is that this was the hajji mentality.

"So what do you think?" he said.

Here was an examination it was very simple to pass. "Their country," I said.

"Damn straight," Terry said. "Who the hell cares where this lady pisses?"

"Not me," I said.

"What you got to understand is that for the towelheads—"

"I hear you, brother."

"Those ladies—"

"They suffer, man. They suffer."

I don't believe Terry had expected me to capitulate so quickly. He seemed unsatisfied. We sat in silence for a moment or two, until from the other table a harsh, cruel laughter broke the early-evening calm. A couple of UNPOLs—one from Burkina Faso, the other from Benin— were trying to feed scraps of barbecued chicken to the chickens pecking under the table and were kicking away the hungry dogs attempting to steal some chicken for themselves. This was cracking the table up. Terry got a disgusted look on his face, seeing that.

"Knock it off," he said. "You don't got to humiliate those damn birds. It's enough you're eating their carcasses."

The Africans laughed. Terry glared at his colleagues for a long time in a way that wasn't friendly. I don't think they understood the menace implicit in his low voice, or they thought laughter would defuse it. The guy from Benin kept feeding the chickens their kin. Terry's stare was a prelude to standing up. It shocked me how swiftly his mood had switched from placid good humor to something nearly violent. An afternoon with Terry White was not necessarily relaxing.

Then the tension was over. The African UNPOLs backed off, still laughing, and Terry grinned at me: we were complicit, if but for a moment, on the side of justice. That gesture endeared him to me.

Terry told me that before coming to Haiti he'd been in law enforcement almost twenty years. "What you gotta understand is that a professionally conducted interrogation isn't fair," he said. Terry talked, he gave examples, and with a little prompting, he talked some more. Later he told me that his testimony had sent a man to death row—that's something. How'd that feel? "Like it was the best thing I ever did," he said, but not callously, rather as the only decent end to an all-around bad business. Terry told me that he'd been active in Florida Republican politics for years: at one point he'd taken a run for sheriff and lost. "Now, that's a brutal game, Florida politics. Those boys don't play." So how'd you end up in Haiti of all places? He told me about Marianne Miller, Marianne Miller being his erstwhile rival back home. The upshot of the narrative cul-de-sac was that no one had appreciated what a terrific law enforcement official he was, not least the new sheriff, who had let Marianne Miller whisper poison in his ear, which had led to the complicated imbroglio that had led to the best interrogator in Florida being out of a job, then going broke, then ending up in Nowhere, Hades.

Terry was not interested in me. Not once did he ask what brought me to Haiti, what my work consisted of, or where my family was from. But had he pressed the issue, I would have told him that I had followed my wife here: she was a civilian employee of the United Nations, working as a procurement officer; and I would have mentioned that I intended to use my time in Haiti, after a decade working as a journalist, to complete a novel. Terry's sole attempt to broach the conversational divide was to ask where my wife and I were living.

We rented our house on the rue Bayard from Maxim Bayard, a member of the Haitian Sénat. The previous tenant had left the Mission to return to Zimbabwe, and we had taken the keys directly from him, completing the details of the rental with the Sénateur by email. The Sénateur had left a small library of spiritualist literature, in both French and English, on the bookshelves: books on the interpretations of dreams, a volume on yoga, guides to communication with the dead, the margins filled with handwritten comments in bright red ink. This was all I knew of the man.

"Maxim Bayard is a maximum asshole," Terry said.

It was like learning that Terry knew Mick Jagger. I leaned forward as he maneuvered his plastic fork and knife around on the table so that the fork was perpendicular to the knife, with a small gap between them.

The fork and the knife represented vehicles in the parking lot of the Bon Temps, a little hotel and restaurant not far from our house, where Terry had been at lunch with colleagues on a Sunday afternoon. "This was my car here"—he indicated the knife—"and this was a white pickup truck here." He gestured to the fork. "And if you were backing up the pickup, maybe it's not easy to get out, but there was plenty of space, if you don't drive like a monkey's ass."

Terry had been gnawing on a chicken bone when he heard the crunch. He looked up. The fork had backed up directly into the knife.

"Whoa!" Terry had shouted, and all the other UNPOLs swung their heads around to see what the commotion was about. He was on his feet and walking toward the lot when the driver pulled forward and slowly rear-ended his vehicle all over again.

What Terry could recall about the Sénateur with overwhelming clarity was the expression of happy unconcern on his face. Terry had spent more than a little time as an ordinary traffic policeman, and he had never seen anyone cause an accident in this manner and subsequently display no trace of anxiety. "What you got to understand is that I was in uniform. I was armed. This was a UN vehicle," Terry said.

And yet this man not only betrayed no sign of worry, he was still maneuvering his pickup to make a third try at the tricky turn. Terry figured that if he hadn't walked over, the older fellow would have kept ramming his vehicle over and over again until sooner or later he succeeded.

"That's my car," Terry said.

"The wife of my driver, she is having a baby," the Sénateur said in heavily accented English. "I cannot ask him to work, with his wife in the hospital."

It all made sense in the Sénateur's mind—you could tell. In his mind, there was some seamless chain of cause and effect that left him blameless and Terry's vehicle dented. Something in his half smile suggested that to the contrary, Terry was at fault here, that Terry didn't care enough about his driver's wife. The Sénateur's smile incarnated what Terry hated most: arrogance, impunity, indifference to the consequence of one's actions. It was the smile of a man who believed—nay, *knew*—that he was above the law.

Then one of those crowds that seems to spring up out of nowhere in Haiti on a moment's notice was watching Terry and the Sénateur. Terry could hear schoolchildren giggling. There is a terrible power in laughter: Terry began to sweat, and his face went red. The Sénateur began to laugh also, and he shouted something in Creole to the onlookers—the only word Terry could understand was "*blan*." Terry felt humiliated in the eyes of his peers, who considered the encounter from the doorway of the hotel.

"But—," Terry said, "but why didn't you just stop after you hit me the first time?"

The man spread his hands out wide, palms upward.

"*Mais mon cher*, I had no idea that it would happen again."

Terry looked at me. His story had captured the attention of the whole table. We all laughed except Balu, who was responsible for the Mission's fleet.

"So that's the Sénateur," Terry said. "Twenty years in criminal justice, I never saw a reaction like that before."

"That's some story."

"It's some country," Terry said.

Something in his voice—

"Do you like it?" I asked.

Terry was quiet for a long time. "What you got to understand is that Haiti is a lot like pussy," he said. "It's hot and it's wet and it smells funny. You didn't know about pussy, somebody told you about pussy, you wouldn't think you'd like it much. Probably think it was something nasty. But you get to know pussy, you can't stop thinking about it ever."

2 In the little seaside village of Anse du Clerc, midway between Bonbon and Abricots, there is a restaurant and hotel. The restaurant is ringed by a neat fence; the grass is short and manicured; there are bungalows with thatched roofs and beds neatly made with white linens. The mosquito nets sway gently in the breeze. The bay is filled with fish, and for a few dollars a local fisherman will take you out in his brightly painted boat for a morning of snorkeling. The water is transparent and clean; the boat's shadow ripples on the seabed. The food is good: redfish, langouste, conch, in sauce or barbecued, accompanied by heaping platters of rice and beans and fried plantains; and for dessert, thick slices of fresh mango, or pineapple and papaya. Solar panels power the refrigerator, so the Coke and beer are icy cold. The toilets flush, the showers run. In the afternoon one can nap in the deck chairs or play dominoes. In the evening a few guys from the village strum guitars. The little hotel is the only place in the several thousand square miles of the Grand'Anse that could remotely be considered a tourist facility; it suggests a labor of love on somebody's part. It is paradise.

There were two stories about the little hotel at Anse du Clerc. The first story, the one told by foreigners, was this: *She was Canadian and he was Haitian. They met in Canada as students and had children and then, when the kids were grown, moved to his native region of Haiti. She designed and he built this little restaurant: she had good taste; he was crafty. The region*

*was inaccessible, but guests still came. Decades passed. They were happy. He
went back to Canada for a few months. She stayed behind. In a storm, the
road to Jérémie, which was hardly a road at all, collapsed into the sea. Ther
she contracted dengue fever; there was no way to take her to the hospital fo
treatment. She died. Several months later, beset by sadness, he had a hea
attack in Canada and died too. Now the servants ran the hotel: the cook u
a competent woman, and she had learned what foreigners liked.*

But there was a second story about Anse du Clerc, a Haitian st
Madame was blan *and Monsieur was Haitian. They met on the other si
the big water. They came back to Haiti. Madame built the hotel and Mon
helped. Decades passed. They were unhappy. Monsieur had an affair wi
cook. When Monsieur went to Canada, the cook seized her opportuni
visited the* boko *with a scrap of Madame's unwashed clothing, and
vided her with a deadly powder. Soon Madame died. Several mont
Monsieur died of grief and guilt and shame. Now the cook ran the
was her hotel now.*

The first story was the story that foreigners told; the second
the local story. The foreigner's chief concern is: Will I get sic
Will my children fall sick? And so he investigates issues of I
disease. He takes what seem to be reasonable precautions, spr;
self with DEET at dusk and dawn. He discreetly asks the
doctors about the risks of dengue. If he is prudent, he will
how to evacuate quickly in case of illness. The world, the
concludes, is a risky place. Danger is mitigated through pru
unpredictable.

The people of Anse du Clerc had different concerns. R
place where life is fragile, transient: any day might be your I
who lived in this world did not want a set of facts. There w
could do to prevent dengue fever. Facts could not buil
Facts did not give the people of Anse du Clerc a way to

And so the people who lived in that world told te
stories—imaginative, inventive, and profound. The s
Anse du Clerc told to explain away misfortune was a
the same theme: grievance led to hatred, hatred to ma
There was a Creole proverb, *"Pa gen mort Bondiei
meant literally, "God doesn't kill anyone in Haiti,"*

that no one in Haiti died of natural causes. Where suffering seemed to lack an obvious cause, they invented one, and the thing that transmitted cause to effect was the supernatural. In this way of thinking, every death was a murder, every misfortune a crime—and the world made an awful, homicidal kind of sense.

But that's the kind of story I'm telling here too.

It was technically the first day of spring when I saw Terry again, a few weeks after the barbecue. But what does spring mean in a tropical country? Flowers weren't blooming, at least no more than normal; the weather wasn't warming; nobody talked about picnics. After a while in Haiti I stopped thinking about spring and I knew that this was the hungry season, the difficult patch of the year before the mangoes and breadfruit were ready but after the manioc and yam were eaten, when the locals thought all day long about their nagging bellies. This was the food riot and revolution season.

But my first year in Haiti, I didn't know that, and the excuse for my trip to the little hotel in Anse du Clerc was that I had written and decided to delete a page of dialogue. It was a windy day, bright peaks on the Caribbean and the sky streaked with long, fine clouds.

Terry didn't notice me as I came walking across the broad crabgrass lawn that came up from the beach. He was dressed in a pale blue policeman's uniform, open-necked, with the American flag on one shoulder and the United Nations insignia on the other. This was the first time I had seen him in uniform, and he looked a little stockier, a little more bull-necked, a little less handsome than I remembered. He was in animated conversation with a tall fat man.

I walked in their direction, and as I got closer, I could see the fat man's light brown face, three chins oily with sweat; and his maroon shoes shined to a high gloss; and a bright red tie matched nicely with a light pink shirt. His cream coat was neatly over the adjoining chair. Then I could hear them, and Terry was saying, "You can't let the sonofabitch talk like that, you got to step up—," at which point he saw me, stopped himself, and said, "Hey now, Michael Dukakis."

I had made the mistake, when I met Terry, of proposing that we

drive to the beach in an Uruguayan armored personnel carrier. It was only a joke, but I suppose the image had sparked his imagination.

I said, "Hey now."

Then Terry introduced me to Judge Johel Célestin.

I reached out and shook the judge's hand, sumptuous like the best leather.

The judge said, "How do you do."

His face was pear-shaped, substantially broader at the jowls than at the temples. He didn't have much of a chin or jawbone, just a bountiful wave of fat. In his precisely trimmed goatee were curled a few snaky gray tendrils.

"Hanging in there," I said.

"The heat not getting you down?"

He spoke with a neutral Northeast accent, the clipped inflections of educated American speech.

"Learning to sweat," I said. "Never knew I could sweat like this until I got to Haiti."

"Good man," he said.

I trust first impressions, and mine was that this man was as out of place in Jérémie as a zebra at Sea World. This brother, I figured, had made a wrong turn somewhere round about the Bahamas. What he'd been aiming for was St. Croix. His handsome clothes; his refined, chubby features; and his general high-toned snooty air—he looked as if he ought to be shanking a 3-iron wide, dressed in knickerbockers and wearing a silly white cap, laughing things over with the senior partners. But here we were in Haiti.

There had been a kid on the beach asking me for money. Now he was at my heels right there in the outdoor restaurant, barefoot and wearing nothing but a filthy T-shirt down to his ankles. His hair was reddish-orange at the roots: protein deficiency. You could have taken his picture and put it on the cover of Save the Children's Annual Report, both from the cherubic cuteness and the desperate poverty POV.

"*Blan, mwem grangou. Blan, ba'm cinq gourdes,*" the kid said. *Blan*, I'm hungry. *Blan*, give me five gourdes.

Terry and the judge were seated at a table on which a large fish had been reduced to a flimsy skeleton. A few grains were what remained of what had once been a rice mountain.

It was Terry, still sucking on a beer, who said no.

The kid looked at his feet, all confused. But he didn't back off. He just stood there looking cute and desperate.

"Ba'm cinq gourdes," the kid said all over again, as if he were turning the key on a stalled engine.

Terry said, *"Ba'm cinq gourdes, s'il vous plaît."*

The kid just stood there. He wasn't in a hurry. He had all the time in the world. He was thinking things over. Then he smiled at us. What a smile! What the good Lord gave this kid in exchange for all his troubles was this smile, as hot as a hundred suns.

"Blan, ba'm cinq gourdes, s'il vous plaît," the kid said, figuring things out.

So Terry turned out his pockets and gave him some coins, and the kid, still smiling, wandered away. You would have needed a scanning tunneling microscope to find a spot of trouble in his soul: he would eat that afternoon. Life would take care of itself.

"I hate to see that," Terry said. "Kid should be in school, not begging for money like that."

This was such an obvious moral truth that nobody else I knew in Haiti but Terry would have said it. I had been in Haiti only a short time, and I was already coming to see that kid and his protein deficiencies as an irritant, like clouds on an otherwise sunny day. The phrase "breaks your heart" can mean many different things.

"Maybe he would be in school if he wasn't making a living begging," the judge said.

"Maybe he'd be fucking hungry if I didn't feed him," Terry said.

The way these two men bantered, you could tell that they bantered back and forth all day long. It was like watching them chuck a football, and after a minute or so, I interrupted them. "So you're a judge?"

Terry had told me that he worked with a Haitian judge: the two somehow collaborated.

"Juge d'instruction," the judge said, just a touch of snootiness in his voice.

"Wait—," I said. "Are you Juge Blan?"

A smile, not modest, broke across his fleshy face.

"Some folks call me that," he said.

I had heard the name a dozen times—from my Creole teacher, from the plumber, from the woman who squeezed our lime juice, and from the woman in the market who hacked up our meat. "Take your problems to Juge Blan," they said, and it had taken me some time to understand that this wasn't some difficult Creole proverb, but an injunction to encounter a living man, a member of the local judiciary who kept offices at the Tribunal.

Terry said, "You want a beer or rum or what?"

"I'll get a Coke," I said.

"Get a beer," Terry said. "Life is good."

"Coke is okay."

"I'm getting another one," he said. "J.?"

"I'm good," the judge said.

"Cherie!"

Cherie was dozing in a chair in the shade. At the sound of Terry's voice Cherie lifted her head, then shifted her torso, then rocked on her haunches, then stood up. With a sigh she ambled over to our table.

"*Oui?*" she said, putting her hand on Terry's shoulder.

"Bring us more beers, and some cigarettes too, and another round of plantains," he said. His Creole, after however long he'd been in the country, was good enough to communicate his needs.

Cherie was the lady, pretty in a fleshy kind of way, accused by rumor of betraying and murdering her patroness. The smile that she flashed Terry, however, suggested only flirtatiousness, sweetness and light.

The judge and Terry had been talking about something heavy when I showed up. They were still both of them thinking about that something heavy. It was weighing on them. They were thinking up one more thing to say to each other, that last and conclusive point. I was about to excuse myself and allow them to conclude their conversation when Johel said, "So how are you liking Haiti?"

I started to say, *You know, Haiti is a lot like pussy,* but instead I told the judge something like the truth: I had never been anyplace so dysfunctional, so rotten, or so very fascinating. I had been in the Caribbean before and had expected the light, the colors, the tastes. But Haiti had something different from Jamaica or Barbados: that profusion of stories. If you enjoy the taste of an overripe peach, then you might like Haiti; it was a place that sunk tentacles down deep into the soul.

"How's your kid?" Terry asked me.

"Toussaint Legrand?"

"What a name!" the judge said.

"Still a fuckup," I said.

And I told them the latest Toussaint Legrand story.

"I think he might have died if I hadn't given him the money," I said. I didn't say it looking for praise or glory, because every foreigner in Haiti who isn't deeply hard has done something like that: it's just part of the Haitian experience.

"I hear a story like that, and I wonder if we were all meant to be here," the judge said.

"Like destiny," I said.

The judge reclined his head rearward and looked down at me, his sharp gaze skimming over his broad nose. I had thought he was drunk, but his eyes were sober and clear and humorless. He had that concentrated attention for which a man in trouble pays ten dollars a minute. "You think we got one?" he asked.

"A what."

"A destiny."

All you can really say to a question like that is "Maybe." It's easy for the guys drinking a cold beer on the beach to figure that this is the way it's all supposed to be.

I glanced at Terry. "Do you?"

"No doubt, brother," said Terry. "I know His strength. We're all here for a reason. That's what I'm telling this guy. I'm saying, 'Judge, you can't escape your destiny. You're like a fish on a line. Destiny is reeling you in, and you're fighting. Just give in, brother.'"

"Sounds like Terry thinks you're a marlin," I said.

The judge didn't laugh.

"Where does Brother Terry think your destiny lies?" I asked.

"Brother Terry thinks I have a vocation."

"I don't really see you in a clerical collar."

Now the judge laughed. "Terry's been telling me to run for senate."

"Where?"

"Right here."

"In Haiti?"

"In the Grand'Anse."

"Against Maxim Bayard?"

"Next year, maybe."

Had the judge announced that he was auditioning for the role of Hamlet at the Old Vic that year, it would have seemed hardly a more grandiose or improbable a project than winning some contest of charisma and wiles against the legendary Sénateur.

And yet I once heard a man declare that he was going to rob a bank— and two weeks later he did it. A roommate in college joined the French Foreign Legion, announcing his decision in a voice no more swelling with excitement than that of the judge. If you meet a thousand people, one will do something that only one in a thousand will do.

"That's ambitious," I said.

"Things have got to change around here," the judge said. "They have to."

A dugout canoe was cutting across the bay, laying down lobster traps. Its motion, the swell and fall of the sea, the lapping of the waves—they were hypnotic. Things changed all the time in Haiti. They just always seemed to change for the worse. Even in the short time I had been there, I saw things declining. The road to Dame Marie was worse for the fall storms. There had been an outbreak of measles. A water pipe burst and now a swath of the town had no water. The standard Haitian response to "How are you?" was *"Pas pi mal"*—No worse. No worse was as good as it got.

"You hear the story about the ice chest?" I said.

"The fingers?"

Every election day, the story went, the Sénateur sent his goons around to the polling stations to offer the poll workers a cold drink, thanking them for their labors. Inside the ice chest, on a bed of ice, there's nothing but human fingers and bottles of Coke, all those fingers stained with the indelible ink which identifies a voting citizen—presumably someone who had voted for the Sénateur's opponent. After that, the poll workers often found their way to slip a ballot or two the Sénateur's way.

"That doesn't scare you?" I asked.

"In six years since we're back, I have yet to meet a nine-fingered man," Johel said. "And believe you me, I've looked."

"Brave man."

"Stories like that, that's the way Maxim is," the judge said. "That's how he maintains and perpetuates power. He's a talker." That didn't seem enough, so he added, "Was it safe for Martin Luther King to march in Birmingham? Was it safe for Gandhi? Was it safe for Nelson Mandela, spending twenty-seven years in prison? Was that safe? Things have got to change around. People can't go on living like this."

Terry seemed to sense that the judge had stumbled. He said, "What you got to understand—Johel and I are in the trenches here every day. You've got no idea what's going on here, really going on here. People come up to us, they say, 'Thank you, Judge. God bless you, Judge.' People say, 'If only you were president, Judge.' People offer him money, he never takes a dime. Real money sometimes. You go anywhere in the Grand'Anse, I bet they know Johel. We go up into the mountains, they know him. And they're asking him for help every day of the week."

"What's wrong with the guy they got?"

Terry said, "Are you kidding me—"

The judge interrupted him. His voice was soothing, calm.

"Is this a—confidential conversation?" he asked.

"I'm not friends with the Sénateur."

"You live in his house."

"I've never met him."

"We're not hiding anything," the judge said. "But I haven't made any decisions, and I'd prefer if this was—between friends."

I nodded, and the judge leaned in. His face was glossy with sweat.

"You know the new road they talk about?" he said.

Jérémie was just one hundred and twenty-five miles or so from Port-au-Prince as the vulture flew, but the trip overland on the old road, the Route Nationale Numéro Deux, could take fourteen or fifteen hours, if the road was passable at all. When the summer rains set in or the fall hurricanes blew through, the road was just mud. Rumor held that a Canadian proposal to build a modern road connecting Jérémie to the southern port city of Les Cayes—where a two-lane highway to Port-au-Prince began—had been rebuffed by the government of Haiti.

"It's true," the judge said.

"I don't believe it."

"I didn't when I first heard it. Something like that, you'd think you'd hear about it. I mean, it's a road. A whole damn road. Seventy million American dollars. Maxim Bayard won't let it go through."

"He wants a cut?" I said.

"Nothing like that. Government gives the okay, the Canadians give the money to the Inter-American Development Bank, the IADB puts out the call for tender, pays the winning bid directly. Last time, they awarded the contract to some Italian outfit to build that one up north. That's a good road now. Government of Haiti never sees a dime, just gets a road."

"So what's the problem?"

"That's just what I asked. I put in a call to Port-au-Prince. And what the minister of finance says is his hands are tied. I say, who's tying them? He says Maxim will bring down the government if he signs the accord. Or worse."

"What's his deal?" I asked.

The judge spread his hands wide.

"Man doesn't want a road," he said.

"But who doesn't want a road?"

"Sénateur Maxim Bayard, that's who."

"Why doesn't anyone mention something like that?" I asked. It seemed to me the kind of story that you'd read in newspapers.

The judge said, "The Canadians are as embarrassed as anyone. That money's just sitting there in an escrow account, waiting for a signature. Once the money's budgeted—that's a slap in the face. Heads roll in Ottawa, that money just sits there."

The thought of decapitated Canadian civil servants distracted me. I was startled to find Cherie standing at the table with our drinks and plantains.

"What would you do if there was a road to Port-au-Prince?" I asked her.

"I'd go to Port-au-Prince and buy a new dress," she said, putting the food and glasses on the table. She spun her skirt in a coquettish circle. "Then I'd never come back."

"I guess a road would make some difference," I said to the judge, watching Cherie amble back to the kitchen.

The plantains were salty and topped with *piklis* so spicy it burned your nostrils before it burned your tongue. The judge ate a plantain, then another. He tilted his head and considered me. What you had in the judge was one of those men who looked at all times as if he were quietly evaluating your intelligence and finding it lacking. Terry looked at all times as if he were quietly evaluating your manliness and finding it lacking. Between the two of them, they had all bases covered. "How much you pay for bananas? Or for mangoes?" the judge asked.

There were at least two dozen varieties of mango in the Grand'Anse, but my favorite was the *mangue Madame Blan*, a mango whose tawny skin sliced open to reveal pale flesh as inviting as the thighs of that long-ago golden-haired plantation mistress for whom the fruit was named. I had once believed that the South Indian mango known as the Alphonso was the finest mango in the world, but this mango was subtler, less fibrous, and more sensual.

"A couple gourdes, maybe?"

"I pay one gourde one banana. And I pay ten gourdes a mango," he said.

"Is that a lot?" I asked.

"You know how much a banana costs in Port-au-Prince? In Port-au-Prince, a capital city of a tropical nation, sometimes you pay twenty-five gourdes for a banana. Sometimes more."

He was waiting for me to respond. When I didn't, he kept talking.

"Rich folk eat bananas in Port-au-Prince. Poor folks don't eat bananas. Poor folks don't eat fruit in Port-au-Prince. You got babies going to bed hungry in Port-au-Prince because they have nothing to eat, you got babies swole-bellied here because all they eat are bananas and mangoes. You think that lady who sold me a banana for one gourde would like to sell her bananas for five gourdes? Sure she would. And you know why she can't? *Because there's no road.*"

He was quiet and I was quiet and so was Terry.

Then the judge said, "People here live on a dollar a day. They had three dollars a day, they'd be okay. Five dollars a day and they'd be great. They'd have enough money to feed their kids, enough money to pay a doctor when the kids get sick, enough money to send their kids to school, maybe even save a few bucks and start a little business. Buy some pigs. There'd be doctors and schools because people could pay for them. That's five dollars a day, and the difference is—a road. It's fine and dandy to build a school or some latrines or give away mosquito nets, but at the end of the day people still have just that one dollar they got to stretch out from sunrise to sunset. Look at that right there—"

And what was there on the fringe of the property but a magnificent *manguier*, dripping with fruit like money . . .

"Up north, a tree like that, you can get maybe twenty gourdes a dozen. A tree like that can give you—what? A hundred dozen in a season. That could be seventy-five bucks, just for gathering the fruit from your own mango tree. Two or three trees, and people around here don't see that kind of cash in a year."

Mangoes! An export fruit! Johel's voice was sincere, eager, persuasive. A mango tree is for a small peasant like a little money machine: a mango tree *and* a road are school fees for your child; a mango tree and a road, and your wife has prenatal care; a mango tree and a road is a concrete cistern to gather rainwater, and that means you're not drinking ditchwater. A mango tree *without* a road is a pile of fruit; a mango tree without a road is a swollen belly; a mango tree without a road is timber. And what happens to the mangoes now? They fall to the ground and rot—the pigs eat the mangoes and the kids go hungry. And why is that? *Because there is no road*. Farmers nowadays were cutting down these trees to make charcoal, the only thing you could transport to market in Port-au-Prince. Things didn't change around here, soon the hills would be denuded, the topsoil washed away, and the last place in Haiti still covered in thick forest would be, like the rest of Haiti, nothing but barren hillside.

When the judge was done talking, his face was covered in a fine sheen of sweat. Terry was with him word for word, nodding when the judge nodded, shaking his head when the judge shook his.

"Good luck with all that," I finally said—one of those rare occasions on which I have succeeded in saying just what I meant, no more and no less.

3 Mild days coalesced into calm weeks, and I heard nothing more from either Terry or the judge. They had their destiny and I had mine; and mine involved swaying in a hammock in the afternoon while my wife was at work—swaying just so *in* and swaying just so *out* of a hot stripe of sunlight, all the while admiring the industry of the hummingbirds. Another portion of my attention was devoted to a chicken pecking lazily at a fallen mango. I was considering writing a poem on the subject. What I had in mind was a kind of dialogue between the chicken and the hummingbird on the theme of love.

I was trying to find a rhyme for "cluck" when a voice startled me from my poetic reverie. "Anybody home?"

"On the terrace," I said.

A blond woman with a fine, thin nose and light blue eyes rounded the corner. She was small, and walked with a graceful step. Her hair was pulled back in a sporty ponytail. She was wearing a white skirt and sandals with a bit of a heel and a pink polo shirt and a very fine gold chain around her neck.

"Cookie lady!" she said with a little laugh.

I was attempting to roll out of the hammock, and I must have looked a little ungainly because she quickly said, "Don't get up—you look so comfy. Just stay where you are." But by then I was vertical, and I offered her my hand, which she shook firmly—professionally, even.

"I'm Kay White. Terry—you know Terry? from the Mission? he's my husband? He said you would be here. I made cookies."

She said all this in one slightly embarrassed, charmingly girlish rush, and her eyes flicked downward to the plate of cookies she was carrying in her hand.

I said, "Would you like some lemonade?"

Micheline, the woman we hired to cook and clean for us, had squeezed a pitcher of juice that morning, sweetened with raw cane sugar. I went to fetch the jug and a pair of glasses from the kitchen and told Kay White to make herself at home. She smoothed out her skirt and sat gingerly in the wicker chair, saying to me as I receded into the kitchen, "Oh, I *feel* at home here. Your house is just lovely, so peaceful."

"It's over one hundred years old."

"I love old houses," she said.

I settled myself in the chair opposite hers. I poured two glasses of lemonade. I said, "Please." She took her glass and sipped.

"Do you want to hear about Micheline?" I said.

"That's *just* why I came."

"She has a cookbook collection. French cookbooks from the 1950s. She looks at them every night. My wife and I were very excited when we first moved in; we thought she must be quite a cook. First night she left out the *Larousse Gastronomique* or whatever it was, told us to pick out whatever we liked. I think we chose a soufflé. That night she served us some rice, some beans, and some boiled bananas. We thought maybe we hadn't understood, but the next night it was the same thing. I don't think she can read."

Kay looked thoughtful. "What does she do with the cookbooks, then?"

"I think she was just hoping the recipe we wanted was rice, beans, and boiled bananas."

Kay laughed, and I asked her how long she would be staying in Haiti.

"Two weeks, and I'm not doing *anything*," she said. "I'm going to read a book and go to the beach and sleep. Maybe we'll eat a fish if we get ambitious."

"First time you're down?"

"Oh, no! Fourth time!"

Her shoulders and calves were nicely toned—it was all the Pilates and yoga, I figured. The delicate tracery radiating from her eyes and thin lips had erased the first blush of youth, but she was still a very pretty woman. I supposed she was in her late thirties. At first glance she had struck me as girlish, but the serious way she held herself now suggested hidden stores of competence, as if you could entrust her with details: a complicated travel itinerary or negotiating escrow. "What you got to understand is that my Lady handles million-dollar properties every day," Terry had told me. She was also a little sexy.

"So I guess you like it," I said.

She had a bracelet of small turquoise stones on her left ankle. The stones flashed as she crossed her legs. Her toenails were painted a rich pink, like the fringe of a coral reef.

"Not at first. At first it just made me think about all the money I used to spend," she said.

It makes me think of all the lovers I used to take—that was her tone of voice; and the intimacy broke the tension between us.

"I love to spend money," I said. "I just wish I had more of it."

"Me too," she confessed. "I feel guilty just thinking about how much money we went through."

"Tell me about it."

"Sheets. Just for example."

"Not diamonds?"

"Have you ever slept on a *really* good sheet? A girl's best friend is definitely her sheets. I got those cotton sheets with superhigh thread counts, you know? Just because I liked the way they felt against my skin? And I replaced them when they weren't soft anymore or if the colors faded? So I get here and a lady asks me for money to send her kids to school for a year, and I do the math and I used to spend that—I didn't spend that on a sheet. Maybe on a pillowcase."

"You spent all that on a pillowcase?"

"It's *easy*," she said. "If you want a good one."

"Had you ever been to a poor country before you came here?"

She said, "You know those commercials on TV? Send money so this kid in Africa can eat? And he's got flies in his eyes? And he's all snotty? That's it. There was this little kid in Kenya? His name was Wilson, that was my little guy. Then Terry came to Haiti, he called me up and said,

'Kay, you can't believe this place, how people are living.' When he got here, I saw the pictures and how beautiful it was and all the kids looked like Wilson and I said, 'Terry, I'm coming to visit, like it or not.'"

I asked her what brought her husband to Haiti in the first place.

"Didn't Terry tell you?"

"He mentioned something—"

"Oh, we went broke!" she said with defiant cheerfulness. "We were broke before everyone else went broke. You could not believe how broke we went. Terry lost his job and I was in real estate, but with the economy— well, you know. We had some properties, investments that didn't—you know with the crash and everything—work out. We went broke, broker, and brokest. When Terry got the job here, it was Haiti or lose the house and move back in with my mom and dad."

Talking about money had made her anxious: she had begun to stare at the cookies.

"Would you like another cookie?" I asked.

"Just one," she said, and took the smallest cookie on the plate.

Conversation faltered for a moment. We sat in silence until, employing that feminine expertise in small and unimportant talk so essential to her métier, she asked how I met my wife—India, temple, lynch mob, *isn't that romantic!*; how I found "inspiration" for my books—I wish I knew; and whether we ate the mangoes that fell from our mango trees—no, they were small and wormy. The sunlight had crawled high enough that it was now in Kay's eyes. She moved her chair closer to mine. Then I asked her how she met her husband.

It was the summer after college, she told me, when a green Cadillac Escalade raced through a red light and hit her yellow Volkswagen Golf, which had been her father's graduation present just three weeks before. She thought she was going to die, and when she looked up, there was Terry, in uniform.

"It was like the baby ducks, you know? Are you my daddy? I guess he just imprinted on my brain. I was like, 'Don't leave,' and he said, 'Don't worry.' The second I saw him, I felt safe."

"I could see that," I said. "He's got that kind of quality."

"You know who hit me? It was a priest—he was drunk. In his clerical collar and everything. They had like this Sunday luncheon after Mass, and there you go. Too much wine or something. After that, Terry came to visit me in the hospital."

"Talk about the hand of fate."

"Terry was so sweet when I was in the hospital. He brought me balloons and flowers. I was there for a long time, and he came just about every day. So I married him."

"Just like that?"

"Just like that," she said. "And you know who married us? The priest who put me in the hospital."

"What an idea!"

"Terry thought of it."

"Did it work out the way you hoped?"

"He got drunk."

"Terry?"

"The priest. We took away his keys at the end of the reception."

"I was asking about the marriage."

She smiled, her lips pursed neatly together. She waved her slender ring finger. "Still together," she said, an inscrutable expression, evocative and compelling, settling again on her pretty lips and eyes. "You have hummingbirds!"

"And woodpeckers. They drive my wife—"

"So we had dinner with Johel last night. You know Johel, don't you? He grilled the most amazing tuna steaks. And Nadia—she's just a beauty."

So that was why Kay was on my porch. She wanted to know things; she was probing. And I *had* heard a story. I didn't know if Kay had heard it also. At the Hotel Patience one could rent a little room for the afternoon. It was here, they said, that Kay's husband and the judge's wife passed an occasional *petit moment*. They said the judge knew; they said the judge didn't know. I knew because everyone knew; and everyone knew because everyone else knew. But I didn't know if it was true. It could have just been a story that people told.

Kay said, "I've never seen an African American lady with blue eyes before."

"I haven't met her," I said.

"It's so striking."

I said, "Some Frenchman raped her mother's great-great-grandmother and some other Frenchman raped her father's great-great-grandmother. Then those genes just floated down through the generations, waiting to meet each other again. You see it here from time to time."

"She was so quiet. She didn't talk all night."

I tried to change the subject. "Did you know he was a national spelling champion?"

"Johel? Where did you hear that?"

"I looked him up," I said.

"I'm a crummy speller," Kay said. "I'm lucky I have a short name."

"He grew up in New York. When he was thirteen, he was the national spelling champion. His word was 'elegiacally.'"

"I admire him, I really do," she said. "He's got so much talent, he could be anywhere doing anything, and still he's here."

"Is he still going ahead with the election thing?"

"What I heard," she said—and what she heard was this, from Terry: "Brother needs to grow himself a fucking pair and not let his woman tell him what to do."

"So he's not going to do it?" I said.

"Terry told me that Nadia is too frightened. She won't let him."

"What is she frightened of?"

Kay lifted her hand and formed it into the shape of a pistol, which she fired at my head.

"Bang, bang," she said.

"It sounds like the woman has a head on her shoulders."

Kay looked disapproving. "I don't like a man who won't make a decision for himself."

"Would Terry listen to you about a thing like that?"

"You mean, would Terry do something I didn't approve of?"

I nodded.

"Hello!" she said. "We're in Haiti!"

Kay looked around as if hidden in the bougainvillea or hibiscus, there might be someone listening.

"Just after Terry got the offer to come here, he got another offer," she said. "Head of security at a shopping mall in Tennessee. And I thought, *Great, now he doesn't have to go to Haiti.* We went up there to visit. I liked the way we could go out at night, the shopping, the music. It was good salary, good hours for Terry, good for me, everything good. But Terry said he wasn't going. We had a big fight. He said, 'I don't want to spend my life protecting the Gap and Zara,' and I said, 'Honey, those places are essential to my way of life.' But in the end Terry got what he wanted."

"And you didn't approve?"

Kay's fine-boned face was immobile, her eyes like slivers of old ice. There was a long conversational silence, filled with callings of innumerable birds and the cry of the ice vendor on the cobblestone street: *"Vann glace! Vann glace!"* Laughter of children from the neighbor's garden. The scratching of lizards on the pebbles. A smell of burning charcoal.

"I was scared for him. For us," she said.

"Why?"

"Terry and I see someone at home," she finally said. "She's an older lady. She has—powers. And when Terry got the offer to come to Haiti, we visited her, like we do. Madame Roccaforte saw two birds. She saw an eagle and a hawk. And the hawk was attacking the eagle. And after that, Madame Roccaforte told me not to let him go."

4 Électricité d'Haïti supplied us with electricity just three times a year—for the festival of the city's patron saint, Saint Louis; for Christmas; and for Carnival—and by electricity I mean two or three hours every evening for a week or so. The rest of the year, the big generator on the rue Abbé Hué lay idle—no fuel—and the city lay in darkness. The house we rented from the Sénateur, though, like the houses of all the wealthy, had a generator, an array of car batteries, and an inverter, and so maintained an autonomous electrical supply, sufficiently powerful for a few lights or even a small refrigerator. A couple of weeks after our arrival the generator groaned, the inverter sparked, and the batteries burst into flames. We stumbled around by candlelight thereafter as a series of increasingly agitated emails to our landlord went unanswered.

Not long after I met Kay White, a caravan of three black SUVs delivered the Sénateur back from Port-au-Prince. He was home to meet with his constituents. The next morning I wandered down to his concrete cottage, on the same large property as our house but separated from us by a bamboo grove.

The Sénateur's cottage was neither so imposing as to frighten the peasants nor so humble as to make his wealthier patrons ill at ease. It was just right. The clay water basins, filled from a muddy well, told the regular folk of Jérémie that the Sénateur lived not much better than they did. A dozen *citoyens* were waiting to see him, all dressed in their Sunday best, the ladies in faded calico dresses, the gentlemen in oversize suits and black ties. A few carried offerings for the Sénateur: some mangoes or avocados or a large sack of beans. One woman was carrying a big silvery fish. When the others saw me, they made little murmuring noises and somebody said, *"Blan,"* indicating a space on the bench beside him. It was warm in the early-morning sun. I waited with the others for perhaps half an hour until somebody else said, *"Blan."* Then I was summoned up the stairs. Now I realized I had passed only from the first waiting area to the second, but here at least I was in sight of the Sénateur.

Maxim Bayard was a scion of one of the town's famous but now disappeared mulatto families: I never met a Haitian man with lighter skin. He had tight curly hair, gone gray. His nose was large and fleshy, bulbous at the end and bumped in the middle. It was an ugly face, as goofy and grotesque as a children's clown. He was a large man, and bulky also, broad-shouldered, round-gutted, thick-handed, long-limbed. He had a gold chain around his heavy neck and wore a white linen shirt.

The Sénateur conducted his business in a wicker chair, leaning close to one of the regular folk, the two of them talking quietly. On a stucco wall, just above the Sénateur's head, a younger version of the Sénateur was shaking a younger version of Fidel Castro's hand, both of them smoking fat cigars. Behind him now were the Sénateur's goons, three large men in black blazers playing cards at a little table, holstered sidearms visible under their jackets. The rest of us sat farther out, our faces in the shade but our backs in the sun.

It was a joy to watch the Sénateur. It really was. It was a pleasure to watch him in the way it is a pleasure to watch any thoroughly competent professional, a major-league shortstop shading toward second base, or a sous-chef in a top restaurant disemboweling a chicken. I watched him dealing with three or four supplicants before my turn came up. I tried to imagine the things people wanted from him: *My well has gone dry. A landslide wiped out my fields. A rich man wants my house. My donkey is ill. My enemies have used magic against me and I need to buy some expensive magic to punish them.*

To each of these complaints, the Sénateur listened patiently. His eyes were by turns focused, kind, authoritative, sympathetic, wise, amused, intelligent, and cruel. From time to time he nodded. You can't fake that level of attention. At the end of each interview he'd hand the supplicant a wad of cash from his wallet or say something to one of his goons or just seize the man's hand between his own and hold it there.

Then finally it was my turn to sit with the Sénateur.

Before he said a word to me, he glanced at his watch. Then he looked into my eyes. I introduced myself and offered him my hand, which he accepted with a handshake that began limply then gained force until his grip was almost painful. His hand swallowed mine. All the while he pulled me nearer to him, until we were very nearly touching. He was much stronger than I was, although I reckoned he was twice my age.

"Maxim Bayard," he said. *"Enchanté."*

I could smell his breath—it was unexpectedly sweet and minty from behind those yellow, crooked teeth. He held on tightly to my hand until he squeezed out of me an admission that I was enchanted also.

Only then did he let my hand go, and I finally had the chance to speak.

"Sénateur, I'm sorry to bother you."

"Bother me! Nonsense! You *delight* me! Pierre, bring coffee for our American friend. Or would you prefer juice?"

"Neither, Sénateur. I'm only here a minute or two."

"I would be offended if you won't try our coffee."

"Coffee then."

"Pierre, make our friend's coffee strong and with plenty of sugar."

"Thank you," I said.

"This is our Haitian hospitality. With a guest we share nothing less than our hearts."

The Sénateur leaned back in his small wicker chair. He cracked his knuckles. It sounded like padlocks springing open.

"The people from Venezuela were here last month."

It was a statement of unexpected familiarity, as if we were gathering up a thread of an old conversation.

"The mayor of Caracas was sitting in your chair. You know he still has the president's ear. We had an argument—a discussion. He warned me to be on the lookout for the North Americans. He said you would be coming. I said, 'We must be friends with the Americans. They are kind-hearted beasts.' And as the philosopher reminds us, the only absolutely good thing in this world is a good will. Do you agree with me?"

"Bien sur," I said.

Pierre brought the coffee to me with a grunt. It was very strong and unpleasantly sweet.

The Sénateur leaned forward until he was at a distance where he could have easily sprung forward and bitten off my nose.

"Then why do you oppress us like this?"

His voice was as friendly as one can be in asking such a question. I thought for a moment that he was referring to my conversation with Terry White and the judge; I thought of innocent-faced Cherie, listening to us.

Then the Sénateur said something about birds. That morning he had been surprised to find in his garden a pair of western Caribbean warblers. The Sénateur wanted to know if I enjoyed also the pleasure of our aviary companions. He mentioned birds in the poems of Ronsard and spoke of hunting birds as a young man with a slingshot—Goliath on the trails of David!—and how, if I were to take the time and opportunity that a man in his position no longer possessed, I would find in the hills other young men today still hunting in this manner. The hills, he said, were like rich museums of the Haitian past: men and women still lived not several hours' walk from where we sat, in the very manner of the men of the revolution. This was at once Haiti's strength and her tragedy. If I was to understand Haiti, I must understand her history. "We have had such a tragic history," the Sénateur said, and he spoke of the crack of the slaver's whip, the whispers of long-ago slave revolution around the flickering campfire. These were our ancestors, *mon cher*, brave men! In all of human history, the only successful revolution of slaves—the casting off of chains—our glorious land of freedom.

The lecture went on for quite a while, and the Sénateur's deep voice mingled with the high buzzing of the bees; the minutes passed neither slowly nor quickly; I was aware only of the sweat stains slowly expanding from my armpits and a fly crawling across the Sénateur's knuckle, which

I restrained myself with effort from shooing away. Then the Sénateur startled slightly. Something had snapped him out of his reverie. He looked at me as if he had never seen me before.

"And what can I do for you, *mon vieux*?"

"It's a little thing," I said. I produced our rental contract from my backpack and handed it to him, explaining that we had rented a house with electricity (gasoline at the charge of the tenant) and now occupied a house without electricity. It was in paragraph two, clause three, the relevant objects clearly listed as functional in the *état des lieux*.

The Sénateur took the papers in hand. He found a pair of spectacles on a side table and settled them down on the bridge of his nose, the gesture lending him a mandarin air. He looked through the papers slowly, for a very long time. He read every line of the document, turned the pages over to see what was written on the back. His ugly face was quivering like a molded aspic by the time he had flipped the last page around and come back to the first. Then he ripped the pages up—once, twice, three times, scattered them on the floor.

"This is my home," the Sénateur said. "If you're not happy in my home, you can leave."

I attempted to speak, but the Sénateur cut me off. He stood up.

"You are my guest. This is not how a guest treats his host. Pierre!"

"Maître!" Pierre cried.

"Would you come to a man's house and accuse him?"

"Jamais!"

"Would you thank him for his hospitality, take his hand, promise him help and kindness?"

"Bien sûr!" Pierre said. "That is basic. That is to be polite."

All the goons were smiling now, enjoying the specter of a *blan* humiliated. The regular people in their seats in the sun were laughing too. They'd go home to their villages and families and tell them how the Sénateur treated me. Thus the story would go out into the world. The Sénateur was a very good politician.

I got up from my seat and offered him my hand. I said, "Thank you for the coffee, Sénateur."

He ignored my hand. "Sit again," he said. Then, after a moment, "We don't have time in this short life for quarrels. Not between friends. I want to be your friend. I have too many enemies. In Creole, we say, 'Only cats have time to fight.'"

Then the Sénateur winked and I sat down.

We sat in silence as a thick cloud covered us in shadow. Finally he said, "I admire the coolness of your blood. Here in Haiti we have hot blood. A foreign scientist has studied the matter. This gentleman discovered that the average Haitian has a temperature of between ninety-nine point seven and one hundred degrees. I myself am never less than that. I have measured! It is a scientific fact."

He fanned himself. He leaned back in his wicker chair. He made a gesture to Pierre, who poured a tall glass of water from a pitcher, placed the glass on a small plate, centered the plate on a wooden tray carved and painted to resemble an eggplant, and brought the ensemble to the Sénateur. The Sénateur sipped from the glass, swished the water in his mouth, and spat on the deck.

"I will give you a story," he said.

He pulled his chair very slightly back and addressed not just me, but everyone on the deck.

He had received the Sacrament of Holy Baptism, he told us, from a priest named Jean Vincent Brierre. Père Brierre was in his day a celebrated man, on account of an incident in his youth, when the great President Sténio Vincent decided to allow the Rara bands to circulate on the feast days of the Church, so long as the bands did not enter the cities themselves. Père Brierre was a man of fierce conviction, and when he saw the peasants leaving their fields, turning their backs on prayer to dance and drink all through the holy days, he was outraged. He sent a telegram to the president himself denouncing the president's decision.

"And, you understand, he used certain words . . ." The Sénateur coughed. Pierre brought him another glass of water. The Sénateur took a drink and continued.

The president sentenced Père Brierre to die by firing squad should he fail to apologize for the offense to the state and the outrage to the presidency. Père Brierre would not do so. He announced from his pulpit that he was defending the soul of his parish and the honor of the Haitian people, and he declared gallantly that he would prefer to die by bullet than to renounce his words. He requested of the president only the honor when in front of the firing squad to cry "Fire!" himself.

The privilege was so granted.

The Sénateur began to chortle.

Père Brierre was arrested and brought in chains to Port-au-Prince, where he demanded the opportunity to exercise his presidential privilege. But the army would not shoot him. The generals declared that it was an outrage to the honor of the army for any soldier to receive an order except from an officer. No civilian would ever order a member of the Forces Armées d'Haïti to fire a shot.

And so nobody would shoot Père Brierre. After a while he was allowed by the army to return to his parish and continue preaching—there was no reason to waste a good priest—until such time as the president would rescind the curé's privilege and the army could shoot him properly.

The Sénateur's chortle had progressed to a guffaw. The peasants were laughing with him. "*Alors,*" he said. "In 1939 my father was crossing the great Grand'Anse on his horse in a storm, when the river was full, when the beast was startled by a lightning stroke and bucked my father off into the raging waters. My father would certainly have drowned had Père Brierre, who was returning from a Mass in Roseaux, not dove into the waters and saved him. Shortly after that, I was conceived. That is why my father asked Père Brierre to baptize me—because I owe my very existence to him. And so I tell you now, so there is no confusion—I too am the kind of man who reserves the right to cry 'Fire!' myself when in front of the firing squad! And *mon cher*, you ask me now to cry 'Fire!' but I'm not ready!"

The Sénateur laughed until his face was a menacing purple. Then he leaned in very close, so close I could smell his clean, minty breath. The ordinary folks faded away, and it was just the two of us, alone on the deck. "You can tell your friends also, the kind of man I am," he said. "Let them know that I'm not ready."

The Sénateur was quiet. I thought the conversation was over. But then he said, "You know that this is a city of poets, don't you?"

"I saw the sign at the airport."

The dirt landing strip was carved into the fields of sugarcane and bananas like a scar. The airport itself was a one-room cement hut. A sign read BIENVENUE À JÉRÉMIE. LA CITÉ DES POÈTES. Seeing that sign had been the first hint that I would love this place.

"Do *you* enjoy poetry?" the Sénateur pursued.

A verse began to round out in my brain, something from high school: *Hear the voice of the Bard / who present, past, and future sees.*

"Of course," I said.

His face brightened.

"Then you will know Docteur Révolus. Jean Joseph Vilaire. Callisthènes Fouchard. General Franck Lavaud. Félix Philantrope. All men of Jérémie—these splendid poets. And those are only some of our more famous poets. When I was a boy, you could not find a man in Jérémie who did not reckon himself a poet. They called us quite correctly the Athens of Haiti."

Hear the voice of the Bard / who present, past, and future sees; / Whose ears have heard / The Holy Word—I couldn't remember the last line of the stanza. *That walk'd*—and what?

"I too am a poet," he said.

The Sénateur paused. He was waiting. He had an almost shy look on his face.

"Perhaps I might read your poems someday," I said.

"What an honor that would be for me! What a pleasure that would be! Then you would know my soul. Pierre!"

"Maître!"

"Bring the man the book."

Pierre went off into some inner room, locking eyes with Fidel on his way out. He came back with a small book. There was a portrait of the Sénateur on the cover, in profile and black-and-white, in a high turtleneck sweater, looking mournful and serious. The book was titled *Les chansons de l'aigle.*

"I very much look forward to this," I said.

"Please do not judge me too harshly."

"I'm in no position to judge anyone when it comes to writing poetry."

"I'm afraid the poems reveal the *man.*"

He said this with such unexpected humility that I felt the first stirrings of fondness for him. By now I had long forgotten electricity.

I was at the top of the stairs when I said, "Sénateur?"

The Sénateur was already talking with the next of his visitors, giving him all the attention he had offered me.

"My friend?" he said.

"Would you mind signing your book?"

His face exploded in a huge, ugly smile. "Pierre!"

"*Maître!*"

"Bring me a pen!"

He wrote in the book in perfect cursive, almost calligraphic handwriting:

> *For an American friend—*
>
> *welcome to my country,*
> *this place of joy and sadness,*
> *where the days shall pass swiftly,*
> *the nights in pleasure,*
> *and to which you will owe no less than your heart.*
>
> *with all respect and affection,*
> *Sénateur Maxim Bayard.*

That evening, nestled under the mosquito net and listening to the drums beating out messages to the other world, I remembered the last line of my stanza. It had been worrying me. *Hear the voice of the Bard / who present, past, and future sees; / Whose ears have heard / The Holy Word / That walk'd among the ancient trees.*

PART TWO

1 Here is Haiti, by every statistical measure the poorest country in the Western Hemisphere, but don't be surprised by the Boucan Grégoire, which would not be out of place at all in Paris or New York, not in its elegance, not in its food, not in its prices. Out front of each arriving car, the young boys gather. Half begging, half menacing, they offer to watch the car as you eat: "*Blan!* Remember me! I'm Fanfan. I'll give you good security! Best security!" At the entrance to the restaurant there is a man with a shotgun. A man with a shotgun stands at the entrance to every place the wealthy in Port-au-Prince cluster—at the supermarket; at the bank, of course; in the driveways of the villas of Pétionville. After a while you no longer see the man with the shotgun, but you know he's there; you wouldn't feel right if he wasn't.

So you sit at the bar of the Boucan Grégoire and look at the other customers. The patrons have plush, oily skin; their well-fed bodies glow. Everyone is quiet, and they lean close over their plates to talk: the world of the wealthy in Haiti is intimate, suspicious, inbred. These people know one another and hate one another; they have green cards and apartments in Miami and cars with bulletproof glass. They live behind high walls topped with barbed wire. What is it Kapuściński wrote? "Money in a poor country and money in a rich country are two different things." Nobody understands money like a rich man in a poor country. A wealthy man in America, in Singapore, in Norway, has a bright, happy, satisfied face. Fortune has favored him; his pleasures are endless.

But if you are wealthy in a poor country, that is something different. You are a fat sheep in a land of wolves. You are always alert, always watchful; the worst is always yet to come. You live on a small island where uncertain winds are blowing. A wealthy man arrives at middle age in Haiti stripped down to a tough, resilient, unsentimental core. A wealthy man in Haiti has narrow, shrewd eyes. You can never relax. Tomorrow somebody might kidnap your beloved nephew—he's careless, that one, coming home from the discothèque by motorbike in the early hours of the morning. Tomorrow there might be mobs on the street, throwing rocks at your car or trying to storm your office. Tomorrow the government might fall—there could be a coup d'état—and you might need to flee again into exile. Soon there will be an election, and elections are precarious: the former president once spoke of placing burning tires around the necks of the wealthy. Such a man could be in office again. Do you send the children abroad for their education? Your father died of a heart attack. There are no facilities to treat a coronary in Haiti. Sometimes you are out of breath when you climb stairs. Your wife says, "Miami." She says, "Jean, now is really the time for Miami." But what would you do in Miami? Sell used cars like your brother-in-law? No, you have your dignity. Do you know what it means to do business in a country such as this one? Tomorrow the Americans might discover a worm in the mangoes, and then where will you be? Tomorrow the president might appoint your enemy as customs inspector. Then where will you be? You will be poor. There is nothing worse than being poor. You know what poverty is: you live in Haiti. How do you live with anxieties like that? You take your wife out for dinner at the Boucan Grégoire. You wave to your friends. You order a rum sour and another, and then—why not?—the smoked salmon with its crème fraîche.

The evening had been made possible by Facebook: it was Kay's birthday, and she had invited all her multitudinous Facebook friends to join her for drinks and dinner.

I arrived at the restaurant early and nursed a glass of rum until Kay's pretty cheek brushed up against my own and Terry's hard hand palpated my shoulder, and their perfumes, like lemons, roses, and musk, settled in a pleasant cloud around me.

"I'm *so* glad to see you," Kay said. "I was afraid nobody was going to come."

"Don't you have many friends?" I asked.

"I'm very popular," she said. "I'm the most popular girl in school."

"Leave Kay alone on a desert island and she'd make friends with a coconut," Terry said.

"I love coconuts," she giggled. "I even married one."

She rapped her hand against his head and ruffled his graying hair.

Terry said, "I need a drink."

"I want something girly," Kay said. "Please."

Terry drifted obediently in the direction of the bar. "And what have you done with yourself all day?" I asked.

She leaned in close and said, "My husband rented a beautiful room for me in a beautiful hotel with a beautiful view, and we turned on the air conditioner and drank champagne and my husband made love to me all afternoon. And now I intend to celebrate."

"It's nice to see you happy," I said.

"It's very nice to *be* so happy," she said.

She must have sensed in me something understanding, because she added, "Promise me you won't let me say anything embarrassing tonight."

"You're very charming," I said. "You don't need to worry."

"You're so diplomatic."

"I'm sincere."

She leaned up close and whispered in my ear. "If I start to say something embarrassing, you just say something about Africa and I'll be quiet like a mouse. That's our signal."

"It's a promise," I said.

"You just say, 'I understand there's a war in Africa,' or 'Have you seen a good movie from Africa?' and zip—"

She zippered her red lips firmly shut.

Then she opened them again to say, "Nadia and Johel are supposed to come."

Terry came back with a flute of champagne reddened with Kir, and for himself a tumbler of rum.

"How pretty!" she said. "It's too pretty to drink!"

"With the prices here, you'd better drink it," Terry said. For a man who had spent all afternoon making love to his wife, he was pretty glum.

"Terry hates places like this," Kay said. "I had to drag him here."

"Kay—," he said, his voice whiny.

"Well, it's *true*," she said. "Terry feels guilty spending all this money when the kids outside are hungry."

"He's got a point," I said.

"Not you too! It's my birthday!"

"And even in Africa, the lions are celebrating. To your birthday!"

2   Kay and I saw each other whenever she was in Jérémie: a trip to the beach, a walk in the mountains, an evening game of Scrabble. She was the kind of woman with ideas: there was a crumbling house twenty minutes out of town—the birthplace of Alexandre Dumas's grandfather. So she piled on the back of my motorcycle and we bumped up and down the back roads until we found the ruined foundation, nothing but some squared-off stones in an empty field where once a mansion had stood. "It's so sad," Kay said. Then there was the time she had heard of a family of Amish missionaries out near Mont Beaumont who sold medicinal honey—wouldn't it be a kick to go find them? Would I want to go and find the *pharmacie vodouisante* with her? She wanted to buy good-luck powder. So we went down to Basse-Ville and hunted for the Pharmacie Zentrailes together.

Or else we just walked. Eight in the morning she'd present herself in leggings, a T-shirt, and pink tennis shoes, her blond hair pulled back in a tight ponytail. "Let's go, early bird," she'd say. Then we'd walk from my house to Carrefour Prince, about an hour and a half each way on a road that surveyed the ocean. Little house after little house, tin roof, thatch roof, children carrying buckets of water on their heads. Donkeys clip-clopping toward the market. Children everywhere, sitting naked in the dirt, dusty faces streaked with tears. Orphanage, distillery, a pair of churches, Protestant and Catholic. Everywhere we went, people waved at us, and shouted *"Blan!"* Mango, papaya, grapefruit, mandarin trees shading the road. Ladies washing themselves bare-breasted. Through the break in the trees, glimpses of the sea, tranquil and teal.

Once upon a time when the times were good, the White family finances had balanced on three pillars, like a stool: the properties, her income in real estate, Terry's salary. The summer before Terry came down to Haiti, all three collapsed.

Kay's job had been the first pillar of the family to crumble. Who in South Florida hadn't sold real estate in those years? With every Tommaso, Ricardo, and Miguel buying a second house or a third, with credit as fluid as tap water, and with housing prices seemingly as buoyant as cork, all Kay needed to make good money in those days was a big smile and a Rolodex. A big smile and a Rolodex were *precisely* the assets Kay possessed in superabundance. People liked Kay and she liked people. *Do you want to see a house? Why not! Let me show you some things. Come on, honey, I'll take you out tomorrow—lemme check my book. No, tomorrow's no good, but first thing Thursday, I've got just the place to show you. We'll catch up while we drive around. I'm so happy.*

She hadn't come to real estate as a passion—as a little girl, she had dreamed of training show jumpers—but she liked having her days filled with people, and she liked the money too. Besides, she'd tried so many other things, and nothing had quite clicked. Before there was real estate, Kay had spent a year in grad school at the University of Florida studying Seminoles—if you can believe that; tried her hand as a potter's apprentice; opened up a dog grooming business called Doggone Chic with her niece; even worked for a spell in human resources at Disney. Nothing had been quite right. Then she'd hooked up with Todd Malgarini and his crew. She'd always had a flair for decorating and design, so Todd had asked her to help him fix up houses for show. Before clients came over, she'd boil a sprig of rosemary with a little lemon and vanilla. Kay's houses smelled like baking and Sunday morning. In the trunk of her car she kept wine bottles filled with M&M's and candy corn. She'd arrange them on the kitchen counters, and people felt, not knowing why, that kids could live there. Then there was the trick she used for the bathrooms, rolling up the towels instead of folding them, so the place felt like a spa.

But when Kay saw Todd's BMW, she thought, *I can do that too*. So she got herself the real estate license, and there never was a better time for someone selling houses in the greater Watsonville area. Once she got going, she very literally did not have enough hours in her day to show houses to all the people who wanted to see houses: people would have been looking at houses at three in the morning if the owners hadn't minded.

And what Kay was seeing every day out in the real estate trenches were people no smarter than she doing *very* well by themselves. Every day she saw people all around her getting second, even third mortgages, riding the market upward, then letting the properties back out onto the market. She saw those people building themselves solid foundations; she saw people turning their sweat and dreams into income, and she wanted to put herself and Terry on a solid foundation too. What was a solid foundation? A solid foundation meant having the same kind of life for herself that her parents had; it meant riding lessons and trips to the Keys and the better kind of lingerie that was flattering but not trampy; and above all, it meant not having to think so much about money. Kay hated thinking about money, but she liked life—that was a basic fact about Kay—and money was just what you needed if you wanted to enjoy it: money meant the wine tasted better and the cotton was softer and the furniture was prettier.

So Kay took equity from her own house—thank you, Wachovia Bank!—for a down payment and spread it across a pair of condos. She knew the market, and she chose good ones, refurbished ones in an old brick building in the city center, not far from the university, but not so close either that they'd be student condos: they were investment grade. Kay was being responsible. That was the irony of the whole situation.

And for a while it worked. She knew what properties like hers were worth—she was selling them every darned day. She looked at what she and Terry had, and she knew the two of them were on a solid foundation. The bank offered her a reverse mortgage: that's how they turned those apartments into the trip to Vail, the BMW, Terry's first run for state senate. Kay liked to throw parties, so there was this time, once, they had a fund-raiser for Terry: two hundred people in the backyard and an ice sculpture. She paid almost four hundred dollars for a swan that, when it started to melt, looked like a penguin. They could afford a couple of cases of good wine to keep in the basement for special occasions. They could afford all the stuff that made life extra fun.

Then the market went sour.

When people talked about "the market," Kay always had in mind some big, slow, friendly, lumbering dinosaur, like Barney. You could tell where Barney was going from a mile off. Barney wasn't going to start sprinting downhill. She figured that if the market turned—and she knew it could turn—it would turn slow. Maybe she wouldn't get out at the peak. But she still had two investment-grade properties under title in downtown Watsonville, not to mention a house and a career.

But it turned out that Barney the Market was some Freakosaurus Rex, capable of sprinting downhill so fast that not even the most personable, prettiest, and most charming of realtors could chase him. There was no way to unload those properties. And Barney the Market wasn't so fucking friendly either. He was loose in their neighborhood, and every house he stopped at and swiped at with his monster claws lost value: *I love you! You love me! There's no longer equity!* Those condos were underwater so deep, so far, and so fast that divers with masks couldn't have found them. Nobody was buying houses now. Kay, after a few months— like the ten zillion other real estate agents in Florida who thought they were geniuses—didn't even try. Soon she was back doing what she had been doing before, fixing up houses for Todd Malgarini, work that had felt fun and creative once upon a time and now felt like a humiliation. There weren't a ton of houses to show, and the Whites fell back on what they had, which was Terry's salary. This is about when Kay stopped sleeping nights, trying to figure out how to stuff those two condos, a house, the health insurance, the car payments, and the subscription to the Wine of the Month Club into one deputy sheriff's salary.

Nothing in Kay's experience had prepared her for being broke. She was terrified. She wished that Terry couldn't sleep either. Why wasn't he awake, too? The two of them could talk about the shadows on the ceiling. That one looked like a dancing walrus. That one looked like a sad weasel. She looked at Terry lying there, and she thought, *What is wrong with him?* So she lay in bed doing the numbers; then, first thing in the morning making coffee, she did them all over again. Kay made plans that didn't pan out and contingency plans that she knew were unrealistic. Kay and Terry had been paying for private school for Terry's nephews. Now they couldn't send that check to Green Valley anymore. They canceled vacations—that wasn't *nearly* enough. Kay's father loaned Kay twenty-five thousand dollars—"against your inheritance," he said. "Daddy, don't talk like that," Kay said. Kay took the money and felt awful in every way. That ran out too.

Then came the moment when the two of them, not exactly holding hands, stepped off the financial cliff, when Terry lost his job after the business with Marianne Miller. He was just outplayed, pure and simple, by that woman. It wasn't fair, but that's what it was. That was the summer Terry took up competitive glowering. He was pretty good at it, too. If you got him talking, he'd head straight to the one subject he was fit to talk on, which was how much he hated Marianne Miller.

Give it a rest, Terry—that's what Kay thought but was (almost) smart enough not to say (too often).

It wasn't as if Terry was exactly a hero to her in that stage of life. Things hadn't exactly been super great between Kay and Terry since forever.

The first thing was about the kids—and don't tell Terry I told you this, okay? But we tried for years, and finally I got him into the clinic, and—and that was a big thing for Kay&Terry, a very big thing, maybe bigger even for Terry than for her. They almost adopted, the process falling through twice at the last minute, the second time when the birth mother backed out, with Ella Marie White's room all decorated and waiting for her. After that, Terry, looking as thoroughly beaten by the world as a man can look, said, "Kay, if you want someone who can give you a family, I'd understand." And Kay rolled over and said, "Like swans, Terry. We're for life."

It was just about that time that Terry and Kay became obsessed with politics, the two of them taking all their energy and despair and boredom and channeling it straight into ambition. When she'd met Terry and married him—why, the guy just glowed with promise. Everyone thought so. It wasn't just Kay. Her sisters, her mom, her friends—people saw him in politics or business, or as a lawyer: anywhere someone smart, articulate, clean-cut, and connected could make it big. They didn't see a cop; they saw Representative White, with a solid background in law enforcement. Maybe even Senator White.

So when Terry threw his hat in the ring, Kay figured that this was when Rocketship Terry, headed straight for Planet Success, finally took off. Only Terry took two shots at it and lost both times. The two of them worked their backsides off trying to get Terry up the ladder, and both times he took a licking. Kay never understood why. You know that business with the pheromones, how you fall in love with people because they have some smell you didn't even know you were smelling? Maybe that's the way it was with Terry. Funny thing was, *she* loved the way he smelled. Sometimes he'd come home at the end of the day and she'd bury her nose in the fleshy place under his jawbone, just inhaling him—like a half packet of Marlboro Reds and two cups of black coffee, like honest sweat, like a man . . .

. . . there was something she wanted to tell me. Do you mind if I tell you these things? It's just that we don't know each other, so I can talk to you . . .

Kay hadn't been the only one who thought Terry smelled great. There was another lady voter who found him mighty attractive. Like the swans, my ass. With her nephew Brett's third-grade teacher. *Seriously?* Terry was coaching Brett's Little League, and Miss Whitman came to a game, introduced herself. It didn't help that Brett was head over heels for Miss Whitman too: all Kay heard that year was Miss Whitman this, Miss Whitman that; the woman made kids laugh and grown men act like pigs.

Oh my fucking Lord, did that hurt. She's staring at the ceiling at night, worrying how they're going to eat and pay the mortgage, and Terry's dreaming about *her.*

That was a couple of years back now, and something about the affair just rankled down to her bones, rankled to this day, rankled in a way that not even her own infidelity expunged. Basically, she knew that Terry, no matter how much he wept and cried and begged her to take him back, would have left her for Miss Whitman—but Miss Whitman wouldn't take him. Terry wasn't good enough for Miss Whitman. He was too good for Kay and not good enough for Miss Whitman, so that pretty much left Kay somewhere down at the bottom of the pile, which was not exactly how Kay thought things should be.

Deepest, longest, hardest pain of her life, and nothing really made it better. Not the counseling thing, not Terry's tears and protestations and affirmations of undying love. Not even the thing with her dentist, and don't laugh, say what you will about Dr. Stern, he was basically single; he was gentle; he had a good sense of humor; he took every Tuesday and Thursday afternoon off all summer long; he had a condo with a pool; and he asked Kay a lot of questions about what it was like to be the woman in Kay's head and body, then listened to her answers with the same air of concentrated attention he offered her in his office when she talked about her incisor, the one that was getting supersensitive to cold. Also—and this wasn't a joke—he really had the best-tasting mouth of any man she had ever kissed. She asked him about that once, and he said that it really made a difference, regular flossing. Kay wasn't exactly sad when Dr. Stern broke it off in the fall—it was just something that she missed. She didn't even change dentists.

Why did she stick with Terry? It's a good question—the question she asked herself approximately twice a minute for the last three years. And is it totally crazy if I just say I still love him? Just not the way that she thought love should be. She hated herself for loving him when her sisters told her that she should be hating him: it made her think she was weak and sick. But the thing is, deep down, Terry was a good person. Like the way—when guys were in county lockup at Christmas, he'd make sure their kids got presents. He'd take orders from the guys in lockup and then spend his own money to make sure some fuckup's three-year-old got a shiny toy truck. Or like the way when his sister was dying (ovarian cancer and only thirty-four), he spent every minute at her house, carrying her to the bathroom, just sitting by her side when, drugged out and dopey, she slept. Kay knew that's the way Terry would be for her.

And then there was something else. It was Dr. Stern who wrote her the first prescription for Vicodin, and before long she was visiting this pain clinic in a strip mall out on the drive. Wait in that waiting room for an hour with the white trash and the pregnant ladies with the stringy hair, not believing that this was how her life was turning out, and then six minutes with that weird old Indian doctor, shaking his head in stupid figure eights. "What is being the problem, Madame?" Being the problem is that my back/nose/spleen/soul won't stop hurting. Then walking out with the scrip. Not that she had ever imagined herself doing that, but that's how she got through those days, and she wasn't making any excuses. It's what allowed her to get through those days and not explode with stress and rage and not kill her husband, and if you want to judge me, go ahead, but try walking a couple of miles in my espadrilles first.

So all that was what was going on in Kay's mind when Terry first packed up and headed down to Haiti. When Terry got the job in Haiti, she thought, *We can pay the mortgage.* Then she thought, *Thank God I won't have to see him anymore.*

Only the strange thing was—Haiti was sort of just like this thing that they had needed.

As soon as Terry got down to Haiti, she started to like him more, just the tone in his voice, the pictures he sent of him and his African colleagues. Kay wasn't too vain, certainly not compared with her sisters, but sometimes she would see an outfit in a fashion magazine—a pretty skirt or blouse, something that under ordinary circumstances she'd never wear in a thousand years—and more than anything she'd want to try it on, see herself wearing that printed skirt in the mirror. See how it transformed her, turned her into another woman. Kay had two fears in life: the first was that she was going to lose everything she loved—her job, her husband, her house—but the other was that it was all just going to stay the same until she died. She knew that didn't make much sense, but where was it written that Kay White had to make a whole lot of sense? Sometimes the thought tormented her, especially in the early evenings, that nothing in her life was ever going to change—and Haiti was change, pure and distilled. She saw Terry's pictures of the beaches and the white dirt roads, the tin-roofed huts and the little kids in nothing but ankle-length old gray T-shirts, and she saw change: she wanted to see herself in that picture too.

Looking at Terry in those photos was like seeing him for the first time, as if she were looking at someone else's foxy husband on Facebook. The little fleck of gray in his hair was new. Kay thought it was handsome. Terry with his arm over his colleague, Terry with his arm around the judge. That was the Good Terry. Terry telling her about that road. This was the Terry she had once loved before life had set them both back on their heels. The Terry who thought huge and made big plans and said yes to everything. The Terry who was going to take her up in the hot-air balloon of life until they were floating weightless in the clouds . . .

. . . the Terry who showed her one day—they were just kids, broke and hopeful—that big Georgian house with the columns and the rolling lawn and told her that was going to be the place where one day their grandkids would play on the lawn. House wasn't even for sale. Terry said, "Come on," rang the doorbell. Old couple answers. Cutest little old people you ever saw. So in love, so old. Terry says, "We'd like to buy your house and raise a family here." This old couple, charmed as all heck, they invited us in, offered us lemonade. Before long, they're showing us the nursery and the pantry, and Terry is telling them we're going to have two boys, and those old people are saying, "We can tell you kids are going to have a wonderful life."

Just a wonderful life.

That Terry was in those photos from Haiti—that same Terry grin and smirk. "Kay, we're going to do some great things down here"—that's what he told her. "Kay, we're going to make a difference."

Welcome back, buddy. I missed you.

So she came down to Haiti, and then she just kept coming. People back home asked her, "What d'you love about it down there?"

And what could she say about Haiti but that it made her happy?

3 Soon some of Kay's other friends arrived at the restaurant. How had she met so many people? That was the miracle of Kay White. "This is my friend Baker, he's from the embassy," she said, and I shook hands with a dreadlocked political attaché whose accent was Texas, whose aspect was the other Caribbean of pretty beaches and steel drums, and whose manner was all pleasant professional charm. Then I met a man named Larry Bayles Jameson who told me to call him LBJ, just like everyone else.

"LBJ is my inspiration," Kay said. "You know what LBJ does?"

I shook my head, and LBJ looked at the floor modestly, and Kay explained that LBJ ran a small Ford dealership outside Terre Haute. He gave his customers the following option when they bought a new vehicle: if they made a donation to one of his water projects in Haiti, the first service was on him. At the end of the year he matched all the donations out of his own pocket. Then he and his sons came to Haiti twice a year to dig wells and install pumps and build cisterns.

Over the course of the next quarter hour, the group swelled out to more than a dozen. On the flight down to Haiti just that morning, Kay had met an Indian telecom engineer who worked for Digicel—he was there too; then I shook the hand of a cartographer who worked for USAID, and I kissed the downy cheek of his French girlfriend, an epidemiologist who worked for the WHO. A few of Terry's colleagues were there. "These are our *good* friends," Kay said. Some of the guests had never even met Kay in the flesh. They were friends only on Twitter and Facebook.

We were soon seated at a long table in the garden, where on Kay's instructions I was nestled between LBJ on my left and Baker on my right. Kay was directly in front of me, talking to the French lady from the WHO. The others in our group, who did not know one another, made polite conversational forays. The only thing that brought us all together was that we were acquaintances of Kay White.

I said, "Now, LBJ, tell me what brought you down to Haiti."

"You want the long version or the short version?"

Seeing me hesitate, LBJ smiled. "Short version is I used to have quite a serious drinking problem. Came to Haiti and stopped drinking."

LBJ picked up a roll from the basket, pulled it open, and smeared it with butter.

"And the long version?"

LBJ said, "Long version is I had more money than I needed and more time than I could handle and I was wasting my life away swimming laps in a bottle of Jack Daniel's. That's a real long story right there. Long version is I got to the point where my wife was going to walk right out the door if I didn't clean up my act. So I went to my pastor, and he told me to come with him down to a village in Haiti for a week."

Up there in Fond Rouge, LBJ continued, the nearest water was from the Artibonite River, an hour away on foot. There was no water for bathing or for washing clothes or for irrigating crops or for drinking— no water except what people could carry on their heads. So the local people walked to the river, then walked back home, picking their way along the rocky paths, five-gallon buckets balanced on their heads. The kids were skipping school just to lug the gallons up the hill. Not only was the water inaccessible, it wasn't even all that clean: it was river water, and there were villages crapping and pissing in the river long before the residents of Fond Rouge got it in their buckets.

Maybe three days into his trip, LBJ told me, he got to watching a local carpenter making a child's coffin. He stopped in the sun and watched the carpenter working. He had never seen a child's coffin before—that's a beautiful fact right there about American life, that you can live an ordinary American life and never see a carpenter making a child-size coffin. An undertaker in the States has to special-order that cruelest box. But this carpenter in the Haitian hills that day was talking with some other fellow and laughing, painting the varnish on this coffin, making it pretty. Brother—how many of those things you make a month? Too many, too many.

On his last night in the mountains, LBJ told me, he got himself a bottle of the local rotgut. He'd been holding out all right until then, more for appearance's sake than anything else, but that last night in Haiti one of the local guys offered him a tot and he was off to the races. This stuff was raw white rum, strong like the call of Satan and as mean as an alley cat. He was halfway through the bottle when he had the thought that would change his life—that he, Larry Bayles Jameson, was in possession of everything necessary to improve the lives of the inhabitants of Fond Rouge, Haiti. What they lacked, he had. He could give them water if he wanted to, and if they had clean drinking water, nobody would be making child-size coffins; and if they *didn't* have water this time next month, next year, or however long it took—it was because he, Larry Bayles Jameson, chose not to give it to them.

Now, twenty years, LBJ said—that's a long time. Lots of twists and turns in that time, and he wasn't going to pretend he never touched another drink or was always a fine husband or a perfect father. But come hell or high water, twice a year every year, three weeks in winter and three in summer, he was down here digging a well or capping a spring, making sure someone who didn't have water had some.

"Now, that's just sheer goodness," Kay said. "Is there anybody who doesn't want to be a good person deep down?"

LBJ smiled modestly and took a sip of his sparkling water.

From Terry's side of the table there were raucous bursts of laughter. Terry said, "The whole thing?" and the man beside him, who I believe came from Brazil, spread his arms out wide. Terry said, "That's not so big." On my side of the table, Kay remained engrossed in conversation with her French friend; and Baker, to my right, was hunched over his phone, tapping out a long description for his Facebook page of the experience of sitting at this table. At one point I started to ask him a question, and he said gently, "I'm sorry—just a minute," and were I to have said something else, I would have been considered an irritant or a scold.

LBJ started talking to Kay about a band they both liked. Only in Haiti do you meet people who find it a diversion to build infrastructure. But in Haiti you meet people like that *all the time*. One hundred percent true story: Fellow makes a fortune down in Texas building big-box retailers. Buys a bulldozer, ships it down to Haiti. Starts building roads. Ends up medevaced out of the country after driving that bulldozer off a cliff. Who just shows up in a sovereign nation with his own private bulldozer and builds roads? How many people do you know who have built a charitable hospital? In Haiti, I met three. Orphanages, latrines, and wells? I lost track. And because in Haiti you meet people like that all the time, it comes to seem normal. That's why so many outsize schemes and megalomaniac ambitions were hatched in Haiti, because it is a place where nobody ever says no.

I had been in poor countries before I came to Haiti, but never in a place—not India, not Africa—where nearly everyone was poor. Walking around Haiti, I sometimes felt like one of those Saudi sheiks who install gold-plated hot tubs in their retrofitted 747s, wealthy beyond imagination or hope. I too had visited villages that, like the village of Fond Rouge in LBJ's story, were without clean drinking water; and like LBJ, I had seen carpenters cutting, sawing, sanding, and planing lumber into a child's coffin. But then I had let the matter slide. Deep, deep inside me there was a voice that said, *Let them walk for their water.* There is no other way to put it: had the voice said anything else, and had it been loud enough, I would have acted. My ability to remain happy while intimately aware of the sufferings of others was a discovery about myself.

Now it was time to order. This proved complicated. Some people at the table had yet to open their menus, and others could not read French; some people were very hungry and wished to order full meals, while others were treating dinner as an opportunity to snack and drink. In the delay and hesitation and confusion you could feel the mood of the table souring. So Kay suggested ordering an assortment of appetizers to be shared. In this way, people could consider the menu at their leisure. Terry from his end of the table said, "You go, girl," which made our end of the table laugh. Then Kay spoke with the waiter, who was glad to have a single interlocutor from this large and demanding group. She ordered efficiently and lavishly: plates of deep-fried okra and bruschetti topped with diced tomatoes and basil, and little bite-size portions of this and that.

I was still waiting for Baker to finish sending his message when Johel and Nadia arrived.

4 I had told Kay that I had never seen her, but I was wrong: I had seen this woman many times in Jérémie, but I had not known that she was Nadia, the judge's wife. I had never made the connection between them. From Kay's stories I had been on the lookout for a woman with a certain kind of beauty. But the woman I had seen at the market or at the *boulangerie* was plain. She was neither tall nor short, but slender, almost willowy, which in consumptive, malnourished Haiti is rarely considered attractive. Her skin was very dark, almost greenish—I had imagined Nadia as cocoa-colored, like the judge. Kay had mentioned her striking eyes, but I had not noticed them. Indeed, I might not have noticed her at all—fixed her as a face and person—if it had not been for one incident.

The meat market in Jérémie was also our abattoir. At dawn, the goats were led here from the hills and sold. Then the *marchandes* would slaughter them on the spot with a machete blow, splitting the heads open. The drainage canal was like a swamp of coagulated blood speckled with fat. Goat heads with glassy eyes were displayed on the concrete benches, side by side with goat paws, the fur still attached. Goats, yet to be butchered, bleated in terror and misery. Huge swarms of flies blackened the exposed meat.

I liked the place: there was a fascination in the organs, entrails, and musculature, the rusty smell of blood; and here I was introduced to that hardiest and most enduring of human beings, the Haitian *marchande*. When you and I and all our kind have long since moldered away—when the last writer and the last reader have grappled each other into a shallow grave—these women's descendants will still be in tropical markets, whacking the heads of goats with blunt machetes, laughing at the horror, and surviving.

Nadia—I did not know her name then—was at the market one morning. This was at the most humid time of the year, thundery days building toward but never reaching climactic rainfall. She was bargaining with a *marchande* and I was bargaining with another when her arm reached out for the table, her knees wobbled, and she sank slowly to the floor. It was such a graceful gesture that I watched her fall with unconcern. (Haitian women, by the way, for reasons I do not know, were very often fainting.) The *marchandes* surrounded her, someone found a chair, and someone else fanned her with the side of a cardboard box. She had landed in a puddle, and her face and hair were caked with goat's blood. Her spooky, flaccid stare, her lips twitching soundlessly—she was not where we were.

That was how I thought of her thereafter—not as Nadia, but as the lady who passed out in the market—until I saw her again that evening at the Boucan Grégoire, trailing two steps behind her husband as they threaded their way through the crowded terrace.

And now she seemed to me a beautiful woman. Perhaps it was a matter of her hair: tonight she wore her hair in long cornrows, which she pulled back into a loose ponytail; what had been to me before a bony face with a high forehead and sharp, jutting cheekbones now seemed feline and dramatic. I had not noticed how lovely her mouth was, her fine lips sculpted. When I had seen her before, she had been dressed in jeans and a tank top that only emphasized how thin she was—her jutting collarbones, her arms as thick at the bicep as at the wrist. Tonight she wore a red dress that I knew without knowing why was both stylish and expensive. She looked as if she had spent her afternoon being groomed. She balanced easily on a pair of high-heeled sandals. Now her skinniness was like the weightlessness of a fine-boned bird. Her fragility, which before had suggested sickliness, was made delicate and desirable by the expensive room she was in.

As Johel led his wife in the direction of our table, he stopped at other tables. Nadia arrested every eye in the room. The judge shook men's hands and gripped shoulders; women stood up, and he gave them kisses. People were pleased to see him. He was dressed, like the other men in the restaurant, in a well-pressed white shirt and blazer, and in this room his fatness, which in Jérémie seemed like superfluous bulk, now seemed masculine and important. As I watched him maneuver his way through the room, his notion that he could be a politician seemed less absurd to me. He had acquired grace and poise. The people he greeted were people with whom he was intimate and familiar. He had left Haiti as a child, but the portion of his family that remained was of old and established Port-au-Prince stock. Now I saw that his return to Haiti had been like a tributary branch of a river returning to broader waters.

Soon they were at our table, and here the judge was also at his ease. He knew some of the people, and others he didn't. To Kay he said, "You look marvelous. I can't believe you're turning twenty-five. Happy birthday." Then to Terry, who had stood up and walked around the table to shake his friend's hand, he added, "Well done, brother. Well done." I wasn't sure what this meant, but Terry seemed pleased by the compliment, which seemed to evaluate positively every facet of Terry's life. Johel shook LBJ's hand and said, "So you're the famous LBJ." He kissed the French epidemiologist on the cheek. When he came to me, he said, "Brother, what a beautiful surprise."

As he moved around the table, he introduced his wife, keeping his hand low on her back. She didn't smile, and her voice was so quiet as to be almost inaudible. When I was introduced to her, she showed no sign of recognizing me. Her eyes drifted down to the tablecloth. Her handshake was fragile, and when I stepped forward to kiss her on the cheek, she stood absolutely still, as if I might be provoked and bite her.

Now there was a problem. The table was too small to accommodate easily the newcomers. We had already been seated elbow-to-elbow. It would have required rearranging the entire group to place two plates side by side. So chairs were moved, and the waiters somewhat clumsily inserted a pair of plates in the remote corners of the table, one plate between Kay and Baker and the other on the far side of the table, near Terry.

"Nadia, you want to sit with your husband, don't you?" Kay asked. "Or do you mind sitting next to me?"

Nadia looked in the direction of her husband, who was talking to Terry. It was obvious that she did want to sit with him. But she said, "No, with you is fine."

"I'm sorry, honey. I didn't hear you."

"It fine with you," Nadia said.

"It's fine?"

"It no problem."

Kay's buzz was fading, and she had turned surly.

Her glance strayed from me to the judge to Nadia to the table, then lingered over the large terrace filled with others just like us, enjoying the last of a long evening before going out to confront the hungry children on the street.

The rumors had persisted: my friend Toussaint Legrand, who had access to subterranean rivers of rumor, told me that when the judge was in Port-au-Prince, as he sometimes was, Terry's car could be seen parked outside the judge's house in Calasse. Yet that seemed natural enough to me, hardly dispositive. I thought of what Terry had told me: "If you ever hear a noise outside the house at night, just give me a call." Here was a woman—you had only to see her slender, haunted face to know—who heard many noises at night.

"Oh, good. I'm glad it's not a problem to sit with me. I hate to make problems." Kay took a sip from her glass and added, "But we can make a place at the other end of the table, if you'd like. Near the boys."

Kay was speaking quickly. She didn't care if Nadia understood her. She wanted me and the other men to understand that her pride had been offended: she had been relegated, at her own party, to the corner of the table reserved for women and children. The center of gravity—the stories, the jokes, the masculine drama—was now at the other end of the long table.

"He's not going anywhere," Kay said. "Don't worry."

"Who?" Nadia said.

"Your husband. He's not going anywhere. He's right there next to my husband."

Nadia didn't say anything. Kay had been right: she had beautiful eyes. Their color gave her skin its hint of greenish pallor. I didn't know what she was thinking; I thought of her vacant expression in the meat market, her face and hair coated in blood. Nadia's eyes gave away nothing but that long-ago liaison between master and slave.

Kay said, "Did you know it's my birthday? In my country, when somebody has a birthday, we say 'Happy birthday' and give them a kiss."

"Happy birthday," Nadia said. "I am very contented for you."

"And when is your birthday? When it's your birthday, we can have a party."

"I don't know."

"What do you mean, you don't know? Honey, everyone has a birthday. It's written on your passport. It's written on your birth certificate. I don't believe—"

I interrupted her. "Kay, did you say you were thinking of going to Africa in the spring? To see the elephants?"

"Well, everybody has to have a birthday. That way we can have a party for Nadia, and if someone's not having a good time—"

"After dinner, let's hear some African music. Or see some African art."

Kay stopped herself. She was thinking of getting angry—you could see it building. But the spark wouldn't catch. From the far end of the table, there was her husband's bullying voice. He had his arm around a colleague. I heard, "This motherfucker—this guy—" Then I heard Johel saying, "Wait—wait—what you mean is—"

Kay picked up her knife and inspected her reflection. She pouted at herself. Then she excused herself to go to the bathroom and walked off singing, "It's my party and I'll pee if I want to—pee if I want to."

When she came back, she was happy again. Baker the diplomat asked Kay if she wanted to hear a funny story.

"I'd *love* to," Kay said.

"This is a true story," Baker said.

"Of course it is," Kay said. "I bet you've never told a lie in your life. You've got that kind of face."

"So we give out visas, that's what we do all day, and the truth is that most folks who want a visa, we say no."

"That's cold," Kay said.

"You don't know the half of it. Listen to the story. The way it works with visas is that applicants have to prove to us that they're not going to live in the States."

Now Nadia was looking at Baker. I had thought the language was too difficult for her, but she was staring at him, her brilliant eyes not blinking.

"Basically, you have to prove you're not broke. Show us a bank account, show us a house, show us a job. And that's not easy to do. Nine out of ten applicants we turn down."

Kay had a little smile on her face, waiting for the punch line.

"So one of my colleagues gets this applicant. Lady makes an appointment, shows up at the window, pays her hundred dollars, and wants a visa. Neatly dressed older lady, says she works at American Airlines, wants to visit her kids in Boston. And for whatever reason, my colleague—we call her Permission Denied, she's such a hard-ass—Permission Denied doesn't believe the story. The letter from the employer looks strange, the bank account is nearly empty, et cetera, et cetera. Decision is final. No appeals."

Baker paused for a second as the waiter delivered the appetizers.

"So a couple of weeks later, Permission Denied is ready to go back to the States on vacation. She gets herself to the airport, waits in line, and who's standing there behind the counter but this lady, the one who got her visa denied. Permission Denied is sweating bullets just because this is so awkward. And this lady, sugar wouldn't melt in her mouth. Doesn't say a thing. 'Enjoy your flight, ma'am.' Permission Denied thinks everything will be fine, just until the moment she's getting on board the plane, when American Airlines security stops her. Seems *she's* been flagged on the No Fly List. And she's sputtering how she works at the American embassy, et cetera, et cetera. She makes such a holy scandal they bring out the head of airport security."

"Don't tell me—," Kay said.

"You got it," Baker said.

"Really?" I said.

"She turned him down for a visa too."

"Oh, no!" Kay said.

"You know what the lady at the counter, the first lady, said?"

"What?" Kay said.

"She looks at Permission Denied and says, 'I didn't want to take my vacation in Port-au-Prince either.'"

"Oh, that's too good," Kay said.

"True story."

Now it was our side of the table that exploded in laughter. Soon all of us were telling jokes. The only one who wasn't laughing was Nadia. But Kay was happy again, as all the men—Baker, LBJ, and me—placated her and made her laugh.

It didn't seem like cruelty to ignore Nadia, maybe even a kindness. She did not look bored. She stared at her husband. From time to time her face would attract my eye, and my glance would linger on her high cheekbones, her tiny ears, and her sculpted lips. Later, when the judge excused himself and went to the bathroom, I do not believe that Nadia's eyes wavered for even a fraction of a second from the pathway leading to the main building in which the toilets were located; and she seemed to respire shallowly until the very instant he returned to the table, where he leaned his big body over hers and whispered in her ear. Whatever he said produced a wan smile. Then he sat down again at the far side of the table.

Baker whispered to me, "Is that Madame Mireille?"

I followed his glance across the room to a distinguished lady in red crêpe de chine, the only woman at a table of older men.

"What are you two talking about?" Kay asked.

Baker said, "Not so loud, she'll hear us."

"Who?" Kay asked, her voice inexplicably louder.

"That's Madame Mireille," I said.

"Where?"

"That lady. That's her."

Our heads all swung around like spectators at a tennis match, and then people at neighboring tables followed our glance.

"She doesn't look like the posters," Kay said.

Madame Mireille's face, admittedly somewhat younger, was on electoral posters all over the capital: she had been a losing candidate in the last presidential election, a partisan of the mulatto urban economic elite. The posters had yet to be taken down. Her husband had been president in the late 1980s before being deposed; on his death a few years back, she entered politics herself. She had lost the election very badly.

"She's a brave woman," Nadia said.

Her voice surprised me.

Kay said, "I never understood that, how some women go into politics when their men die. If Terry died, it's not like I'd see it as a career opportunity."

Then the waiter came back. Now we had had sufficient time to consider our choices, and the process of ordering was efficient. It was interrupted only by Nadia, who had not looked at her menu. Instead she insisted on interrogating the waiter on her choices. And I understood that she could not read the menu.

Kay must have noticed the same thing. "The fish is so good," she said. "They make it with this beurre blanc white sauce and—"

Nadia continued to interrogate the waiter.

"The last time we were here, I loved it," Kay said, as much to me as to Nadia. "I'm just not getting it today because sometimes I need meat, you know? If I don't eat a steak once a week, I feel faint. Terry says I'm a natural-born carnivore."

The waiter in his pressed white shirt and tuxedo jacket seemed to be losing his patience.

"Fish is good," he said.

"See?" Kay said. "You'll love it."

"Give me the fish," Nadia finally said.

But when the food eventually arrived, Nadia did something that surprised me. She took a bite and called the waiter over. Her voice now had lost its timidity.

"This fish slept," she said, the Creole way of saying that the fish wasn't fresh.

"He didn't sleep," the waiter said.

Nadia didn't say anything. She had decided before she tasted the fish that it had slept, I think. It was a point of principle. I had not thought her capable of confronting the white-shirted waiter in this fancy restaurant. She stared the waiter into submission. He glanced helplessly around the table for a moment, as if one of us might intervene, then, his shoulders sagging, took the plate away.

Later, when he came back with another fish—we had almost all of us finished eating by then—Nadia accepted the plate with a curt *"Merci."* Then she ate delicately, flicking little bits of fish off the bone and onto her fork. I have never seen anyone eat a plate of food more slowly. We were all long finished before her fish was half consumed.

5 This is the story, pretty much the way Kay White told it to me.

There was a young Manhattan lawyer who wore a sweater-vest in winter under his dark gray suit and carried an antique pocket watch with a flinty silver face (he collects them) and a fat Waterman fountain pen (he collects them too); a man who looked forty when he was twenty, with a bit of a belly and a receding hairline, and looked just the same at thirty; a man who will look just the same splayed out one day in his gleaming *acajou* coffin.

There was a young man who, from the moment he arrived at the age of eleven on the other side of the water, embraced responsibility and eschewed frivolity; a young man who excelled through the application of discipline, intelligence, and unstinting hard work at every American endeavor thus far essayed, and who has been rewarded by being denied nothing in his American life that is his due.

There was a young man with a pretty honey-blond fiancée named Jennifer McCall, a nice girl whom he met in law school, two highly intelligent, highly learned young creatures, both of them ambitious and kindly and smart, building a beautiful American life together.

The young man is holding his bachelor party at a nightclub called Kombit in Brooklyn.

And what we have here are not strippers, hookers, and tequila shots; what we have here is not some last hurrah of single life before the shackles of domesticity are welded on for life—no, what we have here is a damn good party. The young lawyer has invited everyone to his party because that's the Haitian style. Everyone he knows and loves is there at Kombit on that February night, from his grandparents to his innumerable cousins to his colleagues at work—partners, associates, and secretaries alike—to a dozen friends from law school, who know nothing of Haiti and think of Johel Célestin as a black guy with a French name and a white accent, a fact or condition that Johel Célestin both loves and hates, America effacing and rubbing away the nastiness of the old country, but also imposing a story on him that's not his.

And just what *is* his story?

Jennifer McCall doesn't know—that's what Johel knows in his gut but won't be able to say until years later. ("She never understood who I was, brother, because she wasn't Haitian. That's not a sin. Just a fact.") She doesn't understand that when you come from a country like Haiti, that's as much a part of you as your family. She doesn't know that being Haitian makes you different, it's something that runs deep in your blood and bones. When he was in college, Johel used to dream of writing the great Haitian novel just so he could give it to his girlfriends and say, *This is where I come from*. But his brain didn't work like that: two dozen drafts of twenty pages each, and Johel was applying to law school. His roommate in college was from a family of Somali immigrants, and the two of them got along just fine, members of the fraternity of the fucked-up nations of the earth. Those two didn't need to explain to each other how hard the world is, if you scratch away the shiny surface.

But sweet, wide-hipped, bosomy Jennifer McCall knows only that Johel is kind and generous and dignified and smart, that he likes to sip very good rum from his extensive collection and sit in an easy chair after work listening to good jazz or reading a serious book. She knows that he is the kind of man whom you can spend your life with, who will be good and kind and faithful to her and their children, who is provident and mature. Jennifer McCall was even invited to Johel's bachelor party—although next week she's going out with her girlfriends and, like it or not, he's staying home, because she knows that by midnight Johel will be yawning, her big, cuddly smart teddy bear of a man wanting to snuggle up warm in bed with her.

What a cozy future they have together.

And she would have been at his party, too, enjoying his colleagues and family and keeping an eye on her man, if it hadn't been for Grandma McCall's little stroke, not so serious, thank goodness, but necessitating an unplanned trip back to Boston.

She was sorry to be gone, because Johel had planned that party with the care and discipline and capacity for hard work that he brought to bear on everything in his life, somewhere between neuroticism and obsession, right down to the food, which had to be Haitian enough for his aunts and uncles who are fully and one hundred percent old country—that is to say, the food had to be greasy and hot and piquant enough for Tonton Jean and Tonton Alphonse and Tante Marie, who don't like food if it doesn't make your mouth explode—and still interesting enough to please his yuppie colleagues who regularly put the best restaurants in Manhattan on their expense accounts. So Johel stressed over the menu: huge platters of fried plantains; mountains of *griot* marinated in lemons and Scotch bonnet chiles; beef *tassot* made the way his grandmother liked it, soaked in orange juice for a night, then boiled and fried; and tray after tray of deep-fried *akra*. Everything was drenched in *piklis*, so spicy the waiters carrying the platters out from the kitchen kept rubbing their eyes with the back of their tuxedoed sleeves. Not to mention the drinks: vats of Prestige in big steel buckets, and on every table a bottle of five-star Barbancourt and pitchers of cocktails made from Haitian grapefruit, available at a Haitian greengrocer in Flatbush.

And the music—Johel originally chose the date for the party because Tropicana was touring up the East Coast and he thought, *How about that, if Tropicana could play my party?* But Tropicana dropped out at the last moment owing to the ever-present visa issues, and he sat with Ti Maurice who owns Kombit, listening to demo tapes of all the major Haitian bands who play the East Coast circuit: Miami, Brooklyn, Montreal, and Boston. When he hears Erzulie L'Amour, he says to himself, *That's just right.* He thinks of the old-time bands from the back-in-the-day that he never knew; he thinks of starry tropical nights and a big band playing under a gazebo poolside at the legendary hotels of Port-au-Prince, the El Rancho or the Ibo Lele, a lady's voice wafting out over the palmy night, and all sophisticated Port-au-Prince society dressed in white jackets and pretty dresses, drinking rum sours and dancing until dawn.

With planning like that, how could the party be anything less than a success? Everybody had a great time, even though the band was late and Johel was fretting like a maniac—not that you could tell, if you weren't as close to him as someone like Jennifer McCall, who wasn't there, of course. The associates from the firm had their ties loose and were flirting, like the crazy guys they were deep down, with Johel's pretty Haitian cousins, all of them dancing to the music on the stereo—where *is* that band?—and winking at Johel and saying, "You sure you don't want to marry a nice Haitian girl?" The cousins in their tight dresses and short, flouncy skirts are laughing and saying, "I tell him that every day, but he don't listen!" Even the partners from the law firm seem to be having a good time, there with their wives, drinking cocktails and talking about long-ago vacations down in the Caribbean. The Haitian people of course are having a better time. Tonton Jean is telling jokes in Creole—there's no better language in the world for joke telling, puns, stories, making fun, and having a good time generally. Tonton Jean's telling that story about the time he had to go to Baraderes on a donkey in a hurricane, and when he starts talking in the donkey's voice, there isn't a person in that room who can understand a word he's saying that isn't slapping the table and letting loose monstrous guffaws.

Where *is* that band? Haitian people, Johel is thinking, would be late to their own damn funeral if somebody else wasn't hauling them around in the casket.

Now everybody's sweating a little from the spicy food and cool drinks; everybody's been eating for an hour straight, loading up their plates and wiping their foreheads with their handkerchiefs, complimenting Johel on the delicious salty spicy food and getting up for just one more fried plantain or just a little more chicken. That's when Tonton Jean decides to take the microphone and make a toast to the groom, only he forgets that half the room doesn't speak Creole, so Ti Maurice takes the other microphone to translate, only Ti Maurice's English is not so good either, so what you got was something like this:

"My fwens, my fwens, I wanna tell all you a little thing which touch my heart. This boy, when he get here to New York See Tee, he start learn spelling, and when he goes to Washington to make a big champion, I make a bet, like this. I bet one hundred dollars that he lose."

Everyone in the room giggles.

"And you know who I make this stoo-peed bet with? With his *maman*. She bet that he ween."

And Evelyne Célestin, sitting up at the front table, she's prouder than a victorious general on parade, looking like an overripe fruit sitting in the sun, a big, shiny lady, retiring this very year after forty years of working as a maternity nurse. Not that she needed the money the last few years, mind you: one son a doctor, the other a lawyer, and the family owns four parking lots upstate.

"And she tell this boy, she going to whip him if he loses. She lose her money, she going to whip him until he crying rivers.

"And so this boy, he come to me before—how you call it, the *championnat*? The *shampyon sheep*? What you call it? I don't know. I don't care. And he say me, 'Tomorrow I go lose, *Tonton*, and you give me half de monee, okay?' And I say, 'Boy, you got a deal.' And I think, *Dis boy, he some real Aye-eesyen*. But the next day he make me a big sooprees, and he win everything. That night, I say, 'Boy, I thought we had a deal.' And he says, 'My mamma, she offer me *soixante-quarante!*'"

And now the room is drunken chaos, everyone pounding on the table, hooting and hollering, clapping and whistling. That's when the band arrives, but no one notices but Johel. The band is nine men and a woman, all of them dripping from the late-February rains.

"And so dis boy, when he meet dis bay-oo-tiful girl, I make another bet with his *maman*. I say, 'Evelyne, he going to marry that girl before it make one year.' And she say, 'Not my Johel. She too bay-oo-tiful for my Johel. She say no, she run away laughing. *Ti belle fille comme ca!*' And I say, 'One hun-erd dollars,' and she say, 'Okay.' Now what we say in Creole, we say, 'Money makes a dog dance.' Now this dog, he dancing because Johel and I this time *we* go sixty-forty!"

Sixty-forty! That had them on their feet applauding, whistling, cheering. "He one real Haitian dog!" shouts Tonton Alphonse, to which the senior partner replies, "He's one real Yankee lawyer!"

But Johel Célestin, who is greeting the band in the back and shaking hands with the bandleader and the rest of the band, he's not listening at all—he's hardly hearing a word, not thinking of his opportunity to earn sixty dollars—he's staring into a pair of blue-green eyes set in a sculpted, unsmiling face, the most beautiful face he's ever seen.

After the party, Erzulie L'Amour wants their money, and Johel doesn't want to give it to them.

Not that they didn't work hard for the money; not that they didn't deserve it; not that there was a man or woman in the room of any color, constitution, or ethnicity who didn't feel the rhythm slip into their bones and oscillate there until they grabbed the nearest grateful lady or were gratefully grabbed and headed to the dance floor.

What you have to imagine is Evelyne Célestin's sheer bulk, her massive bosom, her broad behind, her huge thighs, all of it shaking like a maraca or a wild animal as the mama tambour beats faster than a hummingbird's heart.

What you have to imagine is Johel's mentor and guide, the gray-haired senior partner, his Charvet shirt soaked with sweat, mopping himself down with a fringe of tablecloth, spinning like a top across the dance floor.

What you have to imagine is the rhythm slowing and two dozen lawyerly hands venturing down over two dozen rounded and grabbable buttocks of African descent in a slippery one-two, one-two, those Haitian derrieres gliding up and down. That's what this kind of music is all about when the rhythm gets slow. It's the kind of music that invites you to explore a little.

What you have to imagine is Johel sipping a cold beer, his first of the night at his own bachelor party, watching Nadia onstage in her silver lamé dress. Then, late in the evening, Nadia settles herself on a stool, legs crossed, and she and the guitarist offer a little soft *troubadour* together, to calm the evening down and send everyone out into the cold night warm and happy. The ladies drape their arms around the men's necks and hang there happily, bodies rubbing up against bodies while Nadia sings Creole love music in her thin, sweet voice. On every table there is a candle, and the flames keep time to the slow music as the wax slips down drop by drop and Nadia sings what she knows about the suffering and sweetness of love.

When the band is done and the guests are all gone and the waiters have taken off their ties and are eating plates of leftover *griot* and plantains, Nadia and the guitarist get to fighting. Johel wants to pay them, and Nadia is telling Johel to give her half to her directly because she doesn't ever want to see or talk with this lying dog again.

Johel has no problem with that. But Ti Pierre, the guitarist who leads the band, is looking at Johel with laughter in his mouth but menace in his eyes, telling him—*Mon cher, mon frère, mon vieux*—that he's the leader of the band and she's a little *folle*, if you know what I mean, clearly hoping to resolve this whole situation *homme à homme.*

So Johel the contract lawyer, mediator, third-year associate, and champion speller is telling the two of them to work it out between them, and he's not unaware that Nadia's green eyes are piercing him like two daggers of contempt. Nor is he unaware that Ti Pierre has scars on his face and hands, the kind you get from knife fights. So he wanders back to the bar to let them work out their troubles, and soon Ti Pierre is saying to Nadia, "Be quiet, woman, or I'll break your face," to which Johel says, "Calm down, brother," and Nadia says, "Break my face, go on" and adds something about his breath, like the smell of Ti Pierre's mother's hairy cunt. Then Ti Pierre slaps Nadia hard across the face, hard enough to send her reeling out of her chair and onto the floor, where, crouched on all fours in her silver lamé dress, she glares at the men like a wounded animal.

Johel is not a small man, but it's easy to miss that under the jovial layers of blubber. Because he smiles easily and often and chuckles frequently, it's easy to miss or not understand that he had some unyielding kernel of courage and rectitude—or maybe he didn't even know he possessed it himself until that moment.

He says to Ti Pierre, "Don't touch her again, brother."

Here is how calmly he says it: Will you please pass me the salt? Or: And how are you this morning, Fred? But he frightens Ti Pierre. Ti Pierre is a man of the world, a man of experience, and he knows that in this country it is men like Johel who have the power: men who know how to speak the language, who know the law, who don't speak with an accent. He looks at Johel's eyes and knows that this is a man who will not forget, will not forgive. Ti Pierre knows that in this country, when the police come, it is Johel who will talk and it is Ti Pierre who will end up in a cell. Life has taught Ti Pierre to be afraid of men like Johel.

Johel says, "It was a wonderful night. I'll pay everything I owe."

That's the prudent lawyer speaking, the one who knows the value of settling early, even at a cost to one's pride, of resolving problems quickly and efficaciously.

Everything Haitian is always cash business. People who overstay their visas by a decade don't open bank accounts. Johel has cash on hand for Ti Maurice, cash for the food, cash for the bartenders, cash for the drinks. Thousands and thousands of dollars in cash. He puts Ti Pierre's full fee on the table, which Ti Pierre counts and pockets. Then he puts half again more on the table, and he says, "That's for her."

Ti Pierre says to Nadia, "Let's go."

Nadia starts to get up, and when she gets to her feet, she is small and fragile. She has lost a shoe: it has skittered across the nightclub floor. Johel stares at the shoe, its sole scuffed and tarnished. Then he looks at Nadia's tiny stockinged foot.

In Creole, Johel says, "Do you want to go with him?"

"I don't know," Nadia says.

"Let's go," Ti Pierre says. "We got Boston tomorrow."

"I don't know," Nadia says again, looking at Johel, the green eyes pleading with him, looking at him in every way a man wants to be looked at, just once, by a beautiful woman.

So Johel says, "This money is for you. You can take it and go with him if you want. Or you can take it and leave. If you have no place to go tonight, you can come with me."

Eventually the wedding is canceled, and Johel's mother collects a hundred dollars from his uncle.

6 She left almost no trace when she was gone.

Johel went to work, and when he came home, the apartment was empty. Only a hint of her sweat lingered in his good sheets. A little rum was gone from the bottle. A few dark hairs on the pillow. Either out of politeness or indifference, she left the ivory nightgown he gave her hanging from a hook on the bathroom door. She left no other sign or signal—but how would she? She had no idea how to read or write, nothing more than her own name. It wasn't a secret where she had gone: a week later he looked up Erzulie L'Amour on the Internet, found they had played a Miami nightclub, called up, and discovered that she had sung there the night before.

What did Nadia do that first week in Johel's apartment? She slept, mostly. She must have been exhausted, and she was very young. At first she slept on Johel's leather couch, where he installed her with a duvet and his pillows; then on Johel's bed, picking herself up from the couch and putting herself between the sheets. She had so few things of her own: the dress on her back, a small suitcase, and her purse, small and nearly empty. Johel thought it strange that anyone could move across the earth having so little. The only thing that seemed truly hers was a small ceramic figurine, no taller than Johel's outstretched hand, that she had bought for herself when Erzulie L'Amour played Boston. The doll was painted in the thick furs of Russian winter, lips and cheeks bright red against the cold, staring out at the world with twinkling eyes of boundless sadness. Nadia placed the doll on Johel's nightstand, the first thing that she would see when she woke up.

When she woke up, she asked for spaghetti. So he fried her up some the way his mother made it, thick and greasy in tomato paste, with garlic and onions. Then she went back to sleep. From time to time she got up to pee. He had never known a woman could sleep so much. She slept almost without interruption for two full days. Only once did he leave her alone, slipping out to buy some food and then, on impulse, from a little lingerie store on the corner, a satin nightgown, which reached down to her ankles and was worked around the bosom in fine lace—just something soft to sleep in. When she saw the nightgown, she said, *"Merci,"* as if he had brought her a glass of water when she was very thirsty in the night. She slipped into the nightgown, inserted herself between his fine Egyptian cotton sheets, settled her angular head on his pillows, and went back to sleep.

Johel watched her sleep, as surprised by her presence as he would have been by the arrival of a fox in his midtown apartment. The few occasions when she left his bed, she watched TV—midday soap operas whose plots she seemed to intuit immediately and whose dramas she absorbed as her own. Then she told Johel the stories of those television dramas as if she had lived them, her story mingling with those stories in a breathless, boring stream of narrative that held him as enchanted as an audience with the president.

It took almost a week before Johel slipped into his own bed beside her. When she found him there, she rolled over and placed her soft face on his chest. Then Johel did not move more than he possibly could, not even when his arm began to ache or when he started to sweat. He listened to the sound of traffic far below and her soft breathing.

She had been in Johel's house ten days when she came to bed naked. She crossed her small leg over his large one and he could feel her hair on his thigh, her small breasts on his chest. Johel had decided in his mind that he was going to save her from whatever she needed saving from. He wanted to be the kind of man who gave her everything and expected nothing; but when he felt the softness of her skin and her gentle breathing on his neck, he kissed her and rolled his big body over hers.

Only a month. How then to explain Johel's panic when she was gone, his sorrow, his night terrors, his unreasoning sadness? His thoughts slipping around in circles over and over again until they bumped up against themselves coming the other way round. The nausea? Whatever he thought before was love—that wasn't love. Only a woman's sorcery could do this. She must have slipped love powder into his coffee, rubbed it on his body while he was sleeping, kneading love into his muscles and groin and fat. Why would she do such a thing, enchant him and then abandon him? He knew the answer: it was a woman's nature. Tonton Jean, who knew women like a bird knows flight, had once told him that women carry a sachet of love powder in their purses or hide it in their brassieres, and they sprinkle a dash here and there as needed. That is how women survive in this hard world.

The only love powder she had used had been her story. She told it to him lying naked beside him in bed, her delicate, slow voice sweet in his ears. Later he would lie in bed alone and tell it to himself, the only thing of her that he had left.

Her first life had been in the village, seven children in the house and enough money to send one child to school—not her. She had known the smell of the other children as they slept all together in the big bed, their little bodies rubbing hot against each other in the sweaty hut. She had known the river and she had known the hill, and she had known every stump and root and stone on the hill, and she had washed clothes on the bank of the river, and she had known hunger always, and she had learned that when you are hungry, sometimes a song can be like food.

That life came to an end as if she were dead and in her coffin when the man with the mustache came to the village. He had been of the village and he had gone away and he had come back, and now his mustache was thick and waxy and his chest heavy and sweaty and his eyes red. And they took him around to see all the girls of the village, to show him which ones could lift and which ones could sing and which ones could carry, which girl was becoming a woman and had a woman's high breasts, and when he saw Nadia, the bucket of water on her head, spine erect, singing "*Ti kolibri*," he pointed at her.

The negotiations had lasted an afternoon, and Nadia had prayed that her mother would take the cows from the man and let her go, because she knew there was nothing for her there but that high hill and the buckets of water and the hunger and the song. And the man with the mustache told Nadia that if she came with him, she would sing every night and never carry water again and her hands would be soft and she would have long hair like a *blan*. In the end, the man with the mustache offered her mother five cows. He had never paid so much for a girl before.

Now the story was on the ocean in the little boat, when a storm came up. Even the men began to cry because in the black clouds and pelting rain they saw the Baron. So Nadia sang to La Sirene, Erzulie of the Waters, who was so charmed by this maiden's song that she implored her lover Agwe to let the boat ride on his back a little longer. Nadia came to the coast of a place that the others called Miami.

This was another life. She didn't know how much the woman with the belt and the fat man with the golden watch paid for her. Now her story lived in a house with shiny wood floors. She was their *restavek*, their slave, and they told her that just as soon as she paid off her debt, she could leave: step out the door with no money and no language (who spoke Creole but Haitians?) into the vast white emptiness of America. So she stayed. The house was very large and the floors very shiny, and if the floors were not shiny, the woman beat her with a belt; and if the floors were shiny or if the floors were not shiny, the fat man with the golden watch came to her at night and she heard the golden watch ticking against her ear.

And that life lasted a very long time.

The fat man liked to make music. He liked to invite his friends some evenings to drink rum, and he would wake Nadia up and make her sing. Then she would come downstairs, and all the men would watch her as she sang the songs she remembered from the village, the fat man playing on his guitar. She had been in the house long enough that she knew the seasons of the plants in the garden, when one of the fat man's friends took her aside. This was Ti Pierre, asking her if she wanted to come with him. She was tired of mopping the floor and the crack of the lady's belt and the heavy weight of the fat man riding on top of her at the end of the night. So she said, "I don't know." And the man with the mustache and Ti Pierre bargained, and she was sold again. That's how she became Ti Pierre's. It was Ti Pierre who taught her to sing with the band, and Ti Pierre who had bought her shiny clothes, and Ti Pierre who taught her—

All those lives, thought Johel, *and still so young.*

Later, Johel's mother, worried for her big, sad boy, insisted that he visit the family *hougan* in Brooklyn. Here was a man with good understanding of the power of the celestial realm. Johel had known Monsieur Etienne since he was taken as a boy by his mother to visit the dark and cavernous *hounfort* before the great spelling championship. Then the *hougan* had prescribed for the young Johel as follows: to bathe in five liters of water taken from three different rivers and mixed with two liters of rainwater, two liters of springwater, two liters of seawater, and a dash of consecrated water from the altar of the church. The *hougan* had been consulted on all matters of significance since; and Johel's life had been, under Monsieur Etienne's guidance, a series of triumphs.

Monsieur Etienne was now in his late eighties, and from early morning until first starlight he accepted visitors who gathered in the anteroom to his professional chambers as he counseled, consoled, advised, and cured those in need of change of fortune, those who sought to win love, or those who sought to escape love's curse. His face was lined, as if by the daily accretion of sorrows his profession obliged him to absorb. His room was lit by precisely forty-three candles. The raw white rum that Monsieur Etienne spilled on the floor to please the various thirsty members of his pantheon burned Johel's eyes. On the wood floor of the apartment, the two ladies who served as Monsieur Etienne's acolytes had chalked in intricate swirls the *veve* of the great lord Damballah, a pair of snakes whose intertwined forms explained the most profound mysteries of the universe, if one had eyes to see and sense to understand.

When he had heard enough of Johel's sad story to understand it was a matter of love, Monsieur Etienne spoke at length in soft Creole. Monsieur Etienne didn't have a quorum of teeth left in his mouth, and the words went to mush somewhere between palate and lips. Johel had trouble understanding him in ordinary circumstances, but when Monsieur Etienne's red eyes fluttered behind his eyelids and his body trembled and the spirit came down to talk through Monsieur Etienne's dried-out lizard tongue and his thin, drooly lips, it was anyone's guess, really, just what Ogoun was trying to say. Even the acolytes were confused, the fat lady saying that love was like a blessing, and the other lady, who was thin and seemed to Johel generally more sensible, suggesting that love was like a curse. Johel's sorrows had not impeded the acuity of his legal mind, and this seemed to him a significant distinction, but both acolytes were agreed that the remedy to Johel's sorrows could be obtained, Ogoun and the good Lord willing. Johel would be freed of love, Ogoun said, if he could offer Ogoun some trace of her presence.

At first Johel presented the long dark hairs he gathered from his pillow. This proved nearly disastrous because only after the *lampe* had been lit, only after Monsieur Etienne had implored Saint Jacques, only after the libation had been spilled, did one of the acolytes think to ask Johel about the hair. Elaborate discussion ensued, and soon both acolytes were laughing at the innocence and stupidity of men. They very nearly had united Johel for life with some anonymous impoverished woman who had sold her hair once upon a time to make the extensions that now drifted down Nadia's back. "*That* lady, she's broke *and* bald!" the fat acolyte said, eliciting from Monsieur Etienne and the thin acolyte choking squawks of dried-out laughter. When Johel presented the long nightgown he had bought for Nadia, the acolytes ran the cloth between their assessing fingers. They knew from the lace and satin and embroidery right to the penny how much such an object costs. But for the magic to be effective, Monsieur Etienne was obliged to pose intimate questions. Had the lady obtained her pleasure in this item? he asked. Johel affirmed that she had, recalling the nightgown slipped up above her slender waist as she ground herself down onto him, her eyes closed. But Monsieur Etienne leaned close to Johel and cautioned him that the power of the celestial realm was infrangible and unforgiving. He spoke to Johel as an older man speaks to a younger man. He told Johel that he was the father of seventeen children and had known more women in his lifetime than waves break on the shore, and still he hardly knew when the pleasure in a woman's body was genuine or had been feigned—such was the malign trickiness of women. You never knew how fully you had possessed one. Now there could be no mistake.

And Johel recalled the green eyes set in the angular face, and her rapid breathing, and the tensing of her hands on his chest; how her body had paused and gathered strength; how her thin musical voice had made a sound almost like a song. So he said yes, this was the lady's nightgown.

Monsieur Etienne began to look unwell. His head rolled alarmingly from side to side. His breathing was shallow. Johel began to sense that strange tingling in his skin that always accompanied the arrival of Ogoun. The acolytes began to chant, "Open the door! Open the door!" Then the aged prophet sat upright, his yellow eyes commanding, like lights in fog.

Ogoun was a warrior, a being born to command, to plunge into the fray, sword in hand. He feared no mortal nor no thing divine. Now he surveyed the room into which he had been peremptorily summoned. With eyes that saw all that has happened and will come, he regarded Johel.

The acolytes said, "Hail, Ogoun! Master of the snake!"

Ogoun said, "From the place of lightning and darkness I come from the sleep that is not sleep to see a man who will be great and not great."

Johel was never sure where Monsieur Etienne ended and Ogoun began. Some part of him always wondered, until just the moment when Ogoun was present, whether Monsieur Etienne was nothing but a canny old showman. But when Ogoun was present, his doubts were silenced.

Ogoun said, "Black clouds gather fast and wash away the hillsides. Water rises and drowns the women. Trees will come across mountains and fish will live on land. No man walks who can stop you. You are the wave that sweeps and washes clean the shore."

Johel said, "I'm here, Ogoun—"

"—for the hummingbird, the bird of love, who never stops flying, never sups from the same flower twice."

"That's right."

"Put money on the table."

Johel pulled out his wallet and placed a hundred-dollar bill on the table. Ogoun stayed silent, staring off into the distance. Johel added another. His mother always said, "Good magic is expensive." Then Johel added a final bill, and Ogoun said, "We can help you."

The procedure that followed was lengthy, and when a month later there was still no trace of Nadia, when his heart was still like abraded flesh, Johel called Monsieur Etienne on the phone to complain. Patience, the older man advised, patience. There exists the time of men and the time of spirit: there are no clocks or calendars in the celestial realm.

The powerful beings who had taken possession of Johel's amorous dossier required a full year to act. Then she called. She was in jail in Dade County. She had been arrested together with Ti Pierre and two other members of the band as they went up north from Miami; dogs smelled the cocaine in the trunk. This was magic surely of the most powerful order. How many times had the band driven north with no problems whatsoever? How many dogs had sniffed the car and smelled nothing?

What Johel thought on his way down to Miami was this. He thought he'd send her back to Haiti and he'd be free. For months, he had dreamed about her every night, rolling over in his sleep and moaning with sorrow and pain—and then the dreams had stopped. He'd started dating: nice women, professional women, women who understood the kind of life a man like Johel needed. Once, he'd even gone on vacation with a lady. The two of them went to Paris, and for five days Johel didn't think once of Nadia or her green eyes, just thought how nice it was to be in Paris, eating fine French food and seeing the museums. A friend told him that Jennifer McCall was engaged, and he sent her a card, wishing her all the happiness in the world. She wrote back, graciously wishing him the same.

Then, when he saw Nadia in the visitors' room in a prison jumpsuit, he knew he was lost to her forever. He knew that nothing mattered more to him than those eyes. He felt the magic with which she had ensnared him throb in his veins. Johel saw her delicate, almost childlike face and he knew that some prison spell would simply kill her: one day she would close her eyes and her soul would slip away. Johel remembered stories of the days when Haitians were slaves. There was a tribe from

Guinée—his mother had told him, her mother having told her, stories like this one handed down through the Haitian generations—who when the chains were locked on, simply died. A sob, a moan, and then the overseer found the bodies of these strong men and lithe women in the cane fields. That was in Nadia's blood—and it was in his blood too.

When she saw Johel, she did not cry. Her restless green eyes roamed across his swollen face. He knew that she had no one in the world but him. So he called a man whose business card read "Criminal Law" and wrote a check, and then he waited. The law is like this: there is the sea, and there are currents in the sea, and only an expert sailor knows the deep currents where the real force and energy of the sea dominate. Only an expert sailor knows how to navigate the hidden shoals and reefs of the law, knows how to find safe harbor even in a vicious storm. The man with the business card made a deal. In exchange for her cooperation and on account of her youth, she will be deported. Nothing else.

When Johel told her this, she didn't understand. Then she did, and now, for the first time, she began to cry. She had not cried when the police stopped her and Ti Pierre; she had not cried when her cousin called from Haiti the year before and she learned that her mother, the lady who had sold her across the waters, was dead. Nothing brought the water to her eyes until she learned that Johel was sending her back to Haiti. For her, Haiti's the prison: the ocean is a wall, the hills are bars, the guards are everywhere. And she will be alone. Nothing frightens her more. Nowhere is life harder than her Haiti, not even here in some Florida prison. She looks at Johel and sees in his smile the cruelest betrayal.

She looked at Johel and saw that he understood nothing at all.

And so she sat in the chair across from Johel and cried until Johel did understand. Then he didn't think: he made the most important decision of his life as naturally as breathing.

7 The others drifted off, one by one or two by two, until by the end of the evening it was just us Jérémie folk at the table: Terry and Kay, Johel and Nadia, and me. We were like members of some secret society, bound together by geography, intrigue, gossip, and isolation. It felt natural that we would finish the evening just the five of us.

I don't know what prompted me to ask Johel if he was still interested in running for the Haitian Sénat. "No," he said. "That's not right for me."

"So what made you change your mind?"

The judge reached out for his wife's hand. "I guess I just don't want to shake all those hands."

"Bullshit," Terry said. "You just pussied out."

"Meow," said the judge.

Kay laughed.

Terry said, "We got to do this thing, Johel. Just for the road. That's all I'm saying. Just for the road."

"You seemed pretty set on the idea that day at Anse du Clerc," I said.

"Rum and sun," he said. "Just rum and sun, messing with my brain."

"I know *that* story," Kay said. "There was this time in college—"

"Like a couple of kings," Terry interrupted. "One day—one fine day—we'll drive down that road and we'll be like a couple of kings. Then when you and me—when we've got just about six marbles together rolling around upstairs, when we're sitting in the nursing home and the nurses are changing our shitty-ass diapers, I'll look at you and you'll look at me, and we'll just grin. Because we got that road built."

Johel inhaled, started to say something, then stopped. His eyes glanced down at his wife's hand. She was trembling very slightly, as if feverish.

Kay said, "Honey, what's wrong?"

"This is no *game*," Nadia said.

"Of course not, of course it's not a game," Kay said.

"For you this all some funny game. This some funny game you play, and if you win, you feel nice in your heart, and if you lose, you say, 'Too bad.' But you don't know Haiti. Haiti is no funny *game*."

Johel said something to Nadia in Creole. His voice was too soft for me to understand. She shook her head.

"She's tired," he said. "It's been a long day."

Kay said, "Don't talk about her like she's not even here, Johel. If she's tired, she'll say she's tired."

"Kay—," Terry said.

"Kay *what*? Am I too tired also? Is that what you want to say?"

"Maybe we're *all* a little tired," I said. "I know I am."

"Amen," the judge said.

Terry said, "Listen. This is a decision, obviously this is a decision you guys got to make by yourselves. But I want to say one thing."

"You—," Nadia said.

"Just listen to me."

"Where we gonna go now?" she said. "You tell me where. Where I gonna go now?"

"Just listen to me."

"We all listen, listen, listen you. We don't want to listen you no more."

"Let him talk," Johel said.

"The only place we go now is dead," she said.

Terry ran his fingers through his hair. He said, "If this is about security, I will be with Johel every step of the way. Just listen to me. Haiti's no game, but I'm not playing. Kay, you tell her—you tell Nadia that when I make a promise, I keep it. And I'm promising Nadia right here and now, win or lose, that she's going to be just fine."

"That's true," Kay said. "Nadia, you should know that. What Terry is saying is true."

"What I'm saying is you either shit or you get off the pot," Terry said. "Don't just sit there squeezing."

"Thank you, Terry, for that beautiful image," Kay said.

"All I'm saying is that if you're going to do this thing, do it. You're not going to get a chance like this twice. Believe me, I know. And I want you to think long and hard how you're going to feel in twenty-five years, you come back and the people are still dying and there's still no road, and you think, *Oh, I could have done that.*"

The judge started to say something and stopped, then started to say something else and stopped again. He looked at his wife, whose eyes tenaciously sought the floor.

As we were leaving, Terry reached for the check.

"It's on us," he said.

It had been understood that we would all share the cost of the meal, with its rich food and many bottles of good wine. One by one the other guests had offered to contribute and Terry had waved them off. Now Terry made a gaudy, immodest gesture of pulling his credit card out of his wallet and presenting it with a flourish to the waiter. The pleasure he took in our thanks thereafter was evident: he had switched for the evening from cigarettes to cigars, and he puffed grandly as we shook his hand, his ruddy face enveloped in great clouds of Cuban tobacco.

I looked at Kay. She seemed delighted by the gesture, by her husband's audacity, by the story it told of their success and generosity. "It's our pleasure, really," she said when Johel protested. "The only good thing about having a birthday is taking your friends out." When Nadia thanked her, she said, "We're just so happy you could come, honey. We love you and Johel so much."

Where had that warmth and fondness come from, that sudden transformation?

It had come from money.

PART THREE

PART THREE

1 UNPOL is the acronym for United Nations Police, sometimes also called CIVPOL, or Civilian Police; and as the acronyms suggest, the UNPOLs occupied some nether ground between civilian employees of the Mission and military units like the Uruguayans. The UNPOLs came to work dressed in uniforms—the uniforms of their national police force—but unlike the soldiers, they were in Haiti by choice.

Any nation can contribute a police officer to a United Nations Peacekeeping unit: just how many police officers a nation will contribute and to which mission is part of the intense and often inscrutable politics of the UN in New York. There is a lot of arm-twisting involved, and nations heavily invested in the outcome of a mission, as the United States is heavily invested in the success of the Mission in Haiti, will put lots of behind-the-scenes pressure on nations like Senegal or Sri Lanka to muscle up some manpower. (At one point, Senegal had 150 policemen in Haiti. The United States, by way of comparison, had 45.) More or less, the deal between the United Nations and the contributing nations is this: the contributing nation will continue to pay an individual police officer's salary back home, but the UN will pay his housing and travel, plus a per diem and bonus for hazardous duty.* The UN, however, is generous in

*In addition to hiring police officers, the United Nations hired armies: the UN offered $1,038 per month per soldier to the national army of any country that sent soldiers on

its assessment of expenses, and for police officers from poor countries, the expense money will often outstrip by far their salaries back home. So with frugal living in Haiti, cops from Burkina Faso or Sri Lanka or the Philippines, living six to a room and eating nothing but Top Ramen from the PX, can save quite a boodle on Mission. Policemen from the States, on the other hand, are often reluctant to head off to Haiti, so the base salary offered by the State Department through its contractors is significant: this, plus the expense money and hazard pay, is what enticed Terry White to Haiti. Every contributing nation has its own method of selecting UNPOLs. Qualifications are, professionally speaking, minimal: five years' experience in law enforcement, basic physical fitness, a health exam, and working knowledge of one of the official languages, which in the case of the Mission in Haiti were French and English. UNPOLs from poorer nations tended to be at the end of their careers, assigned either as the capstone of long service or, rumor had it, as a result of bribery and corruption back home. Competition for a UN job could be quite intense. One of the ironies of the UN system is this: there are Haitian policemen serving all over the world as UNPOLs themselves, monitoring and mentoring law enforcement officials in places like Congo and Burundi, even as Congo and Burundi send their policemen to serve in Haiti.

When Terry White first came to Hades, he had an interview with the personnel office in Port-au-Prince. The guy who conducted the interview was a pygmy—no kidding! That's the way Terry told it. From the contingent of Congo. He was perhaps five feet tall, with enormous glasses and a face as wrinkled as a walnut. He spoke very slowly, and whatever Terry

---

Mission. This was a very attractive offer to those countries with large, expensive standing armies where the soldiers earned less than $1,038 per month. In addition, the United Nations paid contributing armies for every tank, armored personnel carrier, jeep, and generator they provided. This was how the Uruguayan battalion arrived in Haiti.

Peacekeeping missions are a particularly attractive option for nations with some kind of simmering social disorder at home. Wars are expensive, and sending half the army abroad to keep the peace pays for the other half of the army to stay home and fight your Tamil Tigers, your Ibo petro-guerrillas, or your Maoists, which explains why there were large contingents from Sri Lanka, Nigeria, and Nepal on the ground.

said provoked a copious round of note taking. The interview lasted ten minutes.

"So what do you see yourself doing here?" the pygmy asked, his voice all high and reedy.

"Investigations and interrogations," Terry said.

The pygmy scribbled out the first chapter of his memoirs. Then he looked up.

"Do you speak French?" he asked in French.

"A little," Terry said in French. He'd had four years in high school.

The pygmy wrote out Chapter Two.

"Do you enjoy a challenge?" he asked—*un défi.*

"No," Terry said, thinking that a *défi* was a defeat.

The pygmy went back to Chapter One and began to revise.

"Thank you," the pygmy eventually said.

"My pleasure," Terry said.

The pygmy sent Terry to Jérémie.

When he got to Jérémie, Terry had another interview, this time with the commandant of the UNPOLs, a tough nut of a Québécoise named Marguerite Laurent. You take a group of twenty-four men and women, and you'll have your Morlocks and your Eloi: Marguerite Laurent took one look at Terry, at his beefy face and hands, those slow-moving eyes, and she figured Terry was Morlock. She asked him what he wanted to be doing, and when he said "Interrogations," she assigned him to patrol.

Driving patrol was rough, boring work. In Haiti, UNPOLs dress in full police uniform, carry arms, and drive vehicles marked POLICE, but they don't have executive authority. Executive authority is the power to make decisions, to effect change, to govern, to rule. In Haiti the government retained sovereignty, such as it was, and between the government of Haiti and the United Nations there was the complicated symbiosis of an unhappy marriage, both partners simultaneously powerless, frustrated, and trapped. At any given moment, the government could insist that that man get the hell right out of her house—and the United Nations would. *This ain't no colony: no man be tellin' me what to do in my own state, bought and paid for with nothing but a lifetime of sweat and blood.* But if the United Nations left, the government would collapse—*and don't be calling me, baby, when you got yourself a coup d'état or a revolution or an assassination.*

With you, lady, it's always you don't be needing me till you be needing me. I hope you enjoy exile, Mr. President. Live it up. I'll just be laughing at your sorry ass. So Terry and his colleagues couldn't arrest a suspect or even have him in their possession: if he started to walk away, they'd have no executive authority to haul him back to the vehicle. The Haitian national police, the PNH, on the other hand, had executive authority, but no transport, so pretty much all Terry and his colleagues did was haul Haitian cops around so they could exercise *their* executive authority.

Say you had a suspect sitting in the cell in the commissariat up in Beaumont. Say the guy's been eating his neighbors' goats for months. So one day his fed-up neighbors rope him up, beat his goat-nourished ass near to death, then lead him down to the *juge de paix*, who hears the case and remands this suspected goat rustler into the custody of the PNH, to be transported forthwith to the *pénitencier* in Jérémie, there to await trial on charges of goat thievery. But the two hundred or so PNH who police the 350,000 citizens of the Grand'Anse have a couple of motorcycles and a broken-down pickup truck—that's all. So Terry and his colleagues spent most of their time driving members of the PNH from Jérémie out to one police station or another, then driving back with a goat thief or two in the rear. If all that sounds a lot like chauffeur service, that's how it seemed to Terry too.

There was a story Terry had told me: "So one time these two police in Dame Marie call the commissariat in Jérémie. They need a lift ASAP to Chambellan to execute a warrant. So we drive to Dame Marie, get Tweedledum and his brother Numbnuts, drive them up to this village, where they tell us to wait in the car. Situation is under control. The *blan* might get people riled, and so me and this guy Beyala from Cameroon, we sit there by the car. This is normal. This is every day on Mission. In goes one guy and gets laid, comes out, doesn't even bother to tuck his shirt in. Then in goes the other guy to bust his nut. Two and a half hours on the road to get there, two and a half to get back. Twenty minutes while these guys do their thing. I don't think that's a good use of anyone's resources. They're paying me one hundred K plus to be a taxi driver."

"One hundred K plus?" I said.

"Salary, per diem, hazard pay, et cetera."

"And that's the job?"

"Mentoring, monitoring, and support. That's support. You gotta believe, brother, I know something more about law enforcement than how to drive a four-by-four pimpmobile, but that's what the job was."

"That must have been frustrating for you," I said.

"I was going out of my skull."

"What did you expect you would be doing?"

"Making things better."

But what bothered Terry more than anything was the offense to his pride: almost two decades in law enforcement, and he was the moron who sat in the car. The PNH had a unit doing nothing but investigations and interrogations, the Police Judiciaire, and Gilles, the French guy assigned to monitor, mentor, and support them was a motorcycle cop back in the old country. Terry had known motorcycle patrolmen back home, and French motorcycle cops—let's just say about the same level of mental acuity as their American counterparts. On those long drives up into the mountains Terry had time to brood.

Every morning when the UNPOLs saw one another they shook hands. The office would start filling up at about half past seven, and each newcomer would seek out and shake the hands of those already arrived. Then the Africans felt it impolite to begin the day without asking after one another's families and affairs at home—even though they had seen one another just the evening before. All the UNPOLs quickly adopted this custom, even when shaking non-African hands. They would look deeply into one another's eyes, like women.

"I hope you slept well, *monsieur.*"

"Not badly at all. But the heat!"

"I trust your wife is well?"

"Very well, *grâce à Dieu*! I spoke with her just last night. And yours?"

"*Ça va! Ça va!*"

"And the affairs of your country?"

"There is talk of a coup. And yours?"

"*Tranquille!*"

All this produced considerable bonhomie and also demanded quite a bit of time: the first half hour of every workday was consumed with handshaking and salutations, and in the evening, equally elaborate farewells.

The only one who couldn't stand that crapola was Terry. The others would be shaking hands and bouncing their heads and smiling and being as friendly as a guy trying to unload a used Buick, and Terry would be waiting out in the patrol car, keys in hand. Once, to this guy Beyala from Cameroon, he said, "Doesn't anyone around here want to get something fucking done?"

"Du calme, Monsieur," said Beyala. *"Dans le chaleur, toujours du calme."*

First stop was always the commissariat, where a dozen PNH were lounging in the morning sun. The PNH were playing dominoes and getting their shoes shined. Every now and again the PNH would impound a stolen goat or a pig, and these animals were tethered out front, munching on the dying crabgrass. When the animals got big enough, the PNH would barbecue the evidence. There was a fire truck parked out front too, a gift from the people of Taiwan: whenever Taiwan needs to clinch a close vote in the General Assembly, the Taiwanese buy Haiti a shiny fire truck or a bulldozer. This really ticks off the other Chinese, who make a fuss and threaten to veto the Mission's mandate in the Security Council. In the end, the diplomats squawk and gibber, and every year the mandate gets extended. In any case, the fire truck hadn't much changed the quality of life in Jérémie: a few years back, one of the local political parties burned down the house of a member of a rival political party. The Taiwanese fire truck drove over to the scene of the crime, but the pump didn't work—no water—and the local population turned on the firemen and beat them. The fire spread and destroyed most of the old wooden houses on the waterfront. Since then, the fire truck just stayed at the commissariat when there was a problem—not that it could have gone anywhere anyway, as the PNH had no gas.

Terry and Beyala wait half an hour, until one of the PNH gets himself ready to head up to the mountains. Then they're off.

The roads in the Grand'Anse are terrible. There were a few that were paved, but all in all, probably no more than two or three kilometers, max. Otherwise, every road was half big rock, half dirt. You couldn't even hope to go on these roads if you didn't have a healthy four-by-four. There were huge divots, holes big enough to swallow a rhinoceros, and places where the road was simply washed away and you just had to make your way along the side of a mountain as best you could. Terry and the other UNPOLs had a good car—a solid Nissan Patrol, painted white, letters *UN* on the side—but Terry's back after about a week began to hurt something fierce. He felt every divot and pothole like an electric shock somewhere around his sacrum, a rivulet of pain running over his ass and down the back of his leg. He was starting and ending his days with 800 mg of ibuprofen. He'd get on the phone with Kay back home, and she'd know just from the way he was breathing that his sciatica was killing him.

All along the road, every couple hundred meters, there were big hand-painted signs explaining in French that this was the site of some international development project. A project outside Gommier to help farmers affected by hurricanes, paid for by the government of Japan and executed by the World Food Program. A pilot project to protect the banks of the Roseaux River, paid for by the European Union. The construction of a national school in Chardonette, paid for by the European Union. UNESCO was rebuilding the Adventist college Toussaint Louverture. In a large open field, the Inter-American Development Bank was proposing to build sixty latrines. The project had been scheduled to begin a few years back and would last four months, but the field was still barren and rocky when Terry drove by. USAID began a hillside agricultural program: nowadays the hill was nothing but rocks and stones. The IADB was rehabilitating the water supply of Carrefour Charles. There was a program to encourage the production of yams, paid for by the United Nations Development Program. A faded sign, almost falling down: CARE was putting in place a program designed to guarantee food security.

Two hours of bad road later, Terry White, Beyala, and a PNH were in Beaumont. Beaumont was like the set of some spaghetti western set in a tropical country populated only by dirt-broke black people. A single street, wooden houses, some drinking establishments, folks splay-legged in front of their houses, chewing idly on toothpicks, the ladies in kerchiefs, the gentlemen in big straw hats, tethered donkeys raw to the withers standing there under the burden of an overstuffed saddlebag or a few bags of charcoal, nobody moving, the day hot. Flies buzzing, and every eye is on you.

Terry parked out in front of the local police station, where the *chef* was a little guy with glasses covered in a film of dust and the apologetic air of a disorderly professor, as if he had expected the *blan* tomorrow or the day after that, or was it yesterday.

The *chef* rose with a start when they came in; then, gathering his wits about him, he extended a long, strong hand. The other PNH was unshaved, fat, chewing on his own tongue as if it were a piece of gum. Now he was sitting on a three-legged stool, trying to balance with only moderate success on just two legs while Terry inspected the register.

The names of the suspects and their crimes were written in beautiful cursive, like the names on the Declaration of Independence. The PNH are supposed to write down everybody they arrest and everybody they let go. You subtract the latter from the former, and the remainder should be rotting away in the dank, dark cell. It's not tricky, Terry figured. It really wasn't. He looked at the register, and he looked at it twice.

"Where is Neolién Joassaint?" he said.

They booked him in two weeks ago, still haven't let him go, still haven't charged him with a crime, still haven't transported him to the prison in Jérémie. But he wasn't in the cell either—Terry looked. In theory, that's extrajudicial detainment.

"Neolién Joassaint?"

"Here," Terry said. "Look. He's on your books."

The *chef* looked at the other guy. The other guy looked at the *chef*.

"The *juge de paix* ordered him released," the *chef* finally decided.

Now, this is a pretty darned important detail. You take a prisoner into your custody, you should write down when you let him out. If you don't do that, he takes off for the hills, how do you know the PNH didn't bury him out back of the station? What they were trying to build in Haiti was a system of justice, effective bureaucratic procedures with checks and balances, allowing the police, on the one hand, to maintain public order and safety, but allowing the public, on the other hand, to audit the work of the PNH. Neither dictatorship nor anarchy.

"Did he sign the thing for his liberation?" Terry not remembering the word for "receipt."

"Of course!"

"Can you show it to me?"

The *chef* let out an exasperated sigh. He pulled the whole drawer out of his desk, overturned a massive pile of papers on the floor, papers going back decades, little red bugs scurrying from the light. He started looking through the papers one by one, squinting at each.

Terry went out for a smoke with Beyala while he looked.

"It is not like this in my country," Beyala said.

"Bullshit," Terry said.

Terry had been on patrol with police from a dozen countries, and everybody said their country was better than Haiti. If you listened to the Africans, you'd think Cameroon, Tanzania, Niger, and Benin were little Switzerlands, they were so efficient; the people were so honest; the ladies so fat and lovely. Sri Lanka was swell. No place beat Nepal. The Philippines were fantastic. Only Haiti sucked.

Twenty minutes later the *chef* still couldn't find the receipt. No one had a clue whether the PNH beat the guy to death and buried him, or whether he escaped and they were too embarrassed to mention it, or whether he was released legitimately.

Terry wrote all this down in his notebook. That's all he was expected to do: take notes. That's all he had the power to do.

Thus he had monitored.

Next came "mentoring."

That's when Beyala suggested that they buy some envelopes, organize the receipts by month. The *chef* put his lips together, then inhaled through his nose. He shook his head sadly.

"Unfortunately, we do not have the means to acquire office supplies," he said.

The words "office supplies" sounded soft and effete in his mouth.

"Haiti is a very poor country," he added.

The way Terry saw it, poverty was like a fast-running river sweeping every Haitian and his responsibilities downstream. The poverty of the nation excused every personal fault. *C'est pas faute mwem*, the Haitians said: It's not my fault.

Beyala looked stern. "In my country, if we have no money to buy envelopes, we use our personal funds," he said. "We care about our job. For us, it is a *pleasure* to do one's duty."

The *chef* nodded, as if he had absorbed an important lesson. Pleasure equals duty.

Then Beyala lectured on handcuffs and their proper use. The UNPOLs were supposed to give a little speech to the locals about some aspect of good policing. Somebody gave the UNPOLs the lesson in their Sunday meeting, then they spread the gospel all week long. This week it was handcuffs. Last week it was the role of the *juge de paix*. The week before that it was arrest warrants. The guy chewing his tongue on the stool zoned out. His eyes went glassy—no exaggeration, like he had a 103-degree fever. The *chef* nodded his head seriously.

"The handcuff, what is it?" Beyala began. "It is a tool for the control of the prisoner. When the prisoner is handcuffed, he is in your charge and entirely your responsibility. What are the three circumstances under which the handcuff is to be employed? *Alors . . .*"

Long silence sometime thereafter indicated to all present that Beyala was done.

They have mentored.

Now it was time to "support."

Out came the prisoners. An old guy, a young guy, both handcuffed with the plastic flexi-cuffs the UN gave the PNH. ("The prisoner may be restrained only when the liberty of his or her hands might constitute a menace to the security of others . . .") They looked docile enough, but the young one was accused of threatening to kill his uncle in a beef over a pig. The old one had gone and rooted around in some other guy's field like a wild boar—he was charged with *dévastation de champs*. No one knew why; in Haiti, no one ever knew why. The old one looked guilty, like a dog with his head in the garbage.

The fat PNH stopped chewing on his tongue.

"Au revoir, Messieurs!" he said to the prisoners. "You are going to travel today like a pair of princes!"

When they finally got back to the commissariat, the PNH took the prisoners inside, where they passed out of Terry's life forever.

They have supported.

During Terry's first few months in Jérémie, a couple of other plum posts on the org chart came open. There was the *coordinateur*. Reporting and Planning. Mentoring Support. Admin, Logistic, and Personnel. The guys who did riot prevention. There were maybe three dozen cars in the whole Grand'Anse—and even Traffic would have been a step up. Guys who had less experience than he had, guys who didn't even know how to turn on a computer, were getting those jobs. Traffic went to that little Indian guy, Sunderdarbashan, who was best friends with Marguerite Laurent; when Marguerite Laurent saw him, she wrapped her arm around him and said, "Go get 'em, buddy." That kind of shit drove Terry crazy. He didn't think that was how an office should be run, on the basis of whether Marguerite Laurent thinks you're a cutie-pie.

After the Sunderdarbashan incident, Terry got into it with Marguerite Laurent.

"What is it going to take for me to get treated with some respect around here?" he said.

Terry could be a forceful guy, and the way he said it, in retrospect, was maybe a little heavy-handed, like he was trying to intimidate her.

She was right back in his face. "Terry, what you need to do here is relax."

Terry *was* getting a little obsessive about things—he admitted it later, just that word. The house he was staying in out on the Route Nationale was like a hot concrete box at night. His Jordanian housemate spent all night watching bondage porn, and all night long Terry heard women begging and pleading, "Please, no, please." Terry's back would be killing him on his cheap cotton mattress, so he couldn't sleep.

He felt like this wasn't some isolated incident in his life: that for a good long time now, the Marguerite Laurents of this world had been looking down their long, pointy noses at him, obstructing and impeding him. The way it was supposed to have worked was like this: law enforcement for ten years, then elected office. That's the way it worked in Watsonville County, either law enforcement or military. They told him, "First you carry a gun, then you run." So he carried a gun and ran twice. First he took a shot at state senate, but he never got the kind of full-throttle support from the local big shots that he'd needed to win the primary, which was an injustice after the sheer donkey hours he'd put in over the years. He and Kay had been shaking the money tree for all and sundry for a decade now: cocktail parties, fund-raisers, you name it. Knocking on doors, doing favors. It didn't matter. No gratitude. Then, after Sheriff Shook's heart attack, he'd expected that the sheriff's job would be his, until Tony Guillermez and company decided that the Republican Party needed more Hispanic faces. "I can campaign in a sombrero," Terry said. Not even a chuckle out of Tony. So that was that.

Then even the job was gone, when the new sheriff, a Democrat, fired all the Republicans. His right to do so, Terry would have done the same. Deputy sheriff is a political appointee. Been that way since Hector was piddling the rug. Still a bitter pill to swallow, since no one could really argue with his results, his arrest records, the clearance rates. Heard from a friend of a friend that twice in the last five years he had been very nearly Southeastern Lawman of the Year. Putting Marianne fucking Miller in that job, what a crock. Then came all the money problems. What a man did was provide for his family, and for a long while there, *ipso friggingo facto*, Terry was hardly a man. Now with this new job in Haiti, at least they could pay the mortgage.

Truth be told, Terry hated Haiti. Later, he'd laugh about how much he hated it. At the time, not a whole lot of *ha-ha-ha*. Last place he ever wanted to be in his whole life was Haiti. The number of times Terry had fantasized about one day living in Haiti was precisely zip. Would leave tomorrow if he could, never come back. He didn't like the people, who kept making fun of him; he didn't like the food, which was spicy and greasy. Just didn't see much point in the place. This was his first time in a third world country, not counting a week in a resort in Cancún, and he hadn't liked that much either. Came as a surprise to him that everyone was so fucking broke. He'd seen poverty back home—what cop hasn't?— but Haiti was something else. All his life Terry had dreamed of being rich, and now in Haiti he was rich and he didn't like it. Children walking barefoot with five-gallon drums of water on their heads, kids with hair red at the roots. Babies with swollen bellies, just like on TV. Back home, poverty smelled like fat and grease, like buckets of french fries simmering in the sun. But Haiti was like old sweat, bad fruit, shit, and ammonia. Every day he'd drive back from some small Haitian town with a prisoner or two handcuffed in the backseat, the smell so strong he'd gag.

Everywhere Terry went, people asked him for money, not just kids, but adults too, even fat, sleek, healthy-looking adults, like sea lions barking for fish. How the hell can you be fat when kids are hungry? Damn country made no sense to Terry. It was like a reflex with them, he thought: they saw someone white and the hand came up. *Blan, ba'm yon cadeau*—White, give me a present. He'd say no and they'd start shouting at him. Or he'd give them his change and they'd ask for more. The worst part was that he couldn't criticize, not really. These people just wanted to suck on the same teat he was sucking on. He just had the good fortune to get on it first.

Terry knew what was right and what was wrong. That's why he had gotten into law enforcement. Back in the States, he'd locked up bad guys. Threw them in lockup because they were scumbags. Got them to tell their sad, mean stories. Didn't hate them, didn't love them, just didn't want them on the same streets as the people he loved. He'd felt proud of his work: it was something he could explain to his nephews. His father had once told him, "Never do a job you can't explain to a child." So he told the boys: "I keep good people safe from bad people."

But here he was, and all he saw was wrong. The worst of it all was the prison. Almost every day he visited the prison, dropping off some poor fool. Hundreds of men locked up in a hole, no trial, no nothing, just sitting behind bars in a room about 130 degrees on a hot day, shitting in a little drain, eating next to nothing, with not much hope of ever getting out. Trials were held once a year, if that; and during the solitary several-week session of jurisprudence, of the three hundred prisoners awaiting justice, only a dozen or so might find their way to the courtroom. The rest just sat, all of them together, in an unlit cell so crowded that men were forced to sleep on their feet, and so fetid that the rotting air, like ammonia, burned your eyes and throat. Sometimes a prisoner's file was simply lost, and then the accused could stay in prison, forgotten, until he died. The only way out of prison, innocent or guilty, was to bribe the prosecutor or judge. Getting arrested in Haiti was like getting kidnapped by the police. Terry saw all that, and he felt like a cog in an unjust machine. He tried to explain what he was doing in Haiti to his nephews, and they didn't understand.

Kay White told me later that she started seriously worrying about him all alone out there in Haiti those first few months, before he met the judge. Cops' wives hear a lot of stories about their men and their service revolvers, the way their eyes get to tracing the oily whorls of steel, the gun hypnotizing them, telling them to do bad things.

Terry would get on the phone with her those first few months and she'd say, "Honey, you sound so depressed."

"I'm just not getting enough sleep."

She'd say, "I'm proud of you."

What she meant was, *You're a hero*, but Terry knew that wasn't true. He wasn't a hero at all. He knew what a hero was. A hero was somebody who conquered himself. Broke down his fear into so many little pieces he could ignore them. He came from a family of heroic men. His grandfather had been a hero in Normandy. Never talked about that, didn't need to. His uncle had been a hero in Vietnam. "Did my job"—that's all he said. Terry was forty-two years old when he got to Haiti, and that's an age when men take stock of things. Pretty much all he did was take stock of things. When he was a kid, he thought he'd be president one day. Hah! Then he scaled down his ambitions, and scaled them down way more.

Now he was a taxi driver in Hades.

2 The only thing that really made Terry happy those first few months in Haiti were the afternoons joshing around with this kid, Beatrice. When Terry arrived on Mission, he shared a house out near the Uruguayan base with a couple of other UNPOLs, a Spaniard and that Jordanian guy. The house was tended by a lady named Mirabelle, who swept and straightened and washed the men's clothes and prepared a meal every evening. Mirabelle sometimes came in with her daughter, Beatrice, a studious, pretty girl who wore her hair in cornrows dotted with blue and yellow beads. Beatrice would help her mother finish the household chores, then sit at the kitchen table in the afternoon and do her homework. She was in her final year of lycée and dreamed of attending medical school in Port-au-Prince.

Although the composition of the household had varied over the duration of Mirabelle's tenure as maid, from occupant to occupant an avuncular fondness for Beatrice had been passed down: the men of the household had paid Beatrice's school fees since she had begun lycée. Coming home from patrol, Terry would tutor Beatrice in English in exchange for lessons in French and Creole. In three languages, he chafed her about boys and made her giggle; when he learned of her ambitions, he suggested to her that she could probably study abroad, and he looked up suitable programs for her on the Internet—in Canada, in France, and in the United States also. He liked her clean, well-scrubbed schoolgirl smell, which wafted across the kitchen table like hope, and her intelligence and drive. He liked the thought of this small girl one day wearing a doctor's coat and treating swollen-bellied little babies and toddlers with rusty red hair. Thinking he was going to make it all possible for Beatrice was pretty much what kept Terry going those first few months on Mission.

Then, just six weeks before the final examinations that would have marked the culmination of so many years' effort, Beatrice stopped coming by the house. A day or so passed, and Terry asked Mirabelle if Beatrice was sick. He was eager to see her. There was a transitional under-graduate program at Florida State, his own alma mater, for which he thought she would be ideal; and he had a notion how such a program could be paid for through the Rotarians. Mirabelle shook her head. She told Terry that Beatrice was going to be leaving for her uncle's house in Port-au-Prince on the very next boat; she was dropping out of school. Then Mirabelle began to cry.

Soon Terry, who had two decades' experience in this sort of thing, coaxed the whole story out of Mirabelle.

Mirabelle and Beatrice lived in a neighborhood of small tin-roofed shacks not far from Terry's house. For several months now, an older boy in the neighborhood, from a larger, wealthier household, had been ag-gressively courting Beatrice. Toto Dorsemilus was in his middle twenties, one of the young men in the orbit of Sénateur Maxim Bayard. In the evenings when the Sénateur was in town, Toto would sit and play cards on the Sénateur's terrace as the Sénateur received his guests.

Every afternoon Toto would wait for Beatrice at the gates of the lycée and offer to drive her home on his motorcycle; when popular acts like Jean Jean Roosevelt came to town, he bought Beatrice a ticket. When she refused to go out at night with him alone, he bought tickets for her friends. In this crowd of teenage girls he stood out for his age and size: he wore his beard in a goatee, and on his thick fingers he had a handful of rings—a skull and crossbones, a garnet, and an opal. He wore over-size jeans that hung down over his buttocks and a basketball jersey that showed off his broad shoulders and thick arms. It was his habit to chew on an old toothbrush, as someone else might gnaw an unlit cigar or a toothpick.

Mirabelle told Terry that the other afternoon Toto had been at the gates of the school, waiting for Beatrice on his motorcycle. Beatrice ordinarily refused his offers, but there'd been a big storm that afternoon, and she had just purchased new shoes, a pair of dark leather penny loafers that had cost the better part of her mother's weekly salary. She accepted the ride, and Toto suggested waiting out the rain at his house: the narrow pathway that led to Beatrice's own home was too slippery in the mud to reach by bike.

Had it not been for the bruises across her daughter's face and shoulders left by those heavy rings, Mirabelle might not have realized the next day that anything was wrong, but the bruises, and later the swelling, made it clear that something was very wrong indeed. Beatrice told her mother that she had been raped. Moreover, she was terrified that it would happen again. For this reason, mother and daughter decided together that she would flee—immediately—to Port-au-Prince.

For the first time since his arrival in Haiti Terry felt as if he had a reason for his presence there. He took Mirabelle's hand, which was hard and lined by twenty years of rough manual labor, all invested in her daughter. When there were no houses to clean, she had cut cane, gathered plantains, or walked hours in a burning sun to sell a meager harvest of manioc and yam at far-flung local markets. Plenty of nights had seen Mirabelle go to bed hungry, the food in the family cooking pot reserved for her daughter. Terry, still holding the thick, dry hand, looked in Mirabelle's eyes and told her that he would help.

That evening, Toto Dorsemilus was in the custody of the PNH. Terry was there when they picked him up.

The next morning, Terry's colleague, the young Canadian UNPOL who worked regularly with the sex-crimes unit of the PNH, took him aside and told him a number of disturbing details. The PNH records are poorly maintained, but she had learned from one of her counterparts in the sex-crimes unit that Toto Dorsemilus had been arrested twice before for the same crime under almost identical circumstances. Both times he had been released shortly after his arrest.

Terry passed a number of rough nights thinking of Toto, hearing the scared women cry on the Jordanian's computer. When the PNH arrested him, Toto, chewing on that old toothbrush, had looked Terry straight in the eye, fearless and arrogant. Terry was convinced that Toto Dorsemilus would soon be out on the streets again, and just a week later he was. Terry saw him on his motorcycle, riding down the Grand Rue. When he saw Terry, he slowed his bike down, looked him in the eye, and said, *"Blan."*

It wasn't hard to find out what happened: Mirabelle had bought herself a television set with some of the money the Sénateur had given her and Beatrice, two thousand dollars in all. In exchange, they had agreed to drop the charges. Then the Sénateur had pressured the public prosecutor to release Toto Dorsemilus without further investigation.

"Christ, Mirabelle, what do you need a television for? There's no electricity," Terry said.

"Gen toujou lespwa," Mirabelle said. A Creole proverb: There's always hope.

"And the next girl? How much is she worth?"

"I only have one daughter," Mirabelle said.

"That's a shame. If you had a couple of them, you'd be rich."

3　Terry had been in Haiti four months or so when Kay decided to come down and visit for the first time. She was celebrating her fortieth birthday. She flew down to Haiti with a stomach full of butterflies, and not only because her sisters told her she was crazy to go on vacation in Haiti: "Wake up and smell the State Department travel advisories," they said. But Kay knew that Terry wouldn't invite her if she wasn't going to be safe. No, it was seeing Terry that scared her. He'd been on Mission a couple of months—it was the longest spell they'd been apart since they were married—and for no reason she could explain, even to herself, the prospect of seeing him made her anxious, as if she were going on a blind date. She was worried that he was going to be a weirdo, or boring, or that she was going to hate him.

Just as soon as she saw him, though, waiting for her at the airport in Jérémie, she knew things were going to be okay. He hadn't shaved in a week or so, which was how she liked him best; and he must have dropped ten pounds, making his cheeks lean and angular. His skin was bronzed, and the smile he flashed her when she got off the plane made her know he was excited to see her.

"Well hello, stranger," she said, sliding into his arms. "Know where a girl can find a man around here?"

That evening she sat with Terry drinking beer and eating barbecued chicken on the roof of his rented house. Both of his housemates were on vacation. Then Terry told Kay the whole Mirabelle and Beatrice saga.

"And you fired her?" Kay asked.

"Don't *you* think it's wrong, what she did?"

"Maybe that money could change her whole life. You don't know. Maybe she could pay for school. Maybe she could—"

"If it's wrong to buy justice, it's wrong to sell it," Terry said. "That's not why I'm here."

Kay wasn't sure that Terry was right. But she took it as a sign of his sincerity—and his love for her—that he'd spent two days getting the house clean on his own. He'd even washed the sheets by hand.

The house was dark and charmless, with barred windows and low ceilings, but if you climbed up on the roof, there was a view of the Caribbean, which in the slanting light of sunset was a vast reflecting pool of ochre, crimson, and gold.

"This isn't the way I imagined it at all," she said.

"How did you imagine it?" said Terry.

"Remember *Black Hawk Down*?"

The next day, Terry took Kay to the beach. "You're going to love it. It's the best thing about this place," he said. He'd been swimming every day after patrol for a couple of weeks now, and the regular exercise was starting to loosen up his back.

About halfway between the Uruguayan military base and the airport, the beach was just longer than a football field, covered in all the debris and muck the people of Jérémie threw in the ocean and allowed to drift ashore: plastic bottles and tin cans, old shoes, plastic bags, the occasional rubbery remnant of some late night *faire l'amour*. The garbage skeeved Kay, but past the dirty shore, the water was as beautiful and limpid and as green as one could possibly imagine in a tropical beach, the temperature of a lukewarm bathtub, fringed by high, tumbling cliffs.

There was some kind of sunken ship or submarine about ten minutes' swim from the shore—just a turret perched a couple of feet above the low tide. Terry told Kay a story about that submarine. He said that in the war a German pocket U-boat ran aground there, manned only by a crew of three. The Germans came ashore, took one look at this lush land of brown rivers, gentle breezes, and pliant women, and decided to make for themselves a separate peace. The story seemed improbable to Kay—but she later found out that the town doctor was a guy named Schmidt. On his wall was a black-and-white photo of three white men, arm in arm.

Kay swam and then sat on the turret of the submarine, splashing her feet and looking at Terry. She had always loved to watch him exercise. He cut across the bay with an efficient, muscular crawl, his elbow coming up sharply to his ear, full extension through the elbow and wrist, reaching with his fingertips, breathing only every third stroke, covering distance swiftly and effortlessly. While Terry swam, Kay daydreamed about the house she'd put up on the big bluffs overlooking the sea. If she could do it all over again, she often thought, she'd have developed property. That's where her real passion lay, in making beautiful things. She couldn't believe such a spectacular spot was undeveloped, just ten minutes from the town center, ten minutes from the airport, and two minutes from a white-sand Caribbean beach. Maybe, she thought, Spanish Colonial, with a red tile roof and thick white walls, the house cleverly designed so every room had sea breezes and a view over the open water. She thought of white curtains flapping crisply, and white cotton sheets . . .

Terry and Kay fell into a rhythm that week, their happiest in years. During the days he worked, leaving the house while she was still in bed. Kay read through the morning or did yoga, following videos on her laptop. She sunbathed a little. Then she walked down the white chalk airport road, past Mission HQ, and all the way up the big hill to the Bon Temps, where she had lunch. It was a very strange feeling for Kay to be the only white woman on the streets. As a teenager, she had been friends with one of the few black kids at her school, a pretty girl named Nina. Nina had told Kay that it was exhausting just being different all day, even if most people were nice. Now Kay thought about looking Nina up on Facebook and letting her know that two decades later, she finally understood. In the afternoon she took a motorcycle taxi back to the house: she hadn't been on a motorcycle in decades, and these rides, weaving around donkeys and bumping over rocks and potholes, felt as forbidden and thrilling as when she was a teenager riding home on her high school boyfriend's Yamaha. When Terry came home, he would take her swimming, and they would make dinner together, cobbling together whatever ingredients she found in the market.

Later, Terry and Kay would have a nightcap on the roof of the house. The evening breeze carried hints of honeysuckle, jasmine, lilacs, and passionflower. Bats flashed from tree to to tree, and vast hordes of slow-waltzing constellations danced across the night sky. Later the moon shone so brightly she could see her own sharp-edged shadow. She was happy.

The night before Kay was scheduled to go back to Florida, she and Terry fought. She had planned a romantic evening for her last night in Jérémie, but as soon as she saw him coming home from work, his face drawn tight with anger and irritation, she knew that he was in a lousy mood. He banged around the kitchen, ignoring the pretty dress she had put on for him, muttering to himself until she finally asked him just what was his problem. Terry told her that Marguerite Laurent had passed him over for another decent job, this time as reports officer, a desk job that would have taken him off the patrol roster and given him some time to rest his aching back. When he'd complained, Marguerite Laurent said, "If you're not physically fit for duty, you should consider your future in the Mission."

"What you got to understand is that this woman is a world-class ballbreaker," Terry told Kay. "She's had it in for me since the day I showed up."

"What do you think her deal is?" Kay asked, still hoping to jolly him into an acceptable mood.

"Who knows?" Terry said. "She's Queen Marguerite, and if you don't lick the royal boot, you get patrol."

"Are you the only one who has problems with her, or does everyone else get along with her?"

"What are you trying to say, Kay?"

Kay lost her patience. "I'm just saying that I've seen this play before. The set was all different, and they changed the lady playing the bitch, but otherwise, same actor, same text."

Kay and Terry looked at each other. The thing about being married all these years was that they could have the fight from start to finish, soup to nuts, Alpha to Zulu, without saying one more word. The minute that followed might have seemed to an outsider like nothing more than an attractive couple on the threshold of middle age sitting quietly, but to Kay and Terry, the air was thick with attack, counterattack, defensive parries, sly, stinging remarks, and wounded feelings. There was no need to say another word because they'd said all the relevant ones so many times before. Kay knew that Terry was thinking that he was in Haiti because of her, because she'd driven the family finances off a cliff with her ice sculptures and soft sheets and investment-grade apartments; and Terry knew that Kay was blaming him because she'd given him the best years of her life and she'd come out of it with nothing more to show for it than a persistently bruised heart and debt. Soon the fight degenerated from grievances to assaults on each other's character. Kay said out loud, "Should we open a bottle of wine?" But Terry heard Kay denounce him as his own worst enemy—it was funny, wasn't it, just how many people seemed to have it in for Terry. Kay told Terry that he'd had opportunity after opportunity over the years and he'd gone out of his way to blow them. *And you know why? Because you're frightened, Terry. You'd rather destroy something before it gets going and blame Marguerite Laurent or Marianne Miller or Tony Guillermez than try and* fail. *You're a coward.*

Kay had meant to make Terry angry, and she had succeeded, but she winced when he told her that she was spoiled. She hated the word "spoiled," with its suggestion of rot and age; and she thought to accuse anyone who had worked as hard as she had over the years of being spoiled was *so* unfair. *The truth is*, she told Terry, *is that you think anyone in a good mood is spoiled. Maybe Marguerite Laurent should be considering your mental health issues, Terry, not your back problems. Anyone who isn't miserable, in your book, is spoiled. Maybe if I was a quadriplegic begging on the streets of Calcutta I'd have the right to smile, but otherwise, I'm a spoiled brat. You can't stand it that I'm not depressed.*

Had Terry's phone not rung, the two of them might have continued to fight all through the evening. Even as they prepared dinner, they would have fought: the two of them were entirely capable of discussing whether the pasta was ready, whether the wine was sufficiently chilled, and what time her flight left the next morning in tones an outsider might have considered perfectly amicable, even as another conversation was conducted between them, no words employed, that was cruel and biting and true. The fight might well have lasted until that moment when Kay set foot on her plane back to Port-au-Prince and Miami, the whole otherwise lovely visit clouded by a sense of disgruntlement and marital unease, despite the fact that neither Terry nor Kay had said out loud so much as a single bitter word.

But at that moment Terry's phone rang. He had the phone chiefly to communicate with Kay herself. It might have been the first time since she arrived that she heard its shrill ringtone. She startled slightly.

"Talk to me, brother," Terry said.

Then Terry was moving quickly, listening and standing up at the same time, holstering his pistol. "I'll be there in five minutes," he said. "Get under the bed and stay away from the windows. Don't go outside. I'm on my way."

He slipped the phone into his pocket.

"Who's that?" Kay asked.

"I've got to go."

Kay could tell from the cast of his face that whatever was happening was serious. Something she knew about Terry, something she liked very much, was that he was extremely competent in an emergency. She trusted absolutely his judgment on important matters, matters of life and death: she knew in these moments not to interfere or question him. Then she could hear the siren of his patrol car screaming. She sat alone in the early-evening darkness, wondering what she would do if he never came home.

Terry first met Johel Célestin at Mission HQ when Johel came to give the UNPOLs a presentation on the situation in Les Irois. Presentations like the judge's were a regular feature of UNPOL life, some speaker from Port-au-Prince or per diem king droning on monotonously for an hour or two about arrest warrants or the responsibilities of the local justice of the peace.

But Johel was a lively speaker. Terry admired a good orator, even if the oration was just a PowerPoint slideshow for a couple dozen UNPOLs. He appreciated that Johel switched between English and French, making sure that everyone in the room followed the complicated legal and political details. Moreover, Johel was passionate about his subject. Terry had been surprised how many people associated with the Mission, both Haitian and foreigner, seemed to speak from some dead-souled place of extreme boredom and cynicism. But Terry could see from the judge's animated face and sharp eyes that the situation in Les Irois was keeping him up nights.

The dossier Johel discussed with the UNPOLs dealt with a recent spate of civil unrest in the small seaside town of Les Irois. The mayor of Les Irois, Maximilien "Fanfan" Dorsainville, had for many years enjoyed an intense and combative rivalry with another local politician, a fellow by the name of Hyppolite Aurélienne. Despite their differences, Mayor Fanfan and Député Aurélienne had maintained an uneasy truce, until sometime shortly after the most recent election, when Député Aurélienne achieved for his district a legislative coup, finagling a grant for the creation of a community radio station—the money a gift of the European people, part of a European Union democracy-building program. What Député Aurélienne did not mention to the Europeans was that the man who would own and run this radio station was none other than himself.

The station quickly won loyal listeners by offering a daily diet of Compas music and soccer scores, but the choicest offering came at dusk, when Député Aurélienne, a little man in possession of an incongruously deep voice, sat in the recording booth, opened a bottle of rum, and discussed the faults of his archenemy, the Honorable Mayor Fanfan. This was a subject that could keep him going for hours. He informed his listeners of Mayor Fanfan's corrupt and extravagant ways, his taste for young girls. All this naturally rankled Hizzoner, but what threw the mayor over the top was when the *député* mocked Mayor Fanfan's considerable girth: Mayor Fanfan had a habit of traveling around town by two-stroke motorcycle, and the *député* commiserated with the burdens of that poor vehicle, calling it the "Mayor's Camel" on account of the way the motorbike bobbed lazily up and down on the road as it hauled Mayor Fanfan over the rocks and dirt.

That was really going too far, and one day, with Député Aurélienne in Port-au-Prince attending to the people's business, armed men broke down the door of the small radio station and, live and on the air, shot all four citizens found inside: the *député*'s brother-in-law, his nephew, a radio engineer from the capital who had come to adjust the antenna, and a young lady whose reasons for being inside the station were never made clear. The radio engineer from Port-au-Prince lost his leg, and the young lady lost her eye; the others died. The station at that moment changed both management and political orientation.

The investigation into the shooting was assigned to Johel Célestin.

There is no precise equivalent to the *juge d'instruction* in the Anglo-Saxon system of justice. In the Haitian system of justice, a distant descendant of the Napoleonic Code, the *juge d'instruction* acts as a kind of investigative magistrate, a cross between a detective, a prosecutor, and a judge. The *juge d'instruction* has the power to investigate all manner of serious crimes and to imprison suspects for months at a time while the investigation proceeds. His job is to prepare a dossier that will eventually be submitted to a public prosecutor, who will then, based on the *juge d'instruction*'s research, take the case to trial.

Johel pursued his investigation of the shootings in Les Irois with his customary discipline and hard work. He interviewed dozens of witnesses and took hours of depositions. Soon he had produced a preliminary dossier setting out his findings, a dossier whose conclusion went far beyond the details of the night in question.

Johel explained the facts of the dossier to Terry and the other UNPOLs. Haiti lies roughly midway between Colombia and the southeastern coast of the United States; to transport cocaine from Colombia directly to the United States is both risky and difficult. Far better to ship cocaine to southern Haiti, transport the drug overland to the northern shore, and send the freight on to the Cold Land in many smaller pieces: in cigarette boats and catamarans and slow tankers out of Port-de-Paix in the north; buried in the purses, bellies, and trick-bottom suitcases of nervous-looking Haitian or Dominican immigrants; or across the border, where more efficient Dominican dispatchers would dispatch it north in cruise ships, diplomatic pouches, and cargo holds.

On moonless nights, no place in Haiti was darker than Les Irois, where the nearest electric light was at least fifty miles away. Fishing boats would slip out onto the Caribbean, returning at dawn with bricks of cocaine wedged under their nets. The war in Les Irois then was a battle over who would harvest this lucrative catch.

Judge Célestin's dossier proposed that the man who organized the cocaine trade in Les Irois was not the mayor, but rather his patron, Sénateur Maxim Bayard.

At first the judge had thought the shots were fireworks, like the kinds the kids set off at Carnival. Then the kitchen window exploded, and Nadia shrieked. Nadia's cry made the judge realize that something was wrong, but still he had trouble understanding that somebody meant to do him harm. Nobody had ever wanted to harm him before. There were two different sounds: one was the sound of the shot and the other was a kind of echoing *thwack* as the bullet lodged in the hard cement of the house. The judge saw himself in the mirror: he was smiling, as if this all were some complicated practical joke. Nadia had already left the kitchen and was running down the corridor to the bedroom. The judge saw his own face settle into a scowl, and he followed her, patting his pocket for his phone.

Judge Célestin told the UNPOLs that there was nothing he could do to prosecute the Sénateur, who, like all members of the Haitian legislature, enjoyed the privilege of parliamentary immunity. The phrase "parliamentary immunity" rankled Terry: no one should be above the law. Still, the judge's dossier had potentially broad ramifications. You can't ignore a thing like that, not even in Haiti. In the worst case, it might cause the American embassy to invoke the Oxblood rule, which limited the dispersal of American money to foreign governments known to be involved in the trafficking of narcotics. The U.S. secretary of state was required to certify to Congress that this was not the case—how could she do that with a report like the judge's on record? No one wanted to see that hap-

pen here. This was the kind of case that causes the embassy to start
suspending visas.

The judge told the UNPOLs that he was looking to arrest the mayor,
who still remained at large, and convince him to testify under oath
against the Sénateur. Such testimony, the judge felt, might compel
the *sénat* to lift its esteemed member's immunity and allow him to be
prosecuted.

Terry knew that the judge had long ago issued a *mandat* for the arrest
of the mayor, but he also knew that no one had succeeding in getting
Fanfan in the bracelets. The local PNH had been ordered to arrest him
but, themselves frightened of the mayor and his henchmen, failed to
produce him. Twice pickup trucks of armed PNH had been sent from
Jérémie to arrest the mayor, but both times he had been tipped off to the
operation and slipped into the hills, coming back down when the coast
was clear. Rumor held that Sénateur Maxim Bayard was the mayor's
informant.

At the conclusion of Johel's presentation, Terry invited the judge for
a beer. His own run-in with the Sénateur in the parking lot of the Bon
Temps had made him sympathetic to Johel's work, and he was curious
about this earnest young Haitian judge. More than once in the course of
his investigation, Johel told Terry, he had received telephone calls in the
middle of the night, only to hear the sounds of a funeral Mass played on
the other end of the line. Then there had been an incident just a week
before, when Johel came home to find the cadaver of a dog on his front
steps. The judge's courage moved Terry and made him feel a little ashamed:
here was somebody doing what Terry came to Haiti to do. He gave the
judge his card and told him to call, day or night, if there was anything
he could do to help.

There were varying accounts of just what happened the night that Johel
called Terry, and far and away the most modest was the account offered
by Terry himself. The judge's house was up in Calasse, where Johel, a
few years back, had bought a plot of land. Terry drove up in the darkness,
high beams shining and siren wailing, and the way he told it, the sound
of the siren alone was sufficient to drive off the two men on a motorcycle

who had been firing their pistols at the judge's concrete house. By the time Terry arrived, he said, all he could see was the bouncing crimson of their receding taillight.

When Kay heard this story, she thought it sounded heroic in and of itself. But the judge, when she finally met him a few months later, told her that there was not one motorcycle, but two, four armed men in total. And they weren't firing pistols, he said, but assault rifles. When Terry's headlights hit them, they turned from firing at the judge's house to firing in the direction of his oncoming vehicle—and still he kept coming. Only the fact that they were lousy shots prevented them from shooting Terry or his vehicle. Then they fled on their bikes.

Whatever the precise details, it was a fact that when Terry finally came back from the judge's house late that night, he was shaking with adrenaline. Kay poured him a healthy glass of rum and took one for herself. Then she gave him a long massage, concentrating first on his shoulders and aching back, then kissing all the places where the muscles were knotted and hard. "My hero," she said. Other women might have been frightened by Terry's story, but Kay was exhilarated. That night he made love to her with a ferocious intensity, as if the two of them were breaking rules.

The two stayed up most of the night talking. They talked about Haiti, about all the strange twists of fate and odd coincidences, the setbacks and victories that had brought them to this place at this moment: they were in a town neither of them, six months before, had ever heard of, in a country they had barely known existed.

"Maybe you were here just to answer that phone call tonight," Kay said.

"Maybe," Terry said. "But can I tell you something? And you won't laugh or—"

Kay replied by kissing Terry. He could feel the softness of her breasts on his chest.

"I got here—and you know, I wasn't good here. But ever since I got here, I can't shake the feeling that I'm meant to be here. That this is it."

They were silent for a moment. Somebody observing them might have seen nothing but a couple lying quietly and supposed that they were drifting off to sleep. But Terry was telling Kay, no words necessary, that something important had been missing and he thought he had found it. It was something even more important than happiness: it was something you would give your happiness to obtain. And Kay was telling Terry that this time, finally, they weren't going to waste their opportunity, that she would be with him every step of the way, wherever this new road might lead.

Finally Kay said, speaking out loud, "Have you felt that way before?"

"Only once," he said. "When I met you."

Kay didn't know if Terry was telling the truth, but even if he wasn't, she liked that he loved her enough to lie.

The morning after the attack, Johel Célestin came to Mission HQ, where he asked Marguerite Laurent, the head of the UNPOL program, what the Mission could do to protect him. The judge made it clear that should the Mission be unable to guarantee his security, his inquiries regarding Les Irois would end.

The situation in Les Irois was now a matter of national interest. The radio engineer from Port-au-Prince who lost a leg had filed a complaint with Amnesty International, and soon thereafter *Le Nouvelliste*, the newspaper in Port-au-Prince, ran an article on the rogue mayor of Les Irois. At Port-au-Prince cocktail parties foreign donors mentioned the case to their Haitian counterparts; terms like "judicial impunity" were bandied about in high circles. The American ambassador mentioned the situation in Les Irois to the Special Representative of the UN Secretary-General in their weekly meeting; the SRSG considered the situation an embarrassment and a hindrance to his own personal project of one day becoming a Deputy Secretary-General of the United Nations, and he directed his subordinates to take all necessary measures to bring the situation to an expeditious conclusion.

For all of these reasons, Marguerite Laurent knew that it was important to assist the judge in any way she could. Because the Mission had no executive power in Haiti, and because the Mission's mandate extended only to monitoring and mentoring, she could not directly assign UNPOLs as bodyguards, but she soon spoke with the *directeur départemental* of the PNH, who reluctantly agreed to create a four-man VIP protection unit, with the Mission offering monitoring, mentoring, and support. Then she agreed to Johel's other request, and she assigned Terry to lead the squad.

4 The organizational chart of a large bureaucratic entity is like some baroque habitation, a Sicilian palazzo, say, in which might exist for decades forgotten and unexamined rooms, suites of rooms, and even wings, a film of dust coating equally the ormolu dresser, a bloodstain on the marble floor, and the skeleton of a cat. Once a box exists on an org chart—in this case the box read "Close Personal Protection"—the box will exist forever: no one will question the box's right to exist. With Terry White now assigned to the box, it was understood by all that it was his to occupy indefinitely. No one thought to question him overmuch on his activities, provided that he supply a weekly précis to be included in the situation report. As long as no one complained—and for a very long time no one did—he was allowed to continue occupying the box.

So Johel and Terry got to spending a lot of time together. Terry was officially charged with monitoring, mentoring, and supporting a four-man crew of PNH in the art of close personal protection. The first few weeks on the job went like this: the judge traveled everywhere with two PNH and Terry; two other PNH guarded the judge's house during the night. Terry instructed these men as best he could, bearing in mind that he himself had almost no experience in the bodyguard's art other than what he found on the Internet. He encouraged in the PNH alertness, attentiveness to threats, and an imposing manner. Because he considered the judge's life at risk, Terry committed himself to remaining in his presence as many hours of the day as he could. Here was a job—because he liked the judge, because it was useful, and because he was bored—that he was determined to do well.

Terry's commitment to the judge's welfare, however, was not matched by an equivalent zeal on the part of his trainees. The *directeur départemental* of the PNH was an ally of the Sénateur's and had agreed to create this squad of bodyguards only reluctantly. As the drama of the attempted assassination faded, one by one the *directeur départemental* reassigned the trainees to other duties. In a matter of weeks, Terry found himself traveling the Grand'Anse with the judge alone. No one noticed that Terry was now in charge of the monitoring, mentoring, and support of a squad that no longer existed, except on paper.

Terry and the judge soon were friends. The men shared the kind of easy chemistry that allows a couple of fellows to spend upward of eight hours a day in a car together, navigating the back roads of the Grand'Anse.

The judge, for his part, didn't want to be out of Terry's sight. There had been a minute or seven when the bullets were coming through the house when he knew that he was going to die. Death came into the bedroom as a great white shadow, and Johel felt the *ti bon ange*, his good little angel, separate from his grosser body, filleted out of matter as neatly as a butcher takes fat off meat. Then his big body heard the siren of Terry's car, and tentatively, like a frightened cat, the *ti bon ange* returned home. But Johel's soul was skittish. As the days passed, that feeling of fragile equipoise between this home and the next stayed just as strong as the minute the first bullet broke the window and the adrenaline started coursing in his veins. It made him edgy and nervous and a little nauseated, and he stopped sleeping at night. It wasn't the rational part of his brain, but something reptilian and concerned with survival that felt better if Terry was within eyesight. So at the end of the day he made a point of inviting Terry in for drinks, and on weekends invented excuses to get him over.

As it happened, Johel's house had been shot up just days before the World Series was scheduled to commence. Both men loved watching sports, and so they decided to go fifty-fifty on a new satellite dish to replace the old one, which the bullets had reduced to little more than an oversize colander. In this way, long days on the road visiting remote Haitian villages soon metastasized into lazy evenings at Johel's concrete house, the generator cranked outside to keep the beer cold and the TV rolling.

When Terry told Kay about the judge, she said, "He's got a little man-crush on you."

Terry said, "You think?"

But Terry soon came to admire Johel too, not only for the Ivy League diplomas on the wall, but for the gentle, respectful way he spoke with everyone he met. When Terry took the judge down to the Tribunal in the morning, outside the judge's office there was always a line of Haitian peasants, two dozen long. Terry sat sometimes and talked to the peasants, and what was most notable was the stories he didn't hear: *I was slapped in jail by the judge, kept there two weeks until my lady visited him. Price of freedom was a night with my woman and a thousand dollars.* Nobody told Terry that the judge was shaking him down, wanting a stack of bills just to give Nobody a court case that would end up with Nobody humiliated and embarrassed by a pair of fancy French-speaking *avocats* from town, everyone laughing at Nobody, until finally the judge, upon due and proper consideration, decided that Monsieur Nobody here owed everyone his balls. That wasn't how it was with Juge Blan. The peasants told Terry that this judge was decent. He listened. He was smart. In his courtroom or office, it was just you and the *neg* you're arguing with— he planted crops on my land; he ate my goat, which wandered onto his property—the judge asking questions, rubbing his big fat chin, then saying, "This is the law."

Terry didn't know how to say it precisely, but he had been looking for someone like the judge for a long time.

Soon the two men were talking work. Terry had a lot of hours to watch the judge on the job, and he had advice to offer him. The judge was a fine jurist, but his training was in corporate law. The role of *juge d'instruction*, however, required the skills of both lawyer and lawman. The *juge d'instruction* was a judge, but also a detective and interrogator, someone capable of forming a dossier sufficiently complete to submit to a prosecutor. This was very similar to the work Terry had done for decades. So Terry offered the judge advice on how to pursue his investigative responsibilities: how to interrogate a suspect, how to coax a confession, and how to use that confession to convince others to confess.

The judge, for his part, offered Terry an education on the realities of rural Haiti. This place wasn't just poor like it's just hot, he told Terry. It was made poor. There were forces and people that made these people poor, and it wasn't just an accident. Terry was a history buff: on his bedside table there was generally a presidential biography or a volume of popular military history. So the judge's impromptu lectures fell on congenial ears. The judge explained to Terry that Haiti had been founded as a revolution of slaves, but the revolution hadn't ever really ended, even now, two hundred years after the last slave owner's throat was slit. The country was divided to this day between a very small, very wealthy pale-skinned French-speaking population—the descendants of slave owners or their mulatto offspring—and the vast population of descendants of slaves, most of them living in the country, most of them poor, Creole-speaking, and black. Power in the country tended to flip back and forth between one group and the other, politicians using national office chiefly as a means to enrich themselves and devastate their enemies.

"You mean people like Maxim Bayard?" asked Terry.

Working with trainees back home, Terry had always said, "Give 'em a KISS: Keep It Simple for the Stupid." It was a point of pride over the years, the paucity of broken doors in his territory. As deputy sheriff, he had for years tracked down deadbeat dads just by mailing to their last known address a postcard informing them that they had won a new set of tires from a local dealership. Gentlemen presented themselves as regular as sunshine, no muss and no fuss, no overestimating the folly of Watsonville County's criminal class. Some guys showed up twice for those tires. Then there had been the time some mastermind was hoisting power tools from garages and Terry had put an ad in the local paper, offering to buy power tools. He could tell such stories from tomorrow until the resurrection. Terry's fundamental insight now was that they needed Mayor Fanfan to come to them.

Soon there came a day when the judge and Terry were in the judge's office, the diplomas hanging on the wall, talking over the scandal du jour, the story of the *député* from Jérémie. Story starts with the European Union purchasing for the Haitian Parliament a fleet of brand new SUVs, on the reasonable grounds that parliamentarians needed some way to travel from their district to the capital. Along with the outright gift of the vehicles had been allocated a budget for maintenance of the fleet. Johel tells Terry that the *député*'s tires were rolling out new every week from the parliamentary garage and coming home shredded.

"And that would be on account of . . ."

". . . *Monsieur le Député* taking the tires off his car and selling them," said Johel.

"Naturally."

"So the *député* has those bad boys on and off who knows how many times, when another *député* from up north confronts him on the floor of the Chambre des Députés. He's waving receipts at him like they're winning lottery tickets."

The judge tells Terry that the *député* from Jérémie responded as any man whose dignity has been outraged should: he took his pistol out from under his suit coat and took a shot at his accuser, right there on the spot. He was standing, the judge indicated, about two meters away. Nevertheless, he missed, plugging a clerk of the *chambre* in the shoulder.

An investigation conducted by the leading members of the *chambre* ensued. These men were of the same political party as the *député*. They concluded that the shooting was accidental.

"What kind of country are you people running here, brother?" Terry asked.

The judge put on a four-hundred-dollar-per-hour face. "I'm quite sure that the *député* had no intention of shooting the legislative clerk in the shoulder."

The conversation might have continued on considerably longer had Mayor Fanfan not telephoned. "Reach out to the man, you never know," Terry had said. "Make him think you want to be his friend." So the judge had sent Mayor Fanfan a Facebook friend request. Soon the judge and the mayor were talking most every day, trading text messages, laughing at each other's bons mots, the judge clicking "Like" in response to Mayor Fanfan's daily prayer.

And what you have to appreciate is that Haiti is a nation *tête en bas*, all upside down. What would have been strange in Haiti—not unheard-of, just a little off—would have been if a man in the judge's position was *not* interested in doing a little commerce with a man like Mayor Fanfan. Terry understood that Haiti, end of the day, is all one big family: any two Haitians can talk things over, come to an arrangement. What's that they say? All veins are made for blood. Friend and enemy were labile categories in Haiti. Friend & Enemy, Good & Evil, Alive & Dead: all like the thick, tangled vines that make up the mapou tree, can't take one without the other. One day the judge wants to arrest you, says nasty things about you; the next day, he's your friend. That's no craziness. What wouldn't have made sense is the judge just sitting there in Jérémie, brooding over that dossier like a fat hen.

So now, on the phone, the judge, suddenly inspired, was explaining to Mayor Fanfan what he had heard, that the *blan* were giving away motorcycles to rural elected officials, Honda 250cc off-road bikes, the kind with fat, knobby tires and a high wheelbase, just like they were giving vehicles to deputies and senators.

"That's a beautiful machine," the judge said, explaining that they had twenty of them just sitting on a lot behind the commissariat, waiting for the appropriate official to present himself with identification.

Mayor Fanfan makes a noise.

The judge said, "That's what I'm saying. Maximilien Dorsainville, right there on the list, mayor of Les Irois."

Soon there was an incident that made Terry appreciate with particular keenness the judge's fine character. It consolidated the good impression the man had made on him. They were driving back from Dame Marie around dusk, just past Chambellan, where the mountains are high and lonely. An old man waved at them from the side of the road. Terry's instinct was to keep going, but the judge said, "Stop a minute," so Terry pulled over. A few minutes later Terry and the judge were in a smoky hut.

Terry could hardly see, it was so dark in there, and the occupants of the hut, perhaps a dozen men and women, were weeping and wailing so furiously that it took him a minute to realize that the little girl lying on a mattress in a dirty yellow dress was dead. She was no more than three years old. Terry looked at that girl and thought that no matter how a doctor might have diagnosed her death—malaria, typhoid, bad drinking water, or malnutrition—what she really died of was poverty, straight-out poverty. Her family didn't have enough money to keep her alive, and she died. Terry had seen his share of death, but something in that hot little hut made him, ordinarily so cool in a crisis, want to vomit and run.

What settled him down was the sight of the judge, talking in his deep, calm voice with the family. He was respectful and grieving and solicitous. Terry couldn't understand much of the language, but he figured out after a few minutes that the family couldn't afford to bury their own little girl: not enough money for a coffin or a funeral or even to buy a little cement to build her a crypt in the backyard. Even her dress was old.

The judge told Terry to drive him down to Chambellan. The day was getting dark, and Terry didn't like to be on the roads after sunset, but he didn't say anything. In Chambellan, the judge asked a few questions, and before long he had ordered a carpenter to construct a coffin for the girl, paid for a funeral Mass, and bought three yards of good white cotton. Then he had Terry drive back to the family, and he explained what he had done.

The patriarch of the family insisted on giving the judge a basket of mangoes and limes, straight from his own trees. It was mango season, and there was more fruit than the family could eat. It was falling on the ground and rotting.

On the way back, Terry said, "You ever think that if the Sénateur wasn't the Sénateur, someone else could get that road built?"

So the judge is telling Terry about the time last year the mayor of Jérémie shot a protester in the back, when the phone rings.

It's Mayor Fanfan, wanting to know what he should do about his motorcycle just sitting there.

"Just one left now, Fanfan," says the judge, winking at Terry.

He tells Mayor Fanfan that the mayor of Bonbon and the mayor of Pestel came by to pick up their bikes. Just Fanfan and Beaumont still on the outside looking in, and you *know* Beaumont coming in for that bike.

Mayor Fanfan tells Johel, long time he's been riding the Camel while Député Aurélienne cruised back and forth from the capital in that sweet Pathfinder. Long time he's been feeling that particular insult and ache. Leader of the people of Les Irois, his commune extending outward and upward into the hills, some of his own people not even knowing his face on account of a lack of appropriate transportation. What tears him up double inside, he says, like he's been drinking Clorox and eating rocks, is the thought that all his brother mayors—the mayor of Anse-d'Hainault, the mayor of Dame Marie, the mayor of Chambellan, the mayor of Moron—they all going to get their motorcycles while he's left riding the Camel, on account of this Macoute injustice that makes it impolitic and unwise for him to travel in his own country. Two things matter to the mayor, that's what he always tells his constituents: dignity and justice. That's what he fights for every day while serving the people. And where's the dignity in riding the Camel? And where's the justice?

Judge says he'll make some calls.

Later that day, the judge calls back. It's a problem, he's not going to tell stories; it's a big problem. They're not going to give no motorcycle to just anyone who walks in off the street. No, sir, you can't send your cousin. They want the mayor himself to sign for that motorcycle, watch a video on safety, fill out the forms. Uh-huh. *Oui.* Uh-huh. Fortunately, the judge is in the problem-solving, not the problem-making business. For a little consideration, he would be happy to assist Mayor Fanfan.

The mayor sends his cousin to Jérémie straightaway with the money, grateful that he has a friend, and Johel tells the mayor that he's arranged everything. He's going to send his mechanic out with the motorcycle the next day. Only the next day, the mechanic never shows. Not the day after that either.

The way the judge tells it later, Fanfan gets to calling multiple times every day. Fanfan's got to thinking about that motorcycle so much he's not thinking no more. Fanfan so mad, he could eat a chili pepper and shit flames.

Fanfan's thinking that with a motorcycle like that, no more walking in the mountains, embarrassing himself like that. Now he can head up into the hills, visit his ladies, visit his kids in dignity. Fanfan is thinking that the development of his commune just starts with a motorcycle. You can't be donating a motorcycle if you're not donating money for petrol, maintenance.

He calls the judge up, says, "Where's my motorcycle?"

Judge says, "That motorcycle, it's got a problem with the tires."

Only way a beautiful bike like that got a problem with the tires, somebody been riding it. Mayor Fanfan's not dumb. Fanfan figures only person riding that motorcycle is the judge.

The judge is making excuses.

The judge is telling the mayor that the tires are okay now, but his mechanic has a fever, motorcycle just sitting in the judge's house, waiting for the fever to break.

The next day the judge is telling the mayor that the bike has no gas, and there's a gas shortage in Jérémie, no way to fill it up.

How much more I got to suffer, thinks Fanfan.

Mayor Fanfan looks on his Facebook and sees a photograph of Johel Célestin riding high and proud on a motorbike. Johel Célestin don't even look like he know how to ride that bike, how you got to sit low and nice.

The story germinates, an idea blossoms. The idea gets tossed back and forth, those two guys on those long, bad roads, bouncing and jostling— they've already talked pussy and the four-seam fastball and love powder and pussy again, considered the effects of love powder *on* pussy—and the one guy says to the other, "You know, brother, I was serious what I was saying the other day. We could do this thing, we could get it done. Get that road built."

And the other guy says, "Huh."

Soon the judge was hearing the same thing everywhere, from ordinary people. His neighbor comes over for rum sours and says, You should be senator, Judge. Get that road built.

Huh.

The pharmacist sells him some ibuprofen for his headaches and says,

Judge, this country wouldn't be the way it was, men like you were in charge. We'd get this done.

Everywhere Mayor Fanfan goes, he's hearing laughter. He figures folks laughing at him on account of him still driving the Camel while the other mayors be cruising. He's out near the Protestant church, and he hears a little boy giggling. Mayor Fanfan gets down from the Camel, takes the belt right out of his pants, and teaches that boy that no one laughs at legal authority. Then one of his ladies asks Mayor Fanfan just why his face is so sour, whether he shoved a lemon up his ass. He talks; then she says, "Fanfan, you so angry about the motorcycle, you go get it. Be a man."

Mayor Fanfan starts feeling angry. Calls the judge in the dead of night. Judge wakes himself up and says, "Listen, Fanfan, you want the bike so bad, come and get it yourself."

Mayor Fanfan says he will.

Not that night but the next, Mayor Fanfan gets to drinking *clairin* infused with ginger. That kind of brew makes a mild man headstrong, and a headstrong man wild. What Mayor Fanfan starts thinking is how good it's going to feel driving his new motorcycle back to Les Irois, his people seeing what kind of mayor they got for themselves. How nobody be laughing then, they be seeing him riding low and nice on the *blan*'s motorbike.

That's how it happened that Maximilien "Fanfan" Dorsainville presented himself at Johel Célestin's very home at three in the morning, the judge saying, "Let's go get that motorcycle now, Fanfan." The judge and Fanfan driving right down to the commissariat together. And even in jail Mayor Fanfan was telling the other prisoners that Johel Célestin stole his damn motorcycle.

Then the judge starts thinking it over at night, when he's alone and he's sitting out on the deck nursing a whiskey and listening to Coltrane. Johel thinks of what Ogoun told him: *Trees will come across mountains and fish will live on land.* He thinks of big trucks laden with fruit, of flatbeds filled with mangoes, bananas, breadfruit, avocados, and papayas; he thinks of the fishermen putting their redfish, mahimahi, tuna, and bonito on ice.

The judge starts wondering whether he could win the election. That's what he asks Terry the next day. They're sitting out at that little restaurant at Anse du Clerc, taking a break from the roads and the heat, celebrating the arrest of Mayor Fanfan.

Terry says, "Honestly? You know what I think? I think you and I got a destiny. I think of all the things that brought us here, all the crazy luck and weird chances, and I don't think we're just out here by accident."

A couple of weeks after the arrest of Mayor Fanfan, a Haitian lawyer presented himself at Mission HQ. He represented Toto Dorsemilus, and he said that a member of the Mission had severely violated the rights of his client.

The lawyer for Toto Dorsemilus claimed that his client had been returning to his home from an evening at a Jérémie nightclub when a paralyzing electrical shock caused him to tumble from his motorcycle. The fall caused skin abrasions of the forearms and face. Toto Dorsemilus, lying on the ground, was shocked multiple times. He was then beaten unconscious with a heavy stick, the blows concentrated on his legs, arms, and abdomen. He had lost multiple teeth in the beating. His pants were then pulled down around his knees, and the toothbrush on which his client habitually chewed had been forcibly inserted into his anus. A blow from a boot had caused the toothbrush to puncture his bowel.

Toto Dorsemilus claimed to recognize his assailant as the *"blan"* who had been present at his arrest all those months ago.

The case was referred to the Special Investigations Bureau of the Mission for further investigation. The SIB quickly discovered that Terry White was checked in on the night of the alleged assault to a Port-au-Prince hotel, where he had been traveling with Johel Célestin to attend a judicial conference. Mission travel logs confirmed travel to Port-au-Prince the day before the assault. Investigators from the SIB spoke with Judge Célestin, who confirmed that he had dined with Terry on the evening of the alleged assault. No physical evidence linked Terry White to the assault, and although Toto Dorsemilus insisted that Terry White was his assailant, he failed to pick out Terry White in a photo array.

The investigators from SIB sent the dossier to the review board with a recommendation that no further action be taken, owing to insufficient proof of the assailant's identity. All members of the Mission enjoy complete immunity from local prosecution under the Status of Forces Agreement signed by both the United Nations and the government of Haiti, and the case was dropped.

PART FOUR

PART FOUR

1 I met Toussaint Legrand just a few days after I came to Haiti. I was walking to the beach, about a mile from the center of town, and all along the way, little voices shouted, *"Blan!"* I waved and dispensed casual smiles and received in reply giggles, grins, and suspicious stares. The yellow sun cast sharp, sparkling shadows on the white dirt road. It was cockfighting day, and the men carried roosters, the birds' heads stuffed into socks. The way it works, a rooster can't see, he thinks everything's copacetic: soon as the sock comes off, first thing he sees is some other damn rooster there, disrespecting him.

I was halfway to the beach when a very skinny kid with an incongruously deep bass voice stopped me. If you closed your eyes, it was like talking to Sidney Poitier. Open them, and there was a malnourished kid who looked about twelve, with a large plastic bag of potatoes and manioc balanced on his head. He had a face like a space alien, with very big eyes, a broad forehead, and prominent cheekbones tapering down to an angular chin. I don't remember how he began the conversation—that we were conversing at all was a sign of what a natural salesman he was—but the upshot was this: he was seventeen years old and called himself a student; his family had no money; he had no money; his mother had no money; his little brothers were hungry; and he wanted to be an artist. He asked me for money to feed his little brothers and I gave him the change in my pocket. His name, he told me, was Toussaint Legrand.

A few days later Toussaint presented himself at the front gate of the Sénateur's mother's house. Jérémie is a small place, and Toussaint, going from neighborhood to neighborhood and door to door, had found me. As he waited for me, he had a look on his face of patient, fragile hopefulness. I invited him into the house, where he drank a glass of orange juice. Much later I learned that he was so excited to see me that he hadn't slept the night before. That's exactly the look he had on his face as he sipped his orange juice, as if he couldn't quite believe that he, Toussaint Legrand, of Carrefour Prince, Haiti, was sitting there on my terrace drinking orange juice.

In the weeks and months thereafter, no pretty lady has ever been courted by such an animated and constant suitor as I was courted by Toussaint Legrand. He came by the house all the time. He was unshakable.

My wife and I tried many schemes to convince Toussaint to leave us alone. We told him that he was allowed to visit only every third day. Every third day without fail he showed up at our door. We asked him to visit only after five in the evening, with the result that we had a standing appointment with Toussaint Legrand at 5:01 p.m. Once, we asked him not to visit us at all. *Hah!* He was resistant to hints, oblivious to suggestions. What did he want? Not just to ask for money, but also to say hello, or to eat a meal, or to hang around, or to ask a question. What he wanted more than anything, I think, was to be part of the family. He wanted to sit with us out on the terrace in the evening and *belong*.

In the end, Toussaint wore us down. He was the kind of kid you could horse around with. He was always up for kicking around a soccer ball or taking a trip to the beach. You could send him up the mango tree, and he'd come down with half a dozen fresh, juicy pieces of fruit. He had an easy laugh. You could tease him about girls. My wife taught him to dance. After a couple of months, it got to be an accepted fact of life that two or three or five days a week, Toussaint Legrand would show up at our house and hang around until we told him that he had to leave. It was hard to be mean to somebody so young who wanted so badly to be liked.

Brilliant smile aside, Toussaint wasn't very handsome. He had terrible body odor, and his hair was reddish at the roots—he asked me for money to buy soap and shoe polish, which he rubbed in his head. His red hair bothered him more than hunger, because every girl on the street knew, just by looking at him, that he was broke. Even the qualities of Toussaint's own character weighed against him. He told me he wanted to be an artist but had no talent: only once did I ever see him actually try to make art. Illiterate, years behind his age in a school he rarely bothered to attend—who could even *start* to say how intelligent or capable he was?

It was hard to imagine somebody who had been dealt fewer good cards in life than Toussaint. He and his family had nothing. They had no money, no property, no savings, no skills, nothing but hungry bellies. They were out in the storm. And so the family lurched from crisis to crisis. Shortly after I got to know Toussaint, his mother's stall at the market caught fire. Then Israel, his younger brother, contracted typhoid, and the family spent his brother Junior's school fees on doctors. Then Toussaint's grandmother died, and the family was desperate to give her a decent funeral. About once a week Toussaint would rap at our gate late at night with some new, ever more elaborate story of dramatic need. Some of these stories might even have been true.

Toussaint had only one asset in life, but it was considerable. It was the reason why I gave him money. Despite every disadvantage he suffered, despite every self-inflicted wound, he was nevertheless making his way in the world with radiant, unshakable optimism. One day he bought a hen, whom he named Catalina. This was to be the start of a chicken-breeding empire. Then his family got hungry and ate Catalina. Toussaint was undismayed. He asked me for money to buy another starter chicken. If you gave him fifty gourdes, he'd give half to the kids on the street to buy candy—Toussaint saw himself as somebody who could afford to be generous. When he told me he wanted to be an artist, I think he chose the word almost at random from a list of grand words that to him were synonymous with hope. He would tell me later that he wanted to be a preacher, a doctor, a poet, an engineer. Step by step, he went forward toward an opaque future that he was sure—absolutely, unshakably sure—would one day be glorious.

In the meanwhile, he got by.

The judge had a discussion and study group at his house three times weekly. He started by inviting the smartest high school kids in town, all of them curious about the world and wanting to know what was out there past the sea and the hills; but the group soon expanded to include kids back home from university in Port-au-Prince, seminary students, young lawyers—anyone eager to talk, listen, argue, and think. Nominally a group devoted to human rights issues, they'd come to the judge with stories of abuse of power and corruption and the kinds of things that make up the pages of the Amnesty International country report, but soon it was more like a bull session on Justice and Liberty and Freedom. What does it mean to have the Separation of Powers? How do we get an Independent Judiciary here in Haiti? What is the Rule of Law? Anything with a capital letter was grist for the mill: they'd sit out on the judge's terrace, yakking until sundown. Then the judge, who was a talker, would start talking about whatever was on his mind: building a road to Port-au-Prince, the mangoes, how long it took fish to get to market in the DR. Long before I had sat with Terry and the judge that day out at Anse du Clerc, those kids had heard the speech a hundred times, had started to repeat it around town themselves.

Every time I saw Johel, he was on me. "Brother, why don't you come over and talk to my kids?"

"What do they want to talk to me for?"

"These kids—Port-au-Prince is the end of the world for them. They want to meet anyone who's been *anywhere*."

Next time, same story: "Brother, when are you coming to talk to my kids? And why don't you take Toussaint with you?"

After the shooting incident, Terry had insisted that the judge throw up a wall around his house, so three masons worked ten hours a day for three days, and now when you came up the road, there was a fifteen-foot stone wall topped with razor wire. Open the gate and you'd expect a mansion, something commensurate with that mighty wall, but there was just a tiny concrete cottage, painted sunflower yellow, still pockmarked with bullet holes.

Now keep your eyes on Toussaint Legrand. He's the skinny kid in the back of the room, looking all shy and intimidated by these smart, lycée-educated kids. But the judge is saying with his eyes, *Toussaint, I'm glad you're here.*

The judge was thinking of a funny story. So he was just a little judge, thirteen years old, fresh off the metaphorical boat, just arrived in the Cold Country, and believe me, you people don't know cold until you know an upstate winter, and he was competing in his first spelling bee. Spelling? He barely spoke a word of the language. He would have been better off at a flying bee.

Then he explains to the kids what a spelling bee is, how it works, and they're nodding up and down, locked in on him, emoting with him, sharing his story—even Toussaint.

So this is an ordinary school spelling bee, and he has no idea if he can compete with all these white kids. He's just a little Haitian boy, after all. Strange thing about being a Haitian. We know we kicked Napoleon's ass, won our freedom and independence . . . same time, we're never sure we're as good as anyone. They asked him to spell "I," he might have stuttered and choked, he was so nervous. And what's the very first word that comes up? What did the good Lord ask him to spell right there and then?

Ratatouille.

R-A-T-A-T-O-U-I-L-L-E.

And he knew that word because his Haitian mother had clipped a recipe from *Le Nouvelliste* and left it on his Haitian refrigerator for the first twelve years of his Haitian life. That's when Johel knew he belonged. He knew he could compete. Doesn't matter that he screwed up his next word, "irony." He knew he was as good as anyone anywhere.

Not the next year, but the year after that, the judge was national spelling champion, best speller in the whole country. They put him on TV.

Haitian kid.

Then he finished third in his class, straight off to college, scholarship.

Haitian kid.

Law school, where he was *Law Review*; clerkship for a United States appellate judge.

Haitian kid.

Just like them.

All they needed to do was go down the road, and to go down the road, you *needed* a road.

And there was one kid in particular who was soaking in that message—a kid who couldn't have spelled "ratatouille" to save his life, no less defined it, and that was Toussaint Legrand. I'd hauled him along to the judge's meeting, no agenda or intention on my part, just thinking it might interest him. But this was what Toussaint Legrand—those big space-alien eyes not blinking, his whole being absorbed in the judge's message—had been looking for.

After that, Toussaint didn't stop coming over to my place, but he started heading over to the judge's place too. Soon he was knocking on the judge's door three times a week, the judge inviting him in to sit and watch soccer, the judge asking how his family was doing. When Toussaint asked for money, the judge said no.

He said, "Toussaint, you've got to take your own destiny in your hands. Nobody ever gave me anything in my life but that road. Your road isn't a good road, but you got to get yourself down that road by yourself."

And here's what Toussaint Legrand is thinking about. He's thinking about the mango trees on his uncle's land in Carrefour Prince. He might not be able to spell, but he can sure as hell add, multiply, and divide. And what he's thinking about is how fine he'd look if he could only sell the mangoes in Port-au-Prince. He's thinking that if there was a road, that would change everything. He wouldn't have to paint his hair with shoe polish. He could afford deodorant. He'd find a girl.

All Toussaint knew his whole life had been bad roads.

He was born in a little village about an hour's walk from Jérémie. Out in Carrefour Prince, there was no electricity, no running water, no nothing but sugarcane, goats, beans, and fruit trees: mangoes, bananas, plantains, and breadfruit.

And no road.

Toussaint's bad luck began *before* birth. His daddy was a master of the dark mystical arts, a *boko* named Destiné Eric. When Toussaint was five months in his mamma's belly, Destiné Eric quarreled with an unsatisfied client who swore that he would take his vengeance—which he did, most unmagically, cutting Destiné Eric's throat open with a machete. Toussaint was the thirdborn of a brood that would eventually swell to five brothers by five different fathers, all dead before their children were born.

Madame Legrand sold flour, sugar, rice, corn, and a myriad of Chinese-made plastic housewares at a stall in the market. When Toussaint was twelve, his little brother Junior got into a fistfight after school. Madame Legrand confronted the bully's mother. Words got heated. This other lady cursed her: "Marie, you're too rich. You won't have money again!" After that her products ceased to sell. Weevils invaded the flour. She got too tired to get up and go sell. She ran out of money. She pulled Toussaint out of school, no longer able to pay his school fees.

Out of school, Toussaint got to vagabonding all day long around Jérémie. At the bus station he fell into conversation with a fat lady from the seaside village of Corail. Toussaint looked at the lady's huge thighs and broad behind, her arms as thick as his chest, and he could almost smell the rice and meat in the folds of her clothes. *Where there's fat, there's food*, he thought. So he smiled at Suzette, melting that fat lady's heart, and Toussaint had a new family, three hours' walk down a bad road from his old family.

But things in Corail weren't as Toussaint had hoped. There was a house to clean and dishes to wash and pots to scrub and buckets of water to haul; and although he wanted to be one of Suzette's eight happy kids, he wasn't. All the kids slept in comfy beds, but Toussaint slept on the floor in the kitchen with the rats and the bugs; and when Suzette made big fat-lady meals of rice and beans and meat, first she fed her kids, then herself, only then giving Toussaint the skinny leftovers.

Toussaint had been living twenty-one dog years chez Suzette when there was an incident—a nasty one.

Suzette's husband was a tired, mean man who loved goats; he kept them and raised them and bred them and ate them and sold them. He had a ram that he kept for stud, a hearty, rancorous, endlessly horny beast just like himself, named Cerberus, and one of Toussaint's jobs was keeping an eye on Cerberus when he was at pasture. A goat like Cerberus was the envy of many another goat breeder in the district.

Now, just what happened to Cerberus is a matter of dispute, Toussaint claiming that he asked one of Suzette's kids to watch Cerberus while he himself helpfully hauled buckets of water, said child of Suzette thereupon irresponsibly falling into a deep and typical slumber. The other story was that Toussaint himself had fallen asleep, allowing Cerberus to gnaw his way through his rope. Either way, Cerberus was gone, most likely now rutting his way through some other man's she-goats. Truth in the affair may be indeterminate, but blame was assigned nevertheless to Toussaint, who was beaten with a thick leather strap Suzette's husband maintained for such exigencies, until thick welts like mushrooms sprang up on his slender face and arms and he was huddled in a ball in the kitchen. That's when Toussaint took stock of his life and conditions—he was as skinny as the day he showed up and no closer to glory or a girl—and decided to take the bad road home.

So after three years on his own, Toussaint walked back to his mamma in Jérémie, where he did nothing and had nothing to do, and nothing was the problem that he faced all day every day: nothing to eat, nothing to wear. Toussaint had been back in Jérémie just a few months, and he woke up one morning to hear his little brothers crying on account of their being so hungry and his mamma not being capable of feeding them nothing. So he went out on the road looking for a vision of what to do, and a vision came to him of his mamma's uncle out near the airport. It was a long walk, and when he made it out there, his uncle was boiling up potatoes and manioc, which made it hard for said uncle to deny the existence in his garden of potatoes and manioc. When Toussaint explained that Junior and Israel were crying hungry back home, his mamma's uncle dug him up some potatoes and manioc, which Toussaint tied up in a black plastic bag and balanced on his head, and went walking home, feeling somewhat resentful that he was doing what his mamma should have been doing, begging for food for the little men.

But it's like they say, God comes on a donkey, slow and steady, because on his way back into town, Toussaint Legrand saw me, and he felt certain that the good Lord had put me on that road, the road that led him right to the judge.

The Legrand family had countless cousins and distant relations spread out over almost all of the Grand'Anse; and it was Toussaint's habit to mooch off all of them, drifting around the region in a rhythm of his own devising, his exceedingly sensitive inner compass guiding him to whichever cousin had just come into a little cash or a ripe harvest, or had won some money in the *borlette*, or was simply feeling generous. His cousin Selavi (pronounced "C'est la vie") Legrand, for example, had a husband in Miami who every few months would Western Union her down a small contribution for the upkeep of his children—and within a day or two of the receipt of these funds, Toussaint would arrive on Selavi's doorstep, looking woebegone.

Selavi lived in a village accessible only by foot, perhaps a three-hour hike from the road, which itself necessitated a hike of almost half a day from Jérémie. Toussaint's scrawny body concealed strength and endurance, and he thought nothing of long distances on foot—what else did he have to do, after all? When he arrived in Morne Rouge, his patience did not go unrewarded: the Haitian peasant rebels at parsimony and is generous, and so it was that Selavi offered Toussaint a bowl of chicken stew and a couple hundred gourdes to buy the little men in town a new pair of shoes or to buy Marie Legrand some credit for her phone.

Back in Jérémie, Toussaint told Terry and the judge the following story:

He had been sitting after dinner, as the older men swapped bawdy jokes and the children dozed, when Selavi's father indignantly recalled the last election. He had shown up at the polling center, he said, intending to cast his ballot for the Sénateur, only to find that the box next to the Sénateur's name had already been checked on his ballot. Selavi's father was a *citoyen* and a proud son of the revolution, and it rankled him that what should have been his choice and privilege was now an obligation. When he protested, the head of the voting center informed him that no other ballots were available. Soon other men joined their protests to his, and the situation threatened to become unruly, when a local curé, a man named Abraham Samedi, appeared.

The crowd at the voting center fell silent as Père Samedi descended from his mule. He was in his late sixties, and his hooded black eyes, set deep in his bony face, made the locals think of the illustrations in their Bibles of Old Testament prophets. Selavi's father, well-muscled as he was, stood not much taller than five feet, and Père Samedi towered over him. He wrapped his long arm around the younger man's shoulder. Then the men walked side by side for several minutes. No one in the crowd could hear their conversation, but they could see Selavi's father nodding, and by the time they returned from their brief promenade, it was clear that Selavi's father had seen the wisdom of the old priest's counsel: that a vote for the Eagle (this was the name of the Sénateur's political party, of which he was the only candidate) was a vote for the Eagle, no matter who scrawled an *X* in the box opposite the Sénateur's photograph on the ballot. In the end, the precinct in which Selavi's father voted turned out nearly unanimously for the Sénateur, as they always did, giving the Sénateur 312 votes and his opponent just 6.

What interested Terry and the judge particularly in this story was that neither man had realized the role of Père Samedi in local politics, nor his ardent support for the Sénateur.

And so it was that Terry and the judge offered Toussaint the first job of his young life: he was now the scout.

Back in the days when they were slaves, the judge told Toussaint, there was always a scout, somebody who went below the slave man's radar. A kid, maybe, someone who can slip in and out of anywhere, someone who can talk to anyone. Someone who makes friends easily, can find out what the real lay of the land is. Who's the *gros neg*, the big man? What does he really want or need? Someone who can find out the true story of what happened last time around. What do they really think about the Sénateur? Not a job any of those lycée kids could do—maybe they know how to read and work out chemistry problems, but they show up in Morne Rouge, deep in the mountains, they'd stand out. They don't have Toussaint's natural ability to talk, to listen, to make friends.

The judge had an old, beat-up motorcycle sitting in a shed, and he let Toussaint take it out on the road: one day Corail, one day Pestel, three-day trip from Dame Marie to Les Irois or deep into the mountains. Everywhere he goes, he has a cousin or knows someone who knows someone; they treat him as a friend.

And everywhere he goes, he's coming back telling the judge the same story: not a chance in the world the judge is going to beat the Sénateur. People *like* the Sénateur, yes, but that's not the issue. Problem is, the Sénateur has Bonbon, or Beaumont, or Pestel wired up tight. In Bonbon, they say, last time around, you hardly even needed to bother to vote: there was an *X* already in the Sénateur's box on your ballot. You ask for another ballot, a clean ballot, they'd tell you, "So sorry, brother, all the ballots we have. You like those fingers?" In Beaumont they'd say, "Didn't want to vote for the Sénateur myself, but I couldn't turn down the money. Not with the price of coffee the way it is." In Pestel they'd say, "We didn't like the Sénateur around here, so we just stayed home. Lot of bad things happen on voting day. Funny thing is—when they published the results, seems we all voted anyway."

The judge said, "Sounds like an uphill battle on our hands."

Toussaint said, "I'm with you to the end, Judge."

"Tell me something, Toussaint. You think if they voted fairly and people just voted their hearts, do you think I'd have a chance?"

Toussaint thinks it over. First time in his life anyone ever asked him a thing like that, wanted his opinion. He says, "I do, Judge."

"Why's that?"

"When I tell people about that road—they can't believe it. One thing everyone wants around here is a road. I think you tell people about that road, you just might have a chance."

2 A few years before I came to Haiti, the Mission decided to bring the vast Port-au-Prince bidonville of Cité Soleil under its authority. The neighborhood was said to be dominated by warlords and gang leaders, and the military operation began with a show of force: soldiers from the Mission would parade through the narrow streets in APCs, one after another, like Hannibal's elephants. Somewhere in the middle of the procession a Uruguayan APC came under small-arms fire from gang members on roofs. Then the Uruguayan APC broke down and the Uruguayans abandoned their vehicle in panic, leaving the gang members in possession of an APC, a machine gun, and numerous small arms. The no-nonsense, hyperviolent Brazilian army had to rescue the equipment, leaving who knows how many dead Haitian civilians in their wake. It was not a pretty scene, and shortly thereafter the Uruguayans were sent to Jérémie—in peacekeeping terms, a decided demotion.

Nowadays the Uruguayans would take their APCs out on the back roads of the Grand'Anse from time to time just to see if they ran right. Once, they knocked over the wall of their own base trying to park. That was about the extent of their martial activities. Most mornings you could see a couple dozen of them out on the beach, drinking maté and playing soccer and flopping around in inner tubes.

I found Terry swimming in the deep water out past where the Uruguayans were splashing. I hadn't seen him in a couple of weeks. Kay had been back in Florida, and without her around to animate the barbecues and cocktail hours and trips to the beach, the only time I saw Terry was on the road from Mission HQ around dusk, when he'd wave at me from the window of his SUV.

Even now, we almost didn't speak. He was swimming much farther out than I had ever gone. I had arrived to find him swimming, had swum myself for at least an hour, and had been sitting, watching him, for still longer when he finally came out of the water, his broad chest and shoulders swollen from the sport. He was panting from the exertion. When he saw me, he came and sat beside me.

He was silent for a long time, watching the tide creep higher. Then he started talking to me, the way a man can sometimes talk more openly to an acquaintance than to a friend, about the burden of pain and love he was carrying.

"What you got to understand—what you got to understand, her pussy, it's *sweet*. Almost like—cinnamon, you know?"

Terry pulled a cigarette from a pack he had left in his shoe. He took a drag so deep that half the cigarette was reduced to ash. The smirk fell off his face. His bluster faded, and I realized that his vulgarity was only a mask intended to conceal a tenderness I hadn't thought him capable of. You only had to look at his eyes to see it: the lower eyelid distended by sleeplessness, streaks of red emerging from the mud-colored pupils.

"Listen, brother. We got something—it's serious, brother. That's all I'm saying. She won't talk to me, and you gotta go see her for me. I'm dying here. I don't know who else I can get to go. She likes you, she'll listen to you."

"She doesn't like me," I said, surprised that she even knew my name. We had only exchanged words once, at Kay's birthday party.

"No, she does, bro. Trust me, she does."

"Why won't she talk to you?"

"You were there, man. You saw her. She's not like you can talk to her, she gets in the mood, you know."

"It's the election?"

"That and other things."

"Other things?" I said.

A roar came up from the Uruguayans: someone had scored a goal.

The winning Uruguayans lifted their hero on their shoulders and paraded down the beach with him. The defeated goalie sagged to his knees. He looked about ready to bash his own brains out with the nearest rock.

"She wants me to get her out of here," Terry said.

"Where are you supposed to take her?"

He stubbed out his cigarette in the sand, flipped the pack over onto its back, slipped out another one, and lit it. He was on four-day stubble.

"That's what I say. I say, 'What am I supposed to do?' But she won't listen. I say, 'Even if I marry you, even if you weren't already married, even if I weren't married, I can't get you a visa.'"

"And you told her that?"

He said, "You can't talk to her. She just says, 'You don't love me.' I say—"

Terry didn't finish.

"Does Kay know?"

"She doesn't need to know. I love that woman. But this thing isn't like that. What you have to understand is that I don't have a choice."

Back after that first thing, Kay had dragged Terry into counseling. No, no, I won't go—and then there he was, slouched in a chair like he was at the principal's office. Principal was a middle-aged lady with horn-rimmed glasses, chewing nicotine gum, one piece after another. Louise Whatshername. Christ, what was her name? Three times a week, ninety minutes a session, for about six months, this Louise Something sat there listening, crossing her legs when Kay crossed hers, then talking to Terry, the look in her eyes telling him that she understood, she really did. "I bet that was *very* difficult to resist," she said. Sometimes Kay would jump on Terry's ass, and Louise would say, "Kay, this is Terry's time to talk. Let Terry tell his story. Your time is coming up next."

And Terry knew just what she was doing: this was *his* game. She was taking a bad situation and making it into a story, something both of them could live with. "Love is a story," this Louise Lady said. "A marriage is a story. But you can't have two stories in a marriage. That's my golden rule. If a stranger comes up to you and asks what happened, you both tell the same story. Bad story, good story, but maximum one story per marriage." She was taking two stories and making them one again.

"I can't forgive him," Kay said.

"You don't need to," said Louise. "You two just need to have the same story. And you don't even know it, but you two have been living different stories for a long time. When you two have the same story, you don't need to forgive him, because you were the one who was unfaithful, just like he was unfaithful, and he's the one who suffered, just like you're suffering now."

"I wasn't unfaithful," Kay said. "I was a good, decent, devoted wife."

"The *couple* was unfaithful," said Louise.

"Bullshit," said Terry.

That got a smile out of Kay, first in a long time.

After he got the first confession out of his system, Terry loved confessing. Two decades he'd spent coaxing men to confess their sins, and this was the first time he'd ever seen it from this side of the table. He knew this from the interrogation room, the way getting someone to talk the first time was hard, getting them to stop talking was harder. Sometimes he'd want to tell them, Shut up, you're digging yourself a deeper hole. Same dynamic at work with Louise Something: the urge to talk and talk and talk. Every time you tell the story, you tell it different, you tell it deeper. First story: wasn't me. Second story: was me. Third story: was me and I'm good. Fourth story: was me and I'm bad. Nth story: used to be me. How much it had bothered him that Kay stopped seeing him the way she used to, like he was her hero. How there'd been a place in his heart that was Kay's, and he'd given it to this other lady. How they'd made love twice a week, most times at her place. How they'd watched TV together afterward.

"What did you watch?" Kay asked.

"You know, whatever was on."

Kay wincing, the TV hurting her more than the sex.

"Did you love her?" she asked.

Terry didn't know how to answer that. He'd always known where home was. That should mean something too. He'd never lost his head for her. There was just this thing that was Kay's and he'd given it to *her*. But it was Kay's and if you *knew* that thing was Kay's—doesn't that mean something too?

So that was how the other thing went. Whole time it was happening, the thing inside him that told him what was right and what was wrong was pointed firmly in the direction of wrong. Terry White was the kind of guy—he liked to be able to look everyone in the eye. If you can't look your own wife in the eye, something's wrong. He knew that. And when Kay knew, really knew, that he understood that, that's when she let him come home. Separate Kay and Terry and interrogate them about his thing with Miss Whitman, and they'd have ended up telling pretty much the same story, word for word. That's all you can really hope for: one marriage, one story.

So what you got to understand, what you really have to understand, is that this thing with Nadia was all different. What you got to understand is that the thing inside him was pointing the other way round.

What you got to understand, Terry was saying—what you got to understand is—

He lit a cigarette.

He had never wanted a woman more in his life, from the first time he saw her, which was on the very night he had heard gunfire and, motivated by blind, stupid instinct, headed in the direction of danger. The siren of his vehicle had interrupted the assault. By the time he was at the house, the judge was already half out the door, standing on his front stoop with a shotgun in his hand. Didn't even know how to rack it properly. Terry was worried that the judge would shoot his own balls off. Then they'd gone inside, patrolled the house, rooftop to kitchen, back terrace to bedroom, where Terry had seen Nadia sitting in bed in white underwear and a gray camisole. The judge had slipped into the bedroom, closed the door—the last thing Terry saw was her green eyes staring into his, a straight-out soul connection if there ever was one.

A week later Terry was in charge of a special unit doing close personal protection, officially training the PNH who would be assigned to protect VIPs, in truth, the judge's shadow himself—and those days,

Terry barely saw Nadia: she seemed to flit around the background of the judge's existence like a fawn. Terry was a deer hunter, and he knew that you don't see the does like you saw the bucks. He'd be watching baseball with Johel on the big screen and she'd be listening for the voices of hunters in the glades, those strange green eyes sweeping the room side to side. It took a long time, maybe months, before she could just sit in a room with Terry and be still—we're not talking anything else, brother, but sitting in a room. How many words did they say to each other in all that time? Two dozen? How many smiles? One, two, at the most? If you were a different man than Terry, you might have thought she just didn't like you. But Terry knew just who she was right from the start; he had seen it too many times not to understand it.

Here was a woman who was frightened for her life.

Driving patrol, lying on his cotton mattress, or swimming long sea laps down at the beach, he was thinking about Nadia, what it was like when she and the judge were alone together, what they talked about, what they did. How she felt when she saw his big body coming to her in the night. What Terry always knew, what made him a good cop, was that you could feel this way and the other way all at the same time; he knew that we *all* could feel this way and the other way all at the same time. *Son of a bitch had it coming; worst thing I ever did was shoot that son of a bitch. I'll hate that cunt until the day they put me in the earth; how could I have done that to the woman I loved?* The judge was the best man he ever met, and sometimes he thought the bastard was like one of those creeps who preyed on small children.

No doubt in Terry's mind he'd give his own life to protect the judge's.

No doubt in Terry's mind the judge could make a difference around here.

No doubt in Terry's mind that Nadia was with the judge because she had nowhere else to go.

Nowhere else to go—that's just one of those phrases Terry had never thought about until he got to Haiti. An American always has someplace else to go. That's what it means to live in a big country. Big country is a big way of looking at the world. Haiti was the first time Terry ever thought about life in a little country, like living in someone's armpit, tight and narrow and hot and hairy. Terry got up in the mountains, looked out at the sea: that was the prison wall, right there. One goddamn hill after another, all of them leading to a place like this place. Nadia couldn't get past that wall. Where was she going to go? Some other nasty-ass butt crack of a Haitian village? Port-au-Prince? The Dominican Republic? Live in some Santo Domingo whorehouse, selling herself? She had the judge. That was all she had. Judge plus Nadia equals Ongoing Life. Nadia minus judge equals Death. That was the simple pair of equations that governed this lady's existence.

And believe it or not, Terry had been determined not to touch her, determined to be good. Good husband, good man, good friend. Once in his life, he wanted to do the right thing by everyone—by Kay, by his family, by the judge, by himself, by the hungry kids with red hair. Just look himself in the mirror and know that he could tell his story straight-up to a stranger on the street.

But then came Tuesdays, when the judge's maid washed the laundry out on the back terrace of the concrete house and hung the laundry on a line. The house overlooked the Caribbean, and Terry would sit out there with the judge in the evenings, watching the sun set in the direction of Jamaica and drinking a Prestige, utterly and absolutely soul-struck by the sight of Nadia's underwear swaying and sashaying and cavorting in the breeze, simple white cotton women's panties and bras, stroked gently by the wind.

And still he wanted to be good.

For four months he tried to be good, and when you had it like he had it, four months is a long time, brother. In four months, how many times did the two of them talk one-on-one? Maybe twice. Once, in the kitchen, Terry was making rum cocktails. "Do you want one?" he asked. "I don't care," she said. "Then I won't make you one." "I want one." "Then cut up some lemons." That was conversation number one, reproduced verbatim, interrupted by the lumbering bigfoot presence of the judge, wanting to know if Terry had heard the latest from Les Irois. Terry turns around, and she's gone. Terry had to cut that lemon himself. No rum sour for her.

What you got to understand is that Terry loved them all—that can happen too. Loved the judge like a brother and Kay like a wife and

Nadia like a woman. Those long drives up into the mountains, the judge and Terry had talked about Nadia, the way they talked about everything else. That's when Terry started to fall in love with Nadia, just from hearing Johel talk about her. The judge had come back to Haiti determined to save and reform her, turn her into a solid citizen. Johel knew she was an intelligent woman: sometimes he'd tell her things about the law, and she'd tell him things back that'd make him think long and hard. So the first step was going to be to school her. Second step, teach her a trade or open a little business. Last step of the program, she'd be a free and independent woman. Only thing was, the judge had failed to consult Nadia. She wasn't interested, not at all. Didn't want to make plans. Didn't want to go to school. What do you want to do? No answer. Are you sad? No answer. Happy? No answer. Johel got so frustrated he'd shake, trying to talk to her. Then he'd see her taking a shower, hear her singing, she'd come to bed. So soft, so gentle. Remember that he loved her. Man, she drove the judge crazy. You couldn't fight with that woman. Reason with her, and she'd just stare at you. She was unhappy, she'd just leave. She had a cousin who lived near Carrefour Charles, she'd head up there like a runaway slave. No cell phone reception. Stay there until the judge himself hoofed his way up the mountainside to get her. Johel went a day without her, it was like his heart was breaking into shards of glass. Only place he ever saw her relaxed was up in the village. Watching over her cousin's kids. Every day in the church singing. Making music. Carrying water. Washing clothes at the river. She said she hated the village, but Johel saw a calm in her up there. That was where she belonged. What was she doing with *him*? What was he doing with *her*?

(And Terry knew, not knowing how he knew, what it was to wake up first thing in the morning to that big, unshaven face. The judge never talked to her; he talked *at* her. Came back at night, that mouth opened and shut and opened and shut and opened and shit and Nadia—she didn't understand a word. Words just didn't stop. Johel and Nadia played off each other like this: he talked&talked&talked, and Nadia could see all the while right into his jealous heart—because nothing that the judge felt or wanted was a mystery to her. No woman who had been pawed and loved and struck by as many men as Nadia could fail to understand a man's heart. Terry imagined Nadia telling herself to be grateful that she wasn't still in prison down in Florida. Then Nadia starting to wonder what the difference was. Terry could imagine how once a week the judge climbed on her. That big body riding on her, smelling like onions. Grunting. Sticky. The judge eating, just eating and eating and eating. She wanted to wear pretty things, the judge saying no. She wanted to go to Port-au-Prince, the judge saying no. She wanted to dance, the judge not able to keep his feet in line, move her around right.)

Sometimes Johel would ask Terry questions. Whaddya think? Would you leave Kay home with him? The "him" in question was the gardener. The plumber. The next-door neighbor. Terry said, "You got to be confident, Johel." But the judge was fat, had always been fat. He didn't see himself with a woman like Nadia. Didn't know if he satisfied her. It could torment him, just wondering what she thought of him. She had left him once, and the pain of it had almost killed him: he thought the pain of it the second time around *would* kill him.

But when it came to Terry, the judge was blind. And had he been just a little jealous, Terry might have backed off, put in for a transfer to Port-au-Prince. He'd been in Jérémie long enough. But the judge, who noticed every man and boy in Jérémie who'd ever thought about his wife, didn't want to notice the way Terry's face went red if Nadia was present, didn't want to see Terry's eyes roaming her slender body. Law of nature: a dog's got to growl if he wants to keep the bone.

That's the way it was, those long drives with the judge and Terry. Talk, talk, talk: marriage, marriage, marriage. Not easy for me either, brother. Let me tell you about Kay. Let me tell you about Nadia. Fuck 'em all. Let's get a beer.

And in all that, Terry felt, for the first time since his sister's death, the first—shit, he didn't know what to call it. Call it love, okay? Just call it love. And "love" wasn't the right word at all. It was like the ice was melting in his heart.

Louise McPherson. Christ alive, that was her name. That was going to drive me crazy. Louise McPherson. Good ol' Louise.

Nice lady, but didn't know shit about marriage.

So there was this incident—made him think long and hard.

Sometimes, if Marguerite Laurent was shorthanded and the judge was out in Port-au-Prince, she'd ask Terry to take a turn on patrol. So he was riding shotgun on the way to Chambellan with Eric, from Quebec. Eric spent his free afternoons at a local orphanage, fixing the roof and carrying the kids around on his shoulders, acting like the grandfather none of these kids had. When he went home on leave, he organized a toy drive, his whole community pitching in to buy a couple hundred stuffed animals. That's how all those little bears and otters and ocelots could be found on sale in the *marché*, right next to the mosquito nets distributed to the poor by the WHO.

Terry asked Eric, just to pass the miles, not really wanting an answer, what brought him to Haiti.

Eric tells him that all his marriage he'd been a first-class dog. He saw a pretty girl, he'd call his wife, tell her that a case came up. "I was a bone on legs," he says in that Canadian way, as if he's got a sinus infection from hell. He tells Terry he cheated on his wife in hotels, motels, bars, lounges, rented apartments, and the back of his car. "I hear you," Terry says, thinking all of a sudden about Kay, about how he wants to do right by her.

So Eric knew every sleazy motel in Quebec. He'd had mistresses, girlfriends, lovers, ladies who gave him a romp if he gave them a call once a year. When they were younger, he and his madame had these big fights—knock-down, drag-out, change-the-locks, call-the-other-cops fights. Then she'd just resigned herself, got this sad look in her eyes. Made him want to get out of the house, that look. So it was just three years ago, Eric said, after thirty-three years of marriage on his terms, that he woke up one morning, his wife (he says whatever the name of his fat-ass Canadian wife is, but what Terry hears is *Kay*) in bed beside him, made himself a cup of coffee, went off to work. Later Eric left a message on the answering machine telling (Terry hears it again: *Kay*) that he was working a case late. He didn't come home until it was almost dawn. He found (*Kay*) just where he'd left her, still lying in bed, just like she was when he got up the day before. The doctors said it was an aneurism. (*Kay's*) body was already going stiff.

When the paramedics took Eric's wife away, they had some trouble getting her through the door into the hall. They had to bend her this way and that. There was some talk of having to get her out through the window. Somebody, not realizing that Eric was in earshot, made a joke about a saw.

Then, when she was gone, Eric hit the button on the answering machine. There was his voice saying "Honey, working a double shift tonight. Back late." The worst part of it all was that he couldn't look at his kids now. They were just the spitting image of his wife. It was as if she were looking at him, hating him, wondering how he could have been off loving up some other woman while (*Kay*) was lying un-mourned, unwept, unnoticed in her deathbed. When the kids looked at him, their eyes said, *You bastard.* So now he was in Haiti, working with the orphans just so he didn't have to be back in Quebec looking into his kids' eyes.

Eric finishes his story and looks at Terry. Appropriately somber-eyed.

And what happens is, they're still driving, and this big old hawk came swinging up over the cliff, hunting down some cute mouse for breakfast. Terry never could forget that hawk, how it came swooping down out of nowhere until it was about this close to the windshield, then swung out over the mountainside. Terry thought that bird was going to come right through the fucking window.

He says to Eric, like nothing happened, "I hear what you're saying, brother. I really do."

After that Terry stayed away from Nadia, best he could. Man can have two desires in his head. Man can discipline himself. Man can say no. Man can stay away. That was when he started thinking seriously about the road. That was when he started pushing the judge on the road. It's more like a game than anything else. Man's never gonna build a road. Pushing the judge, just a way of marking the miles out, you know? Banter. Talking smack. Bullshitting.

Only the judge was listening. Every time he tells the judge, "You got a destiny," son of a bitch hears *destiny-destiny-destiny*, like footsteps echoing down a marble corridor. He wants to listen, though, Terry's happy to talk. Because he believes in destiny, because he believes we're meant for greatness. That's when he starts believing in that road himself. He starts seeing it. He stops thinking about Nadia so much and starts thinking tarmac. He's thinking how he'll tell his nephews, *I built a road*. He thinks he's out of the woods with Nadia. Judge says, "Come on in for a drink." Terry says, "Nadia home?" Judge says, "Most likely." Terry says, "Maybe tomorrow, brother. Got Kay on Skype tonight."

Four months. Kay visiting. Making love to his wife. Driving out with the judge. Talking politics. Thinking about the future, even after Haiti. Building. Planning. Lot of serious talks. Long swims. Road. Feeling like everything is getting solid again.

And then—just like that—just like that goddamn hawk coming down on the car, Eric throwing on the brakes, the patrol fishtailing and throwing up a cloud of dust—just like that—

Start with this. Terry had this thing he did, walking around cemeteries. Some people don't know the dead can talk. That's their secret. But someone's got to be listening.

In any case, it's something he's done since he was a kid—spending an hour or two every now and again prowling around the cemetery, looking at gravestones, looking at the flowers, thinking about the ancestors. One of the few truly effective antistress things he knew, taking a walk in the cemetery. Quiet place, put every damn thing in your life in perspective. Spend an hour visiting the dearly departed, come away with your brain rearranged.

Cemetery in Jérémie was a spooky, beautiful place. Not some neatly tended country club of a cemetery, the kind you find back home: The Garden of the Eternal Snooze. Our Lady of Rot and Repose. In Jérémie, the bodies were all parked aboveground, in concrete tombs. The better class of Jérémie family owned a tomb to give their loved ones perennial shelter, but for the most part, the people in Jérémie could only afford to rent a vault for a year or two. When the rental period was concluded, no ceremony at all, the tomb's owner jacked open the grave and tossed the current occupant out into the cemetery's high grass and weeds and vines. If there's still some flesh on the cadaver, they'll toss on some kerosene and let it burn. That's that. The cemetery was riddled with these evicted skeletons and skulls. Sometimes a dog trotted off, chewing on a femur. Those days, when the shit started building up between his temples, Terry found it very calming going over there to that cemetery, watching the bodies coming in, the skeletons going out.

And that morning, she was doing the same thing he was doing. Wandering around the tombs, looking at the skeletons. Maybe she'd been up all night with the drums and Erzulie—she did that. She was in a white dress—how'd she keep it so clean? She had this smile on her face, like she could hear the dead talking too, telling her she was pretty. Some of those graves went back a century. Lot of the graves have padlocks on them so nobody can come and open them up, turn the cadavers into zombies.

And Nadia is looking at him. Tell yourself all the lies you want, when there's that thing, it's there. They ended up sitting on the tombstone of Monsieur Maximilien St. Valois, who lived in Jérémie from 1876 until 1932. How many women had he loved? Father, husband, grandfather, *citoyen*. Now his tomb was empty—he was gone. No one remembered him. No one remembered anyone who remembered him. Some dog is gonna chew your leg. That'll be your skull right there. That's where he was headed, Terry thought. That was his worst fear, to leave this earth never having built something, made something. To be forgotten. He could smell Nadia's perfume, like wildflowers, and he could hear her breathing, like life. Better build something while you can. Better live while you can. Better love while you can.

What you got to understand, if you think about it a certain way, is that she's like the judge's prisoner, and what you got to understand also is that Terry hadn't always been able to protect the ones he loved. Maybe without the one fact the other fact wouldn't have been so strong. But memory weighs on present. Maybe if he hadn't known sorrow, he wouldn't have been so frightened of sorrow. Now he looks at Nadia and thinks of his sister, her head like a skeleton at the end, as thin as a bird, equally fragile, looking at him with deep, scared eyes that said, *Save me. Help me. Make it stop.* And what could he do for her but nothing?

There was a place he took her, the Hotel Patience. It must have been a grand old place in the day: a large foyer and a sweeping staircase leading up to little rooms, all sharing a balcony on the Grand Rue. Nowadays there was a pig sleeping on the floor and a blind man sitting alone. That was Emile Sever, and people came to the Hotel Patience because just so long as the gentleman did the talking, Emile Sever would never be able to identify the owner of the high-heeled footsteps.

First time they were in that little room, the place reeking of old semen and sweat, she starts to tremble. Room lit only by the barest light of flickering candles. Terry can still taste her, like something spicy, can still smell her on his face. He's watching the mosquitoes dive in frustration at the net. Then her teeth are chattering, she starts to moan.

And he knew what to do because this was something his sister used to do when they were kids: the fainting . . . not quite gone, not quite present . . . like everything she was feeling, even happiness and sadness, was stuck up there in the—he doesn't know the word, the synapses or something, and some switch in the brain goes off and she can't stop trembling . . .

So what he did was what he did with his sister. He got out from under the mosquito net, and he started to juggle, with whatever was at hand. He started juggling with his shoes and a bar of soap and some other stuff. At first she's not even looking at him, just sitting under the net, trembling. But then he started dropping stuff, half on purpose and half because he was clumsy.

It took him a few minutes, but he got her to smile.

Terry wanted me to talk to her. That was all he was asking. Just go and talk to her. He wasn't afraid to admit that he was frightened. He hadn't slept in a week, not really: a couple of hours rolling around, four in the morning, wide awake, watching sunrise, his head pounding. Thing was, Terry figured, he was all she had. And now she didn't want him. And if that were true, she had nothing left. Every instinct he had told him to protect her. There wasn't much arguing with a feeling like that.

Terry wanted me to talk to her, but he didn't even have her phone number. About a week before, her phone had stopped ringing. He figured she'd changed numbers.

"That's a sign," I said.

"Just go see her. Make sure everything's okay. Tell her—"

"Tell her what?"

"Tell her I'm still here."

3   May is rainy, hour after hour, water tumbling down from the rooftops, making sticky the mango leaves, splashing loudly on the broad banana leaves, sliding down the palms' ringed trunks. Out of town, people went wet and desolate on muddy roads to dripping mud houses, the women tying plastic bags on their heads. Yellow rivers scattered garbage down the hills. Soaked pigs rooted in the trash. Clothes mildewed. Young and old huddled in doorways and porticos, watching the rain or throwing down dominoes or staring with ruminant patience at the overflowing gutters. The rain washed down the sides of the hills; the topsoil turned to mud and silted the three rivers—the Grand'Anse, the Voldrogue, and the Roseaux. The rivers rose, and the gray-brown waters colored the sea gray. A *voilier* from Pestel collapsed in the rough seas: seven drowned. A landslide near Les Corberas cut the road to Port-au-Prince.

With the road cut, there was no way in or out of Jérémie for the poor but the night ferry. It was the breadfruit harvest, and so the people came down from the hills with engorged gunnysacks. The *Trois Rivières* was late coming out of Port-au-Prince, and so they waited some more, until the wharf was like an encampment of peasants and *marchandes* interlaced between mountains of breadfruit. The *Trois Rivières* was almost three days late, and every day the crowds on the wharf grew.

Everyone would later agree that the boat, which had never been meant to navigate on the high seas, was wildly overcrowded. There had been no plan in the loading of the *Trois Rivières*. The cargo was all on deck: tens of thousands of pounds of breadfruit, charcoal, waterlogged hardwoods, yams, and rotting mangoes. Nobody knows just how many people were aboard, but under ordinary circumstances the ship transported a thousand passengers or more: some estimated that the traffic that evening was twice that. The passengers arranged themselves on top of the cargo, prepared to sit all night in the open air, in the rain, on the high seas.

The ship had been scheduled to leave harbor in the early afternoon, but so great was the crowd, and so complicated the project of loading the vessel, that she first attempted to pull out into the open sea just after dark.

The wharf at Jérémie was short, the harbor had not been dredged in decades, and in the rainy season the high tides washed into shore all the silt that ran down from the mountains. It was low tide. Biting mud held fast the *Trois Rivières*. The engines whined, and the ship strained—the sound of the engines, survivors would later say, like an ox pulling a plow. The ship didn't move.

The captain of the *Trois Rivières*, a pale-skinned Cuban, made three attempts to pull the ship out to sea and then shut down the engines, and the ship sat at harbor. Soon the mood of the passengers grew surly. The patience of the Haitian peasant is legendary, but it is not infinite. The men and women on this ship had sat on the wharf for days in the rain, then endured the chaos of the ship's loading. Few things in life are as enervating as sitting in wet clothes. The captain spoke no Creole, and when he stepped out onto the deck of the bridge, he did not see tired travelers impatient for the journey to begin so that it could soon end; he had no words to explain the situation to his passengers; he saw only a vast sea of angry faces hurling furious epithets in his direction.

By chance, there was a second vessel in the harbor that evening. This ship wandered the coast of Haiti, delivering its cargo of fifty-pound sacks of cement. The captain of the *Trois Rivières* contacted the captain of the cement ship, and the two captains devised a plan.

The cement ship pulled to the flank of the *Trois Rivières*, and crewmen laid lines between the vessels. Then the cement ship reversed her engines, intending to pull the *Trois Rivières* off the reef of mud that held her.

As the ropes grew taught, they produced a high whine, like the buzzing of innumerable bees or static on the radio, a noise that echoed across the waters and into the slums. People as far away as Sainte-Hélène or Caracolie could hear the hempen ropes.

Aboard the *Trois Rivières* there was at first a moment of pleased satisfaction as the ship swayed at harbor. Then a bag of breadfruit opened, and the fruit, the size of bowling balls and just as hard, began to bound and skitter across the deck. A woman cried—those were her fruit! Soon the *Trois Rivières* was inclined to the horizon and the hands of the passengers sought something solid to cling to. Children tried to balance. A wave of laughter swept the boat from stern to tip as it swung out into the harbor, only the rear of the ship still low in the muck.

Now the *Trois Rivières* was at a severe angle to the horizon. Now the mothers were grabbing their children. Now the cargo was shifting, and things were tumbling. Now the ropes were extended full-length. Now the engines of the cement ship and the engines of the *Trois Rivières* droned powerfully. Now there was a noise louder than a gunshot, like the crack of thunder overhead—even in my house on the rue Bayard I heard it. The lines had snapped.

What happened next happened very, very fast. The *Trois Rivières* swung back in the other direction. She had been leaning one way, and now she leaned the other way. Nobody aboard had been prepared for this movement. Hundreds of passengers were thrown into the shallow water. Very few could swim.

I was reading on the terrace when I began to hear voices. They were coming down from the hill, some passing at a run, others ambling. I followed the voices in the direction of Hôpital Saint-Antoine, where, at the entrance to the hospital grounds, a woman wearing a short skirt and nothing else lay howling, beating her head slowly and insistently against the ground. Near her a cluster of young girls was inexplicably dancing, and from the interior of the hospital walls emerged a groaning sound, like a car in low gear straining. This was the roar of a large crowd. Soon the only ambulance in Jérémie, a gift from the people of Japan, attempted to part the crowd, and the crowd surged to surround it. The faces surrounding the ambulance flashed red and blue. The driver honked, and still the crowd didn't move.

A policeman climbed down from the passenger side of the vehicle. I watched him unholster his revolver, aim roughly in the direction of Venus, and squeeze the trigger. The crack of the shot silenced the crowd, as if someone had depressed the mute button. Then a wave of hysterical laughter swept the throng, which moved to let the ambulance pass.

There was a powerful smell in the air, of urine and sea salt and ammonia and old sweat. It was the smell of fear. The smell of shit repulses and the smell of sex arouses; so too the smell of fear spooks. Everyone there, whether they had been on the *Trois Rivières* or had just wandered down the hill to rubberneck, was soon under its sway. I began to sweat myself, a cold, clammy, unpleasant dampness at the small of my back.

The entrance to the hospital was like a chute or a ramp. Soon I was swept up into the crowd. Some of these people had been separated from their traveling companions in the accident. Now they wanted to get to the hospital as quickly as possible and find their missing. Others had put someone on the boat. I was pushed from the sides and behind. I felt hands on my back and sides, grasping at my feet. Everywhere, I heard voices saying, *Blan—blan—blan*. The crowd pressed up in a huge mass at the steel doors of the hospital, which were closed and held fast with a steel chain. Then the crowd spilled out to press up against the steel security bars of the hospital windows, and the more athletic young men tried to shinny up the drainage spout to reach the roof. From there they could drop into the courtyard.

The victims came up the hill on the backs of motorcycle taxis, wedged unconscious between the driver and some Samaritan riding shotgun, legs dangling helter-skelter; others staggered in on their own, clutching scraps of bloodstained shirts to their heads. For some of these newcomers the crowd parted, as if guided by an invisible hand, but others, too weak to press forward, simply recoiled to the margins of the crowd and sat on the ground to nurse their wounds alone.

I must have stayed on the fringe of the crowd five minutes or more. Two women saw each other: they had lost each other in the accident.

They began to dance and sing in a spontaneous thanksgiving, spinning each other around. Next to them a lady cried in an open-throated, unforgettable howl of grief. Angry voices, sorrowful voices, reasonable voices all intermingled incomprehensibly.

Somebody grabbed my shoulder: somebody was making eye contact with me, talking to me. I couldn't understand a word. I nodded my head. Then I heard the word "*médecin*." The word echoed through the crowd: *médecin—médecin—médecin*. Hearing the word, a woman thrust a small boy at me. He might have been two. He was wearing a T-shirt and shorts still wet from the sea. The boy saw me and began to cry. I didn't want to accept the child, but the crowd had seized me and the boy and placed us together. The woman who handed me the child merged back into the throng of faces. The crowd was now maneuvering us toward the steel doors of the hospital. The doors opened a crack to admit us, then slammed shut behind us.

The Hôpital Saint-Antoine is a square of concrete with an open courtyard in the center. There was a nurse in blue scrubs at a counter, writing in a ledger, a look on her face of acute boredom. I have since tried with no success to imagine how she had arrived at that moment—that vast sea of frantic faces peering in at her through the barred windows of the hospital—and produced that face, but here is the limit to my capacity for empathy.

"This child—," I began.

"You need to wait," the nurse said.

"This child isn't mine," I said. But talking to this woman was like throwing pebbles into the sea. She returned to her ledger.

The boy in my arms seemed to suffer from no ailment but that he was in my arms and not the arms of his mother. This was enough. He writhed in my arms with surprising strength and wailed as if I were pricking him with a sharp needle. I put him down and he stopped crying. He looked up at me solemnly.

I leaned over and said, "What's your name?"

He looked at the ground.

"Where's your mommy?"

The boy stood there.

We were standing in front of the open doors of the *salle d'urgence*, where a doctor, a Haitian, was occupied with a man who had cut his head. On the floor were puddles of coagulating blood. The doctor, who could have been no older than thirty, attended to the wound with meticulous attention. Those waiting to see him sat on the floor or lay sprawled out in the corridors. Many had lost their clothing in the accident: a woman with massive breasts moaned and swayed. Another woman massaged the back of a man—to what end, I'm not sure, for he was dead.

The boy, for all his unhappiness, seemed to need nothing but his mother. He began to cry again, and I picked him up and balanced him on my hip. He allowed himself to be consoled. I wandered the hospital, bouncing the boy on my hip. I was looking for that person who in Haiti does not exist—the man in charge.

The wards were small and poorly lit and overcrowded. The patients lay in beds and in the spaces between the beds, on the floor. There was the sharp chemical smell of carbolic acid and Betadine. Haitians come to the hospital either to give birth or to die. The boy and I walked down the hall and turned left into the maternity ward, with its air of teeming fecundity and rows of fussing, immensely pregnant women. When they saw me and that child, a murmur of laughter arose. I had thought for a moment that one of these women might be the child's mother. Perhaps he had been playing outdoors and had been overwhelmed by the arriving crowds. But he wasn't.

We wandered out into the courtyard. Your brain in moments of stress is meant to work a certain way, and those things that do not move and make no noise are stimuli of lesser importance. So before your brain notices the dead, your brain will see the fat rat scurrying through the grass, and before your brain understands the dead, your brain will see the rosebush, which had no business being in that courtyard but was nevertheless in glorious bloom. Only then does your brain comprehend that the men, women, and children piled in a heap are not shadows on the wall or broken furniture.

The rat stopped at a Styrofoam box in which had been left behind the remnants of somebody's dinner of rice and beans.

Watching a rat eat his supper and confronted with a hill of cadavers, I couldn't think of what else to do at that moment but call Terry White.

"Nice kid," Terry said.

"It's not mine."

"Really?" he said. Terry's calm was contagious. "That boat was a fucking death trap. First time I saw that thing, I said it was only a matter of time until we're fishing bodies out of the sink."

"Sénateur owns that boat," I said, repeating the rumor I had heard from the crowd.

"Fucking Haiti."

The judge showed up a few minutes later. Terry had called him on his way down the hill.

I said, "You should sit down. You look like you're going to hurl."

"Not me," Johel said.

"It's pretty fucked-up."

"That it is, brother, that it is," he said.

"You got any idea what I should do with this guy?" I asked.

Terry said, "Somebody just handed him to you?"

"I think somebody figured his mother was in here. But I don't see her."

Johel said, "The water rises and drowns the women."

The little boy reached for Johel's hand. Maybe because of his size, Johel seemed like a more comforting presence. Johel held the boy's hand with the stiffly self-conscious air of a man unused to children, but who is pleased to be liked by them.

A few minutes later two men from the morgue began to pick up the bodies from the pile and arrange them in rows. It was a two-man job: one for the arms, one for the legs. As each body rose up in the air, the head flopped backward. The men were straining hard, lifting the bodies over the others and dragging them into rectilinear order. Soon the men were sweating, drops of sweat flopping off their faces onto the faces of the dead. The men from the morgue rifled through their pockets, looking for money or phones.

Johel was trying to keep the kid from seeing his mother come out of that pile. But kids aren't stupid. Johel turned him around and tried to keep him looking at something else, but there was nothing to look at, and the child turned around and stared at the bodies as they came out from the pile and the men from the morgue lined them up. Then Johel tried to pick him up and take him for a walk, but he squirmed out of Johel's arms, walked back to the same spot in the courtyard where he had been standing, and stood there watching.

She never came out of that pile. The bodies were lined up in a row of eight and in a row of seven, and never once did that kid cry out *Maman!*—although he was looking for her, believe me he was.

Lined up in neat rows, they were like something else entirely from cadavers tossed in a heap. There is a difference between being tossed aside and being lined up in a row with your head neatly balanced between your shoulders and your eyes closed. Maybe the dead don't care, but the living do. There was a man with a broad, muscled chest—mid-forties, a workingman—wearing one Timberland boot. He might have cared a lot about losing his shoe if he cared about anything. There was a teenager wearing a shirt that read LIFE IS SHORT. EAT DESSERT FIRST, the publicity for a bakery in Paulson, Minnesota. His face was smeared with a weird smile of sputum and sea foam, like being dead was better than cake.

Terry lit a cigarette and said, "Do what you want, Judge, but for me this isn't acceptable. I had it in my power to change something like this, I'd do it."

When we left the hospital, the boy's mother saw him. He was still holding the judge's hand. She had no idea if he had lived and he had no idea if she had lived. When she saw him, she cried out. He ran to her without looking back. A roar of applause rose up from the crowd.

"*Merci Jezi,*" a woman cried out.

"*Merci Juge Blan,*" another woman cried.

Thank you Jesus and Juge Blan! That crowd camped outside the hospital, which had seemed so recently threatening and unreadable, now became festive and rejoicing, not at their own good fortune, but at the happiness of another. The generous crowd swarmed around the judge, the men shaking his hand and the women embracing him. Johel's face was soon streaked with tears.

In the weeks to come, he thought often of that moment in the foyer of the hospital, the crowd chanting his name.

4 Thank goodness for Kay! If it were not for Kay, I don't think the judge's campaign would have gotten much past "Hey! I *would* like to be *sénateur*!" When Kay heard that the judge had decided to contest the election, she put in place what she called Plan Kay, which consisted of her telling Todd Malgarini that she was out of commission for a while, flying down from Florida ASAP, and putting on her get-stuff-done hat, the actual hat in question being a tennis visor. Twenty-four hours after the judge announced his intention to run and just two weeks after the grounding of the *Trois Rivières*, Kay had already begun to turn a shaggy wooden house just off the Place Dumas into campaign HQ. The rental was concluded so fast that she must have organized it all, in typical Kay style, weeks or even months in advance. "Thank goodness for Kay!" we said when a large generator began to throb in the back; it was thanks to Kay that there was a fifty-five-gallon drum of petrol beside the generator; and it was thanks—yet again!—to Kay that there were desks, chairs, lights, and pens. Kay and the judge covered the walls of the office with maps of the Grand'Anse, each village, hamlet, and town shaded according to the size of its population. Kay even thought of push-pins, bright yellow, red, and green, sunk into the map in those places where the judge, after consultation with Toussaint, intended to campaign.

Not that there was much campaigning yet to do—the election was still months away. The judge hadn't even gotten himself on the ballot yet. So in the absence of actual activity, there was an almost nonstop evening party, where the judge's friends, disciples, acolytes, and acquaintances presented themselves at dusk for cocktails.

Jérémie was a small town, and the hours could stretch out. So it was nice to have a little social club where in the evenings we could repair for drinks. There was usually music on the stereo—Haitian Compas, Dominican merengue, or reggae. It all depended on who was closest to the stereo at a given time. Sometimes my wife would come and we would dance. Somebody would bring in a huge pot of rice and another huge pot of beans and plates of deep-fried plantains. The judge would be in shirtsleeves, collar loosened, sitting on the edge of his desk, talking about whatever was on his mind: some recent Supreme Court decision up in the States, his experience as a champion speller, the advantages of a road. He often wore a white Greek maritime captain's hat perched on his large head—I have no idea where it came from, but it suited him in a kind of lighthearted, self-mocking way. Terry was in charge of the blender, mixing up drinks and pouring them with a bartender's flair into the outstretched cups. (And it was thanks to Kay that there was a refrigerator that was cold and full of beer and ice . . .) It was the kind of place where people would bring a friend of a friend, just to talk politics and get a drink; it got so bad after a while that Terry had Toussaint hire two friends to serve as security guards to make sure no one walked off with the judge's laptop.

The judge called all of this "holding a meeting."

I found it strange to see Terry and Kay together. One evening I watched them dance the *bachata*. Both of them were light on their feet, with a good sense of rhythm, and to see their glowing, sweaty faces, you would have thought they were the most contented of couples. She was wearing a pretty sundress, and his hand lay authoritatively across her lower back, fingers splayed wide. Then he whispered something in her ear that made her laugh and blush.

But just that afternoon Terry had asked me if I had gone to see Nadia yet.

"I don't want to get involved," I said. "Kay's my friend too."

"Just tell me she's okay. That's all I have to know," Terry said.

"And if she's just fine?"

"Life goes on," he said.

I was watching Terry and Kay dance and thinking about the mystery that is a man and a woman when I felt the heavy weight of the judge's hand on my shoulder. I startled slightly at the unexpected touch.

"Easy now," the judge said.

The smile on his face was so sincere—seeing me, his smile said, was the latest but certainly not the least significant in the string of happy moments and coincidences that made up an altogether happy life—that I was tempted for a moment to hug him. I enjoyed the smell of his aftershave.

"So you're doing it after all," I said.

The judge sipped from his beer. He was dressed as casually as I had ever seen him, in an immaculately pressed white shirt, open at the collar and rolled halfway up his chubby forearms.

"I took a long look in the mirror."

"What did you see?"

"A lot of lines. Gray hair. Time passing."

"A senatorial look, sort of."

Through the open doors of the campaign HQ there was the Place Dumas. Citizens had come to enjoy the warm night air, playing dominoes and drinking rum. Terry dipped Kay and she giggled. Toussaint was talking to one of the judge's prettier female students. "That night at the hospital, I made a promise to God," the judge said. "I promised God when they were lifting up those bodies that if He gave that child back to his mother, I would do the right thing. I told God that He had to give me a sign."

"I don't know if you're contractually obliged to keep that promise."

His face settled into thoughtfulness. "There was offer and acceptance," he said. "Due consideration. Not sure about the precedents. Probably a conflict of interest with the magistrate, but it's not going to be easy to change venue. I'll keep my side of the bargain."

"How's Nadia taking the decision?"

"She's barely spoken to me since I told her."

"And you're still doing it?" I asked. "I wouldn't have the balls."

He started to chuckle, but the smile didn't get past the corner of his lips. He nodded very slowly, his big chin merging into the wide neck. Then in his pleasant baritone he began to recite:

> *Ah, Love! could you and I with Fate conspire*
> *To grasp this sorry Scheme of Things entire!*
> *Would not we shatter it to bits—and then*
> *Remold it nearer to the Heart's Desire.*

I told the judge that I was writing a piece about deportees. They were a distinct subculture in Haitian life: formed on the island, finished in the States, and then sent back to Haiti, sometimes penniless, sometimes not, as a result of some sin or failing after decades abroad. The stories of deportees were inevitably fascinating. The judge called Nadia on the spot, and she agreed to see me the next day at four.

When I saw her the next day on the sun-dappled terrace of the judge's small house, I wondered how I could ever have thought that this was anything but a beautiful woman. She wore a white skirt and an apple-green blouse, a silver scarf wrapped tightly around her head. The ensemble lent her an air of faraway glamour, as if she had been transplanted that afternoon to Jérémie from the chicest café of Dakar or Abidjan. I had not noticed before how graceful she was. This was the first time I was alone with her, the first time she gave me her full attention. Her sea-colored eyes glittered.

"I'm happy to be here," I said.

When a man describes a woman's smile as "enigmatic," it generally means only one thing: he is wondering what she thinks of *him*. Nadia now smiled enigmatically.

My notebook rested on the table between us. Nadia picked it up and began to thumb through it. From time to time I had attempted pen-and-ink sketches of interesting places in the Grand'Anse. "That's Dame Marie," I said.

"Very nice."

Then she looked at sketches of the beach at Anse d'Azur and the fish market at Abricots and the hot springs near Sources Chaudes. Over her shoulder I could see the judge's boxer shorts hanging on the laundry line, baggy, shapeless things, like hopelessness incarnated in an undergarment. They inspired me to say, "Terry asked me to come. He's hurting something terrible."

From time to time over the last five years (Nadia told me, her voice very low and soft, her remarkable eyes glancing at mine or resting on the horizon where the *voiliers* dipped and glided on the breeze) she had sung, when the mood struck her, with a local band. Galaxy was not a very good band, but they had a steady diet of gigs at nightclubs, feasts of patronal saints, political rallies, and private parties. For Nadia, having sung for years with a top East Coast Compas band like Erzulie L'Amour, Galaxy was just an excuse to get out of the house and onstage and let a little life back into her veins.

Nadia's participation in Galaxy had produced a dozen fights or more with Johel. Perhaps because he couldn't even carry a tune—Nadia winced when he tried to sing "Happy Birthday"—he couldn't imagine the shared intimacy of the stage. Perhaps the look of transfixed passion on Nadia's face as she sang disturbed him: that face, he thought, should be his alone. But the story he told her was that the back roads of the Grand'Anse were too dangerous for her to travel alone. Still, in five years, nothing had happened, if you didn't count a few flat tires, until the incident in Dame Marie.

Nadia had just completed her set and was relaxing with the band when a shadow loomed across her table.

"Madame Johel," the Sénateur said. "I salute you."

The Sénateur bowed low, and his callused hand took her fingers and raised them to his lips. He spoke to her so softly that although she shared her table with a half dozen men, only she could hear him.

"Would you do an old man the honor of accompanying me on the dance floor? You must not refuse me! My heart is weak."

She felt herself being lifted out of her chair. A hand materialized on her back. The Compas is not a complicated dance, a sinuous one-two rhythm, bounced along by limitless energy and a suggestive sashaying of the hips, but in the wrong hands (those of the judge, for example) it could be a tedious affair. The Sénateur, however, danced very well, not taking the vulgar liberties younger men took when they danced with her, but holding her close and maneuvering her with facility and grace.

He never stopped talking.

"Madame, I will not tell you—I would not wish you to report this to your husband!—the admiration—the trance that your remarkable eyes have cast over my soul. Be discreet! I have too many enemies already! Let this be our secret."

He spun her in a half circle. She could feel the strength in his arms and hands.

"Do you know when I last saw eyes such as yours? She was the great love of my life—she was my nursemaid—I could have been no older than six—and I knew love such as I have never known before or since. And after a lifetime of wandering, hoping, and despair, those eyes have returned to me!"

Nadia said nothing as the Sénateur spoke, but it would be a lie to say that dancing with the man was unpleasant. Pressed up against his chest, she could smell the soap in which his white shirt had been laundered and his cologne, the clean, sharp, musky smell of a man who liked women. He guided her around the dance floor, the other couples clearing space for them. Sometimes—it was not the first time—when she was closest to the Fear, she felt it least intensely. She could not lie. Some part of her longed for the Fear.

They were done dancing, and the Sénateur led Nadia to a table in the back. The Sénateur had his private table in every nightclub in the Grand'Anse, all of them, like this one, out of sight and recessed from public view, where he met with important men and sat with pretty women. The Sénateur prepared drinks, pouring heavy shots of thick, molasses-like rum into two tall glasses, the ice heaving and cracking like ships pulling on ropes, then adding half a bottle of good Haitian Coca-Cola, which fizzed and crackled over the glass's rim. He gestured to Pierre and said, "Bring me a lime and a knife." Nadia admired the way Pierre sprang to attention. After a moment, Pierre came back with three small limes and a butcher's knife. The Sénateur cut the lime into wedges—Nadia felt droplets of juice on her forearms—and squeezed them into the drinks.

He took a tall spoon and stirred the glasses, the ice rattling the concoction. Then he handed Nadia her glass.

"*Santé,*" he said.

"*Santé,*" Nadia said.

They touched their glasses rim to rim.

After all the dancing and singing in the sultry heat, Nadia was thirsty. She drank greedily. She could remember being carried by her uncle as a child, going home from the market on long mountain paths, drifting in and out of sleep as he marched steadily upward. These were some of her earliest memories. She had no say in where she traveled: she had yet to even possess the capacity for words. She was in the grip of someone more powerful than she was. There was no question of resistance.

The drink went swiftly to her head. She looked around and saw that in this private area of the nightclub there was only the Sénateur and his strongmen. She started to stand up, and the Sénateur's hand was on her forearm.

"Finish your drink," he said.

His light touch coaxed her back into her chair. The feel of his hand dissipated her skittishness. The Sénateur was talking about his childhood, and then, to her surprise, she was talking also: the Sénateur had coaxed words out of her. "Child, how long were you on the other side of the water? When did you come home?" She enjoyed the feel of his strong hand on her arm, the intensity of his stare. Here was a man who understood her, who needed no complicated explanations. The Sénateur poured her another drink.

"So you're with Juge Blan?" he said.

"He's not *blan.*"

"He's not from here," the Sénateur said.

"His ancestors are my ancestors," she said loyally.

The Sénateur put his hand on hers and held it tight.

"This is a Haitian hand. This hand cut cane. This hand held a machete. What kind of hand does the judge have?"

She thought of the judge's hands, soft like butter in the sun.

The Sénateur answered his own question. "*Blan* hands."

"Gentle hands," Nadia said.

The Sénateur put his hand on her thigh. She was wearing a dress that she wished were longer. He rubbed her thigh with his thick thumb, and she felt the Fear flicker inside her. He leaned in close, and she could smell his cologne, his hair oil, his breath, rich with rum and mint. Now she felt her heart trembling. In the market Nadia had seen the *marchandes* slit the breasts of the butchered animals, and she could see the young beasts' hearts trembling. Now she felt as she did when Baron Samedi slid down the *poteau-mitan* and wandered the dance floor, selecting this one, selecting that one, to be his concubine for the night. The Sénateur's rough hand moved up her thigh. She could not get away from him.

"I spent my nights at the Hotel Patience also," the Sénateur said. "Beautiful nights I would wish to stay private."

Her breath was nervous as the Sénateur's thumb caressed her thigh.

"Tell your husband something for me," he said.

Now the Sénateur's hand was higher. She felt his hand at her center, pressing against her, inside of her.

The Sénateur said, "I am a rooster. Is Juge Blan a rooster too?"

Nadia was aware of everything and nothing. Her soul was fleeing her body. She saw a woman trembling and the Sénateur leaning over her, his hand between her legs.

The Sénateur repeated, "Is your husband a rooster too?"

She shook her head. Her hips moved back into her chair: she ground against his long fingers. He was inside her. The music in the room was louder. She felt beads of sweat on her back. She could only feel the Sénateur's fingers and hear his voice. The Sénateur leaned back. He smiled at her—a gentle smile. She saw her dampness on his fingers. The Sénateur put his finger in his mouth and tasted her. Then he reached for his drink.

"Madame Johel, here's a lesson in politics for your husband. Tell him losers have no friends. Tell him he wants to fight the roosters, he better win. He seems like a nice boy, your *blan*. But he's no rooster. Tell him to leave rooster business to the roosters."

Nadia went back to the judge the next day. Now the Fear was very close. The thought of the Sénateur's hands on her thigh or probing inside her nauseated her.

It was then that she began to beg the judge to abandon his political plans. She had not thought much about them before: they had been to her like his regular proposals to lose weight. These projects had foundered on shoals of deep-fried plantains or guacamole rich with garlic and onions, strips of goat meat sautéed in oil.

But now she heard his voice and heard "road" and heard "election" and heard "democracy" and heard "the people's will" and heard "Mandela" and heard "Martin Luther King" and heard "freedom," and Nadia felt the Sénateur's fingers like cold snakes sliming the inside of her thigh. She thought of what would happen if the judge learned about the Hotel Patience: he would put her out. Then she would be alone in the high mountains with the *loup-garou* and the hunger, rain coming, nothing to eat and no place to go. That was the place where the Baron came hunting.

Only once in her lifetime had she been so frightened—not even when the police had arrested her and Ti Pierre in Miami, because then in some recess of her mind she had known there was Johel.

No, the precursor to this fear was in childhood. In her village, there had been a *boko* who knew the recipe for *poud' zombie*. He was an old, slobbery man who took as his right the deflowering of all the village girls: nobody dared refuse him for fear of dying and awakening from death in idiot slavery. When she was twelve and blossoming into beauty, she came home from the river with a bucket of water balanced neatly on her head and found the old *boko* sitting on her front porch. She saw his yellow eyes and narrow serpent tongue flickering around a cavernous mouth, his smell filling the family hut like the smell of old meat.

Seeing the *boko*, she had collapsed to the ground, the heavy water splashing down the hill. She had begun to tremble and then to forget, and when she began to remember again, they told her that the *boko* had not come for her. It was not her time yet. But he would come, oh yes . . .

That was the Fear.

When she first heard the bullets break into her bedroom, and again when she felt the Sénateur's touch, her first thought had been betrayal. She and Johel had a bargain: he would keep Fear away from her, and in exchange she would be his. The bargain had never been stated, but Nadia had understood it clearly; she thought Johel understood it also. The night the bullets came, she lay under the bed in her underwear and Fear looked at her and fitted her and Johel for mahogany his-and-hers coffins.

Fear smiled at her and laughed and said, *Child, I'm ready for you.* Now, when Nadia thought of the election, she would start to shiver as the Fear seeped out from inside her, carried from viscera to skin by way of high, cold sweat.

The judge looked at her with generous confusion. Nadia knew that what he felt for her was love. He pulled her against his warm body and she shivered there, and she promised herself that if only he would give up his plans, she would love him too, only him.

"What's your problem?" the judge said.

But Nadia couldn't find the words to tell him what she feared. "This isn't your thing," she said. "Leave this alone."

This was incident number one, and then there was incident number two and incident number three and incident number twenty-six, and then the judge said, "Okay."

"Really?" she said. *"Vraiment vrai?"*

"Vraiment vrai," said the judge.

And Nadia remembered her promise and folded herself into his arms, where she became small against his bigness. Her gratitude was like love. Johel would do what he had promised—he would protect her—and she would do what she had promised: she would love him. If there was one moment in which she found happiness with Johel it was then. Happiness for Nadia meant that things were no worse than they had been. She threw her phone into the sea. Sometimes she imagined the phone ringing under the waves, Terry's calls provoking the curiosity of the gray-nosed fish.

The events of the world have consequences, and from consequences arise new events. Nadia sometimes wondered where things started and where things ended, or whether things ever ended at all, and the world was just a continuous blur of action. The *Trois Rivières* threw her passengers into the sea, and the judge decided, despite Nadia's tears, to play politician.

Nadia thought frequently of the boy the judge found at the hospital. She didn't know how to swim, and deep water was a particular terror to her. She wondered how long the boy had foundered before hands pulled him out. Had he struggled against the warm water or had he lain very still and floated, as she knew some children will do by instinct? She wondered whether he had been frightened in the blackness of night and water, or whether he found the nothingness soothing. How long had he been in the water? Nadia lay in the darkness of her bedroom at night, the judge asleep beside her, imagining the little boy floating calmly as the engines of the big boat churned and the frightened passengers shouted. She waited for the hands to grab and pull her out of the water too.

Nadia began to dream nightly of the boat and the sea, dreams of remarkable vividness and power. The boat was headed to New York. All the men she had known were there: the man with the mustache and Ti Pierre, the Fat Man from Miami and the Sénateur; Johel was there, and so was Terry. And she was in the middle between them, and they were throwing the Fat Man's golden watch back and forth. Someone had told her that the watch was worth as much as a car. Nadia had understood intuitively why someone would pay so much money for something so beautiful; she would have given anything to have such a beautiful thing herself. Nadia loved the intricacy of tiny objects: the minute precision of an earring clasp, or the well-wrought, neatly balanced heft of a chain necklace, or the gleaming, glinting light of color in a sparkling stone. Now, in her dream, Nadia's tripe twisted in horror as she watched the men throw the watch. It seemed to her a crime that such a beautiful thing should smash on the boat's deck or fall uselessly into the sea. The men were giggling like schoolgirls.

Nadia grew enraged at the carelessness of men. She had never known anger like this before. Only a woman knew the value of things; only women knew how hard it was to make things. Men were forever smashing, playing, throwing, shouting, screaming, hitting, cursing. Men broke things. So she ran between the men as they tossed the beautiful watch into the air. She saw it glinting high as it flew. She grabbed at the men, but they were so much stronger, so much larger, and the watch flew higher. She scratched at the men's faces and kicked at their shins: it was like scratching concrete or hitting stone. The men hardly noticed her, so absorbed were they in their men's game, and the watch looped and tumbled high in the sky. Why would you throw around such a lovely little thing? Then the boat tipped, and Nadia stumbled. The men laughed.

Every night, the watch, arcing high across the sky, fell into the black and empty sea.

We sat in silence for a long time. Shadows had lengthened through the course of the afternoon from nubs at the base of the palms until they were longer than the palms themselves, and the palms were just black silhouettes against the last of the evening's light. It was warm, but I shivered slightly nevertheless.

Nadia told me that the dreams of the boat, of men, and of precarious and lovely little things had come every night. She knew that a dream that comes nightly is *Bon Dieu* or the *Loa* speaking to you with persistence of important matters, and she visited a lady she knew in Sainte-Hélène who was skilled in the interpretation of difficult dreams. Then Nadia told me that she was pregnant.

I wasn't surprised. She had that aureate glow some women achieve in the first flush of incipient motherhood, when Nature, for no reason at all, renders women particularly desirable.

"Does either of them know about the baby?" I asked.

She shook her head.

"Do you know who—"

I couldn't finish the question, and she didn't answer it. I don't think she knew if it was Terry's child or the judge's, or even the Sénateur's: women in Haiti told stories of *homme mystiques* who could make a woman heavy just by staring at them. Some women were impregnated in their dreams, and others touched by the *Loa*.

A tear ran down her face, and she wiped it away with a casual, almost masculine gesture of her fingertips. I can't imagine there was a man on the planet who would have been indifferent to this woman's sorrow. She inspired a silly, hopeless tenderness. "Do you want the baby?" I said.

She nodded.

"He's my passport and my visa," she said.

A passport and a visa. What you need at the border. Nothing more precious in the world.

PART FIVE

1 A copper plaque on the wall of the Bibliothèque Nationale "Sténio Vincent" announced that the library had been rehabilitated thanks to a charitable intervention by the Honorable Sénateur Maxim Bayard. The Sénateur had reroofed the library, purchased chairs and tables, and installed a ceiling fan, which, owing to the lack of electricity, hung immobile, cobwebs dangling from the blades.

I have very few mementos of my time in Haiti—no art, no metal-work from Croix-des-Bouquets, no papier-mâché Carnival masks from Jacmel—but in my wallet I carry at all times my library card. The library consisted of nothing but a reading room that, in the absence of a breeze and under the Sénateur's tin roof, grew stiflingly hot in the late after-noons, and a small back room where the stacks were maintained. There were some newspapers imported from the capital, none more current than the previous week, and a table dedicated to the poets of Jérémie, the Séna-teur's own book having pride of place. To select a book from the collec-tion, you first consulted the catalog, a handwritten list of titles affixed to the wall with Scotch tape; then you prepared a written request for the librarian. Monsieur Duval was a man of antique vintage, gray-haired, with a pair of reading glasses so thick they might have been bulletproof. He would rise, with a thousand creaking joints, from his chair, where he had been comfortably reading the same volume since the fall of the Ber-lin Wall, and trundle slowly into the back room. Then you waited. I have many lovely memories of the library. They are not dramatic. There was a young man, a motorcycle taxi driver, reading *Les Misérables* and a young woman, her baby asleep on the floor, her legs tucked neatly under her haunches, nodding in sympathy to a tattered edition of *Le Deuxième Sexe*. There were high school students reciting from *Le Cid*. There was an older gentleman who every morning read from the library's not insubstantial collection of Latin poetry—the high schools of Jérémie had once taught Latin as a matter of course.

Père Abraham Samedi was another regular in our ranks. I knew his name from Toussaint Legrand, who had told the judge, Terry, and me of the important role the priest played in local politics. I saw him for the first time as I read *Maigret et le corps sans tête* and he read, at the adjacent table, *Un Américain bien tranquille* by Monsieur Graham Greene. He was a tall, thick man in a clerical collar, a coeval of the librarian, with sooty dark skin, holding his book at arm's length, as if unwilling to admit that he might be ready for spectacles. Something in his manner suggested that a conversational overture would not be unwelcome.

Thereafter, whenever I drove in the direction of Anse du Clerc, I would stop by Père Samedi's house. He was usually able to spare me no more than a few minutes from the crush of his duties, but in those moments we would drink a cup of coffee and he would tell me some amusing tale of daily life in the forgotten stretch of the universe that lay on the southwest coast of Haiti between Jérémie and Bonbon.

This was territory Père Samedi famously patrolled on foot, until his recent bouts with gout, when he had allowed himself to be transported on muleback. Here there was little tin- or thatch-roofed house after little house, interspersed with gardens or small fields. Père Samedi, at one time or another in the quarter century since his return from exile, had slept in every one of those huts, dossing down without fuss on the stone or dirt floor. He was as likely to arrive with a substantial and well-timed present as without: for a family with a new baby, he would have a pair of squealing, healthy piglets, a glossy young goat, or a half dozen chicks; or for a family recovering from illness, a sack of seed, which he imported personally from the capital. I met one family in Anse du Clerc that had tumbled from poverty to bitter poverty by the loss of the ten-dollar diving mask that had formerly allowed the father of the family to set lobster traps. I mentioned this story to Père Samedi, who made a note of it on a scrap of paper. On my next visit to Anse du Clerc, I learned that Père Samedi had replaced the mask.

Although I had drunk half a dozen cups of gritty black coffee with him, I had not thought us friends. He required a moment each time he saw me at the library to remember me, and once, when I passed him in the *marché*, where he was buying supplies, he did not so much as glance at me, as if out of my usual context, I had become invisible.

So it was a surprise when my phone rang just after dawn and a gravelly voice said, *"Père Samedi à l'appareil."*

"How are you, Father?" I said.

"One maintains," he said.

He cleared his throat.

"Bring your friend Johel Célestin to visit one of these days," he said.

"Can I tell him what this is about?"

"He'll understand."

Two days later, the judge, Terry, and I drove to Bonbon to meet with Père Samedi.

The judge was riding shotgun, and I got into the back.

"Either of you guys see that moon last night?" I asked.

It had been a night of almost perfect darkness when a gap emerged in the clouds to reveal, low on the horizon, the full moon. Silvery moonlight reflected off the undersides of the clouds, producing an unexpected dawn, so bright that the palms cast long, straight moon shadows. The dogs awoke and began to howl, the chickens crowed—even the songbirds began to trill. It was the precise opposite, I suppose, of the disturbing moment in a solar eclipse when the midday sun disappears, but no less unsettling.

"Nadia woke me up," the judge said. "Spooked her out."

"It was pretty amazing," I said.

"She calm down?" Terry asked.

"I put her to sleep."

Then he chuckled, his laughter greasy and suggestive, and started to talk about tobacco. What he wanted to know was why a rich, value-added crop like tobacco wasn't being grown right here. This was tobacco country. Dominican Republic. Cuba. Same latitude, same climate, same soil. So why not here? When he had the opportunity, that was something he wanted to explore, some kind of cooperation on importing some Dominican tobacco farmers, cigar makers, exchange some skills—why not hand-rolled Haitian cigars? Wouldn't that be fine, driving down our road, puffing on a big fat Haitian cigar?

Now we were in front of the Uruguayan military base. There was always a crowd of children and teenage girls loitering there. Sometimes the girls traded favors with the soldiers in the garbage pit behind the base. The enlisted men had no money, but they could pilfer rations and supplies from the base, which the girls gave to their mothers to sell in the market. This was a seasonal traffic: new battalion commanders arrived, industrious and idealistic, from Montevideo, and the skin trade disappeared. By the time the battalion left nine months later, the girls lounged in front of the base unabashedly.

The judge was in a garrulous mood. "You know these farmers here are eating their seed?" He wanted to talk about seed supplies and fertilizer. "Now, fertilizer—basic agricultural input. Only in Haiti does seed cost more than the agricultural output. You want to know why they don't have vegetables around—"

"Do you ever shut up?" Terry said. His face had been drawn since the judge mentioned Nadia's name. "Could you just give it a rest?"

The judge looked like a child reprimanded unjustly by an overtired parent.

Terry said, "What's the color of my skin? Basically pink and rosy? I'm not Haitian. I can't vote. If I were from around here, and thank fucking Christ I'm not, you'd have my vote. But could you give it a rest?"

The judge looked forlorn. I regret now that I didn't tell him that I found his conversation interesting.

The airport flashed by on the seaward side of the road.

"Slow down, brother," the judge said. "We'll get there when we get there."

"I got to take a shit," Terry said.

"Be that as it may, son, you hit a donkey or a kid, I'll be the Haitian judge who puts you in a prison cell."

I couldn't figure out if this was banter or something rawer: two men, too many hours alone in a car together.

I said, "Johel, I thought UN personnel had immunity here in Haiti."

He looked over his shoulder at me. "Well, they do, technically speaking. But it can be a long while before the court orders his release."

Whatever internal censor deployed in response to Terry's reproach was lifted, and the judge began to discourse on the history of United Nations Peacekeeping in Haiti, and the Status of Forces Agreement under which the government of Haiti accepted the presence of ten thousand foreign troops.

Terry said, "These aren't billable hours, are they?"

The judge chuckled good-naturedly. "Alas, no. Those were beautiful, bountiful days."

"You miss it?" I asked.

Now he was serious, and I liked him for his earnest face. He said, "Just look at it, how beautiful it is out there. This is some kind of beautiful country."

The peasants had burned the hillside the year before, and it had grown back in tender shades of green and lilac. Bright flowers, as red as poppies but broader-leafed, broke through the new foliage. The sky was a blue just a shade darker than any sky I had ever seen. In the gap between hills, there was the sea.

(All that keen, nerdish enthusiasm on the subject of the vegetables of the Grand'Anse—this was Johel Célestin at his very best. If anyone ever asks me one day to tell them all about Johel Célestin, that's where I'd start—with the vegetables.

(By no vegetables, the judge meant no tomatoes, no eggplant, no zucchini, no cucumbers, no lettuce, no spinach, no broccoli, no chard, no snap peas, no green peas, no snow peas, no green beans, no corn, no arugula, no endive, and certainly no radicchio. Cabbage, carrots, potatoes, and garlic were imported on the weekly boat from Port-au-Prince, usually arriving bedraggled, mildewed, rotten, and nasty. Otherwise, we had the occasional okra, plantains, sweet potatoes, many varieties of beans, breadfruit, manioc, yam *e basta*.

(Let me now eliminate the hypothesis that local farmers did not grow vegetables because they were not to the taste of the population. These vegetables were all for sale in the markets of Port-au-Prince and other provincial cities: a cook in Cap-Haïtien would have found an eggplant or a tomato as commonplace as you would. I think it's fair to say that the absence of vegetables was in the most literal sense a failure of the market, as in: no vegetables in the market, despite demand.

(The effect of the dearth of vegetables was twofold: on the one hand, the diet was impoverished, both from the point of view of taste and nutritional diversity; but it also created greater poverty, because vegetable gardens in other places in Haiti were tended by women as a supplemental source of income. Generally speaking, food in Jérémie was in short supply and incomes limited. Vegetable gardens would have helped to resolve both issues.

(The absence of vegetables from the market was in fact just the last link in a catena of market failures. Begin with seeds—if you can find them. You won't find vegetable seeds in Jérémie, however. A small farmer who wished to supplement his meager income by growing tomatoes was immediately foiled: no shop or merchant in Jérémie sold seeds. This is so astounding a fact it requires repetition: no shop or merchant in the leading city of a province subsisting exclusively on agriculture sold the sine qua non of life. Not even in Port-au-Prince could one easily find vegetable seeds: nobody was importing seeds on a commercial scale to Haiti. And why was this? Because just about every year I was in Haiti, bureaucrats from the WFP and the FAO and USAID, reproducing the glory that was Soviet agronomics, would launch some new program giving away bushels of seeds to farmers, hoping to stimulate local production of vegetables. Somehow the programs inevitably faltered—either failing to produce marketable goods or failing to produce goods for which there was demand, or by providing the appropriate seeds, but not fertilizer, or by providing seeds for a hardy bean that tasted like cow dung—but succeeded in choking the market for seeds. Who would buy tomato seeds when mung bean seeds were being given away freely? And who would import seeds and invest in a distribution network when in competition with the immense resources of the international aid community?

(Suppose, however, you did find seeds. Then you were faced with the triple problem of fertilizer, insecticide, and water. Fertilizer and insecticide could be found in Jérémie, but both were expensive. The absence of a road from Port-au-Prince meant that everything imported was imported on the boat by small merchants, buying from middlemen in Port-au-Prince who themselves imported from the States or the Dominican Republic. Moreover, fertilizer distribution in Haiti has been as compromised by the interference of central planners, both in the form of Haitian state and foreign aid, as seed distribution. Depending on the whims of foreign bureaucrats (in this case, largely Japanese bureaucrats, offering Japanese fertilizer to Haitian peasants) the government of Haiti has either subsidized or failed to subsidize the price of fertilizer: the price rises and lowers dramatically from year to year. As a result, honest fertilizer importers are driven out of the market in bad years, producing a country of peasant farmers for whom it is frequently impossible to buy fertilizer. Anyone who has ever attempted to grow a tomato will testify that without fertilizer or insecticide, your results are probably going to be sad. The tomato is a heartbreaking plant.

(Then there was the problem of good old H_2O. Basically, water in the Grand'Anse was what fell from the sky or what you carried on your head. A cement cistern to catch rainwater was to the Haitian peasant a luxurious dream. Even if you lived in that rare community serviced by a well, most of the population still needed to lug water in a plastic bucket the last kilometer to the house; lots of people lugged water much, much farther. So agriculture in the Grand'Anse depended exclusively on rainwater. Vegetables, to a far greater extent than coffee, say, or cocoa or plantains, require regular irrigation.

(Even in the city, water was undependable, mercy to the whimsy of one Monsieur Theobald Augustin Darcy, an employee of the municipal water company. If sober, for a bribe of one hundred gourdes, or about three dollars, Monsieur Darcy would unlock a cement cabinet up the hill from us, turn a little knob, and replenish our water tank. This was high luxury: the average folks in Jérémie sent their children out with five-gallon buckets. But left to his own devices, Monsieur Darcy would forget to do his duty and our house would be dry. Our tomatoes, zucchini, and eggplants were promising until Monsieur Darcy went on a monumental bender one late-summer weekend, in the course of which he lost his key ring. I am not exaggerating when I say that a goodly portion of the population of Jérémie was enlisted in the hunt for Monsieur Darcy's keys, and by the time they were retrieved, the hot sun had killed our tender tomatoes.

(Last but not least was the absence of decent roads. Here the judge's speech, which I was to hear in its entirety many times, mounted to a manly peroration. Lack of a road massively inflated the price of all commodities entering the Grand'Anse and made it impossible for perishable goods to exit the province. Should a small farmer in the mountains, suffused with entrepreneurial zeal, through industry, luck, talent, and foresight produce a brilliant green *salade* of a garden, brimming with bloodred tomatoes and magnificent aubergines, he still had no way to transport his wares to market but on the back of his donkey.)

Père Samedi's ecclesiastical residence, if the grandest house in Bonbon, was nevertheless modest: a bungalow of stucco and cement, receded from the dirt road and surrounded by a high wall. On earlier visits, the cottage was abuzz with visitors and life. The curé was well tended by a flock of servants: the toothless gardener who opened the broad gate and would send me home with a bag of fresh mangoes or limes; a washerwoman who sang hymns as she hung linens; and a housekeeper, a fleshy, bosomy young woman with the placid, tranquil face of a being unequivocally secure in His love. There was in addition a large herd of children, the older ones in school uniforms, the younger ones naked, shrieking maniacally and darting about like geckos.

The house, which I had always thought a cheerful place, seemed now infected by some sorrow. The gardener had opened the gate for us with a forlorn tread. When I asked the washerwoman how she was, she had replied with a stoical "*Nou là*"—we're there. She seemed to expect some gesture of commiseration, and when none was forthcoming, she shambled off on heavy legs to dunk dirty clothes in gray wash water.

We were ushered into the house. There was a crucifix on the wall and ceramic knickknacks on the bureau shelves. Other rooms and a staircase were hidden by lace curtains that ruffled and waved in the gentle breeze. The place smelled of incense and rice. The highly polished mahogany table in Père Samedi's parlor reflected four faces: my own, looking confused; Terry's, still looking distinctly irritable; the judge's, solicitous and intelligent; and finally the cadaverous reflection of our host.

The old priest stared now for a long time at his own reflection in the dark table. He was unshaven, his light gray beard sparse on his dark skin. The judge inhaled deeply, held his breath a moment, and exhaled. The room in which we sat was close and humid and uncomfortable.

There was a sepia photograph on the wall that on my earlier visits had aroused my curiosity. It depicted two young men standing on the steps of the Sénateur's mother's house. One man was dark-complected and the other light; both were handsome. They looked as if they might have been wrestling on the front porch or playing lawn tennis when someone called them to the camera: there was a high sheen to their skin, and a bit of color in the cheeks of the paler man. Their faces were creased with smiles.

I had asked Père Samedi about the photo.

"This was me," he said. "And this was Maxim Bayard."

Then I could start to see the faces: where the wrinkles had set in or the ears drooped or the nose, in the case of the Sénateur, had elongated. The Sénateur over the years had acquired jowls, and from Père Samedi's neck had swollen out a large, bobbing Adam's apple. Père Samedi then was thick across the shoulders. But the change that haunted me was in the men's eyes, although just what changed and how escapes my vocabulary of adjectives. They were not deadened now, nor had they grown somber—I would in fact have noted a zestful glint in the Sénateur's current eyes. The eyes in the photograph did not shine with youthful innocence now dimmed, because they were not innocent then. But drastically changed they were, proving once again the wisdom of proverbs and clichés, such as the one that describes the eyes as the windows to the soul.

2 Abraham Samedi first met Maxim Bayard early in his career at the Lycée Saint Louis. Abraham was the discovery of a Jesuit missionary in Dame Marie who had noted the young boy's intelligence and discipline and arranged for this son of an illiterate fisherman to be educated in Jérémie, as the Jesuits did every year for two or three of the brightest children of the remote provinces, particularly those whom the fathers suspected of harboring a vocation.

Abraham would not have survived the first weeks of school at the intimidating lycée were it not for the assistance of Maxim Bayard. At the beginning of every week, students at the lycée were given ten cards. Any student who caught another speaking Creole had the right to demand his card. At the end of the week, students with the most cards would be rewarded, while the student with the fewest cards would be flogged. Young Abraham could read and write French with all the fluency of his wealthier classmates, but never having been exposed to French as a living language, he found himself spontaneously bursting into Creole when attempting to address his peers and teachers. Nobody in Samedi's family had ever spoken French or understood the language, and during the first month of Samedi's career at the lycée, he suffered the double indignity at the conclusion of each week of watching his classmates cheerfully eat rich slices of homemade chocolate or *komparet*, the spicy ginger cake that was the town's specialty, while he himself was struck a dozen times across the knuckles with the *rigoise*.

With every passing week, Abraham Samedi found it more difficult, not easier, to speak French. He was utterly unsure what language would come out of his mouth at any time, so great was his anxiety. Even when he had composed and practiced a sentence in French, under the stress of performance a Creole word was capable of emerging, and that would be sufficient for one of the students or another, ever eager to amass another card, to spring up and shout, *"Donnez-moi vot' cat'!"*

The tension of the situation so overwhelmed young Samedi that after six weeks or so, he considered leaving school and returning to his father's fishing boat. The past week had been particularly difficult. Nine times he had been caught speaking in Creole; the other boys sat staring at him now like the hungry vultures who circled the fields, waiting for him to slip up so they could pocket one more card. At night in the dormitory, Abraham remembered the days on the fishing boat with his father and brothers, telling stories and jokes about the sea, and the pleasant evenings with his mother and sisters, mending lines and salting fish, the hours passing swiftly in a babble of words.

Abraham begin to pray for deliverance morning, afternoon, and night. He imagined his heavenly Father as a kindly village father, and he spoke to him in Creole, certain the Lord spoke all languages with equal facility. He demanded that his Savior remove the terrible stones that had been placed in his mouth, which prevented him from expressing himself in the language of the *blan* and threatened to impede a life in His great service. He asked the Lord for the gift of simple speech.

It was just before school began, the hour when the Jesuit fathers demanded that each student present his cards to be counted, when Maxim Bayard first approached Abraham Samedi.

Although the two boys shared a common nation and a common language, they might have been from different continents, so different were their childhoods. Maxim was a product of Haute Ville, the elegant old mulatto aristocracy. His father owned a *guildive*, a distillery, producing the raw clear rum called *taffia*; he traded in coffee, cocoa, and rubber. The Bayard men dressed in English twills imported directly from the manufacturer and cut by the best tailor in Jérémie. The future Sénateur had been the middle child of six, four daughters and two sons, all living in a riotous confusion of amateur theatricals, declaimed bits of home-spun poetry, or the scratching of the Sénateur's brother's ill-tuned violin, accompanied by Maxim's mother's far more accomplished performance on the piano. The garden was a profusion of the Sénateur's mother's roses: every marriage, feast, and burial in Jérémie was garnished with her 'Paul Néron,' her 'Frau Karl Druschki,' or her 'Radiance.' In the eve-ning the children gathered on the terrace at the feet of Maxim's father, who read aloud in his mellifluous tenor from Balzac, Zola, or Hugo.

The two students, in the course of the still-short school year, had hardly spoken: Maxim was the center of a social whirl, effortlessly charm-ing and witty, but a terrible student, flogged as often for inattention as Abraham was for speaking Creole. Maxim, however, did not seem to take the teacher's whippings with the air of humiliation that so tormented Abraham. Maxim winced as the beef tendon came down on his knuck-les but thereafter laughed with the Jesuit fathers, who seemed no less immune to his carefree charms than were his peers.

"How many cards do you have?" Maxim said in Creole.

Abraham looked at Maxim, wondering if this was some trick.

"Two," he said.

"I have nine," Maxim said, still in Creole.

Abraham stared at his classmate until Maxim, still speaking Creole, said, "Ask me for my card."

"Give me your card," said Abraham, so flustered that he was not sure if he had asked in Creole or in French.

"Here you go," said Maxim, and handed Abraham not one card, but his whole stack of them. That morning at the habitual assembly, Maxim allowed the priest to strike his knuckles, and later, Abraham's eleven cards were sufficient to allow him to taste *komparet* for the first time.

Young Père Samedi, nearly graduated from seminary, was consumed by a singular ambition: to instruct his illiterate parishioners in the art of reading, that they might read for themselves in their maternal language,

Creole, the Testament of their Lord. To this end, he labored very nearly day and night. It was known that any man or woman who stopped by Père Samedi's modest hut might receive a simple lesson in the art of literacy; he organized not only a school for children but schools for adults as well. The bookish priest, with his thick neck and bull-like body but strangely fine and thoughtful features, was a familiar face on the trails and mountain byways of his parish, hectoring his parishioners not only to receive Mass in the whitewashed churches that dotted the countryside but to remain thereafter for an hour or two of instruction.

In 1964 Père Samedi's modest life intersected with history when a band of thirteen idealistic adventurers calling themselves Jeune Haiti arrived on the shores of the Grand'Anse. These young men were all exiles from the dictatorship of François Duvalier, and they proposed, beginning first in the distant villages of the Grand'Anse, to spark a revolution.

Haiti was absolutely in the madman's grip now: he had been eliminating his enemies (they were everywhere) and consolidating his power (it was at once absolute and insufficient) since his election seven years earlier. The results of his political work could be seen in the excellent results of his reelection, in which three million of his subjects voted in his favor, only 3200 opposing him. Even 3200 was too many: a worrisome and hostile trend, to the One and Absolute ruler of the state. François Duvalier bayoneted, shot, bludgeoned, electrocuted, eviscerated, and starved his opponents, real and imaginary; he divided them one against another and pursued power, more power, and still more power with a monomaniacal zeal no preceding Haitian dictator, king, emperor, strongman, or president had ever considered possible.

The Doc came to power after a career as a country physician, a champion of the doctrine known as *Noirisme*—the power of black. Haiti was a nation divided between the descendants of slaveholder and slave, between France and Africa, French and Creole, Catholic and *vodouisant*, pale skin and dark, urban and rural, a few very wealthy and the vast majority very poor. *Noirisme* was Duvalier's radical untying of the complex knot of Haitian life, the favoring of the latter over the former. If in campaigning he had been motivated by his vision of social justice, in power he was motivated by a single transcendently important goal: the elimination of his enemies. Like all evil men, Duvalier knew that he had enemies everywhere. But there was no place where he suspected that he had more enemies than Jérémie, that town like an island off the edge of Haiti, where the poets wrote in French, where the commerce was direct with Le Havre, and where the wealthy families were pale-skinned. They represented all that *Noirisme* and the Doc abhorred.

The young men of Jeune Haiti had no notion of how cruel was the personality to whom they had put themselves in opposition. One by one, the dictator hunted them down, dragged them to Port-au-Prince, tortured them, shot them live on Haitian television, and left their decapitated bodies to rot openly in the streets, a warning to any who might indulge in like-minded folly. Then the dictator put his mind to eradicating their accomplices. The dictator was not of a mind to be subtle, and he counted as Jeune Haiti's abettors the entire mulatto community of Jeune Haiti's natal town, Jérémie.

Père Samedi found his old friend Maxim huddled in the small barn where he kept his donkey and pigs. He was dressed in the ill-fitting overalls of a peasant—his friend who took such pleasure in his tailored suits. His face was covered in blood, and his eyes, ordinarily so insouciant and charming, flickered from shadow to shadow. Père Samedi could not imagine what might have produced so dramatic a transformation of his old school comrade, who passed his days, to the frustration of his mother, composing mildly erotic verse, painting, and seducing village girls, the blacker and more full-breasted the better. Père Samedi did not have it in his heart to censure Maxim's conduct, but neither had it been a friendship he had been eager to sustain after lycée and his years at seminary in Port-au-Prince. So it was a surprise to see his old school comrade prostrate in his barn, trembling in fear, pleading for his assistance.

"My Father, you must help me," Maxim said.

Maxim had never before addressed Abraham by his title, and the young priest's first thought was that Maxim had seduced the wrong girl, and some outraged boyfriend or father had taken his correct revenge. Or perhaps an outraged woman, Abraham thought: the image of one of

Maxim's slighted amours assaulting the runabout produced a hint of a smile on Abraham's face. He wondered why Maxim had thought to come to him, of all people.

"What happened to you?" he asked.

"My Father, don't you know?" said Maxim.

"Know what?"

Maxim stared at the priest. In that moment the priest knew that this was no matter of jilted hearts or wounded honor.

"We're all dead. All of us."

The priest stifled his instinct to demand an explanation. His own hut afforded greater privacy than the barn, which fronted a path where villagers would sometimes walk in the night, so he led Maxim through the *lakou* and into his dusty dwelling. He started a fire and brewed coffee, which he laced liberally with rum. "More," said Maxim, and the priest topped up the mug until it contained more rum than coffee. Maxim sipped at the strong beverage until he found the strength to speak.

There had been rumors for some time, of course, that the Macoutes would come for them, but Maxim did not believe it: no one would let such a thing happen in that small town, where *mulâtre* and *noir* had so long lived side by side in easy friendship.

(Père Samedi stayed silent as he recalled the pews of the cathedral, the first ranks reserved for the mulattos, the remainder for the blacks. He recalled the time when Maxim had invited him to a literary evening at the Excelsior Club, a night dedicated to the *poètes maudits*, and some mulatto wag had set the room aflame by declaring that a fly had landed in the milk.)

Maxim had been at home with his sisters and mother when Sanette Balmir, the leader of the local band of Tontons Macoutes, came to the terrace of the family gingerbread accompanied by half a dozen of her men. Sanette Balmir! Who could have imagined that this woman could rise to such prominence? She was old and fat, a diabetic—too old to ply her quondam trade as whore and thief, but not so old that she didn't remember every disparaging word the townsfolk had ever muttered at her hunched-over figure as she swept the streets of Jérémie in penal servitude—and there was no family she loathed more than the Bayards. This was because it was the testimony of Evelyne Bayard herself that had placed Sanette in the hands of justice after Sanette Balmir stole an entire harvest of roses from her garden. Sanette had made no secret of her loathing for this wealthy, privileged clan, and of her desire to take revenge. Now she was a great Macoute, and she awaited only the word of her patron and chief, the Doc himself, to obtain her satisfaction. The telephone call from Port-au-Prince soon arrived.

When she arrived at Maxim's house, it was clear straightaway on what kind of errand she had come. The Macoutes stood under the spreading mango tree, their sunglasses, worn even at night, reflecting the torches they carried.

Maxim was in his middle twenties, but in such a moment it was nevertheless the family matriarch, Evelyne Bayard, who took command. (Maxim's father had been dead now almost three years.) She said, "Sanette Balmir, what do you want with us?"

"How are your roses this year, Evelyne?" asked Sanette Balmir.

"Healthy and beautiful. If you or these gentlemen have some happy occasion, I'll be pleased to clip you a dozen."

"A dozen will not be enough." Sanette Balmir handed a machete to Maxim. "Boy, go and clip me as many flowers as you can carry."

Maxim took the knife, warm still from the fat woman's hand. He trembled as he walked toward the rosebushes, accompanied by another of the Macoutes, a young man his own age, Dieuseul Bontemps, someone he had known, in the way of small towns, since earliest childhood. They had tangled numerous times on the soccer pitch. Now Dieuseul refused to meet Maxim's eyes, an evasion that frightened Maxim more than a glare of outright hatred. Maxim gripped the machete harder— but he knew that his mother and sisters were alone with Sanette Balmir. He would not risk upsetting her further.

It took Maxim twenty minutes to cut down an entire season of his mother's roses. His hands and arms were bleeding from the thorns as he carried the stems bare-handed. Then he made his way back up the hill, where Sanette Balmir, the Macoutes, and Maxim's family stood where he had left them. Sanette walked over to Maxim's mother, and with a stroke of her machete cut open the older woman's dress. Then she cut off her underwear, not caring whether she sliced open Evelyne Bayard in the process. Evelyne Bayard stood naked in front of her family and her attackers, a film of red sliding across her breasts. Groaning loudly, Sanette began to massage the blood into the older woman's skin. Mosquitoes attracted by the smell of blood began to swarm.

The Bayards were taken on foot to the commissariat, walking through the streets where they had strolled every day of their lives. No one ran to their aid. No one cried that generations of Bayards had been their friends, benefactors, and neighbors for a hundred years or more. They felt eyes on them from behind every window and door. Maxim's sisters began to cry. It was Evelyne Bayard who silenced them, hissing sharply through her teeth. They were kept in the prison for almost half a day, united in their cell with the large Sansaricq clan and the Guilbauds. Half the daughters in the room had succumbed at one time or another to Maxim's touch. Now the women stood naked and shook in fear.

The three families—the first of what would eventually be a massacre that consumed the entire mulatto community of Jérémie—were taken on the white road that led past the beach at Anse d'Azur to an empty plain near the airport. The Macoutes, displaying rare efficiency, had dug a pit already. The shots came in volleys. Maxim had the presence of mind, when he saw his family crumple, to fall into the pit as well. The bodies of the Sansaricqs fell on the bodies of the Bayards, and the bodies of the Guilbauds fell on the bodies of the Sansaricqs.

Sanette Balmir tossed roses on the open grave.

His fingertips trembling, Père Samedi crossed himself.

"I came on foot," said Maxim.

"The Macoutes didn't see you?" asked Père Samedi.

"They were too drunk by the end of the night to notice. They were too drunk even to bury the dead."

Père Samedi thought for a moment that he could hear Sanette Balmir's raucous breathing in the very room itself. He excused himself from the small front room and retired to his bedroom, where he kept a private altar. He dropped to his knees and asked his Lord for guidance. Where did his duty lie? To his friend or to his parishioners? He asked his Lord to give him the courage to decide. When he was done praying, Père Samedi felt certain that the Lord wanted him to tend his flock. Père Samedi thought of his namesake, the great Abraham, obeying the Lord's injunction to slaughter his beloved Isaac. Père Samedi adjusted his cassock and decided that he would offer his old friend the opportunity to confess his sins. He would prepare for Maxim a decent meal—and then he would ask Maxim to leave his hut and render himself unto Caesar.

Père Samedi stepped back into the small *salon*. Maxim was seated at the low table, a look on his face of utter confusion. Before there is sorrow or even anger, there is surprise. He looked at Père Samedi as if he had never seen him before. At that moment, recalling the taste of *komparet*, Père Samedi decided—it was an instinct, not a decision—to abandon the narrow course of his decent and obedient life. He begged the Lord to pardon him, then told Maxim to hide in the back room of the hut before his maid arrived.

When she arrived shortly thereafter, he told the woman, whom he did not entirely trust to keep a secret, that he had hankered all night for a variety of shrimp found chiefly in Dame Marie—a morning's walk and an afternoon's return. Grumbling loudly, she left the priest alone in his hut to plot.

That morning, Père Maxim Bayard of Bretagne, dressed in clerical robes, accompanied by Père Samedi, set off in the direction of Port-au-Prince. They traveled in Père Samedi's beat-up but serviceable old Citroën, on roads that in those days could still convey the traveler to the capital in a matter of hours. At military checkpoints the two priests blessed the soldiers in their work. A Catholic priest in Haiti is still a man of considerable influence, and the soldiers allowed them to pass without incident, all the way to the Dominican frontier, which Maxim Bayard crossed on foot.

Père Samedi's scheming was not without repercussion, however.

It was the same maid who found the poems in the pockets of the dirty pants that Père Samedi gave her to wash. She had never washed these pants before. Scraps of paper, strange verse—it was Père Samedi who had taught her to read. Now she read the name Maxim Bayard and was horrified. She understood immediately that he had been in the house, that her priest had harbored him. She thought of her babies. Were it to come out that Maxim Bayard had stayed the night in Père Samedi's hut, who would believe that she didn't know?

Père Samedi spent the next year in Fort Dimanche, the place where the Doc tortured his enemies before he murdered them. He emerged only thanks to the influence of the Vatican: even the dictator hesitated before shooting a priest. (The Doc had watched his Macoutes torture the young priest, burning his feet with cigarettes and placing electric probes on his genitals, and had developed also a strange and merciful fondness for the young cleric. It did not bother him to let this one go . . .) The Jesuits found the priest a new position in the Vatican, but it was quite some time before his eyes adjusted from darkness to light and he was able to read again.

François Duvalier was a man little satisfied with the destruction of his enemies: the Doc believed in sowing their fields with salt. The key to Jérémie's prosperity had long been direct commerce with the world, exporting coffee, cocoa, and rubber directly from her port on ships serving the Caribbean and Europe. Now Duvalier ordered all international vessels to serve Port-au-Prince and Port-au-Prince alone, and the prosperous town of Jérémie was effectively cut off from the world.

From that moment, the town began to wither. Nothing came in or out but what came on the boat from Port-au-Prince. The great wooden houses went untended as those families not murdered by the regime fled, some to Port-au-Prince, others abroad. The road to Les Cayes, built under the American occupation and so solid in the Sénateur's youth that a man could travel to Port-au-Prince and return on the same day, was left to deteriorate. Farmers ceased to plant anything that required access to roads or markets, and the most prosperous region of Haiti soon became the territory of subsistence farmers. Forty years later, no trace of the road was left, just massed rocks and crevasses of mud.

The years that followed the massacre were the happiest of Sanette Balmir's life. She soon moved into the Bayard house, together with her menagerie of flunkies, followers, lovers, and acolytes. The large Bayard library was fed, sheet by sheet, to the flames to start cooking fires. Sanette was too fat to fit in Evelyne Bayard's clothes, but the dresses of the Bayard women were cut open and stitched together to make nightclothes for her. She enjoyed the feel of Evelyne Bayard's soft sheets against her ample skin at night. She drank her way through the Bayards' excellent collection of wine imported from France, and she was known for the rose she inevitably wore in her hair.

3 There were other photographs on the walls of Père Samedi's study: Père Samedi leaning on a knee, surrounded by a large crowd of somber children—the orphans he harbored in the orphanage he had constructed at Bonbon. Père Samedi had restored the lovely church at Abricots, and Père Samedi, hard hat on his head, stood looking over an architectural blueprint with the French architect who had volunteered his time (at Père Samedi's suggestion) to oversee the project. In another photo, Père Samedi was holding a shovel, digging out the ceremonial first scoop of dirt at his health clinic; and in another he was arm in arm with three *blans* at the prow of one of the fishing boats that Québécois Catholics had donated to Père Samedi's parishioners following the passage of a hurricane.

I had been looking at the photographs on Père Samedi's wall for five minutes or more, the room quiet and animated only by the swirling dust motes, when the priest finally spoke: "Let me see your teeth."

"I'm sorry?" said the judge.

"I want to see your teeth."

The judge bared his teeth—neat, square, small, and regular. They were neither attractive nor unattractive, and in no way particularly notable.

"Open wide," Père Samedi said.

"Why?" he said.

"Open."

The judge did as he was ordered. The priest peered inside his mouth carefully, as if looking in very much the wrong place for a lost button. Then Père Samedi stood up. He stood tall, like some complexly articulated skinny spider, and he ambled over to Terry. He said, "Now you. Show me yours."

"These are for me and Dr. Stern," Terry said.

"Show me your teeth," Père Samedi said, and his voice was so mild that Terry smiled and opened his mouth wide.

The priest looked inside Terry's mouth attentively. I could see Terry's pink tongue. Terry's eyes were smiling: one more Haiti story to tell back home.

"Now you," the priest said.

He held my chin gingerly between an old leathery forefinger and an old leathery thumb. He looked at my tongue and my gold-capped molars. His examination lasted a long time. Then he released my face, returned to his place, and shouted, "François!"

After a moment, the gardener ambled in.

"François, show the men your teeth, if you please. It's very important."

With no hint of embarrassment, François opened his mouth.

We sat in our seats, nodding, until Père Samedi said, "No, gentlemen, I insist. Come and look at these teeth. *Look.*"

"It's okay," said the judge, embarrassed for François.

"François doesn't mind," said Père Samedi.

François didn't seem to mind. His smile suggested that he might even take a perverse pride in the condition of his teeth. There were teeth in his mouth, technically speaking, but very few. It was a cul-de-sac of dental destruction. It was like looking at a rose garden after a hurricane rips through. François was opening his mouth wide and leaning over the judge's face, and the judge was trying to maintain a neutral aspect, not wanting to alienate a voter.

Terry leaned over and whispered to me, "What the hell are we doing here?"

"Looking at François's teeth," I said.

Père Samedi lit a cigarette, and Terry took that as permission to do the same. Then Terry offered François one from his pack; he accepted it happily.

"I sometimes wonder what His intentions were in giving us these fragile mouths," Père Samedi said. "Surely He was aware of the conditions we would face. Why add yet another burden to our shoulders?"

The judge was thinking about those billable hours. He said, "So you need a dentist."

"François needs dentures," Père Samedi said.

"I imagine a lot of folks around here need good dental care," said the judge.

"The children," Terry added.

"Not just the children, everyone," said the judge.

"We had a dentist once," Père Samedi said.

"What happened to him?"

"He died!" Père Samedi began to laugh, a dismaying caw. "It was a long time ago. He drilled a cavity, somebody bit him, the blood became infected, and he died!"

"Doesn't sound like he was much of a dentist," said the judge.

"He wasn't," Père Samedi agreed. "He treated François."

"Maybe we could find you another one," said the judge.

Then the judge began to talk. It was as if he'd been thinking about rural Haitian dentistry for months. In Jacmel, he'd seen a volunteer dentistry program. Real model for how it should be done. An American dentist flew in every month or two for a marathon of oral care. Cavity. Boom. Extraction. Boom. Saw more patients in three days than he probably saw up north in a month. Now, if Père Samedi could supply a working space, nothing fancy, just a room, and maybe a place at the guest house, then Johel was betting he could find the dentist. Somebody who'd love to take his hygienist down to the little hotel at Anse du Clerc, fill cavities in the morning, snorkel in the afternoon, boff the hygienist at night— excuse my language, Father—why this could really work.

This could be the start right here of a lot of good things.

There was one photograph not on Père Samedi's wall that well belonged there, but it exists only in my imagination. It is a portrait of an immensely fat woman dressed in a green silk gown hiked up around her waist. She is wearing no underwear. The woman, her skin the color of wet mud, is lying in a patch of wet mud, being nosed by a snowy white sow. Her arms and legs are askew, in a position that the viewer, not knowing why, knows immediately is unnatural. Her head lies a meter away from her body. Her mouth is open, and her tongue lolls out. In her eyes there is a wide-eyed, unblinking stare of perfect terror.

Stories circulated still about Père Samedi in the year immediately after his return from exile. Papa Doc and Baby Doc were only recently gone, and the parish was still divided between those who had supported the dictatorship and those who had opposed it: everyone knew which way their neighbor had gone. Père Samedi, returned to his parish after so many years away, now attracted vast crowds with his furious sermons. He urged his parishioners to rough-and-ready justice. It was said—whispered, hinted—that Père Samedi himself led bands of men armed with machetes to lonesome houses where once-powerful Macoutes now trembled. They said that the priest made lists of his friends and lists of his enemies, and he scratched names off one list and inserted them on the other. It was around this time that the head of the aged Sanette Balmir was discovered in a pigsty.

They say that it was Maxim Bayard, returned from exile also, who tempered Père Samedi's righteous anger. Both men had suffered the depredations of the dictator: nobody understood Père Samedi's anger so well. Maxim had spent his exile in Paris, driving a taxicab. Not a day had passed when he did not feel the sadness and longing that only an exile can understand. The very day that Baby Doc fled Port-au-Prince, Maxim Bayard came home. He swore that he would never again sleep in the house that Sanette Balmir had profaned, and he built himself a small hut on the edge of his large property. Then he sought out his old friend Abraham Samedi. The two men, together with half a dozen like-minded men in various districts of the Grand'Anse, devised a plan for justice. Soon Maxim Bayard was Sénateur Maxim Bayard, and Père Samedi spoke to him as an equal.

Nowadays, it was said that in Père Samedi's parish, there was only one voter, and that was Père Samedi. He had learned in his youth a hard lesson in the importance of politics. At the pulpit, he was not afraid to identify the candidate in each election whom he supposed would best benefit his flock. For a great many of his parishioners, confident in his judgment and grateful for his assistance, that would be enough. His parishioners knew that those who had voted for the candidate of Père Samedi's choice would be rewarded. Père Samedi seemed to always know who had voted for whom, and he could be trusted to arrive at your homestead with a small envelope in which could be found a *petit cadeau* in appreciation of one's trust and fidelity. Others of independent mind who persisted in rallying or campaigning for the opponents of the lanky priest would find themselves visited at night by Père Samedi, who would sit for hours in attempts at gentle persuasion.

But when this failed, fields would mysteriously be set aflame. Women who crossed Père Samedi would sit in the market and not sell so much as a clove of garlic. Yet the most dramatic sanction the priest could impose was to withhold Communion: for many years, Père Samedi had seen to it that there were no Protestant churches in his parish, and to be outside the safe confines of the Church was to lay oneself open to every kind of danger.

By one means or another, Père Samedi succeeded in delivering the votes of his parish, *all* of them, election after election, for the Sénateur or for some other candidate of his choosing. It was to deliver his votes to the judge that we were in Abricots.

4 The judge had been selling himself vigorously to Père Samedi for maybe twenty minutes when he asked Terry and me to wait for him outside. The judge was a professional negotiator, and he knew that the only people who belonged in a room when final terms were discussed were the principals themselves.

Terry and I went outside. He had the kind of pale Scotch-Irish complexion that turned crimson the instant it was in the sun.

"Christ, it's hot," he said.

"He's good," I said.

"I told you. And he will get it done. These people will have that dentist if he says they'll have a dentist."

Terry pulled a packet of Marlboro Reds out of his pocket. "I hate these things. Eight years I didn't smoke. First cigarette was twelve minutes exactly after I landed. That's what this country does to you."

I looked at Terry for a long time. His face was too irregular, too puffy to be handsome, but he'd seen a lot of life, and that gives a man's face something attractive also.

He said, "You ever wonder why he doesn't want to build that road?"

"The Sénateur?"

"I've got a theory," he said. "I used to think he was after the money. I didn't know how it all worked, but I figured if you traced it all back to where it came from, you'd find money. But I got to thinking more and . . ."

Terry walked over to the car and pulled out a bottle of water. He took a long swig from it and handed it to me. "What you got to understand is that they're *his*. That's how he sees it. If they build that road, what the hell do they need Sénateur Maxim for? They'll sell the frigging mangoes in Port-au-Prince, or fish, or they'll plant gardens and sell tomatoes. The way Maxim Bayard sees things, these people don't need him, it's like he doesn't even exist."

There was an open cement cistern covered in a scum of rainwater and algae. Mosquitoes danced across the surface. Terry bent over, picked up some loose gravel, and started tossing pebbles into the water.

"He says they're his children, but I tell you, a father can hate his children too. It doesn't happen often, but it does happen. I once had a guy who found out his wife was cheating on him, he took his two kids and slit their throats. This guy told me he felt evil in their hearts. That was my death-row case. And that's the way Maxim Bayard loves his quote-unquote children. He feels evil in their hearts."

The world makes you, and then you see it through the eyes it gives you. Another man sees the same world, but he doesn't have the same eyes. I didn't want to debate Terry. I just let him talk.

Terry said, "There was this time—I guess it must have been, I don't know, 2004. Something like that. Rainy night, right in front of me, two out-of-state vehicles, head-on. One guy died, name was Terry Moore, still remember that, Terry just like me, and the car that hit him, that was this old couple, down from Maine. Here I was in Florida, one car was from Virginia and the other car from Bangor, Maine, and they meet two hundred yards in front of me."

Terry started laughing.

"So why I remember all this, is what I had to do was call this guy's wife and tell her that her husband was dead in Florida. And she's like, 'Florida? What's he doing in Florida? He told me he was going to Graceland with Al. You tell that fat bastard I never want to hear from him again. Tell him I die, he ain't invited to my fucking funeral.' She was going nuts, that lady. Finally, I was just, 'Lady, I'm going to go tell his cadaver everything you just said.' Next thing I know, the woman's wailing into the phone. 'Please don't tell him nothing. Oh, he knows, he knows!'"

Terry kept chucking gravel. The pebbles formed small circles in the water that expanded and encroached and interfered with one another.

"Any case, what I keep thinking to myself, you know, couple thousand miles of road between them, and if those old folks had just gone a touch slower or Terry Moore had stopped for an extra cup of coffee, everyone would have been fine. You ever think what a thing like that means? I mean, really think about it? It's just—there's gotta be some kind of plan. Some kind of plan that makes those two cars slam into each other. Like you ever think of all the fucked-up things that had to happen before I meet Nadia? It's some crazy shit."

I picked up a branch and tossed it into the water. It broke up Terry's circles.

"So you think there's a point to it all?" I said.

"There better damn be," he finally said.

Terry and I didn't talk for a while. That house was making both of us feel pretty lugubrious. I let Terry chuck gravel in the water like he was taking aim at bad memories, and I walked out onto the road. Nobody shouted at me or asked me for money. People just averted their eyes when they walked in front of Père Samedi's house. I was so grateful when a little kid ran up to me with a big smile that I gave him all the change in my pocket.

Finally the judge came out of the house.

"Père Samedi sends you his best," he said.

"I wanted to say goodbye," I said.

"He's not feeling well."

A few minutes later we were on the road back to Jérémie.

"How'd it go?" Terry said.

"He told me he's had the same donkey a lot of years, but it wasn't carrying its weight. He told me he's in the market for a new beast of burden."

"And what'd you say?"

"Hee-haw."

He said it with so little affect that I couldn't figure out what happened.

"So that's good news?" I said.

"He's got it in for the Sénateur, that's for sure."

"That's good for you, then," I said.

The judge nodded. His face was like a mask. He had imported the heavy air of the priest's house into the vehicle. It wasn't easy to breathe.

"It's about the dentist?" I said.

The judge shook his head. "No. The Sénateur could find a dentist, that's what it took. No, there was a little girl on the *Trois Rivières*. That's what this is about."

"What about her?" I asked.

But Terry had already understood. "Man, have I got to take a crap."

"I had no idea," I said, thinking of that flock of children I had seen playing in the priest's garden. Even if you're looking, even if it's all right in front of you, sometimes you don't see the story. Then you wonder why you're always so surprised by how the world turns out.

Johel nodded. We didn't talk. Out at sea, you could see thick clouds and rain, a heavy storm over a small patch of big ocean. But it was sunny where we were.

She was nine. Her mother was taking her to Port-au-Prince. She had a toothache.

PART SIX

PART SIX

1 Coming in from the airport, just out front of the police commissariat, the first thing you saw was the judge's face, twelve feet high and fake-smiling. He fake-smiled at the *marchandes* walking up the coast with baskets of fish on their heads, at the kids in parrot-bright uniforms heading off to school, at the old men rocking in their chairs and admiring the goats. The judge fake-smiled at the UNPOLs dropping off prisoners at the police station, at Balu, the *chef de transport,* buying beer at Marché Soleil, and at the Uruguayan soldiers heading down to the beach. He fake-smiled at the motorcycle taxi drivers and at the vendors of used American clothing. He fake-smiled at all of Jérémie, his bright, round face reminding every voter of the promise of a new day.

The new billboard was the start of the electoral campaign. Kay told me that the judge had hired a company out of Port-au-Prince to execute the work and had personally approved the heavily photoshopped image that hung there: the man that overlooked the rue Abbé Hué was some twenty pounds lighter than his fleshy reality. He had settled on his campaign emblem: a hawk soaring above two lines that suggested a road. This was Toussaint Legrand's only successful artistic accomplishment. He had created the image in a single, perfect moment of inspiration. Beneath the judge's face was written "Célestin: The Road to Prosperity."

Although the campaign was in its earliest days, I couldn't imagine that the judge had spent less than ten thousand dollars already and seemed prepared to spend much more. Johel in his own financial affairs was generally parsimonious. I had seen him pass ten infuriating minutes patiently bargaining down the price of a basket of bananas. His salary as a judge was barely more than an honorarium, if the government succeeded in paying him at all; but I understood that he had some family money and savings from his career in corporate law on which he relied, and he had inherited two apartment buildings in Port-au-Prince, one near Canapé Vert and the other in Pétionville. The rental income from these properties was probably sufficient for his needs.

Still, the prospect of financing a senatorial race out of his own pocket was daunting. Haiti is poor, and the Grand'Anse is the most remote corner of Haiti; but politics in the Grand'Anse were not cheap. I made a back-of-the-envelope calculation: the judge needed SUVs to transport him, his aides, and his security from place to place; he probably needed at least three vehicles, and he needed them for at least three months. He needed radio time, and pigs and goats to feed people at his campaign rallies. He needed tens of thousands of T-shirts imprinted with his smiling face. He needed to pay campaign staff and people to walk around the hills telling his story. He needed big crowds to attract big crowds at his rallies, and crowds of paid supporters don't come cheap. He needed to pay kids to graffiti his name all over town. And above all, he needed to buy votes, because what poor man is ever going to give away something as valuable as a vote for free? And even that's not enough, because the judge needed to buy the people who counted the votes.

There were diverse rumors explaining how the judge funded his campaign. One story, widely repeated, was that he was funded by the CIA. The story was not implausible: the United States did have a sordid history of meddling in Haitian politics, both covertly and overtly, and the Sénateur, with his socialist politics and fervent denunciations of the "cold nation" to the north, had not made himself any friends among that small coterie of powerful Americans who interested themselves in Haitian affairs. (I also heard stories that the Sénateur, whose campaign was equally expensive, was himself funded by the CIA, his rhetoric and ostensible political convictions an elaborate ruse.) Variants on these stories had the role of the CIA played by the secret services of Cuba, Venezuela, and Russia; or various narco-traffickers; or a consortium of real estate speculators eager to profit from the construction of the road.

There was one story, however, more widely diffused than any other, a story that had the additional merit of being true. I heard the story first from Toussaint Legrand, who, after his success with the logo, had painted a portrait of a three-legged yellow dog (he ran out of paint before applying the final limb) that he was proposing to sell to me. With the proceeds of the sale, he intended to buy a bottle of cologne, brewed locally and known as Lightning, so-called for its effect on the ladies. Toussaint indicated the subsequent step in his plan with a sheepish smile. I bought the painting, and Toussaint threw in the story for free. I later gave the painting to Kay White, who said, "That's *interesting.*" She had heard the story also, and fleshed out further details. But the definitive version was told to me by the judge himself, speaking on the dual condition that the story would remain confidential for as long as he pursued or held political office, and that I remove Toussaint's painting from the wall above the toilet of campaign HQ, where Kay had hung it.

Even the lowliest peasant in the most remote village of the Haitian hills will know the name Andrés Richard, or they will call him by his nickname, La Gueule d'Haïti—the snout of Haiti. What the nickname meant was this: What came into Haiti, and fed the nation and nourished it and was essential for survival, passed through him. He chewed upon and digested the meat of the nation. If you spend a dollar in Haiti, some portion of that dollar will filter upward through middlemen and merchants until it has settled in the Richard family coffers. Haiti is an island nation that produces nearly nothing: what is consumed must be imported. So every drop of gasoline in the nation came through Andrés Richard's oil terminal, and every grain of imported rice was stored in his warehouses. Groupe Richard held a controlling stake in the leading distributor of filtered water; they owned the leading bank *and* its competitor. It was said that the Richard family alone possessed more wealth than the Haitian peasantry combined; of the great mulatto families who lived in the hills above Port-au-Prince, his by far was the greatest and most powerful.

Otherwise sober men and women in Port-au-Prince swore that Andrés Richard owed his fabulous success to human sacrifice.

"Abraham Samedi had told me that you have political ambitions," Andrés Richard said to the judge, his voice faint and palsied over the telephone. "Haiti needs men like you."

Château Richard was accessible only by private road—or helicopter. Johel had never been in a helicopter before. The thing rose up in a swirling cloud of dust, then banked, and the city swung skyward, slums spreading like concrete fungus up the sides of elephant-hide mountains. Hulks of rusting ships gleamed grotesquely in the bay. As the helicopter circled over the hills, Johel could see vast neighborhoods of shimmering tin shacks, and in the streets, brilliantly colored cars like jewels, the sun reflecting off each emerald, amethyst, or topaz roof. The last concrete roofs of Port-au-Prince receded into the lower distance as the helicopter rose; then they disappeared entirely from view, the helicopter following the bowls of great canyons and mountain ridges until, at a distance, Johel could see, set on an immense green lawn, the marmoreal whiteness of Andrés Richard's house. Andrés Richard had purchased not only the mountain on which his own house was situated but also the two mountains visible from his home, to ensure that his view was never marred by the encroaching bidonvilles.

A uniformed servant led Johel to the terrace of the house, where a large parrot in a cage that might comfortably have accommodated a family of three regarded Johel with mild curiosity. Johel waited on the terrace for several minutes, considering the splendid lines of the deck furniture, the tranquillity of the pool, and the undulating form of a large steel sculpture, until another servant emerged from the dark interior of the house pushing an aged lizard in a wheelchair.

"Don't get up," the lizard croaked. "I can't!"

The lizard then flicked out his tongue to gather up a spot of spittle on his lower lip and began to laugh.

"Andrés Richard," he said, extending a hand. "At your service."

There was a hole in Andrés Richard's wall, and now that he was old and was going to die, that hole bothered him, worried him at night, and deranged what little sleep he had. What he had built and what he had accomplished, when weighed in the balance of his soul, meant little against the hole in his wall. He had raised children and seen them grow to be wastrels, failures, drinkers, scoundrels—but that troubled him less than the hole in the wall. He had built an empire. He had made love to scores of beautiful women, had made and unmade presidents. He had held private audiences with three popes. He had made his peace with his Lord, but evidently his Lord had yet to make His peace with him.

The hole was in the wall of Andrés Richard's private chapel.

It had been a decade at least since Andrés Richard had left his mountain sanctuary; and on his return from his last descent into the valley and country below, he had decided that to complete his estate and solidify his soul, he needed a space of solitary refuge and prayer. A man of impeccable taste himself, he had called on other men of superior taste to accomplish the work, providing them with all the resources at his command. He wished for a place of simplicity and beauty, and on the fringe of his estate, in a grove of pine and *acajou*, such a place had been erected: not large, not ostentatious, open windows overlooking only the grandeur of nature, and at the altar, the brilliant triptych by Michel Dumartin depicting his Lord's crucifixion and resurrection.

Now Andrés Richard knew that death was very, very near, and one piece escaped his grasp, the third painting of the triptych. To complete the triptych would be to complete his collection and his chapel, and this, Andrés Richard felt sure, was necessary to ensure the survival of his soul in the world to come.

"Have you made the Sénateur an offer for the piece?" Johel asked.

How easily he slipped into the role of counselor. This was how he felt most at ease in the world, contemplating the problems of others and applying his intelligence in the search for a solution. Johel took Andrés Richard's problem seriously: it was obviously of great importance to Andrés Richard, and whatever is of great importance to a man like Andrés Richard is important.

"Of course I've made him an offer for the painting! I've offered him buckets of money for that piece!"

"And he won't take it?"

"Young man, do you really think Maxim Bayard wants my money? If you do, then your reputation for cleverness is severely overvalued."

"I suppose he wouldn't."

"I suppose not."

Johel knew that the problem was the former president. Andrés Richard had been one of the organizers of the coup d'état that forced him out of office and into exile. On the day the former president left the country, the Sénateur, interviewed on Haitian national television, had wept convulsively. A documentary filmmaker from Oregon had put the moment in his film, *Haiti: Tragedy of a Nation*, set to a Haitian soprano singing funereal songs.

The terrible irony of the situation was that before the departure of the former president, the Sénateur had agreed to sell Andrés Richard the painting. Andrés Richard had never imagined that a matter of politics would interfere with business between reasonable men; had he known that the Sénateur would be so troubled, he would have held his hand until the painting was in his possession. This was one of the great miscalculations of his life.

But Monsieur Richard's role in the ouster of the former president had made the Sénateur an implacable enemy. When Andrés Richard contacted the Sénateur again to complete the transaction, the Sénateur had said, "Monsieur Richard, I look upon that painting every morning to remind me that the path to salvation is straight. If keeping that painting in my possession preserves my soul and damns yours, then it is an object to me of inestimable worth."

Thereafter, Andrés Richard, for all his wealth, power, and influence, had never succeeded in convincing the Sénateur to part with his painting.

In the subsequent years, Monsieur Richard told the judge, he had tried many schemes to convince the Sénateur to sell the painting. He had hired a man from France to pose as a collector, and he had attempted to convince the current president to seize the painting as part of the national patrimony. (This plan had foundered only when the Sénateur had threatened to burn the painting before he relinquished it, at which point Andrés Richard had ordered the president to desist.) He had used all his political influence to stall the Sénateur's projects. The Sénateur remained indifferent.

Andrés Richard recounted all of this, then, despite the heat of the day, began to shiver.

"I don't recommend dying, young man," said Andrés Richard. "It is an unpleasant business."

"I will try to keep that in mind," Johel said.

"Are you at peace with your Savior?"

"We're cordial."

Andrés Richard began to laugh. His laughter drew the attention of his bird, who from his cage regarded the old man with alarm.

"That will not be sufficient, young man. That will not do! You see things clearer when the end is near. You see the necessity of things. I do not wish to confront my Maker with unresolved affairs here on this earth. You will see as you grow older that the walls of Hell are thick like mountains."

The parrot began to squawk. Its perch began to swing. It flapped its broad wings, revealing a confusion of reds and blues.

"And how can I help you with your problems, Monsieur Richard?" Johel asked.

Monsieur Richard shook in his chair.

"Why, I thought it was obvious! I thought that was as clear as day!"

At the altitude at which the château was situated, the day was indeed immensely clear.

Andrés Richard lifted up his bony hand, which calmed itself as if by the force of the old man's will into something like a staff or rod. He extended his forefinger until it pointed directly at Johel's heart.

"I am going to make you the next *sénateur* of the Grand'Anse," he said.

Then, exhausted by the gesture, the hand flopped down into Andrés Richard's lap, and the old man closed his eyes.

2 They had been a threesome: Sénateur Maxim Bayard, Père Abraham Samedi, and Docteur Auguste Philistin. The Three Musketeers of the Lycée Saint Louis, the three survivors. Once a year they had met on the anniversary of the death of François Duvalier to drink a pair of toasts: the first was to their dead, tossed by the Macoutes into unmarked graves; and the second, to the Hell-Fiend who supervised the eternal torment of their enemy. Père Samedi's defection meant that the table was set for two, just the Sénateur and his physician.

(Dr. Philistin himself later recounted to me the details of his last dinner with the Sénateur. Our appointment came about in the following manner. Some months after the election and the terrible events that followed, Dr. Philistin published in *Le Nouvelliste* a short appreciation of the Sénateur's life, and included his email address, inviting others who had known the Sénateur to exchange reminiscences. He was gathering material for a biographical essay. We met at Dr. Philistin's art-filled house in the hills above Port-au-Prince. He had only recently retired when I met him, but his firm handshake, his energetic manner, and his unlined face all suggested to me that had he wished to, he might have continued his practice a good deal longer. On the coffee table was an edition of the Sénateur's poems. The volume, I noticed for the first time, had been dedicated to "Auguste Philistin, Master of the Healing Arts and Friend of Liberty.")

Dr. Philistin had accompanied Maxim throughout his political career. Both were men of the Left, firmly convinced that the only solution to Haiti's poverty and backwardness was in an ideology of their deriving, which they called Caribbean Socialism, hashed out by them in a hundred letters when Maxim was in exile. The chief tenet of their philosophy was a conviction that the river of wealth, so long flowing from the Haitian peasantry to the Great Powers, needed to be rerouted in the opposite direction, avoiding the bloodsucking mulatto elites like Andrés Richard. When Maxim returned from exile, Dr. Philistin had encouraged him in his political ambitions and then had revealed himself over the years a shrewd, well-informed adviser. It was Dr. Philistin who had the unfortunate duty of informing the Sénateur that Andrés Richard had decided to invest his resources in Johel Célestin's campaign.

Dr. Philistin told me that he had never seen the Sénateur so agitated as that night at the Boucan Grégoire. The Sénateur's bladder was spasmodic when its owner was anxious, and the Sénateur excused himself to the toilet three times even before the main course arrived. Then he sharply reprimanded the waiter when he allowed a few drops of the wine to stain the tablecloth. A telephone rang too long at a neighboring table, and the Sénateur's face curled into snarl. Only the doctor's calm hand on the Sénateur's forearm had prevented him from confronting the offending device's owner.

"I am being devoured alive by gnats!" the Sénateur exclaimed.

The judge was not the Sénateur's only opposition in the coming election. A dozen candidates had presented their credentials to the electoral authorities. There was Emile Villesaint of the old Villesaints—he ran in every election and was always opposed, as in this election, by his daughter Emmanuelle. Old Emile must have been pushing eighty and Emmanuelle fifty: they lived in Miami and flew back to Jérémie just for elections. There was a Protestant preacher named Erasmus Callisthenes, who, it was said, could preach the Gospel twenty-four hours straight. Thibault Antoine Erick of the well-known clan out of Dame Marie was in the race as part of a wager with his brother-in-law: three hectares of arable land said he could take ten thousand votes. A lady doctor from Jérémie whose intentions were said to be honorable registered herself at election headquarters surrounded by a hundred children dressed in white.

But the judge, Dr. Philistin reckoned, was certainly Maxim's chief opposition. That was the significance of Père Samedi's defection. That news had infuriated the Sénateur. The notion that years of friendship be tossed aside for—for *what*? Père Samedi had not so much as called the Sénateur to explain himself. It was not only the loss of the priest's solid block of votes, it was the signal it sent to the Sénateur's other allies that the old man was weak.

Dr. Philistin was too politic to remind the Sénateur that he had predicted the priest's treachery. The priesthood, he had long insisted, was a reactionary force.

The doctor studied his friend's face. It had never been a handsome face, but its blunt, large, ill-proportioned features had communicated that unbridled energy, that enthusiasm for this curious business of being alive that was the essence of Maxim Bayard. He could remember Maxim's first campaign all those years ago. *Mon Dieu*, the man was tireless: up at dawn, out on foot, stopping at every hut and hamlet, shaking hands, kissing ladies—and with every footfall so gaining in strength and energy that Dr. Philistin had to actively dissuade him from campaigning through the night as well, for fear of disturbing his constituents. The Sénateur had been determined to meet each and every voter and present his vision of the socialist paradise the Grand'Anse could become. Two or three hours of sleep a night, often on the floor of some peasant's hut, half a mango for breakfast, a boiled banana for lunch: that was all the Sénateur needed as he marched across the great Grand'Anse. He had won that election in a landslide.

This evening, though, there was no doubt: the Sénateur was tired. Dr. Philistin noticed him yawning. This was not Maxim. At one point during the meal he closed his eyes and held very still. His skin had the pallor of ash.

"Are you sleeping at night?" the doctor asked.

"A few hours."

"When was the last time, my friend, that you saw the inside of a doctor's office?"

"Are you proposing to bleed me, Doctor, or apply leeches?" asked the Sénateur.

No evidence could dissuade Maxim from his intimate belief that the leaf doctors in the hills were infinitely more capable healers than the doctor and his white-coated peers. There was a variety of yam that grew in the Grand'Anse, the so-called English yam, that was said to enhance the virility of men and give to all and sundry the energy of a young ram. It was in a daily boiled English yam as a cure-all that the Sénateur reposed his confidence.

Dr. Philistin wondered how the Sénateur and his English yams would navigate their way through two rounds of fierce campaigning should the Sénateur fail to win a majority in the first round; and given Andrés Richard's support, along with the defection of Père Samedi, it was hard to imagine the Sénateur winning outright in the first electoral turn. Even as the judge's financial position had solidified, the Sénateur's had weakened: with the mayor of Les Irois in prison, the river of money that flowed from Colombia to the Cold Land had shifted course to the Département de Sud, where the Sénateur and the people of the Grand'Anse were not in a position to profit. Perhaps, Dr. Philistin reckoned, the Sénateur's energy and money would tide him over for the first round. But a second round of campaigning would double his expenses.

By long-standing convention, the men did not discuss politics until they had arrived at the digestif. They traded recollections of their youth and discussed literature. Both men felt the absence of Père Samedi keenly. The Sénateur was drinking an aged sipping rum, thick like syrup, full on the palate, a belly warmer of a rum.

"It is an insult," he finally said.

"Have you met this judge?"

"He speaks with an accent."

"But he's popular."

"If I give a child nothing but bonbons and chocolate, I will be popular. But it will not produce a healthy child. We have yet to arrive, Doctor, at the stage of social evolution where our citizens are able to discern a true friend from a friendly face. I will never cease to be amazed at how devious, how cynical our enemies are."

The Sénateur swirled the amber liquid in his glass.

"I tell you now, Doctor, I would welcome retirement. If a suitable man were to oppose me, I would gladly step aside. I have a little piece of land near Dame Marie, and I can see in my mind's eye a cottage with a garden. I would grow bananas and paint, and in the afternoons I would nap. Do you know, my friend, the last time that I permitted myself the luxury of an afternoon nap?"

Dr. Philistin said, "You're not obligated to fight this election."

Maxim's eyes narrowed to slits. His face colored.

Dr. Philistin could read the Sénateur's thoughts. Other men of the *sénat*, even men of lesser stature, hardly bothered to campaign, so assured were they of their constituents' devotion. The Sénateur was sure that he would be in this position also, had this foreigner, this *blan*, this intriguer not arrived.

There was something unseemly about the endless traipsing on the hustings. He had done so much already. Hadn't he brought in the Cuban doctors? Was he not responsible for the solar streetlights in so many villages, which allowed the village children to study at night? The fishing boats at Dame Marie were his creation, the dispensary in Beaumont, the corn mill in Carrefour Charles. To how many of his *citoyens* had he offered his personal assistance? The line of peasants outside his door was proof that he lived his creed: a man of the Grand'Anse had only to give his hand in friendship to the Sénateur to receive an embrace. Dr. Philistin knew that the Sénateur believed himself to be more than a mere politician: he was the creator of a *social system*. He had found a way to transform the isolation of the Grand'Anse to wealth: men and women merely had to ask him for assistance, and money that would have otherwise lingered in the Cold Land was theirs.

Dr. Philistin stared at Maxim's face as it hardened into resolution. He had not understood his friend's mood. What had seemed indecisiveness was merely a moment of reflection. What had seemed exhaustion was a husbanding of strength. What had seemed defeat was a prelude to victory.

There comes a time in a statesman's career, the Sénateur told the doctor, after so many trials and such great successes, when it was appropriate, dignified even, that he stand before his public and, like a father to his wayward children, declare, "Take me as I am: you'll find none better. No man will ever love you more. We are as one, my children—joined in heart and soul. I am your voice and you my lungs. I merit your fidelity

and you merit my leadership. Together we shall endeavor onward!"
That was all the campaign a great man required.

The Sénateur's glass was empty. He gestured to the waiter to bring
him another. The Sénateur seemed restored to vigor. He sat tall in
his seat, his face flushed with color. Then he explained his plan to
Dr. Philistin.

Perhaps, Dr. Philistin thought, there was something to the English
yam after all.

Dr. Philistin told me that he and the Sénateur stayed up late that night
planning the campaign to come: what towns and villages were vulner-
able, who remained solidly in the Sénateur's camp. Where the traitors
were likely to be hiding. Who was faithful, and who was weak. How
much support could they count on from the president. What would be
the role of the scoundrels in the United Nations Mission? Money: Could
they count on the usual arrangements? Were additional funds necessary?

At the conclusion of the evening, the Sénateur took his old friend's
hand. The Sénateur was a larger man than Dr. Philistin, and his thick,
callused paw swallowed up the doctor's wiry fingers.

"*Mon vieux*, I have been haunted by a dream. I am standing on a
hillside watching birds fighting. What could such a dream mean?"

"I've never understood dreams," murmured Dr. Philistin.

"I have understood the dream to mean that there are perils ahead.
It is for this reason that I wish to ask you an immense favor. I have
been to a lawyer and prepared a final testament. May I mention you as a
legatee?"

Dr. Philistin was shocked. He loved the Sénateur, but he had not
realized that the Sénateur loved him also.

"I would be honored," he finally said.

I watched Dr. Philistin stand up from the couch where we had been
sitting. He told me that the Sénateur had bequeathed him Michel Dumartin's final painting, the last in the triptych Andrés Richard so fervently
coveted. The first painting had depicted the realm of the underworld,
the second terrestrial life. This painting portrayed Paradise.

This was a landscape of heaven. It looked a lot like Haiti, a place of color, light, and shadow. Heaven was a banquet, a table so long it curved around itself like a snake. You could have spent all day looking at that painting, picking out the faces, identifying those lucky enough to eat from the good Lord's pigs, yams, crabs, and mangoes. A dark-skinned Jesus sat at the head of the table, laughing uproariously at the story Moses was telling. All manner of saints and prophets were eating and drinking, slapping each other on the back, flirting and kissing, dancing to the music of angels, and enjoying a nice long break from all the troubles they had endured below. Adam and Eve were fighting, and I figured out why: Adam's hand was on Erzulie's behind. Children played under the big table; a few of them were dancing on top of it. Toussaint L'Ouverture was in the crowd, being served his plate by Napoleon Bonaparte. The table was long enough for ordinary people too, and after staring awhile, I saw the lady who hacked up my goat meat, and the motorcycle taxi drivers who camped out on the Place Dumas, and Micheline, the woman who squeezed our juice. The only face I couldn't find in that crowd was mine.

3 I was drinking my juice and watching a spider devour a fly when Toussaint Legrand showed up one sultry August morning. I had harbored an ambition of working that morning, a project not compatible with the presence of Toussaint on my terrace. I could smell the stench of Lightning, Toussaint's new cologne, at once spicy and sweet and altogether nauseating. I tried to ignore him in the hope that he would grow bored and go away. I got up and fetched myself another glass of juice, not offering him one. He stared at me somberly. The spider had completed its breakfast, and now it settled into immobility. I picked up my book and began to read, but the words refused to form sentences. When I looked up, I noticed glistening teardrops rolling down Toussaint's cheeks. Toussaint in tears made me think of ice cream on the sidewalk, the last day of summer, and the mocking laughter of pretty girls.

Then, in his incongruous, improbably deep voice, Toussaint told me that the Conseil Electoral Haïtien* had published that morning the final

---

*The Conseil Electoral Haïtien, known as the CEH, was the bureaucratic organ in charge of organizing the election, from registering voters to preparing ballots to establishing voting centers to counting the votes themselves. One of the prerogatives of the CEH was to ensure that every candidate on the ballot met the requirements of the Haitian Constitution for the office in question. Candidates for the *sénat* needed to be thirty years old, have a clean criminal record, have lived four years in the territory they wished to represent, own property, exercise a profession in the territory they wished to ballot for the upcoming election. He had heard the announcement on the radio. Johel's name had not been listed as a candidate for the office of *sénateur* from the Grand'Anse.

"It must have been a mistake," I said.

For the first time in our relationship, Toussaint looked at me with the cynical eyes of a grown man.

A little later, Kay called. She was waiting for Terry and the judge at his campaign headquarters.

"Come on down, will you?" she said.

"Is anything wrong?"

"I just want to see a friendly face."

I had seen Jérémie only hours before the anticipated landfall of a Class 3 hurricane, and the town had remained unfathomably calm. There had been no lines to buy water; the families who lived on the banks of the river, which would rise if the hurricane hit and drown them, stayed right where they were. The women shopped, the men played dominoes, and the children went to school in their bright uniforms even as radio forecasters predicted imminent doom. But the townies were right: Hurricane Gilda changed course at the last minute and blew harmlessly out to sea.

Now the moment was different.

There was a corner of the Place Dumas where the *marchandes* who came down from the mountains sat. I bought some mangoes on my way to campaign HQ.

"A pile of problems today," said the lady who sold bananas.

"Always a pile of problems. The good Lord will save us," said the mango lady.

"They eliminated Juge Blan."

---

represent—and be a citizen of one nation, and just one nation, on God's green earth: Haiti. (Haitian law did not recognize double nationality.) The CEH was ostensibly a neutral administrative body, its members selected by all three branches of government, but no one in Haiti believed that it was anything but the well-trained pet of the president himself. To further isolate the CEH from partisan politics, it was, by constitutional imperative, subservient to no court of appeals. Its decisions—whether about the location of a voting center or the outcome of a close election—were final.

"Juge Blan won't accept that," said Banana. "People won't accept that."

"Juge Blan won't accept that at all," said Mango resolutely.

"The Devil's motorcycle never breaks down," said Banana proverbially.

Mango nodded. Then she said, "Juge Blan, he saved me one time."

"Didn't know that."

"It's true, it's true. Juge Blan didn't help me, my little one would be in the coffin today."

"Didn't know that."

"Juge Blan put money in my pocket when he had the fever."

"Didn't know that."

"People will take the streets today for Juge Blan."

"The Devil's motorcycle," said Banana, putting her bananas back in the basket. "A pile of problems."

Campaign HQ, when I eventually arrived, was packed: the usual gang, but others also, people I had never seen before who had come to the office that morning out of solidarity with the judge. The big room with its impermeable cinder-block walls was hot and smelled of old sweat. People had been there since the night before, when the CEH held its press conference.

I found Kay sitting at her desk, her back to the wall, headphones on, watching a video of blond yogi performing a series of unnatural complications. Kay's hair was matted with sweat.

"You startled me," she said.

"I wonder how he's going to get out of that," I said.

"I watch this when I get stressed."

I sat on the edge of Kay's desk. She closed her laptop. Her eyes were red-rimmed and tired.

"Can you believe?" she said. "I heard in the middle of the night. Terry woke me up and said, 'Kay, they eliminated Johel.' 'They shot him?' I said. I swear to God, that's what I thought. He was like, no, they eliminated him from the ballot."

"Did they give a reason?"

"Terry said he heard from his guy on the CEH that Johel wasn't a Haitian citizen."

"He told me he never got American citizenship. Just a green card."

"Of course he's Haitian," she said.

"And no one can stop them?"

She said, "Johel said it was legal."

"How's he taking it?"

She said, "Terry said he's not going to take it lying down."

"Does he have a choice?"

"I guess he's going to take it standing up."

The ceiling fans succeeded only in swirling the anxiety around the room, producing eddies, ripples, and riptides of unease. We were about to be submerged by a rogue wave when I proposed that we get something cold to drink.

There was a small crowd milling outside of campaign headquarters. Mid-August in the Caribbean is a month to be endured. The sky was gray like steel. I thought the dog on the Place Dumas was dead, but then it scratched its snout. A small crowd was assembling in front of head-quarters. It didn't take much to get a crowd together in Jérémie—any hint of excitement would do—and Radio Jérémie had already announced that the judge was going to speak later that morning.

We followed the dusty road to the little bar kitty-corner to campaign HQ. A dozen children shouted, *"Blan!"* and each time, Kay winced. The bar was a dark place with a bead curtain to keep out the flies, and there was a scent of sea salt and sewage in the air. Kay had a drop of sweat on her upper lip. I asked her what she wanted to drink and she asked for a Coke. I ordered one too.

"Boat's not here yet," the waitress said. We'd been waiting for the overdue boat for days. The shelves of every store were empty.

Kay attempted to order a Sprite, a Fanta, a Cola Couronne, a Limon-ade, and a Tampico; I asked for Prestige; we settled on a bottle of water, which came to the table warm enough to make cocoa.

"What does Terry say about this?" I said.

"Who cares?"

I raised an eyebrow.

"Don't look at me like that," she said. "I look awful."

"No you don't."

"Yes I do, and you know it. I haven't slept in two days—"

She rubbed her eyes with the back of her hand. She breathed deeply, held the breath a heartbeat, and exhaled raggedly.

"How long have you known?" I asked.

"I always knew. I just didn't want to know."

"How did you find out for sure?"

"He was talking to her on the phone, saying, you know. Two days ago. Saying things." She looked away and swallowed. "You always think it's not going to matter, or you're going to be adult about it all, but when it happens, it does matter. It matters so much."

"What does he say?"

"He tells me that I don't understand."

"And what do you say?"

"I tell him he's right. That I just don't understand."

Kay looked at anything but me for a minute. She looked at the refrigerator that wasn't cold, at the ceiling fan that didn't spin, at the clock that didn't tell the time. She looked at her fingernails, which were, despite everything, neatly painted. She looked at the sign on the wall that informed clients that credit made enemies.

"Maybe you should be thinking of going home," I said.

"It's too hot. The inverter's broken, we don't even have a fan—"

"Home, home. Back to wherever you come from. Back to the Gap and Zara. Not here."

Her face was covered in a film of sweat. Little blond tendrils clung to her temples. She seemed so intensely alive, so present in the moment: sometime in the future, when she was showing couples starter homes, I thought, she might even remember this moment, improbable as it seemed, with something like affection.

"I want to help Johel," she said. She meant it. She had been building something too. We could hear people chanting the judge's name out front of headquarters.

I said, "Have you ever met the guy who owns this place? Ti Blan François? I got to talking to him once. He's a deportee, he's been back a decade. I asked him what happened, and he said, 'I driving drunk and I kill my wife.' He spent five years in jail for vehicular manslaughter, then got sent back here. You know what he told me? He said it was the best thing that ever happened to him."

"Oh, God, that's awful."

"But you know what? The man is happy. He sold his house in Miami, lives like a king here, has a pretty, young girlfriend, just a perfectly fine life."

When Kay didn't say anything, I said, "I don't know if you want to hear this, but I don't think I'd count on a man's conscience to make sure that things work out the way you want them to. And I'm a man. You don't want to end up like Ti Blan François's wife, roadkill on the way to Terry's new life."

That came out rougher than I intended. Kay looked a little stunned, and wiped the sweat from her forehead. Some kids came in and ordered a Coca-Cola. The waitress explained that there wasn't any. Then it happened again a few minutes later.

She said, "Terry told me today that he's never going back. I said, 'What are you going to do? Stay here forever?' He said, 'Maybe.' It would be so much easier if I just knew what he was thinking."

"I don't know," I said.

"I just don't get what he sees in her."

"He's fallen in love with some story he's telling himself."

"What story is that?" Kay said.

"An ordinary man with an ordinary life sees a burning house and hears a child crying and he runs inside."

Kay looked at me. She was such a pretty woman when her pale face was reddened by a touch of anger.

She said, "He didn't have an ordinary life—he was married to me. Being married to me is wonderful."

"I'm sure it is," I finally said. "You have many charms as a woman. But you're not a helpless child crying in a burning house. Terry knows that you're perfectly capable of opening a window and climbing out all by yourself. By the time he showed up, you'd have put out the fire, remodeled the house, and sold it for a profit."

By early afternoon the crowd filled the Place Dumas. Kids were shinnying up electrical poles to see the judge. Women fanned themselves with scraps of cardboard.

The crowd was Toussaint Legrand's doing. It was Toussaint's job to turn out bespoke crowds on the judge's behalf, masses of enthusiastic paid supporters. It wasn't the strangest profession that I came across in Haiti—that was the *femmes pleureuses*, the women who were paid to weep at funerals. Haitian funerals aimed for a malarial fever of high emotion with god-awful wailing, breast-beating, rending of garments, and eventual hysterical collapse, women carried out of the funeral parlor face-first, writhing and moaning. Toward this end, the *pleureuses* would amp the emotional temperature up past scalding by sobbing convulsively until a frenzy of mourning spread contagiously through the crowd. It was a gesture of respect for the dead.

I later learned that Toussaint had paid five hundred young men and women to come and manifest their loyalty to the judge, but there were many more who came of their own initiative. The paid supporters that day were not so very far in their passion from the *femmes pleureuses*, and the effect on the crowd was the same: men grew soberly angry, but soon the women began to wail. *"Amway!"* they cried, an untranslatable Creole word that meant something like "Disaster!"

Here was my introduction to Haitian politics. I had no idea what kind of place Haiti was until I saw that crowd. The intensity of the day reminded me of something I had seen years before, when I attended the funeral of a revered guru in Tamil Nadu. Mourners that day were convinced that by throwing themselves under the chariot conducting the swami to his funeral pyre, they too would escape the cycle of suffering; the police held the crowd back with whips. Both the demonstration on the Place Dumas and the funeral in India produced the same sound, like the vastly amplified buzzing of a hive. On both days I saw something human beings ordinarily keep hidden. Both encounters left me frightened and exhilarated, as such encounters inevitably do.

Soon the shabby, malnourished crowd was chanting for the judge. They were waving little photos of him that Toussaint had distributed, or green boughs, making a small forest; women banged on pots and pans, the drumming assembling spontaneously into complicated, hectic rhythms. They chanted, "What we want, is to vote." Women were dancing, singing, clapping.

I don't know how long we waited before the judge and Terry drove up in the judge's black SUV. This was the moment the crowd had been waiting for. Now the drumming came to a crescendo, and the wailing intensified. I noticed that I was grinding my teeth as I watched the judge get down from his car, the crowd surging around him. "Come on," I said to myself. Johel was in a dark suit, Terry in his uniform. At first the judge looked pleased by the crowd, waving and smiling, but then he seemed frightened as people pressed so tightly against him that he couldn't move. Terry put his arm up, and the judge took a step, and another. Still, it took him almost ten minutes until he could work his way across the street.

When the judge and Terry were finally inside HQ, the dark room was filled with light as the flash of one cell phone camera exploded and then another.

Terry came and stood beside me. His beefy face was flushed. He was almost shaking with adrenaline. He was bouncing on the balls of his feet.

"God damn," he said. "You ever see something like that?"

"Kay's looking for you," I said.

He blinked, as if startled by the name. He looked around the room, through the doors of the HQ, where the crowd was seething in a mass. It wasn't like a person, that crowd, or like a thousand people. It was just its own kind of thing.

"That man is a rock," Terry said. "What you got to understand is, that man has some big-ass balls. We've been preparing for this for weeks."

"Why'd they do it?"

"The way Johel's guy heard it, the Sénateur paid the head of the CEH."

"What are you going to do?"

"We're headed to Port-au-Prince this afternoon. You know he's not alone in this."

"And what about—Nadia and Kay?" It seemed almost wrong to say their names in the same sentence.

"They're coming too," he said.

"Both of them?"

But I don't think Terry heard me over the roar of the crowd. Johel had stepped out onto the upstairs balcony.

"We'll get there," the judge finally said. "We'll get there."

I submit that there is a natural sympathy between certain languages and certain forms of speech. Sibilant, formal French is certainly, in my experience, the language of seduction and diplomacy, the language of lies; bouncy Italian, with its diminutives, is ideal for conversation with children. Attic Greek does triple duty as the language of epic, tragedy, and philosophy. I would go into battle with any commander who spoke Latin, so brutal and so punchy; and I can't really imagine why anyone would ever wish to write a novel in anything but English, with its massive vocabulary and remarkable ability to leapfrog effortlessly between the lyric and the vulgar, the raw and the fucking sublime.

But if I had to harangue a crowd, I'd do it in Creole.

There was to Creole a compression of sense and thought, a pithiness, a violence that rendered even tongue-tied Haitian orators compelling—and in the hands of someone who could really talk, it was superb.

The judge spoke with a microphone, but between the noise of the crowd and the noise of the generator powering the loudspeakers, I heard only words and phrases of his speech. He spoke for no more than twenty minutes, and of that, perhaps ten minutes were devoted to the judge waving at the crowd and waiting for it to calm down sufficiently that he might be heard. Then I heard him say that he was looking at a crowd of slaves. Master Hunger holds one whip and Master Corruption holds another. Master Empty Cooking Pot locks the chains on in the morning and Master Can't Afford the Doctor counts heads at night.

And Master Maxim Bayard is chasing down runaways.

That's why Master Maxim doesn't want a road. Because he wants his slaves down home where he can keep an eye on them. Because Master Bayard knows what there is at the end of the road.

Someone in the crowd shouts "Port-au-Prince," and the judge shakes his head. The city at the end of the road—it's a beautiful city, the most beautiful city there is. It's a city where justice isn't bought and sold. It's a city where children aren't hungry. It's a city where the water is clean.

At the other end of the long road was a city called Freedom.

Kay and Terry fought while the judge spoke. He just wanted her to be reasonable and get in the car, and she said, "Reasonable? You're talking to *me* about reasonable?" He said, "Kay, it's not the way you think," and she said, "Don't tell me what to think." He said, "Kay, we're getting in the car, and we are going to Port-au-Prince." I don't know what she said to him. The last thing I heard him say was that he loved her. Then there was a loud noise from the crowd, and when I looked back, Terry was standing alone. Kay had slipped out the back door of campaign HQ, maybe expecting Terry to follow her. But Terry had let her go.

The judge finished his speech on the Place Dumas by asking the crowd to march with him to Port-au-Prince. The crowd had calmed down. The drums began to beat out a stately, almost funereal rhythm. Johel descended the stairs, and the crowd parted to let him pass. He crossed the Place Dumas. Terry walked beside him, a few steps to his right. The procession filled the Grand Rue, absorbing greater numbers as it went along until it filled the whole Grand Rue from Basse-Ville to the ice factory, a half mile or so long. They walked through the *quartier populaire* of Sainte-Hélène, with its dense, winding passages of cinder-block houses and the smell of shit coming from the black beach that served as the neighborhood's latrine. At the rear of the procession were white Mission SUVS manned by UNPOLs, watching them.

I walked with the crowd just as far as the iron suspension bridge over the Grand'Anse, a gift of the government of France back in the 1950s. The judge's SUV was waiting for him at the far side of the bridge, the last paved road until Les Cayes, six hours to the south. I saw that Nadia was already in the car. The judge wanted to give another speech, but Terry whispered something in his ear. So Johel just waved at the crowd. Then he, Nadia, and Terry were gone in a cloud of white dust. Little children ran after them until they were out of sight.

4 The next day, Johel Célestin became a legend. He awoke as a minor Haitian politician, little known even in the Grand'Anse. By nightfall his name was known from Ouanaminthe to the Île-à-Vache, from Marmelade to Jacmel. If his name is still remembered today, it is because of what happened that August day in Port-au-Prince.

I was not there, but I followed events on the radio. I was at the library the next morning when I heard the judge's voice exhorting a crowd, and I knew that he was hitting all the right notes when Monsieur Duval, the librarian, put aside his book to listen. Then, when I stopped at the Marché Soleil to buy tinned anchovies, I heard the roar of a large crowd singing the Haitian national anthem. By now the streets of Jérémie had come to a halt as little clusters of voters gathered around each transistor radio.

On Radio Vision 2000, the journalist on the spot estimated the size of the crowd on the Champs de Mars at about five thousand. Radio Metropole told us that the crowd fully filled the immense square. Signal FM said that women had begun to pass out, either from dehydration or from overexcitement. Radio Kiskeya reported that a fistfight had broken out but was quickly calmed.

Now the announcers began to speak more quickly as the crowd descended the rue des Miracles, marching from the front gates of the Presidential Palace to the headquarters of the CEH. The *marchandes* who lined the streets around the Iron Market packed their wares and fled.

The journalists were now agitated. The marchers found the rue des Miracles barred by the PNH and a squadron of Nigerian riot police, several hundred helmeted men carrying shields and waving batons. Behind them were water cannons. In the middle of the block was CEP headquarters, a modest concrete bungalow surrounded by a high fence. Soon the marchers were throwing rocks in the direction of the police, who responded by lofting back bombs of tear gas. *"C'est la guerre! C'est la guerre! C'est la guerre!"* cried the voice on the radio. The marchers remained resolute, drifting back until the gas was taken up into the southern-swirling wind, then moving forward again to assault the CEH's protectors.

Terry would later claim that what happened next was his idea. He had scouted CEH headquarters a week earlier and noticed that while security was tight out front, there was almost no one protecting the rear flank of the building. Another part of the crowd disbursed onto the street running parallel to the rue des Miracles, where they found the back entrance to the CEH guarded only by a single unarmed security guard, who, seeing this immense crowd pullulating with testosterone, armed with machetes, and advancing on him, fled his post. The mob surged. Now the crowd was sweeping over the iron fence and swarming up the very sides of the building, Spider-Man style, pulling themselves up the drainpipes and into the open second-story windows.

CEH headquarters had been empty that day, owing to the menace of the protest. Before long, the building was overrun. The marchers now had the high ground and began to rain down anything they could find on the PNH and Nigerian soldiers below, from tea bags to boxes of printer toner. Out through the window and down onto the narrow street went reams of paper and three-ring binders that contained the numerous reports of well-paid electoral consultants; from the office of the director general came photographs of his three boys and his diploma from the Université d'Etat d'Haïti, class of 1971.

Soon the PNH and the Nigerians gave ground. The crowd, cheering, could hardly believe that the battle was over so quickly. CEH headquarters was now in Johel Célestin's hands.

———

(Just where did those immense crowds in Port-au-Prince come from? I would wonder about this also, until, from Radio Toussaint Legrand, I heard the following story.

(Arriving by air in Port-au-Prince, whether setting out from Miami or Jérémie, you fly low over the vast slum of Cité Soleil. In the midst of the squalor and the garbage, the pigs rutting in mud and the tin shacks, there is—your eyes will hardly believe it—a walled compound with an azure pool. The house figures on no deed or bill of sale, but it was every bit the property of a man named Ti Jean Roosevelt.

(Ti Jean, under indictment in the Southern District of Florida and seeking the safe harbor of parliamentary immunity, wished to be the *deputé* representing Cité Soleil in Parliament—and he surely would have been, given the ironfisted control he had over the bidonville, if the CEH hadn't eliminated his name also from the ballot. Not a property owner, they said.

(In the weeks leading up to the CEP's announcement of the electoral roster, Toussaint told me, Ti Jean and the judge, both men anticipating their elimination from the ballot, had talked long hours in Ti Jean's compound in Cité Soleil. There, Toussaint told me, the two politicians agreed to unite Ti Jean's soldiers with the judge's voice.

(That's the crowd on the Champs des Mars listening to the judge.)

The sacking of CEH headquarters was, even by Haitian standards, dramatic news. Even as the protesters were settling themselves into CEH headquarters, the airwaves were straightaway abuzz. Commentators on the national Right lamented the lack of an army to shoot the protesters, and commentators on the Left denounced the commentators on the Right, calling them Tontons Macoutes and fascists. Being so denounced infuriated the commentators on the Right, who wondered in what *real* nation demonstrators could seize a national treasure like CEH headquarters with impunity. A popular radio comedian joked that the demonstrators hadn't meant to loot headquarters, they'd just been wandering around downtown Port-au-Prince looking for a lost goat. The phrase "Lost Goat" soon became synonymous with all manner of electoral malfeasance.

The special representative of the secretary-general of the United

Nations issued his usual statement in times of crisis, calling on all "political stakeholders to refrain from violence and negotiate a good-faith resolution to the political crisis in accordance with the rule of law." The president of the Haitian Sénat implored the president of Haiti to suspend Parliament and impose martial law; his rival in the Sénat demanded that the president resign. Reporters sought out Etienne Brutus, *directeur générale* of the CEH, and found him at his home, where he announced from his doorstep, reading from a handwritten text, that he and his colleagues in the CEH had acted in accordance with the law. He declared Johel's accusation an assault on his honor. He called on the PNH to shoot the vagabonds, criminals, and gangsters who had "disrupted democracy." A spokesman for the United States embassy declared that it considered Haiti's electoral process "subject to Haitian law." Followers of Haitian politics understood this to mean that the embassy had no rooster in this fight. Then the embassy sent an email to all American citizens in Haiti, advising them to avoid unnecessary travel in downtown Port-au-Prince.

That afternoon, the judge spoke to the press from a conference room at the Hotel Montana. "We're a nonviolent movement," he said. "We don't have guns, we don't have knives, we don't have bombs—we've just had *enough*. Enough of the dirty tricks. Enough of these electoral games." The judge looked into the television cameras and said the phrase that would make him, in Haiti, famous: "Enough of the lost goats."

5   The special representative in Haiti of the secretary-general of the United Nations was the point man for the international community in its efforts to keep the peace in Haiti, a job, the SRSG would sometimes joke, not unlike being appointed chairman of an international committee to make soup—only the Russians wanted to make borscht, the Spanish gazpacho, the Americans chowder, the French bisque, and they didn't have much to work with but pepper, water, and ketchup. Everyone blamed him that the soup turned out lousy. Nobody asked the Haitians if they wanted soup at all.

That morning, the SRSG received a phone call from the ambassador of the United States.

"How are you, Anne?" the SRSG said.

"Frankly, Dag, I'm exhausted."

The American ambassador is expected to do one thing: she must keep Haiti out of the newspapers. That is how her tenure in Haiti will be judged. If Haiti has not made the headlines while she is ambassador, she will be considered a success. She will have succeeded if American troops are not deployed to Haiti, if Haitian refugees are not flooding the beaches of Florida, if the president of the United States is not required to trouble his busy day with Haitian affairs. This morning Haiti is in the newspapers. The Associated Press put the story on the wires: ELECTION

VIOLENCE FLARES IN HAITI. Then the story made *The New York Times*: ONGOING ELECTION VIOLENCE PARALYZES HAITIAN CAPITAL.

"He was on the phone at three in the morning. He's in a mood, Dag."

Every afternoon at the Presidential Palace is naptime. The president dresses himself in pajamas, pulls tightly shut the thick curtains, and cannot be disturbed. But he comes alive at night, pacing the long corridors of the palace. If you wish to deal with PoH, it must be done between midnight and dawn.

The SRSG's rise through the bureaucratic ranks had been lubricated by a special noise he makes. It comes from the back of his throat; it is somewhere between the sound of clearing his throat and sighing. It acknowledges the suffering of others without himself accepting any portion of the blame.

The SRSG made his special noise, and the ambassador continued.

"This can't go on," she said.

The government of the United States felt it an embarrassment, having invested so many hundreds of millions of dollars in Haitian peacekeeping and Haitian nation building, to see the headquarters of the Haitian electoral process under siege. It was a *personal* embarrassment to the secretary of state, who not two weeks earlier in congressional testimony had mentioned "continuing and ongoing progress" in Haitian reform as justification of the administration's policies in the Caribbean and Latin America.

"We are under *pressure* here, Dag."

The SRSG hung up the phone and massaged his face with his fingertips. It was indeed a delicate situation—but it was to resolve situations like this one that there were peacekeepers, after all, and diplomats, and men like the SRSG, who make special noises. On the one hand, there was the president of Haiti, who was quite correct in denouncing the illegal occupation of the headquarters of the electoral authority. On the other hand (and the SRSG knew, from long experience, there was always a countervailing hand), you had these protesters who were also quite correct. How sad it was that they couldn't vote. The tragedy of peacekeeping, he reflected, was that you are inevitably on the wrong side of someone who is in the right. Perhaps, he thought, that was the tragedy of life.

The SRSG invited Johel to lunch at his private residence in Bourdon.

I awoke around dawn to see the *marchandes* and their donkeys coming down from the hills, saddlebags stuffed with the first breadfruit and avocados of the season, or leading goats to their doom. These women were the Haiti that I loved best—indomitable, mystical, courageous. Nothing would have stopped their slow progression down the hill to market, certainly not politics: that was Port-au-Prince business, something that got the menfolk huddled around the radios all heated up. Even if Jérémie were in flames, they would have kept coming, setting up the breadfruit on a groundsheet, sitting patiently until the good Lord saw fit to send them a client.

That morning, from his pulpit in the cathedral, the bishop called for calm. As always in moments of crisis, the cathedral was full, and the bishop advised his flock to avoid those old devil twins: rage and pride. Later, the town would discuss the sermon, trying to understand the political implications. The bishop had been a prominent supporter of the Sénateur: Was he again coming to his longtime friend's assistance? Or had his speech been aimed at a narrower audience—the chief of the PNH, who took Communion from his habitual central pew? Was it a tailored message to this man alone, urging him to *break* with the Sénateur? Nobody supposed that in Haiti the Church represented God alone.

At Monsieur Brunel's *borlette* shop, there was a long line. Toussaint Legrand had told me that people were playing the lottery in record numbers that week, employing every numerological system they could devise, the numbers all originating somehow in either the name or the birth date of Johel Célestin. Then Toussaint asked me for money so that he could play the lottery himself, which I gave him.

The judge remembered something in the night, an incident from his childhood. When he was eleven and just recently arrived in America, he had been invited by a classmate, Reginald McKnight, to the public swimming pool. Johel, unusually for a Haitian kid, had learned the basic strokes in his home country, and he felt comfortable enough in the water that he could enjoy a summer's afternoon horsing around and splashing in the crowded pool. But the afternoon turned nasty when Reginald McKnight and the other kids started jumping off the high dive and the judge, not realizing how high the high dive really was, had followed the boys up to the edge of the board, stared down at the water below, and froze. Kids down below were shouting, "Jump! Go! Move your fat ass!" The situation would have been all right if Johel could have just backed up and climbed down the ladder, but he couldn't make himself do that either. That would have been humiliating. His fear of jumping and his fear of humiliation produced paralysis, and his body refused to move. He had never forgotten that sensation of being frozen on the edge of the board.

That morning, the judge no longer wanted to be the *sénateur* from the Grand'Anse. He tried to summon up the passion that had motivated him. He repeated to himself, "What we need is a road." He tried to remember that good, strong feeling back in Jérémie when the crowd was chanting his name, the way it felt when the people said "We need a man like you, Judge."

Terry was the first to see that the judge was off the reservation, mentally speaking.

"You got your game, brother?" Terry said.

The judge didn't say anything—that said everything.

"They're going to try and roll you," Terry said. "You got to get your game face on."

Still the judge didn't say anything.

"Talk to me, brother. Let me in. You can't back down now."

But the judge didn't feel that either—the connection with Terry, the way they used to feel driving down the back roads of the Grand'Anse. He wondered what Terry really wanted from him.

Later that morning, Terry drove Johel up to the residence of the SRSG, honked the horn twice, waited for the SRSG's security detail to sweep the car for explosives. Then he pulled into the long driveway leading to the large white house.

Before the judge got down from the vehicle, Terry put his hand on his forearm. The look in Terry's eyes was almost imploring. He said, "Nobody's going to do this if you don't do it."

The judge started to say something, stopped, started again.

Terry said, "My daddy used to take me out camping up in Georgia, on the shores of Lake Lanier. That's a big lake. Every spring, young birds would try and fly it."

The judge rubbed his eyes, thinking, *Young birds? Fly?*

"And the birds, not all of them understood that you get to a certain point on that lake, you got to keep flying. You get past the halfway point, it's shorter to wing it on over to the other side. Some birds don't know that, they get tired, they want to fly back where they came from. But now it's too far for them. On the way back, they fall into the lake. That's where we are now, brother. We're just about midway over that lake. And when all you see is water and your wings are tired, that ain't the time to stop flapping."

The judge was too tired to argue. He said, "Doing my best," and got out of the car.

The SRSG was waiting for him in the foyer of the house. Ceiling fans stirred breezes down long white corridors.

"It's good that you're here," the SRSG said. "I'm grateful that you've made time for me."

The SRSG was small, an elegant man, lithe and controlled. The judge noted his handsomely groomed fingernails.

"Let me show you the place," said the SRSG. The house was only a rental, but the SRSG took pride in it nevertheless. He led Johel from room to room: the drawing room, the gazebo, the music room, the dining room, on whose walls hung portraits of great Haitian statesmen. From time to time he pointed out a feature of the house—a picture on the wall, a sconce, the high arches—and the judge would nod appreciatively.

Eventually the SRSG led Johel to the dining room, where a table had been set for two.

"May I offer you a drink?" said the SRSG.

"Just water," the judge said. "If you don't mind."

"Not at all," said the SRSG. "It's certainly the easiest thing I've had to deal with in days."

The SRSG chuckled wryly, as if to suggest that the riots, the seizure of CEH headquarters, and the paralysis of the nation were only minor inconveniences. He poured the glass for Johel with his own hands, his manner suggesting that he was both humble and proud of being so. Then he invited Johel to the table, which had been set with white linen.

"I was once a political man myself," the SRSG said. "I was a candidate for the Parliament of Sweden three times."

"Did you win?"

"Let's just say I survived the experience. My wife likes to say that I'm too honest to be a politician. I lost all three times."

The judge said, "So you entered diplomacy instead."

"I have found honesty remarkably successful in my line of work. It's so rarely employed that it stuns everyone."

A waiter came in with a shrimp and avocado salad set in elegant geometrical patterns on a pair of small plates. The judge waited for the SRSG to reach for his fork, then reached for his own.

"I should thank you," said the SRSG. "There had been talk of moving into a Mission reduction phase. I suppose now we'll be able to fight that off another year. From a budgetary perspective, this couldn't have been better timed."

"You *are* honest," said the judge.

"Too honest, my wife says."

"Mine just complains that I'm too fat," said the judge.

"It sounds like she and I share the same vice of speaking our minds."

The SRSG chewed delicately and then continued.

"It's a fine balance. If this country is too peaceful, they will eliminate our Mission. And if this country is too disorderly, I will be accused of incompetence. Neither is optimal."

"Optimal for whom?"

The SRSG made his special noise, soothing, like the purring of a cat.

"For me! For me, of course! The president called me this morning. He wants to storm the CEH headquarters, and he wants logistical support from the Mission. I said, 'Mister President, allow me to achieve a peaceful resolution to this crisis.' And if I can't, I'll let him use my Brazilian APCs. Then he'll owe me something. For now he wants something from me. The Americans want this to wind down calmly, I don't know why, and now I have something to offer them also. All of this is very, very good for me."

"I see why you didn't make it in politics," said the judge.

"I'm too honest."

"These shrimp are rancid."

"You see how lovely it feels to let an honest word escape your mouth?"

"I prefer fresh shrimp to truth."

"I'll let the cook know that you weren't happy," the SRSG said.

"Be careful, or she'll put poison in your morning coffee," Johel said. "Our Haitian ladies can be temperamental."

The SRSG allowed himself a smile, but now his face grew grave. The judge had all his life felt that the world of men was divided into two categories, the serious and the frivolous, and he had endeavored always to ally himself with the serious. Now he wondered in what camp the SRSG placed him.

"You might be an honest man also," the SRSG said. "The essential thing for an honest man is to know it, and to adjust his behavior accordingly."

Johel was silent. Through the windows, he could see a garden, and in the garden, a gardener clipped roses.

"This situation cannot continue," the SRSG said.

The judge was startled to find the conversation come around so directly to essentials.

"My colleagues and I—"

"Your colleagues and you are running a foolish, grave risk. I invited you here today to tell you that you will lose. You must choose *how* you wish to lose. I say this as an honest man to another honest man."

"We have an honest grievance."

"Take your honest grievance to an honest judge, if you can find one, and win an honest verdict. Then enforce it. I didn't say that you were in the wrong—I said that you were going to lose. And it's a terrible shame if Haiti loses a man like you. I saw you on television yesterday, and I said to myself, 'Here is a man who can help this country. So full of ideas. So mature.'"

"Some might say that the place for such a man is in government," the judge said.

"Yes, if you could win an election, but they won't even allow you on the ballot. They will *never* allow you on the ballot."

"How can you be so sure of that?"

"My office is on the top floor of the Hotel Christopher. I have a view that extends to the sea—it might well be the broadest view in Port-au-Prince. Just from looking out the window, I can see whether there is smoke in Cité Soleil, if the airport is open, if the president's limousine is parked at his mistress's house, or if he has slept at home with the First Lady. And so I know before he knows himself if the president is in a good mood or a bad one."

The SRSG leaned forward. "If I could, I'd make you president of Haiti tomorrow—I would. That's how certain I am that your heart is in the right place. I think Haiti would be a better place for a man like you in power. But I don't have that power."

"I don't want to be president," said the judge.

"I know you better than you know yourself. You have a presidential heart."

"I want to build a road."

"And I thought you were an honest man."

The judge watched the gardener take a towel from his pocket and rub the sweat off his face. "What do you want from me?" he asked.

"Peace. I want you to do what you have to do, and relinquish the CEH headquarters. I want you to tell your protesters to go home. I want schools to open and the ladies to sell their mangoes and spaghetti in the markets, and I want those children to stop throwing rocks."

"And what will you do for me?"

The SRSG made his special noise. Buying rugs in Isfahan, he had found it an effective way to commence negotiations; it suggested that he was a connoisseur of rugs and well acquainted with their market values.

"We'll let you come round to our side of the desk, see the world from on high. We'll establish a commission of the best and the brightest on electoral reform, and we'll need a chairman, someone honest. The chairman will find a place on the payroll of the Mission, and his report will be submitted to a grateful president, who will use all of his powers to see that its recommendations are implemented."

"Will I be on the ballot?"

"That remains in the hands of the current, *legally constituted* authority."

The judge understood the diplomatic subterfuge.

A waiter came into the room to clear the table. He was a dead ringer,

Johel thought, for his Tonton Jean. Johel hadn't seen Tonton Jean since his bachelor party. They said that in the last few years he didn't recognize anyone, with the Alzheimer's and all. But Tonton Jean in his day would have known just what advice to give his nephew: he'd had an instinctive, canny shrewdness when giving advice to others, at sharp odds with his notorious inability to manage his own affairs. Johel studied the waiter's face as if Tonton Jean could incarnate himself in this stranger, returned to vigor across time and distance. The waiter's blank-faced stare of practiced servility gave away nothing at all, but Johel knew that this man went home to his wife and children bursting with the opinions he had concealed throughout the day, then entranced the neighbors with brilliant mimicry of the powerful men who dined in the SRSG's private dining room.

"Will you excuse me?" the judge asked the SRSG.

"To your left."

The bathroom was just down the hall, the walls decorated with paintings of women in the market. *A commission*, the judge thought. *Now that might be enough.* Enough to let everyone stand down with honor. Enough to look himself in the mirror.

The judge opened his fly and pulled out the gavel. He knew (the SRSG hadn't needed to mention it) that the money would be more than decent—and beyond this commission, there would be others. That's the way the system worked. He felt an almost giddy sense of relief. The SRSG had been right, he reckoned: he was an honest man, and truth be told, he had wanted a way out. He'd gotten himself in too deep—who knows how these things happen? Blessed be the Peacemakers, for theirs is the Kingdom—

In the otherwise immaculate toilet of the SRSG's guest bathroom there was an immense turd, eight inches of muscular excrement, tan in color, formed like a submarine, a perfect specimen.

The judge, fastidious about all things fecal, flushed the toilet. The turd rolled slightly to one side and settled back into place, a sturdy bark in unruly waters. The judge pissed into the toilet (he could hold back no longer) and flushed again; and again the turd, fine craft that she was, rode out the water's blast.

This, the judge reckoned, was the kind of turd that required breaking up. He looked for a toilet brush. There was none. Would the household staff have dared to crap in the SRSG's guest toilet? Unlikely, but surely the SRSG himself had a private toilet in which to do his business. In any case, this turd was almost as large as the SRSG himself.

The judge tried flushing the toilet a third time. The turd began to move along the toilet's floor, like a jellyfish drifting, and then disappeared from view. The judge reinserted his manhood in his pants—and the turd came swimming back into the bowl.

And the judge knew: no matter who had produced this turd, it was now his. There was no flushing away this fact: this turd was on him. No matter who was its author, he would be blamed for this turd. And tonight at the waiter's house, the neighbors would laugh as the waiter who looked like Tonton Jean told how the judge had eaten the SRSG's rich food, been made a fool of by the silver-tongued *blan*, and left behind the turd of the century for the servants to clean up.

The judge knew that only by defiance could he escape the SRSG's trap. Only by walking out now—head high, proud, independent, free—could he escape that turd's shame.

6   The next morning, very early, first sun slanting across the hotel room floor, Nadia curls naked in the judge's arms. The judge breathes in her smell. He feels her tongue, quick and agile, graze along his lip. She is weightless, like a bird. Her shallow breath. His thick hands on her smooth skin. She sighs. He slips inside her and the room is filled with yellow sunlight, so strong the judge shuts his eyes.

Afterward Nadia says, "You can't stop now."

She has been thinking, calculating. She senses the child, the precarious little thing inside of her: its presence is not yet weight, but heat. She still dreams at night about the men and the golden watch. Sometimes the Sénateur comes to her in the night, and she can feel his cool breath, hear the ticking of the watch. Sometimes Ti Pierre comes, and she can feel his heavy hands holding her down, the watch's clasp scratching her back. She sees the watch sinking in the water.

"This is all I want," the judge says. His voice is languorous.

"I know," she says. "But they won't let us stop now. There was a moment—"

"We could go back."

"To where?"

It's the same problem, the eternal problem: a passport and a visa.

"We could go away," he says.

Nadia knows from her dreams that the wheel of possibility has turned. "We can't."

"We could have everything," he says.

"Only if we win."

The judge runs his hands over her shoulders, amazed as always by the knots of marbled muscle under her smooth skin.

"You are the wave," Nadia says. "Remember what you are. The wave that sweeps and washes clean the shore."

The judge thinks, *Or breaks, crashes, and is heard no more.*

The airport was closed, and Kay was trapped in Jérémie until it opened again. So, at my invitation, she dropped by the Sénateur's mother's house daily, sometimes having breakfast with my wife and me, sometimes spending a quiet hour in the afternoon reading and dozing in the hammock, and almost every evening, eating with us.

I admired Kay's courage. She never came by the house unless she was carefully groomed, with a bright, false smile on her painted lips. One day she made us a cake, and the next day she spent the morning chopping fruit to produce a salad. Jérémie had remained more or less tranquil throughout the crisis, but there had been a few moments of disorder: the day before, a few dozen of the judge's supporters, inspired by the events in Port-au-Prince, had decided to seize city hall. They had been rebuffed by the police with tear gas. Kay nevertheless came zipping up the hill to our house on a motorcycle taxi.

"If I stay home and just stare at the walls, I'll go insane," she said.

My wife had just left for work, and Kay and I decided to make a second pot of coffee.

"Terry told me they're almost out of money," she said.

"You guys are talking?"

"We're *texting*," she said. "Andrés Richard told them he's not paying for anything else until he sees some results. Terry said that Johel came out of the meeting with the SRSG all fired up. But last night he started talking about sending everyone home. Then he started shivering and vomiting and saying he couldn't breathe."

"Maybe it's over," I said.

"I wouldn't mind if it were."

The coffee was ready. By now Kay was comfortable enough in the house that she said, "I'll get it." She went into the kitchen and came back out to the terrace with two cups. She even knew how much sugar I liked.

"You know who I just don't get?" I said. "Like the person in this story who I can't figure out?"

"She thinks he's going to take her away."

"No, that's not who I meant. I know what *she's* thinking. I meant you."

Kay smiled, as if she had been complimented. "What do you mean?"

"I can't figure out how a sensible woman like yourself got mixed up in a mess like this."

She sipped her coffee.

"I wish we had ice," she said.

"They say cold drinks just make you hotter. In the tropics—"

"You do it for the money," she said.

The word "money," when Kay said it, was like the kiss of a woman one has long desired. It was something serious and exciting. It made you nervous.

I said, "I thought you wanted to build the road and sell mangoes and fish and—"

"Maybe that's how it started, but those two win this election, there's so many things we can do."

"You think?" I said.

"You might be the only person in Haiti who doesn't think so. My God, we're sitting on some of the most lucrative real estate in the Caribbean. Everyone knows what this is all about."

"Even Terry?" I asked.

Kay stood up and walked over to the little mirror that hung on the wall. She stared at her reflection, fixing her hair and wiping away a smudge of dirt.

She said, "Terry likes to tell himself a lot of stories, I guess all men do. Women are different—we have to be, we have to live with you people. A man will tell himself he's building a road. Or saving an orphan from a burning building. Or whatever the hell he's doing with that woman. And if the story is good enough, a man will tell himself it's okay to go to bed at night. But truth is, men don't have a clue. Terry doesn't even know why he gets out of bed in the morning. But I sure know why *I* do."

At the hotel, Terry and Nadia get the judge dressed and walking. Maybe around the second pot of coffee he's roaring like a lion. He's sloughing off the doubts like old skin. He had the idea in the shower, comes bursting out of the bathroom wearing nothing but a towel.

"I don't need to see that, brother," Terry says.

"What do you think—"

"I think you should get that thing covered."

"We're going to walk to the CEH."

CEH headquarters is still being held by the loose coalitions of thugs, students, and paid protesters, maybe a hundred young men holed up in there. Every hour, every day a few are drifting out the back stairs.

What the judge is proposing is a march from the Presidential Palace right to CEH headquarters, carrying boxes of food and supplies for the Democracy Warriors (the phrase came to the judge in the shower) holed up inside. Then the judge will give a speech, right out the window of the CEH, to a crowd of demonstrators assembled in the street below.

He's on the phone, and by early afternoon there are two thousand men and women ready to march. This is the last of their money, on the street. There are drums and a pickup truck packed with loudspeakers. And walking slowly, at the head of the march, is the judge, microphone in hand.

It doesn't matter what Johel says, because no one can hear him over the roar of the crowd.

The press is there, both the Haitian press and the international press: at the start of the riots, there were a handful of foreign reporters; now there are more than a dozen, mainly photographers, some print, couple of camera crews. It's nice to shoot Haiti in a crisis—just four hours from New York, two from Miami. Especially in cold weather up north it's a good gig: you can shoot civil unrest in the day and drink rum sours at night poolside at the Hotel Oloffson. Rumor has it that the correspondent for CNN has a Haitian lover—he's been down since day two of the crisis, doing stand-ups in front of the Presidential Palace, wearing a bulletproof vest and helmet.

Nobody wants a peaceful protest. The journalists can't sell pictures of a peaceful protest, and if the journalists can't sell pictures, what is the point of protesting? The Nigerian riot police backed by Brazilian soldiers don't want peace: If there is peace, what are they there for? The kids in the crowd have been paid to throw rocks. The PNH have been paid to fire back tear gas.

The procession turns onto the rue des Miracles, and the PNH fire a barrage of tear gas, the projectiles rising and falling the distance of a city block in long, parabolic arcs, beautiful and deadly, then releasing on contact with the ground thick clouds of silver-gray poison.

Tear gas is an insidious weapon because it preys on two of the body's most powerful defensive instincts. The first is to hyperventilate when panicked, and the second is to move quickly away from danger. Moving quickly causes one to breathe still more deeply, and in this way inhale still more of the gas. Lungs register the gas most immediately and provoke the first sensation of panic, but it is the exposed skin of the face and hands that causes the most intense pain, like dipping your face into boiling water, every bit as terrifying as the initial realization that the air you are breathing has been poisoned.

The photographers dart forward into the gas, many of them prepared for just this eventuality with gas masks of their own.

Johel felt the tear gas and began to die. The world tilted and swirled. The pain took him to a place beyond thought: he felt his skin slough off his bones, his heart explode, his lungs shred into a thousand jagged edges. Pain traveled from his eyes to his brain on nerves he had never before known existed. He could not move, he could not breathe. His great bulk settled on his knees.

Then the world went black.

Those watching Johel saw him collapse, then rise again. But Johel was gone. The riot police of the PNH firing tear gas projectiles and the protesters alike knew that Ogoun the warrior was in their midst. Ogoun rose to his feet, now taller than Johel had ever stood. He surveyed the scene with the cool of a veteran to whom battle is the natural condition of man. Ogoun felt the pain but felt no pain, knowing that to a soldier pain is only a distraction. At his feet a projectile canister leaked its deadly gas. Ogoun picked up the hot metal tube and considered it, then tossed it imperiously aside. *"Grains mwem fret!"* he cried. My balls are cold! This was his way of announcing that the battle had been well and truly joined.

And because courage is infectious, it takes only one such person to render an entire crowd, which would otherwise have been thoroughly dominated by tear gas, immune to the effects of the drug. Seeing Ogoun move in slow time away from the riot police, the crowd marched again.

Johel would later remember none of this.

7 Senator Charles Oxblood, Democrat of Florida, chairman of the Senate Appropriations Committee Subcommittee on Foreign Aid, keeps a papier-mâché lion's head on the wall of his office. He acquired it on his honeymoon in Haiti, thirty years back. Those two weeks made Haiti an area of sentimental interest to him—but no senator from Florida could afford to ignore Haiti, any more than a senator from Florida could ignore Cuba. What did they say in the cloakroom? "Our esteemed friend from the Caribbean." Let them laugh. He is the most powerful man in Haiti, although, of course, he is not *in* Haiti.

The senator likes to say, when it comes to Haiti, that he's done what he can. At town hall meetings with constituents, questions about Haiti come up (and they do come up, this being Florida) and the senator ticks off his accomplishments on his fingers. The USAID budget comes out of his committee, and he makes sure that Haiti has not been overlooked. The senator was instrumental in passing favorable trade tariffs for Haiti. The United States pays a hefty chunk of the cost of the Mission, and there are members who'd see that budget whacked, but few are eager to wrangle with Senator Oxblood over the matter. State is forever trying to slip out of the Oxblood rule, the complicated series of vetting regulations that the senator has enshrined in American law to ensure that taxpayer dollars don't fund drug traffickers or human rights abusers, but the senator does his best to rein State in. His committee holds regular hearings on Haitian affairs, and when he can, he schedules a fact-finding trip down there.

Still, when Senator Oxblood considers the work his subcommittee has done on Haiti over the years, if the conversation is private and his mood is mellow, he'll tell you that it doesn't seem to have done much good. He wonders if they've been on the right track at all. Haiti has broken the senator's heart a dozen times over the years. Every year that country seems to get poorer, every year it seems like there's some kind of damn riot in the streets—who can keep track of it all anymore? The senator sometimes felt that when it came to that country, twenty years of hard work had just been turning around in a circle.

Destiny comes for the judge and Senator Oxblood on the front page of the print edition of *The New York Times*. Senator Oxblood still reads the *Times* in print, being a man of a certain age. Nobody had planned for this, could have planned this. Destiny is on assignment in Haiti, shooting a story on deforestation for *National Geographic*, trapped in the Hotel Oloffson by the riots. Destiny is bored and gets a day rate from the *Times* to shoot the disorder. Destiny's photo is one of those miracles of composition and storytelling, a photo so compelling that the editors at the *Times* agree there is no place for it but above the fold, A-1. Destiny is a photograph of a little boy carrying an honest-to-god white dove, the boy cowering in fear as three policemen with gas masks come at him with batons. Over the boy's shoulder is the huge banner the protesters have hung on the looted building: DEMOCRACY IN HAITI NOW.

Senator Oxblood sees Destiny's photograph as he drinks his morning coffee with Madame Oxblood. There is a power in a perfect photograph like nothing else. The flower of anger blossoms in the senator's soul. Manipulated elections. Corruption. Sometimes the senator wonders what the hell the point of it is if he can't do some good now and again. The damn country can't catch a break. Ivy League–educated reformer illegally eliminated by a drug-trafficking socialist—and guess what side of the fence the pussies at State were on. Nothing enrages Senator Oxblood quite like the pussies at State. Secretary of Pussy. Undersecretary of Pussy. Department of Pussy. Same as it ever was.

Had life meted out its rewards in proportion to talent, Etienne Brutus would not have been the *directeur générale* of the CEH, responsible for the integrity of Haitian democracy, a burden that would have crippled a far more competent man. Strangers would not have approached him on the street and begun to *bah*.

No, had life slotted Etienne Brutus into the role he was meant to play in the vast drama of Haitian life, he would have been sous-chef in a hotel kitchen: not creative enough to set the menu nor charismatic enough to lead, but competent with a knife, a man who followed orders gladly and was willing to work hard. In addition, he was passionate about sauces. His ability to produce a decent meal was one of precisely three things in which he took pride; the others were his loyalty to his patron, the president of Haiti, and the umbrella of loving protection he offered his three sons.

Etienne Brutus's career had been facilitated by his late wife's cousin, now the president of Haiti. On her premature deathbed, Madame Brutus had exacted a vow from her husband—that he would not touch another drop of liquor until the last of their boys had completed his education—and she exacted a reciprocal vow from her cousin, that he would facilitate the boys' rise in society. Neither man dared violate a promise to the dead. And so it was that this mild, colorless, sober figure rose under the president's tutelage through diverse bureaucratic ranks, displaying himself always the most loyal of servants. He had been the president's man in the Ministry of Finance, in the Ministry of Ports, and in the Ministry of Agriculture. Now he was head of the CEH, the other members selected by him with the same attention to obedience that he offered the president. He had accepted the Sénateur's bribe only after confirming that his action in no way displeased his patron. The president liked Sénateur Bayard and so permitted the transaction to proceed— although if the president or DG Brutus had been asked to identify the judge in a photo array or to explain in what way the judge offended electoral law, both men would have been at a loss.

The object of the DG's labors, and the proximate cause of his corruption, was the education of his three sons. Enrico, the eldest, was now in his second year of medical school at Stanford, while Luciano, the middle boy, slender and intellectual, had been accepted at Swarthmore. The youngest boy, fourteen-year-old Placido, showed promise as an oboist and attended a Florida music academy. Etienne Brutus thought about school fees and tuition very nearly every waking moment. The DG began each day by telephoning all three boys in succession and then in the evening called them again.

All three boys were in the United States on student visas.

At 11:14 the judge receives a call from Senator Oxblood. He retires to the bedroom, closes the door behind him.

At 11:36 Johel walks back into the room.

He looks at Terry, sitting in the chair by the window; at Nadia, sitting on the couch.

"Well?" Terry says.

The judge doesn't say anything. His face is cadaverous, sober. He walks into the bathroom. Terry can hear water running. Terry looks at Nadia: she is staring at a point on the wall. Terry doesn't see where this is going to go now. There is no higher court of appeal than Oxblood— the ultimate arbiter. The judge is out. Terry starts to wonder what's going to happen to him and Nadia now, him and Kay now. His Mission is over.

Nadia is thinking of a place in the mountains where she likes to go, a little spring and brook. There the ladies from the village wash clothes and tell stories about the men they've loved. She's thinking of the golden watch glinting in the streambed, of bathing the baby in the cold, sparkling waters. Now there's no place else to go.

The judge comes back into the room. His face is gleaming with water.

"You want to know the strangest thing?" he says. "It turns out that Charles Oxblood's kid was once the Florida state spelling champion. He competed for the national title and lost. That's what we talked about for twenty minutes—what a thrill that was."

"That's all?" said Terry.

"You can't imagine what that is for a young kid, that kind of attention."

"A lot of pressure, too," said Terry.

"All those lights, all those people—you'd forget how to spell your own name."

"Especially if you spell it all weird, the way you do."

Johel puts on his tie. He's a Windsor man. Only when the knot is centered on his shirt does he turn back to Terry and Nadia.

He says, "He's making a statement at noon. It's already prepared."

"C'est vrai?" says Nadia.

"And he's going to write a letter to State."

"How did you do that?"

The judge smiles, all teeth.

At twelve o'clock, as promised, the office of Senator Oxblood released the text of his letter to the secretary of state:

The Honorable Secretary of State
Department of State
Washington, DC 20520

Dear Madam Secretary:

When I was in Haiti recently, I heard many people remark that the Haitian people deserve a government that cares more about the people than about itself. I could not agree more. As if Haiti did not have enough problems, now, once again, those in power there are trying to subvert the will of the people.

The Haitian Electoral Council's unexplained exclusion of fifteen legitimate candidates from parliamentary races is alarming. Haiti's future depends on a Parliament that is recognized as legitimate. Given the support the United States has provided to the government and people of Haiti in this election and the failure to promptly remedy this apparent fraud, I am writing to urge the department to take appropriate steps to convey our concern. By suspending direct aid to the central government and visas for top officials and their immediate family members, the United States would be sending that message. It is critical that the outcome of the electoral process is recognized as free and fair by the international community and, most important, by the Haitian people.

The United States must come down squarely in support of the Haitian people's right to choose their leaders freely and fairly.

Thank you for your consideration.

Sincerely,

Charles Oxblood
Chairman
State and Foreign Operations Subcommittee

The SRSG was in his office that afternoon when the ambassador called. He was not displeased to hear from her. He enjoyed the sound of her voice; had she been a younger woman, he might have courted her.

"Anne, what a pleasant surprise," he said.

The ambassador had a womanly laugh, and she knew the effect it had on men. It was her secret weapon. It was somewhere between a giggle and a moan: it suggested a hidden reservoir of pleasure.

"Dag, you've seen the way things are going," she said.

"To my surprise—and at my age, I very rarely say that."

"Chuck Oxblood has taken an interest, it seems."

"I wish he hadn't."

"I'll grant you that it's unfortunate, Dag, but that's the world we live in."

She told the SRSG that she has had her staff prepare a list of visas for suspension. The secretary of state needed something to show Senator Oxblood as soon as possible.

"It's budget time in Washington. We're not going to cross the chairman on this one. If it matters to him—"

She let the sentence dangle.

"And what can I do for you, Anne?"

But he knew the answer to his own question. The embassy wanted him to talk to DG Brutus. They wanted his fingerprints on the knife protruding from DG Brutus's back. And what choice did the SRSG have, really? You can't cross State and aspire one day to be deputy secretary-general of the United Nations. That simply isn't realistic.

The SRSG called around sunset with an offer: DG Brutus had agreed to "review" the exclusions if Johel would get his guys out of CEH headquarters. The embassy would hold off on suspending his sons' student visas.

It was Nadia who insisted that they go out dancing, Johel and Terry both being steak-and-a-bottle-of-wine kind of guys. But she winked and pouted at both of them until they relented. They ended up at one of the big dance halls in Pétionville. Nadia danced first with Terry and then with Johel as the threesome drank their way steadily through a bottle of Barbancourt. Everyone in the club recognized Johel. His appearances on television had made him famous, and all night long, strangers came up to him and offered him a drink or clapped him on the shoulder or asked if he'd found his "lost goat."

While Johel circulated through the crowd, Nadia danced with Terry. She felt as light in his arms as a sparrow, but a childhood spent hauling water had given her shoulders and back a surprising hardness. He stood half a head taller, and he could brush her hair, arranged in cornrows, with his chin. He could feel her small breasts press against him, and her dress seemed to his hands as if it were made of gossamer: he took pleasure in the warmth of her body through the fabric. He had never wanted a woman more. He said, "I love you." He had never said this to her before, but as soon as the words escaped his lips, he knew it was the truth. He wasn't sure if Nadia heard him over the loud music, but she seemed to press her fragile body closer to his, as if in response. He thought that after the election, anything was possible.

Inspired by the moment, he kissed her. She reared back, beestung. "He's not looking," Terry said, and he tried to kiss her again. She writhed in his arms, and Terry realized that she was serious, that she would not kiss him. The mood was broken. Terry could see in Nadia's green eyes reproach and contempt. His high emotions were like a bubble, as quick to explode as to expand. All the drama and the tension of the long week settled on his shoulders. He wanted to sleep.

But the judge didn't want to leave the club. Soon Terry and Nadia were seated at a table with the judge and a half dozen other men, beefy men with bad skin, gold chains, and expensive wristwatches. Terry knew some of these men by name. They were members of the Port-au-Prince political world: a couple of deputies from up north, and a man who worked in the prime minister's office. Terry's Creole wasn't good enough to understand the conversation, which came to him as isolated words floating through the loud music. Terry understood that in these men's eyes, he was the judge's pet *blan*. He wondered whether it had been worth all the struggle: maybe Johel was just another Haitian politician. Terry watched couples dancing, their laughing faces like masks. Loneliness assaulted him with a violence that was almost physical. His life, he thought, had amounted to nothing: he had built nothing, made nothing, begat no one. He wondered, should he disappear tomorrow from the planet, whether anyone would truly mourn him.

Then he felt a pressure on his thigh. It was Nadia's hand. Her face gave nothing away: it stared into the distance, pretty and impassive. He could see Johel's face, fat and shiny with sweat, laughing at some joke, exulting in his triumph. Someone slapped Johel on the back. Terry sipped his drink, melted ice and lemon juice and sweet, thick rum.

8 I took Kay to the airport the next morning, the first flight out
   of Jérémie in a week.
      "I don't want to see him," Kay said when she learned that
Terry and Johel were coming back from Port-au-Prince that evening.

"Then you should go home," I said.

"And do what?"

We sat under the sign that read BIENVENUE À JÉRÉMIE. LA CITÉ
DES POÈTES, and watched the *marchandes* sell spiky-headed pineapples,
immense grapefruit, finger bananas, and oversweet mandarins. You
would never have known driving through Jérémie that morning that
there had been any disorder at all, except for the Uruguayan APCs
parked at aggressive angles to the street in front of Mission headquarters.

"I guess I lost," Kay said with a brave, unhappy chuckle.

"Don't think about it that way."

"How should I think about it? I came to Haiti with a husband and a
dream, and I'm going home—"

"That's how you should think about it. You're going home."

Kay offered me a banana. Then she peeled one of her own.

"Are you going to miss me?" she said.

"Of course."

"Well, I'm going to miss you."

We might have gone back and forth like this had my phone not rung. Kay saw me glancing at it and said, "Go on."

I let it ring—it seemed the least I could do—but as soon as it was done ringing, it rang again.

This time I did answer it. It was Marie Legrand, Toussaint's mother. I couldn't understand a word she was saying. It was as if she were falling from a very high place. Finally I understood what she was telling me.

Nadia, Johel, and Terry drove back that day from Port-au-Prince. They left the city after breakfast, the three of them hungover. Between them, they'd slept no more than a dozen hours.

It took a couple of hours to get out of town, crawling through downtown and past the Martissant slum, then through Carrefour, the traffic tight. This stretch of road leading out of Port-au-Prince was as nasty a corner of the planet as any Terry had ever seen: tin-roofed shacks festering in sun-scorched chaos all the way to the sea. Nadia dozed in the backseat while the judge and Terry nudged their way through town, no one talking.

But when they got on the open road, the judge slapped his thigh and said, "Holy shit." Terry and Nadia understood: they were warriors coming home from battle, and they'd won. Soon Andrés Richard called, congratulating Johel. Then Père Samedi. In the light of day, the judge's victory was an even more amazing accomplishment than it had seemed the night before. Terry knew that even Nadia had been caught up in the dream. When they stopped to buy gas in Les Cayes, a small crowd gathered around the pump, all of them wanting to see the judge or shake his hand.

Terry could see Nadia's eyes in the rearview mirror. It made him happy to be so close to her. He felt as if the two of them could speak with no words, his sighs sufficient to tell her that he loved her, her glances in the mirror enough to let Terry know that she was proud.

The night before, Kay had called him. She told him that she was headed home.

"I think that's for the best," Terry said.

"There's still time for you to come too," Kay said.

That Kay would even suggest such a thing—that's how little faith in him she had. The trip to Port-au-Prince had been *his* plan; *his* force of will had animated their adventure. It was strange to Terry that Nadia understood so much more clearly the dimensions of his soul than his own wife.

They had been driving all morning, Terry and Johel switching places behind the wheel, when Johel's phone rang.

Rumors, like fire, drift in subterranean currents until exploding promiscuously: some had known for days that there was a dead boy lying behind the market, and others knew that he had died in the riots, hit in the chest by a tear gas grenade, and still others whispered that the PNH had taken his body and thrown it behind the market, where the pigs gathered. Then everyone knew about the dead boy who was lying in the field, until eventually the *juge de paix* heard the story, came to the market, and ordered the cadaver transported to the morgue, where the attendants rifled through his pockets, found his phone, and called his mother, wanting to know if she knew what everyone knew, that Toussaint was dead.

I went with Madame Legrand to retrieve Toussaint's body from the morgue. She owed morgue fees for the three days they'd held him.

They hadn't done much for him in the morgue. You sure wouldn't want your mother to see you like that. It was just a concrete box with three dead people on the floor, and one of them was Toussaint. He was lying on the stained concrete floor, facedown, butt in the air, no shirt, blue jeans down around his hips, no underwear. His chest had been bruised by the force of the projectile, but the thing that got your eye wasn't the wounds, it was Toussaint's ass, hanging out in the air. What the dead don't have is any dignity.

Madame Legrand looked at her son. I thought for a moment that she was going to vomit or faint, but she just stood there trembling, as if she were very cold. We watched Toussaint for a long time, both of us waiting for him to move, but he didn't, not so much as a twitch. The room smelled of decomposing flesh and Lightning. Then we walked into the morgue attendant's little office.

"He's mine," Madame Legrand said. "He's my child."

The morgue attendant was fiddling with a pencil, trying to figure out the secrets of the lottery. It was all in the numbers, and he was adding and subtracting long columns. He looked up from his work and said, "You got to give him a good funeral now."

"I didn't know that," Madame Legrand said.

The morgue attendant scratched at the paper, wrote some more.

"You can't leave him here," he said.

"It's the first child I lost," she explained.

"You'll lose them all."

"All of them?"

"Even if you have ten, they'll all come here."

"All ten?"

"A good funeral's what you need."

"Did you lose your children?" she asked.

"Not yet."

"Who killed my child?"

Madame Legrand took a step toward the morgue attendant. I guess the numbers were getting somewhere, because it took him a couple of minutes before he answered.

"I didn't see, I didn't hear."

Madame Legrand said, "It's not my child who's dead. Don't you tell me my child is dead."

He looked up, looked down again at his papers. "Madame, you go see. It's you who tells me your child is lying there."

"It's not Toussaint. It's not Toussaint who's lying there."

She was angry now. But the morgue attendant only said, "Go see. I got work to do."

Madame Legrand went back into the morgue. I was still standing there when we heard her cry out. The morgue attendant just kept adding up rows and rows of numbers, crossing some out, subtracting others.

———

There was to have been a celebration for the judge on the Place Dumas when he came back into town, but with Toussaint dead, that had been canceled. In any case, Toussaint would have organized it and hired the paid supporters, who would have cheered and danced until the judge rolled up his shirtsleeves and gave a speech.

The judge, Terry, and Nadia rolled into town late that evening, all three exhausted. The road had been brutal. A bus had broken an axle near the Rivière Glace, where the route was narrow, and they'd had to sit by the side of the car until a mechanic from Les Cayes could weld the axle in place, four hours of waiting in the hot sun. Then, an hour later, their own car had a flat. Terry had fixed it, cursing under his breath, while Nadia and Johel sat side by side on a rock, staring at him.

Back in the car, not even the judge wanted to talk. Terry could hear him muttering under his breath.

"What are you saying?" Terry finally asked.

The judge looked at Terry, startled. "Who?"

"You. You've been talking to yourself for an hour."

The judge smiled. "He told me he wanted to be a poet."

After a minute Terry said, "What he told me was that he was going to be a neurosurgeon."

It didn't seem right to the judge to laugh, but he couldn't help himself.

The sound of the men's laughter irritated Nadia. She wanted to tell them to be quiet, but her own voice wouldn't come. She had met Toussaint only once. He had come by the house to drop off the judge's motorcycle at the conclusion of one of his scouting missions, and they had ended up talking for an afternoon. When he learned that she sang with Galaxy and had sung with a famous band like Erzulie L'Amour, he admitted his own ambition, to one day be a musician himself. He knew the region, if not the village, that she came from, and they were able to exchange stories about a dozen or more local personages. Toussaint reminded Nadia of her own older brother, another skinny layabout big talker with a charming smile. She had wanted that afternoon to warn Toussaint. She had wanted to tell him to stay away from the judge.

It was a moonless night. The headlights of the car lit up only the short stretch of bad road ahead, and looking out the window, Nadia could see nothing of the hills through which they traveled. She had never lost her girlhood fear of the dark. Soon she was aware that she was hardly breathing. She had heard stories as a child of the *loup-garou*: the neighbor who shed his humanity at sunset to steal a feast of children. The *loup-garou* might be your neighbor, your friend. The *loup-garou* had come for Toussaint.

She could hear the judge's voice and then Terry's. It occurred to her that she and the baby she carried were at their mercy. She imagined them looking back at her, their eyes bright red, fangs elongated; she wondered how she would defend herself if they came for her. She felt the child inside her, still not strong enough to kick, but rolling weight. Nadia felt her body pitch forward and sway backward. They were descending the final hills before the bridge over the Grand'Anse. Now they were in Jérémie.

PART SEVEN

PART SEVEN

1 On his first morning back from Port-au-Prince, the judge called his staff one by one, asking them to meet him at his campaign headquarters. There had been some doubt the night before whether he would even continue the campaign in Toussaint's absence. Johel himself had considered dropping out of the race.

But that morning, still sore from the road, he had awoken early and sat on his back porch as the first sun lit up the town. He heard a chorus of children singing at the Baptist church, their song faint at first, and then louder as the music caught on the wind and echoed through the town's bowls and canyons. He had never heard singing at this early hour, and he sat up straighter in his chair. Soon the choir sang the Haitian national anthem. It was vigorous music, expressing all the martial energy of a great warrior people. *"Marchons unis, marchons unis,"* the choir sang. For a moment Johel imagined his enslaved forebears rising up to fight the *blan*, dying, and with each death encouraging a dozen like-minded patriot souls. The swelling of young voices in the apricot light of dawn stiffened his resolve.

Later that morning, when his campaign staff was assembled, Johel told the crew of students, professionals, and lawyers of his emotions as he listened to the stirring verse. His obvious sincerity inspired in his staff similar feelings. Even Terry, who did not understand the lyrics of the song, was moved, and he rose with everyone else when the judge suggested that they sing the anthem in Toussaint's honor. Toussaint's friends and colleagues placed their hands over their hearts and promised to form ranks for the country and the flag. The anthem had a special meaning to each of them that day. There was no thought of retreat. They sang, *"Mourir est beau, mourir est beau / Pour le Drapeau, pour la Patrie."* When they were finished, the room was silent, as if they had all taken a solemn oath.

Then Nadia spoke. She had surprised her husband, who had supposed that she would be intimidated by this crowd of fast-talking, educated young people, by insisting on attending the strategy session. Then she surprised him still more.

"We have to bury him right," she said. "We won't get another moment like this one."

Nadia understood that the way to win a heart was to tell a story, and that the funeral was like a stage that would attract an audience of ten thousand or more, all of them eager to see the patriot's body. She told the men that Toussaint's flag-draped coffin could say more than the judge's words and that in each of Madame Legrand's tears there would be a thousand votes.

The suggestion shocked the judge.

"Should I take his shirt and pants too?" the judge said. "The boy is dead. Let's bury him in peace."

"You don't understand how a dead man thinks," Nadia said.

"And you do?"

"I know he fought for you when he was alive, and you won't fight for him when he's dead."

"What does his mother want?" asked the judge.

"She wants to bury him right."

That afternoon Nadia went to sit beside Marie Legrand in the bereft woman's hut. Nadia rocked her body in sympathetic rhythm to Madame Legrand, the women crying together. Nadia told Madame Legrand that the judge wanted to put Toussaint in the ground with all due respect.

Madame Legrand's tears subsided.

"The boy loved his mother," she said.

"He was a fine child," Nadia said.

"The boy always worried how his family would eat."

"We need to send him home right."

"Will Juge Blan take care of us now?" asked Madame Legrand. "That's the way Toussaint would want it."

The two women, both veterans of the *marché*, understood each other. A Haitian funeral is expensive, and nothing brings more honor to a woman than burying her son right.

Toussaint's death and burial would never have been a significant political or social occasion had the judge himself not acquired such notoriety over the course of the last weeks. He had gone to Port-au-Prince, confronted the *blan*, and come home a hero.

The next day, the judge, as he did most every morning, went on foot to buy fresh *cabiche*. He enjoyed eating the hot rolls spread thickly with homemade peanut butter. Soon the *boulangerie* was overwhelmed with a quickly growing crowd, all pushing and shoving to get closer to him. Women wanted to touch his face. The shouting of the crowd was too loud to allow the judge to speak, and eventually he had to call Terry to come and get him.

Then, that afternoon, there was a scary moment. The judge was in his office when one of his students received a call from an acquaintance in Camp-Perrin. A black SUV had stopped there on its way to Jérémie, the caller said, with four men inside, heavily armed. The story soon spread that the men were on their way to Jérémie to assassinate the judge, and Terry attempted to convince him that he should take refuge for the day on the grounds of the Uruguayan military base, where he would be surrounded by machine-gun nests, watchtowers, and barbed wire.

"Not going to happen," Johel said.

"Just for a day, buddy," Terry said. "Until we figure out what's going on."

"No man walks who can stop us."

"That's fine, but these folks are in a car."

Johel looked at Terry, and Terry knew there was no use arguing the point further.

That evening, *a brigade vigilance* met the black SUV at the bridge over the Grand'Anse. The four men inside the vehicle, flustered by the large crowd that surrounded them, explained that they had flown in from New York the day before. The car was a rental. They were tourists, members of the Haitian diaspora, on their way to visit family in Dame

Marie. Two of the four men barely spoke Creole. All were unarmed, and none of them had ever heard the name Johel Célestin.

The bishop of the Grand'Anse made his political affiliations clear by agreeing to conduct Toussaint's obsequies in the cathedral. On the morning of the funeral, the Place Dumas was overwhelmed by mourners. They came from every corner of the Grand'Anse, many on foot, still others by the fleet of buses the judge had chartered, those tough old yellow school buses, long retired from hauling American children, that found a second life on the battered Haitian roads.

There was, however, a problem that the judge had not been able to overcome. He had hired on Madame Legrand's behalf a private morgue to hold the body and prepare it for burial. But the PNH refused to release the body, claiming that the criminal investigation into Toussaint's death required an autopsy. There were, however, neither forensic pathologists in the Grand'Anse nor facilities to autopsy a corpse, and it was widely assumed that the chief of police was acting on behalf of the Sénateur, who wished to forestall the political rally that the funeral would entail.

Johel had been negotiating now for three days to obtain the body, but on the morning of the funeral, the crowds already massing, the body still lay under lock and key at the Bon Repos. The family had not been admitted to wash the body and dress it and pray over it. The judge had presumed that the urgency of the funeral would cause the PNH to relent, but instead, battle lines had hardened as the chief of the PNH, declaring that the law came before tears, threatened with impeccable logic to burn the body in the courtyard of the commissariat rather than release it under blackmail.

There was an additional complication: the Sénateur himself was back in town. An old political hand, he announced that he was going to kick off *his* own campaign with a massive rally on the day of the funeral. At the very hour that the judge was going to bury Toussaint, he was going to be roasting pigs and serving them with mountains of rice and beans. He suggested slyly on Radio Vision 2000 that in grief and sorrow, nothing was more important than a good meal.

Things boiled over in the early afternoon. The crowd had been waiting

a long time in the hot sun for the funeral to start. Crowds are temperamental beasts, and when it was well past lunch, the mourners, who had
all set out that morning in the earnest, peaceful, and reflective mood
that accompanies the burial of a young man, started getting antsy. When
someone on the fringe of the crowd was accused of being a supporter of
the Sénateur, it took the efforts of half a dozen strong men to break up
the fight.

The judge was still working the phones at campaign HQ, trying to
get Toussaint's body so that he could eulogize the defunct, when one of
his students rushed in, waving his hands wildly and babbling insanely.
Johel couldn't understand a word. "Go *look*," the student finally said.

From the upstairs balcony of campaign headquarters, we could see
the crowd moving and slithering around. Someone said, "Oh my!" and
the judge said, "Holy shit." Toussaint Legrand was crowd-surfing
across the Place. The crowd had broken into the Bon Repos and stolen
his corpse. You couldn't really tell if he was alive or dead, because someone in the crowd had his head and others were holding on to his feet.
He was dressed in the clothes he had died in, jeans and his favorite
Barcelona jersey.

Now, crowds don't make decisions the way individuals do, but decisions are made, and the crowd decided first to parade around the Place
Dumas with Toussaint. Then they did that again. Now that they were in
possession of the body, the crowd seemed good-natured again, chanting
slogans and dancing happily.

Then someone in the crowd got the bright idea to combine the two
events of the day and take Toussaint's body to the Sénateur's rally, perhaps because it was well past lunch, and no funeral being evident, a lot of
folks were thinking they'd like some pig. Crowds can move with strange
speed: Toussaint's body was around the corner and gone in an instant,
and Terry, the judge, Nadia, and I were left staring at the nearly empty
Place Dumas. Even Nadia, who prided herself on being surprised by
nothing, was shaking her head. I supposed that when the Sénateur's
pig-eaters and Toussaint's funeral cortege met up, it was going to be
trouble. I heard the wail of sirens.

But the two crowds intermingled peacefully. By the time I got down
there, you couldn't tell who was for the Sénateur and who was for the

judge. There was good music playing and pig being eaten and beer being drunk, and because nobody quite knew what to do with Toussaint at that point, they had him up on the dais, slouched in a chair, where he had a strange smile on his face, like he had finally met a lady. Neither the Sénateur nor the judge gave a speech that day.

2 I was reading in bed when the phone rang. The judge said something, and I said, "I was about to." He spoke some more, and I
said, "It's fine."

My wife said, "Who is it?" but fell back asleep before I could answer.

I lay for a while in the dark, listening to the high whine of frustrated
mosquitoes on the far side of the mosquito net. I had been expecting a
call like this for a long time. Then I went downstairs, where Johel was
already waiting for me on the terrace.

I hadn't seen the judge in person since Toussaint's funeral, although
his face, on campaign posters plastered on every flat surface in town,
had become omnipresent. Since the funeral he had been campaigning
fiercely, holding rallies, sometimes two in a day, in every corner of the
region.

"This campaign is kicking your ass," I said.

"It's work, brother, hard work."

He looked terrible. His eyes were red and his skin had the washed-
out, bloodless gray of dark men who haven't slept well.

"Drink?" I asked.

"Whatever you've got," he said.

I poured a shot of rum for the judge and one for myself. Then we
sat in silence for a few minutes. I was hoping he had got me out of bed
to talk about an attractive low-risk investment opportunity. He exhaled

slowly, stretched his neck, cracked his knuckles, and rubbed his eyes. He was in a torment of embarrassment.

"I want to know why Kay left," he said.

My heart quickened. I've always felt honesty a severely overvalued virtue. I could see no advantage to it in the present instance.

"She told me her mother was sick."

"Why didn't she tell me?"

"Maybe she thought you had enough on your plate."

"Terry told me that her father was sick."

"He's married to her. He knows more about her family than I do."

The judge's eyes wandered to the edge of the terrace, then back to me. He decided to take a different approach.

"What do you think about Terry?"

"Seems decent enough," I said.

He pounced. "Seems?"

"Is."

Johel kept looking at me and looking at me, so I added, "From what I know."

"What do you know?"

"I don't know him any better than you do."

"And what do you think?"

"I don't think. Very often."

Johel exhaled and leaned forward. I had not quite realized what a large man he was.

"Have you seen anything?"

"Nothing," I said.

He paused, his agile, lawyerly mind working.

"Heard?" he asked.

"About Terry?"

"About me. About either of us. About Nadia."

"Nothing," I said. "I like you. I like all of you."

The judge tilted his head. He smiled, a rearrangement of his face that in no way suggested mirth and in no way diminished the impression he gave of high intelligence struggling with a difficult problem. He closed his eyes and kept them shut for long enough that I almost thought he was asleep. Then he opened them and looked around.

Three days back, the judge told me, he had gone with Terry to a large rally in the town of Abricots. By now, the campaign had become a serious production, and they traveled in a caravan of four vehicles—three pick-ups and the judge's SUV. The first truck was stuffed with speakers as tall as a man and a generator to power them, along with the seven members of Nadia's old band, Galaxy, whom Nadia had convinced the judge to hire for the duration of the campaign. A free concert was a pretty good draw, and Galaxy had written a number of catchy campaign tunes, some of them enthusiastic encomia to the judge, others nasty satires about the Sénateur.

The second truck was the swag wagon. Every kid in the Grand'Anse that month was wearing a T-shirt and kicking a soccer ball with the judge's face on it. (Kay had ordered all the swag from an importer in the Dominican Republic.) Then, if the free gear wasn't enough, Johel had hired a squad of six *marchandes* to prepare vast feasts of rice, beans, *piklis*, and grilled chicken. These ladies would stay up half the night cooking, and then at the rallies would serve up big plates, telling each voter, "It's Juge Blan who gives you this. Let him give you something more." Just getting that much food into Jérémie from Port-au-Prince was an immense logistical challenge, requiring the full-time attention of three of the judge's students.

Abricots is certainly a contender for the title of Prettiest Town on the Face of the Planet. The white sails of the two-masted fishing boats were sharp against the tranquil green waters, and the forested hills rolled right down to the edge of town. There was a church painted powder blue and white, a little cobblestoned town square, and a big tree under whose bower, if sleepiness took you in the afternoon, you could take a long nap. Folks who left Abricots for whatever reason—love, money, or necessity—never thought, as the years passed, that they'd ended up anyplace better.

The town itself had a tiny population (978, according to the census), but there were thousands more citizens living in the hills. This had never been country where the Sénateur's popularity had run particularly deep, and the judge thought that if the voters went to the polls, and if the votes were fairly counted, they might turn out in substantial numbers for him. The double "if" depended chiefly on the goodwill of a *mambo* named Madame Trésor, and it was to woo Madame Trésor, as much as to woo the voters, that the judge had traveled to Abricots.

"People in Port-au-Prince eat canned fish imported from Peru," the judge told the crowd. "You have got the sea on every side of this beautiful country, and you cannot buy a fresh fish in the capital unless you win the *borlette*. You go over to the Dominican Republic, they are eating fish soup, fish stew, fried fish, baked fish, whole fish, fish fillets, and fish steaks. Dominican fishermen go fishing, come back with some nice big fish, they pack it on ice, they drive it in three hours on their good paved roads to the capital. *Because they have roads.*

"But here, what are you going to do with that fish? Drive it two days to Port-au-Prince under a hot sun? That'll smell terrific."

The judge waved his hand in front of his face and pantomimed a rotten smell. The crowd tittered.

"Our problem here is this: Fishermen have little boats, no ice, and the big fish are too far out to sea for the little boats. Maybe you can catch a few itsy-bitsy fish to feed your family. But to lay nets, haul in a serious catch, you need a more serious craft. And who can afford to buy a boat like that if you can't get your fish to market?" This, the judge said, was the poverty trap, when no matter what you do to get ahead sees you running in place.

The judge started running in place on the stage, huffing and puffing as he went.

"You're not poor if you can work hard and get ahead." The judge began to pant. "If you can work hard—and get ahead—then you just don't have a lot of money. No sin, no crime in that." The judge stopped running. "But if you work and work and work some more, and you're still as broke the next day as the day before—then you need a road."

When the judge started talking about the poverty trap, the man standing next to Terry, whose lined and leathery face suggested a lifetime on the seas, said, "That's right," and Terry knew that Johel had earned himself that man's vote.

If the vote was counted.

In the last election, Abricots had not been peaceful. Armed partisans of opposing candidates had frightened the bulk of the population into hunkering down at home rather than venturing out to the polls. Turnout in Abricots had been extremely low.

This was the problem the judge proposed to discuss with Madame Trésor. Madame Trésor had never taken an active role in formal politics, seeing the business of elections and the state as beneath the dignity of an empress of the night. An incident the year before, however, had changed her perspective: her beloved younger brother had been imprisoned in Port-au-Prince, accused of being a member of a gang of kidnappers. Madame Trésor, whose power in her own commune was immense, was helpless to affect affairs in the capital, and so she had done what she was loath to do: she traveled all the way to Jérémie, a long and dusty road for a woman of her size, and made her way to the Sénateur's house, where she was made to sit in the sun for hours, like a peasant, only to have the Sénateur's security at the end of the day dismiss the crowd of supplicants, telling them to return in the morning. Madame Trésor was a woman whose capacity to perceive a slight was of infinite delicacy, and she returned that evening, in the dark, to her home in the hills of Abricots.

If it was known that she supported a candidate, the judge felt, his enemies would think twice before intimidating his supporters.

Madame Trésor lived in a stucco house about a mile out of town, not accessible by road, and the judge and Terry walked there after the rally. By the time they reached Madame Tresor's little cabin, the judge's face was swampy with sweat. Only after sitting down for five minutes on a mossy rock, breathing hard, and rubbing his forehead with a handkerchief was he able to concentrate on the business at hand.

Madame Trésor had been expecting Johel and she greeted him with the exaggerated, flirtatious warmth of beautiful fat women. She invited him to sit beside her on the couch and insisted that he drink a glass of grapefruit juice, made from the fruit of her own tree.

People told many stories about Madame Trésor, and some of them might even have been true: She could transform herself into a bat and fly through the night on gossamer wings. She was said to know the recipe for the *poud'* that turned men into zombies and for the *poud'* that made a man's heart swell up until it exploded from his chest. People came to her to complain of their enemies or to avenge themselves on unfaithful husbands or to find relief from tormented dreams.

She was a large woman, with a nearly square head attached to an oval body. Her small dark eyes fastened on Johel and did not blink or move away. He wondered how she navigated her way up and down these hills. She didn't look much like the feared empress of a secret society that ruled the Night—but then again, Johel figured, it was a *secret* society. She had a habit of saying "My Lord! My Lord!" but otherwise she listened patiently as Johel explained the reasons for his visit.

By now, he had become an excellent pitchman for himself. He had been trying to convince one important personage of the Grand'Anse after another to support his candidacy—and had been successful more often than not. Some wanted a school refurbished, others a new well, and still others just wanted cash. Johel thought seriously about each request and promised what he could. So he told Madame Trésor about the Canadians and the road and, having heard of her problems with the Sénateur, made sure to mention the Sénateur's arrogance. He thought what she wanted chiefly was respect—and possibly vengeance—and her brother's freedom. That was something, he suggested, that he could provide.

"My Lord! My Lord!" said Madame Trésor.

The little room was uncomfortably hot, and Johel felt himself sweating heavily as he spoke. Finally he finished talking, and a grave silence filled the room.

"I had a revelation about you," Madame Trésor said. "A heavy revelation."

Johel didn't know if this was a good thing or a bad thing.

"I want you to see my babies," she said.

She rose to her feet and shuffled out of the room. She came back a minute later with a Mason jar in which some strange thing floated in a tea-colored liquid. It was certainly a biological thing—maybe a squid? Not identifiably mammalian.

"That's my femininity," Madame Trésor said.

Johel was not sure if he was expected to compliment it, but the lady explained. When she was in her early twenties, the doctors had removed her uterus and ovaries. That was the *thing* floating in the jar. She had been until then without mystical powers. She had come home from the hospital in Jérémie unsexed but gifted with Sight.

"Take my children," she said, and handed the jar to Johel. He didn't want to, but he didn't know how to say no. Despite the warmth of the room, he felt a chill of fear pass up his spine. The jar was heavy in his hands and sticky, and the thing inside seemed to vibrate and buzz. Johel suddenly was seized by a wave of nausea. He worried that he was going to vomit the juice on the floor. He saw children playing on the floor, a schoolgirl with yellow ribbons in her hair, a boy climbing a palm tree and flinging down coconuts . . .

Johel, frightened that he was going to drop the jar on the unfinished cement floor, handed it back to Madame Trésor, who accepted it gravely and kissed it, as a mother kisses her babies before sleep. Then she buried the jar between her immense breasts.

"My Lord! My Lord!" she murmured, her eyes closed, rocking back and forth on her heavy haunches. "Come to me, my Lord!"

She must have rocked like that, moaning and crying, for ten minutes or more before she finally sat up straight, her eyes so wide they seemed as if they might burst from her head. She stood up, saying not a word, and walked with the jar into the back room.

When Madame Trésor came back, she said, "My children like you."

"I'm glad," Johel said, not sure if that was the correct word at all.

"They tell me I need to help you."

Johel found it hard to calm his racing heart. His mouth tasted sour, and it was difficult to understand just what Madame Trésor was saying. She was going to support his candidacy. But she looked him in the eye. Her children had warned her—"You have a traitor, a traitor in your camp. Your victory is in unity. You need to look left, look right, look high, look low. Look!"

That was two days ago, Johel told me, and he hadn't slept since. Madame Trésor's warning was dominating him. It was as if she were telling him something he already knew. He had never known a pain like this. Not a minute of sleep in two nights, just lying next to her, watching her breathe, thinking of Terry, each breath like a knife in his belly . . .

"Seriously?" I said. "You get me up in the dead of night *seriously* because some lady talked to her uterus, and so now you think—I don't even want to know what you think."

"I have to know the truth," Johel said.

"The truth is that this lady is a professional mind-fuck. That's what she does. People go to her to get their minds fucked and she fucks their minds. Congratulations, you got mind-fucked. It's happened to better men than you."

"It's killing me," he said.

"I think you need to get some sleep."

"I can't. I just lie there thinking."

"Thinking about this lady's uterus."

"Just tell me what you think, and I'll go home," he said.

"Maybe I'd buy it if this lady had some dead kids that were talking to her. Dead kids can channel like fuck. But that's not the way this situation is. You were talking to a flappy old uterus. That's different."

Johel could endure anything but mockery.

"The whole thing just got me thinking," he said.

"It can happen," I said. "We've all been there. You don't get enough sleep and your brain gets on top of you and before you know it . . ."

"I just wish I was sleeping better."

"Maybe I've got something for you."

I went upstairs and found an old bottle of Ambien. "Take two of these and a big shot of rum. If that doesn't work, double the recipe. You'll feel better in the morning."

"You think?"

"It couldn't seem any worse."

After Johel went home, I followed my own prescription. I dreamed that I had been assigned by the Red Cross to teach the second grade. No matter what I did, no matter how I shouted, I could not get the kids' attention, and they wandered one by one out of the room until just two remained, a boy and a girl. They were monstrous little creatures. In the morning, my wife told me that I had writhed and moaned in my sleep.

3 In the context of Haitian politics, handing out small cash payments to potential voters was not considered a disreputable practice. Although giving a few dollars to a potential voter in no way guaranteed his loyalty, failure to do so was perceived as an insult. Things might have been better for both the Sénateur and the judge had they mutually agreed to quit the practice, but the Sénateur, having distributed cash in each of his previous elections, did not feel that he could now stop. Voters, relying on the privacy of a secret ballot, accepted cash from both candidates, and voted their conscience.

But voters also sold their votes to a particular candidate. The challenge for the voter and the candidate was to find some way to demonstrate to the satisfaction of the candidate that the promised vote had, in fact, been delivered. Many schemes were devised to defeat the secrecy of the ballot box.

In past elections in Carrefour Charles, for example, the poll workers would examine the ballot, and if a voter's X had been placed in the Sénateur's box, they would paint his pinkie, not his forefinger, with indelible ink. The voter could then present himself later at the house of the local *juge de paix*, who represented the Sénateur in Carrefour Charles. In Beaumont, voters simply showed up at the voting center on election day, signed the electoral register, and walked away. The electoral officials would then complete the ballot and deposit it in the appropriate ballot box.

Somewhat more complicated was the scheme in Les Irois, where Mayor Fanfan in elections past had "rented" willing voters' voter identification cards, which he would then distribute to his followers. Again, complicit election officials were required who would overlook the miracle that restored Monsieur François Simonard, age seventy-six, to the bloom of youth. The advantage of this scheme was that voters, who might be frightened to venture out on election day, could stay home.

All of these schemes required the cooperation of the local electoral officials.* The Haitian system of elections gave these officials tremendous power: in addition to administering the vote, they were responsible for counting the vote. At the end of election day, the urns were opened on the spot and the votes tallied in the presence of the public, neutral electoral observers, and partisan observers from the camp of each candidate.

Local electoral officials had lots of opportunities, then, to sway an election one way or another. The most prevalent practice was ballot stuffing—officials simply filling out ballots and shoving them into the ballot box, then counting them at the end of the day. You'd be surprised how many ballot boxes turned out 400–0 for one candidate or another; and even if *all* the votes didn't end up for one candidate or another, it was easy for the officials to slip in a few extra votes for their patron in the course of election day. That could be enough, distributed across an entire commune or department, to sway the election.

Counting the votes also gave the local election officials the opportunity to fudge the numbers. In Jérémie, for example, I heard this story: The Sénateur had won a particular ballot box in the last election by a ratio of 137 votes to 100. But the president of the Voting Bureau, having verbally announced the correct total to the assembled crowd, hand-corrected the tally sheet to read 337 votes to 100, which nobody noticed until soldiers from the Mission had taken away both ballot box and tally sheets.

If Johel led the public campaign on his own behalf, Nadia led his

---

*These local officials were chosen by the Departmental Electoral Office in Jérémie, whose members were selected by the CEH in Port-au-Prince, and to the extent that the CEH was a biased and partisan body, so too the local electoral officials.

private campaign to hand out cash to voters, buy votes, and influence local election officials. At first he had been reluctant to involve her in this aspect of his affairs, but he quickly came to rely on her political sense and judgment: she knew the back roads of Haiti better than anyone on his staff. Precisely because she was from the village, she was the only person the judge's counterparts trusted to show up at their homes and offices to discuss these very sensitive matters.

Soon Johel was sending Nadia around the Grand'Anse with a car and driver. More suspicious than her husband, she had a fine instinct for who could be counted on and who was trying to swindle the judge and his campaign. More than once, Nadia told Johel that someone's claim to control a bloc of a thousand votes was only so much bluff and bravado. If, on the other hand, Nadia told Johel that someone had made a fair offer and was serious, he trusted her instincts, and quickly the deal was done.

The only person who didn't approve of the judge's private campaign was Terry. He overheard the judge negotiating some arrangement on the phone, and his beefy face went dark red.

"You're crossing the line," Terry said.

The judge looked up from his laptop, confused.

"A man's got to have a line," Terry continued. "And that's my line, right there. Those poor assholes don't have anything, not even enough to eat, not enough to pay for their kids' school, living on mangoes—what he's got is a vote and a pulse, and I'm not touching either one."

The judge rubbed the bridge of his nose.

"What good is it to have some line if the other guy just walks all over it?" he said.

"You still have the line. The line is the line. That doesn't go away."

"And what happens if on election day we lose because the Sénateur crossed the line and we didn't do anything? We just sit and stare at our line and tell ourselves what a great line it is?"

"They don't break all the mirrors the night they announce the results. You still got to wake up and see yourself."

The judge rubbed his stubbly face.

"I've never been one for looking in the mirror myself," he said. "There are no lines. You're old enough to hear the truth, son. You got some other guy out there crossing the line, and if you don't do the same thing, you might as well stay home."

Terry couldn't find the flaw in the argument. But he wasn't convinced either.

"Most men don't know where right and wrong are, but you and I— we know," the judge said. "Don't tell me we don't know, because we do. That's what it means to have power. That's what this is all about. You get to be the one who decides."

That evening, Terry went for a swim after dark. There was enough of a moon to keep an eye on the shore, and Terry thought that if he didn't move, the humidity, mosquitoes, and small-town claustrophobia might eat him alive. He was grateful for the water, just cool enough to bite, and for the waves, bigger that evening than normal, high enough that he could wrestle with them. The waves came in rhythm: two or three small ones, easy to ride out, then a big one, surprising him in the darkness, picking him up and sending him crashing shoreward.

That afternoon, he had decided to tell Johel that he was headed home, that this wasn't the way he wanted to play the game. But the words wouldn't come, because he knew that if he left, he wouldn't see Nadia again. It was that simple. When Johel had told him that Nadia had used love powder long ago to ensnare him, Terry had laughed. "More like poontang powder," he said. Now he wondered whether there wasn't something to the story.

Terry rode the waves for an hour or so, letting himself float and splashing. When he finally got to shore, he discovered that someone had stolen his pants, shoes, and shirt. The keys to his vehicle had been in his pants. His phone and wallet were locked in the car. Terry stood there cursing. He was facing a long walk back to the base, barefoot, in his dripping swimsuit, and he was aware for the moment of the ridiculous figure he would cut on the road.

Terry smashed the window of the car with a rock. He knew he would catch hell the next day from Balu, the *chef de transport*, but he figured he could bluff it out. Then he called Johel, who was out there to get him in twenty minutes. When Johel saw Terry standing there in his wet swim-suit, he started to laugh, and Terry laughed too. All the acrimony of their fight dissipated in the warm night air.

Sometimes on those long drives Nadia would drift off to sleep in the jouncing car and Toussaint would come to visit her. That's how she knew that Toussaint had been in love with her. He never spoke to her in her dreams, but simply watched her, his hollowed-out stare miserable with adolescent lust and desire. She didn't think that he had ever touched a woman. Sometimes he'd come to her naked, and she'd marvel at the erec-tion protruding from the undernourished, hairless body; and she would feel a tender pity for his suffering. She took him in her hands and caressed him, or she let him rub his thin, long fingers over her body. He'd just arrive at the very precipice of his desire when the shaking of the car would wake her up.

The dead are nothing if not persistent, and she'd drift back off to sleep and he'd come back into her dream, the big car bouncing and rut-ting across the rocky back roads, her head balanced on the strap of the seat belt.

The dreams came to her so often that she visited the woman in Sainte-Hélène who knew how to interpret such things. This lady listened to Nadia seriously and advised her that the dreams would continue until she pleased Toussaint. But the dead would only lie with a woman who was pure.

There was a little spring that Nadia knew in the mountains, a place called Source Bleu, where the water ran clean. It was a holy place, a place for the spirits. Nadia knew that women who could not get preg-nant sometimes came to this pool in the hopes of finding a child. On the way back from visiting the *juge de paix* of Roseaux, Nadia instructed her driver to stop by the side of the road, and she hiked inland to the source, where she bathed herself in the cold waters, murmuring the prayers she had learned as a girl.

That night, she dreamed that she was in the village, following a funeral cortege to the cemetery. The ladies were in white and the men in suits, and everyone was singing, walking through the green-leafed, red-dirt mountain behind the painted white coffin. Such a pretty coffin, she was thinking, a lady's coffin. She was asking everyone where they were taking the body, but no one would talk to her; she didn't know any of these folks, and nobody wants to talk to a stranger on the day you bury someone. She fell into step beside Toussaint.

She didn't expect him to talk to her either, but he said, "That's a lady who died too young."

"What happened to her, Toussaint?" she said.

"Her man found her in the wrong arms and took her head from her shoulders."

"Some men are like that."

"All men are like that," he said.

She and Toussaint followed the funeral cortege for a long spell, marching side by side with the villagers. Then she found herself alone with Toussaint. She was so happy not to be dead that she allowed him to make love to her. But dreams being what they are, she knew as soon as he touched her that this was not Toussaint, but the man with the mustache, the first man who ever touched her. Every man who had ever touched her was inside her, none of them good, liars and cheats and deceivers all of them. She struggled with Toussaint and he held her down, strong and firm, like they all did, taking her wrists in his thick hands, pushing against her until she opened up with a cry of pain, panting on her with his thick smell of old sweat and sour breath, death and Lightning. Nadia never dreamed about Toussaint again.

4 The ballots had been impregnated with swine flu—that was the
rumor that hit four days before the election. We first started
hearing the story in Jérémie, then reports came to us from all
the coastal towns, until even in the most remote mountain villages, voters
had heard that the ballot itself was poison.

"Goatfucker," the judge said when his campaign workers started talking about the rumor. "This is the Sénateur. This is just like him."

The swine flu story infected all of the Grand'Anse in about a day.
Nobody knew what the symptoms of swine flu were, how to identify a
sufferer of swine flu, or whether it could be treated. Although the rumor
was specifically associated with the ballots, people began to visit the
hospital and clinic, where doctors were unable to reassure them that they
were healthy. A fight broke out at the bank when somebody sneezed. A
hysterical mother came up to me in tears, holding a healthy-looking
baby, insisting that the baby had been looked upon by a woman known
to have contracted the disease.

That final week of the campaign, the judge pushed himself and everyone around him to the edge of nervous collapse. But he wouldn't stop.
He could feel the wind at his back.

Just a few days before election day the judge made a four-day swing
down the coast, hitting Dame Marie and Anse-d'Hainault, even visiting

Les Irois, where the residents did not forget that the judge had put Mayor Fanfan in prison. Still, they turned out to hear the judge talk, eat his pigs, dance to his music, and drink his beer. Then he'd held a rally all the way inland at Source Chaude, going deep into the mountains, a stretch in the middle on donkeys and horses.

And he was making progress.

On his way back to Jérémie, word spread that the judge was coming over the mountains. At first it was just the curious, but soon there were hundreds and then thousands, standing on the side of the road. So the judge told Terry he was going to walk, and there he was, walking back home through the mountains—*rara* music sounding and someone beating a drum—carrying a little kid on his big shoulders, telling the people the story of the road they were going to build themselves.

When citizens heard the judge was coming, they would take the furniture from their huts and assemble couches, beds, chairs, and tables by the side of the road. This was their way of saying, *Judge, my house is your house.* Then they would dress themselves in their best clothes, the ones they reserved for church services and baptisms and funerals, and sit themselves down on their ratty old furniture, just waiting for his convoy to pass. It was a bad day for the goats, chickens, and pigs when the judge came to town, because it seemed that every family in the Grand'Anse had prepared a meal for him, stewing up something, on the grounds that he might just be hungry from his drive. Johel insisted on taking a bite or two from every pot. Long after Terry couldn't stand the smell of another boiled chicken, the judge would still be moving from house to house and table to table, accepting a small plate or drinking another glass of rum, tucking some scrawny old lady under his big shoulder, and declaring that this was surely the finest goat meat he'd ever tasted.

For the last week of the campaign, at every rally, the judge changed his peroration. He'd had some of the guys at campaign HQ stitch him up something that looked like a ballot, and he'd wave it in the air.

"Swine flu is our ignorance!" he said. "Swine flu is our poverty! We're broker than pigs in this country; the pigs ought to be worrying about catching *our* disease!"

He waved the ballot.

"There's just one remedy for our disease! You don't get better from our disease at the hospital!"

"Non, monsieur, non!" shouted someone.

"Don't get better at no doctor's office!"

"Uh-huh!"

"Don't ask the leaf doctor brew you up some tea, make you feel all right!"

"C'est vrai!"

"This here is the medicine you want to cure our disease," he said, waving the ballot. "I hear people say that this ballot is poison. But this ballot here is *our* medicine! This ballot here is poison only if you want to keep folks ignorant! This is poison only if you want to keep folks poor! This ballot here is poison only if you want to keep our people down, down lower than dogs and pigs! This ballot here is poison for Maxim Bayard and medicine for the rest of us! Look here—"

The judge ripped off a corner of that ballot and shoved it into his mouth.

"Mmmm-hmmmm good!" he said. "That ballot tastes good! *Li bon, oui!* That ballot tastes freedom! That ballot tastes progress! That ballot tastes hope! Gimme more of that ballot, I could eat it twice!"

In the course of that campaign the judge must have eaten a couple of dozen ballots, and you'd have thought nothing ever tasted better each time he wadded one down his throat.

I awoke to find the Sénateur, dressed in white linen, sitting on the terrace of his mother's house. It was like finding a bear rummaging through your campsite.

"Sénateur, this is a surprise," I said.

In the years my wife and I had lived in his house, he had never before visited us, although his own cement bungalow was no more than minutes away. From time to time I saw his caravan of black SUVs drive by on the back road that connected his house to the rue Bayard: that's how I knew he was in town. Lately they had been rumbling out at dawn to campaign in the far corners of the *département* and coming back well after midnight.

"I have been having a lovely conversation with your cat," the Sénateur said. "She has been telling me extraordinary things. For example, she has told me that you are good friends with Johel Célestin."

The treacherous cat was curled up in the wicker chair adjacent to the Sénateur's, staring attentively at his ugly face.

"Would you like coffee?" I asked.

"With plenty of sugar."

I went into the house to make coffee, and when I came back with two cups, the cat had crawled onto the Sénateur's lap and was allowing her head to be stroked gently.

"You never told me how you liked my poetry," he said. "I awoke in the night concerned that I might be lodging a critic. I was awake very early and determined to know your true opinion."

"They were beautiful poems," I said.

It was true: they *were* beautiful poems, elegiac and wistful. The Sénateur wrote in a charming but difficult admixture of French and Creole that took me hours to puzzle out. *"La fesse de ma fille"*—that's how he titled a sonnet praising his lover's derriere. A longish history of the town of Jérémie in couplets. There was a successful plea from a fish on a line; the fish liberated from the hook proved to be a god and rewarded the fisherman with a castle. "The Baron's Lament," in the voice of Baron Samedi, lord of the underworld.

"I am so relieved that you enjoyed them," he said.

We sat without talking for a minute or two. There was a woodpecker hammering away, and although it was well past dawn, when the wind shifted, the last drumming from a *bal vodou* down in Basse-Ville came in on the breeze and filled the terrace with its melancholy, frantic song.

"There was nothing we cared for as youth but poetry," the Sénateur said. "We sat on this terrace. There was a group of five or six of us. We called ourselves the Héliotropes—we were a generation of innocents! I remember Georges Clérié, with his yellow bow tie; and Fernand Martineau, who sang; and Roger Boncy, who had such a beautiful sister— what was her name? Marcelle, and her friend Paulette Martineau . . . You have no idea, young man, what time has done to us. But we were once as optimistic as you and your—your friend. I know of your long interest in our Jérémie poets, our history. That's why I thought this morning that I would come and talk to you."

"I appreciate the visit," I said.

"I will be the last of the Bayards to sit on this terrace and discuss the miracle of literature. My grandfather built this house—and I am not a young man! I heard it said from my mother that he was the tallest man in the Caribbean, and for that reason he insisted on these high arched doors. He would not stoop entering his own home! It is a family trait."

He stared past me at the winter flamboyant just coming into bloom, a crimson cloud.

"I was in exile for twenty years," he said. "For twenty years I didn't see this house. I would wander through it in my dreams. When I came back, it was much smaller than I recalled it."

He leaned forward and put his hand on my forearm.

"You think I will lose, don't you?"

There was no such thing, of course, as public opinion polling in the Grand'Anse, and it was impossible to know for sure who was likely to win the election. But I had the sense—the Sénateur must have shared it also—that the electoral winds were blowing in the judge's favor. People seemed to smile when the judge's name was spoken and frown when the name Maxim Bayard was uttered. Both men had been campaigning vigorously, crisscrossing the *département* from morning till night, holding two or even three rallies in the course of a day. But the judge's rallies were better attended.

The Sénateur didn't wait for my answer. He said, "Tell your friend I wish to speak with him. Informally. A friendly chat. He need not be frightened. This is a private conversation. I have never had the pleasure of shaking his hand."

When the Sénateur and the judge finally met, not that evening but the next, I was reminded of large animals sniffing each other. They were almost shy, as if, having imagined and supposed the worst about each other for so long, they could not quite wrap their heads around their adversary's corporeal reality.

I said, "I'll let you gentlemen talk."

But the Sénateur said, "We have no secrets—not even from our northern friends."

"Stay, brother," the judge said.

So I sat back down. The cat strolled out on the terrace and surprised me by once again hopping into the Sénateur's lap. She was ordinarily a timid creature. The Sénateur took her lightly veined ears between his thick fingers and massaged them.

"She likes you," the judge said as the cat began to purr.

"If only she could vote!"

The Sénateur roared with laughter at his own joke, and the cat, frightened, jumped off his lap. Inside the house, I heard my telephone ringing. I went inside to answer it, and when I came back five minutes later, the two men were discussing the election with surprisingly good-natured civility. They were gossiping about the various personages of the Grand'Anse and the places they had visited in the course of the campaign. They had declared a truce for the evening.

"And *his* grandfather was Noé Fourcand," said the Sénateur. "You, Monsieur, remind me quite a bit of Avocat Fourcand."

The judge smiled indulgently. He expected to win the election now and was happy to be deferential.

The Sénateur took a sip from his rum. He had been no older than ten when Noé Fourcand had made his reputation—"And you, Monsieur, will find this story of particular interest. Noé Fourcand was a great orator, like you, Monsieur, and a magnificent conscience of our city—and like you, Monsieur, a substantial man, broad and strong. You might be his twin."

The Sénateur closed his eyes as he recalled the long-ago afternoon when Père Fouquet, bishop of Jérémie, found Josué Jean, town beggar and thief, rifling through the collection plate:

"We followed Josué Jean through the streets of Jérémie, tossing stones at this man who dared violate the sanctity of the holy space. As you and your supporters would stone me! We took him before the *juge de paix*, and I recall even now the smell of sweat and fear as the *commissaire de gouvernement* rose up to condemn poor Josué Jean, who stole from our church two gourdes! Thank goodness for the alert and dedicated priest who noticed this impious villainy in action! The *commissaire* demanded a sentence on Josué Jean's head of six months' seclusion, as a gesture of respect that one owes our saints and holy places.

"Josué Jean, simpleminded in his rags, regarded his accusers in stupefaction, his dark face lightened with dust from the street. Would no one dare rise to say a word on his behalf, offer up for him a defense, advocate his cause?

"And it was Noé Fourcand who taught us all a lesson in courage. He arrived just as the noontime bell from the Cathédrale had sounded.

"And I remember, Monsieur, his bass voice, his grave demeanor— all of these things, Monsieur, in which you seem to reincarnate his presence.

"And he said, 'It is at midday, my brother and sisters, when the Angelus sounds, that the Christian man ought to grant himself a minute of retirement to consider his actions from the first portion of the day. Retire now, magistrate! Retire now, citizens! Retire now, implacable priest! Demand of God to inspire in you a decision marrying wisdom to your power! Act now in the spirit of a true Christian!'

"His words, Monsieur, caused me to drop the stone I had in my hand.

"Noé Fourcand said, 'Before us we have a poor man, a man whose eyes alone tell us of his days and nights of hunger. His stomach and his entrails are tangled by the knots of hunger! Feel his suffering pain, oh Christian brothers! This man could turn for compassion only to Christ Almighty, friend of the poor and suffering! And what does he see, entering the holy space of Mother Church, but the words of our Lord, "Come unto me, those who are hungry?" And what does he spy but the collection box? And what does he feel but the Divine presence? And what does he do but break the box open, his weakened hands trembling, in obedience to Divine commandment and answered prayers? And who among us would condemn him, whose only crime is to be poor?'

"And I tell you, Monsieur, this speech had an effect on the crowd I have not seen since you also began to inspire our people with your grandiloquent oratory. The rage fled from my heart as swiftly as it had once arrived. Not only did we liberate Josué Jean and feed him, but at the next election thereafter, we made Avocat Fourcand our *sénateur*.

"Noé Fourcand!" the Sénateur said. "And how many years has it been since I've said that name. And here he is again!"

The Sénateur put his hand on the judge's thigh. He looked at the judge with an expression on his ugly face not unlike tenderness. "You don't want this burden."

"I think I do."

"I remember Noé Fourcand's funeral. He was hardly in office a year before his heart gave way beneath the weight of his new responsibility. How his widow wailed!" the Sénateur said.

The cat wandered back out onto the deck, and the Sénateur leaned over, picked her up, and settled her on his lap.

The judge smiled. "Sénateur, you should write these stories down. When you're no longer here, our history will be lost. When you are in retirement, I advise you to write a history of this town."

The Sénateur shook his head.

"You have misunderstood me, young man. Men like you and Noé are not meant for the burden of public office."

"And why is that?"

The Sénateur took the judge's hand in his. The judge bridled at the touch, but allowed the Sénateur to hold his hand.

The Sénateur said, "Because you and Noé are too fine. That is a compliment, my friend, that no one will any longer extend to me. My mother always said to cherish every kind word."

The judge took his hand back.

"Sénateur—," the judge began.

The Sénateur interrupted. "Life is too short for us to be enemies. Only cats have time to fight. You and I must be friends."

The judge said, "When they call me Sénateur, you and I will be friends."

"In politics, you will learn to concentrate on essentials. I am proposing friendship. Can we not—compromise?"

The judge was quiet for a long time. Then he started to laugh. I thought he was going to choke. His body shook.

"Would you build the road?" Johel asked.

"I am not opposed."

"And traffic on the road?"

"We could share," the Sénateur said. He spread his hands wide, as if to encompass between them endless bounty. "We could serve each other's needs. Eat at each other's tables. Laugh at each other's jokes. And share the harvest of our beautiful land."

"And you would be?"

"What I am. The Sénateur of the Grand'Anse."

"And I would be?"

The Sénateur slapped his hands together. "You will be young!"

The Sénateur stood up, groaning slightly. He extended his hand in my direction and the judge's. The judge started to stand up also, but the Sénateur said, "Sit on my mother's porch and enjoy the night air. It is wisdom to learn from the mistakes of your elders. I should have spent more time sitting on this porch and thinking of the most pleasant things in life."

The judge sat silently on the Sénateur's mother's porch. I thought, just for a moment, that he might accept the Sénateur's offer. He was a tired man imagining a quiet life: a house by the sea, a library of books, a garden. His face grew peaceful in his fantasy. The stress and tension and anxiety of his campaign ebbed from his fat features. His eyes closed. Then, like a film run backward, his face reacquired its former rigidity. He stood up, took his leave of me, and drove down to campaign HQ, where, I learned the next day, he stayed at his desk working by gas lamp until the early hours of the morning.

5   I was hired as an election day observer by the Organization of American States, which put in place a three-hundred-member observation team distributed throughout the entire country. I was assigned to the mountain town of Chambellan, about forty-five minutes from Jérémie on the road to Dame Marie.

Haiti was a good teacher in the arts of gratitude, and only the coldest hearts would have remained unmoved by the long lines of solemn voters, dressed in their Sunday best, congregating from dawn onward at the Lycée Jean Rabel, a one-story concrete block house. I hadn't expected to see anyone come and vote, on account of the swine flu, but the line stretched out through the schoolyard and down the side of the mountain. The morning had a chill, and the voters shifted from side to side to stay warm, with that remarkable capacity for fortitude that those who do not know Haiti well confuse with patience. The villages around Chambellan had been heavily contested by both the Sénateur and the judge; both men had rallied more than once in the town. The voters today weren't just braving swine flu. The short history of Haitian democracy had been punctuated by many elections that degenerated into violence. At any time, a gunshot could ring out, and who would stand in line then?

In Chambellan, only one incident threatened to disrupt the calm of the day.

It must have been midmorning when the voters in line began to shout. An elderly man was lying on the ground, looking dazed. He was wearing a bow tie and a neatly pressed suit, and the folks in line were insisting that the man was dead.

What happened was this.

The man on the ground, whose name was Berthillus Simeon, had been a partisan of the Sénateur's in this election and in elections past, a member of the older generation whose loyalty to the Sénateur could not be shaken by any promise of a road or riches, and he had made no attempt to hide his scorn for the younger voters of the village who had come to admire the judge. He was an ornery old cuss whose ultimate answer to any political argument was to spit on his opponents' shoes.

It was just two days' back that Monsieur Simeon had drunk himself a bottle of *clairin* and died in the night. Given his age and fragile health, no one in the village was much surprised by the man's demise, not even his children or his wife. Until the coffin was ready, the family was keeping the cadaver right in his bed, with an iron on his chest to keep him from rotting. They were proposing to bury him that day or the next— which is why his presence on the voting line was arousing considerable agitation.

Not only was old Monsieur Simeon present, he was insisting that he be allowed to vote. The judge's supporters, sensing trickery, had surrounded him, and he had responded by hocking a wet loogie at his antagonists' feet. The subsequent pushing had gotten to shoving, and in this way Monsieur Simeon ended up on the ground, looking dazed.

So the questions for the election officials were complicated: Was this in fact Monsieur Simeon? If so, was Monsieur Simeon dead? If he was dead but still capable of voting, was his vote valid?

Voting was suspended for almost an hour as the election officials treated the case of Monsieur Simeon. Partisans of the judge were soon shouting that the whole election was fraudulent—who knows how many of the dead had been allowed to vote?—while partisans of the Sénateur were yelling that the election was a fraud, too, one man waving a copy of the Haitian Constitution in the air and demanding to know just where it said that only the living were entitled to vote.

The second secretary of the Voting Bureau was a skinny schoolmistress brought in from Dame Marie, who gave Monsieur Simeon a glass of water and asked him if he was dead. But Monsieur Simeon seemed to think the question was offensive and wouldn't answer.

A voice in the crowd proposed that this monsieur was a ringer, someone who had taken the deceased's voter identification card and was proposing to cast a ballot in his name. The only problem with this theory was that first, the man calling himself Monsieur Simeon and the man on the voter identification card were very nearly identical; and second, there were at least two dozen citizens in line insisting that this *was* Monsieur Simeon, only he was dead.

As it happened, one of the ladies in line worked as a nurse at the clinic in Chambellan, and she was enlisted to ascertain whether Monsieur Simeon was, medically speaking, alive or dead, a fact whose juridical relevance remained uncertain. A hush came over the crowd as this lady, clearly more accustomed to laboring women and newborns than walking cadavers, pressed two fingers to the old man's scrawny neck and sought out a heartbeat. She waited a minute, felt the faint tapping of the man's old pulsing blood, and said, "He's alive."

A roar went up from half the crowd as the other half shouted wildly: even zombies had heartbeats. Out on the margins of the crowd, the debate was philosophical, as so often in Haiti, folks wondering just what life consisted of. Someone was sent for a mirror, on account of the widely known fact that a cadaver doesn't have a reflection, but no one could seem to find one.

The situation threatened to explode out of control. The president of the Voting Bureau was trying to reestablish order, the muscles in his neck straining as he shouted at the voters to get back in line; and the first secretary was on the phone with the PNH, asking them to send a vehicle. But the PNH were overwhelmed, on account of the situation in Marfranc, where a brace of toughs, armed with machetes, had been hired by a local candidate for *député* to storm the polling center. By the time the PNH responded to the disorder, the ballots and the ballot boxes were in flames. The violence had nothing to do with either the Sénateur or the judge—they were equally collateral damage to the disorder—but the effect was that no voters voted in Marfranc that day for any candidate whatsoever, and the PNH had neither vehicle nor officers to spare.

The day was saved by the arrival of Monsieur Simeon's son. The son of Simeon had the thick hands and flat feet of a true scion of the Haitian soil. He said that he didn't know for sure if his papa were alive or dead, but he could confirm that all and sundry had sincerely believed the old man dead for the past two days. This morning, he continued, he had gone into the bedroom where the cadaver was reposing, expecting to salute his deceased father, only to find the bed empty. So either his daddy had risen from death or he hadn't been dead at all, and he expected it was the latter.

But there was an easy way to know for sure if the old man was a zombie. Zombies couldn't abide the taste of salt, so if Monsieur Simeon was willing to taste salt, then he should be allowed to vote. Everyone seemed to think this was fair except Monsieur Simeon himself, but by now most folks' patience with Simeon was limited, and it was decided to make him eat salt whether he wanted to or not. Soon one of the *marchandes* selling deep-fried plantains was enlisted to produce a specimen glistening with grease and salt, of which Monsieur Simeon, looking around nervously at the crowd, took a healthy bite and then another.

When fifteen minutes passed and Monsieur Simeon wasn't dead of salt poisoning, the president of the Voting Bureau made his official ruling: Monsieur Simeon was not dead, had never been dead, and was therefore entitled to vote. Monsieur Simeon, like all other voters, was escorted into the polling center, where his documents were inspected, and he made his mark on the voting sheet. He was handed one ballot for the senatorial race and another for the local deputy race, and was escorted to the private voting booth. A few minutes later he handed the ballots, folded neatly, to the second secretary of the Voting Bureau, who placed them in their respective boxes. Monsieur Simeon's fingernail was painted with black dye.

At four in the afternoon they counted the ballots.

There were twenty or more of us in the concrete schoolroom. On the chalkboard were the remains of the lessons from the day before: arithmetic exercises and the conjugations of the French verb *avoir*. The local election officials were seated at a long table, the ballot boxes arrayed in front of them, and the observers squeezed themselves into the students' rickety chairs. No wind tempered the still heat of the room.

Until the moment that the president of the Voting Bureau cut the seal on the ballot box, the room was filled with nervous laughter, but when the ballot box was open, the room went quiet.

All across the Grand'Anse—indeed, all across Haiti—the ballot boxes were being opened at that moment, and all across the Grand'Anse—all across Haiti—we were leaning forward, hardly breathing.

The president of the Voting Bureau reached into the plastic box and pulled out the first ballot. He unfolded it and inhaled. He looked at it with a puzzled expression and whispered in the ear of the first secretary.

"Blank," he said.

He showed the ballot to the audience of observers, who all began simultaneously to roar in protest, like sprinters after a false start.

The first secretary said, "I confirm it's blank," and placed the ballot on her desk, faceup in front of her. She made a check on her tally sheet, the president made a check on his tally sheet, and the observers all scratched a mark in their notebooks.

The president removed a second ballot from the box and unfolded it. He held it between his thumb and forefinger.

He said, "Sénateur Maxim Bayard."

He passed the ballot to the first secretary, who said, "Maxim Bayard."

She placed the ballot on a new pile.

The president said, "Sénateur Maxim Bayard," and handed another ballot to the first secretary.

"Maxim Bayard," said the first secretary.

The judge got his first vote on the fourth ballot. When the president said, "Johel Célestin," the observer for the judge in the rear of the room began to clap.

"Silence!" the president said.

"Johel Célestin," the first secretary said.

The counting of votes continued in this manner for several hours— there were three separate ballot boxes of almost three hundred votes each. The president did not hurry, and he read out the results of each ballot as if the name were a surprise. From time to time the Sénateur or the judge would go on a little run of votes—three or four for one candidate or for the other, and you'd think one of them was tearing away with the race; but whenever one candidate would pull ahead, the other would come back.

The only time the counting of the votes was interrupted was when a sparrow flew into the schoolroom and could not find its way out. The small bird flew in frantic circles from desk to desk. The president interrupted the counting of the votes, and the observers laughed as one after another tried to catch the bird and failed. When the sparrow found the window and flew out, the president resumed his count.

When he was done, the president announced his official tally, ballot box by ballot box.

In ballot box number one, there were 280 votes counted. Seven were blank, 5 showed votes for both the Sénateur and the judge. There were 123 votes for the Sénateur, 101 for the judge, the remaining votes disbursed among the minor candidates.

In ballot box number two there were eleven blank votes, three double votes, 130 votes for the judge, and 109 for the Sénateur.

In ballot box number three there were two blank votes, one double vote, 119 votes for the judge, and 99 for the Sénateur.

The judge's observers disagreed with the count of the third ballot box. Their count showed the Sénateur with 96 votes, not 99. The president agreed to recount the vote. By now night had fallen and the room was lit only by gas lantern. The president and first secretary, by the same slow and methodical method as the first count, arrived again at 99 votes. The judge's observers admitted that the count was correct.

"I declare the count official and valid," the president said. "Long live Haiti! Long live democracy!"

Then the first and second secretaries carefully sealed the ballots and the tally sheets where the president had kept the official vote counts. The results of the election were affixed to the wall of the schoolroom:

the judge had, by a slender margin, won this polling station. But there were many other polling centers throughout the Grand'Anse. Out in front of the polling center there was a Uruguayan armored vehicle to collect the ballots and tally sheets. More remote corners of the province were being reached by helicopter, and a few polling centers were accessible only by donkey. The ballots and tally sheets would be transported to Jérémie, then sent on to the national tabulation center in Port-au-Prince.

6 The judge counted the votes collected by his electoral observers and knew that he had won. He had a substantial plurality and was very close to a majority. Everybody supposed that if the election went to a second round, the judge would win easily.

But nobody knew how the CEH would produce the official election results. Just as the CEH had the power to choose illegitimate candidates, so too the CEH had the power to eliminate obviously fraudulent results—a ballot box, say, in which the voters unanimously favored one candidate over his rivals, or a box in which the number of votes counted far exceeded the number of voters assigned to that urn. The judge knew that these powers could be easily abused, and there was no court of appeals to decisions of the CEH but the CEH itself. The judge was worried that the CEH, either through incompetence or malfeasance, would hand the victory to the Sénateur at the last moment.

It took almost three weeks before the CEH announced the results. The town and nation passed the time in a frenzy of anxious anticipation. Almost daily we were assaulted by rumors. But the manifest content of these rumors was never political, reminding me that the Freudian notion of displacement could apply to entities larger than a single troubled soul. In the weeks we awaited the final decision of the CEH, an invisible zombie with a lethal touch prowled the streets. Schools closed as worried parents kept their children home, and the annual Miss Creole Beauty Pageant was suspended. Then the cathedral was burgled and the chalice of the Eucharist stolen, presumably to serve black magic ends. The night before the election results were announced, a woman in Sainte-Hélène began to rave about red water; and in the slum behind the *grand marché*, two men died at the same time in different houses, the last words on both men's lips inexplicably the same.

Late in December, the CEH in Port-au-Prince called a press conference. The judge decided to hold a party at his election headquarters to watch the election results on television with his supporters.

The press conference was scheduled for seven in the evening, but it was midnight before the CEH spokesman ventured out into the ballroom of the Hotel Montana. The delay was designed to reduce the possibility of violence on the part of supporters of the defeated candidates. Grinding tension took over campaign HQ as we waited. Terry chain-smoked on the terrace, and Nadia sat cross-legged, rocking quietly and staring out at the Place Dumas, where a small crowd of the judge's supporters were assembled. The judge walked around the room, shaking hands and rubbing shoulders. The campaign staff and volunteers were drinking beer. A phone rang, someone answered and then told the group that his friend in Port-au-Prince reported that riot police were beating a protester in front of the Hotel Montana. Then another phone rang and someone's friend in Port-au-Prince informed us that we would soon learn that the election had been canceled entirely. Out front, a chant went up, "Judge Blan today / A road tomorrow."

Around midnight, the spokesman for the CEH appeared on the television. He was visibly nervous: his face would be associated across Haiti with election results that would be criticized the next day, whether fairly or unfairly, by half the candidates as fraudulent. Dark pools of sweat colored his shirt.

"Man's deodorant is definitely not working as hard as he is," said Terry.

The judge chuckled, but truth be told, he didn't look much better than the spokesman for the CEH.

The spokesman began with the campaign for deputy, the lower house of Parliament. His voice was a monotonous drone as he read out vote totals for each candidate. There were nearly a hundred races, and in some of the races, there were a dozen candidates or more, some taking as little as a dozen votes. A few of the races seemed like omens: up in the north near Ouanaminthe, there had been another candidate who had promised to build a road. He lost, and a groan echoed around the room.

"Does not matter, does not matter at all," said the judge.

Nadia sat still as the results were read. It was only from her billowy shirt that I knew that her pregnancy was advancing, but I don't know if anyone else in the room was aware of her secret.

Then a candidate for deputy who had favored building a road was announced a victor. The room began to cheer and clap.

"That's what I'm talking about," said the judge. "Now, that's what I'm talking about."

The reading of the deputies lasted a long time, and I stepped outside onto the Place Dumas. Now the crowd was thick: unable to sleep in the hot, nervous night, they had come down to the Place Dumas to observe first-hand the electoral results.

I went back inside as the spokesman began reading the results of the senatorial races. The judge turned up the volume on the television. Then the spokesman read the results from the senatorial election in Port-au-Prince.

"Jean-Emmanuel Robert, *quarante-sept mille, deux cent vingt-trois*," he intoned. That was Ti Jean. He had won.

We all began to applaud enthusiastically, stomp on the ground.

Then finally it was time for the judge's race. I heard the spokesman read off names and numbers—I remember that Thibault Antoine Erick just missed winning his ten thousand votes and three hectares of arable land—and I tried to keep a written tally. But in my excitement I couldn't translate the French into digits with sufficient dexterity. I remember that the Sénateur had something-something-*cinquante-six* votes and I was trying to figure out what percentage of the vote that was.

Then the room exploded.

The judge had won 42 percent of the votes in the first round, the Sénateur down at 28 percent, the motley crew of also-rans dividing up the rest. Every car in town was honking all at once, cheap Chinese fire-crackers were going off like ammunition. There wasn't a throat in the room that wasn't shouting in joy.

"Congratulations, Sénateur," Terry said.

"We still got to do it all over again," the judge said, thinking about the second round, but the way he was smiling, Terry knew the judge wasn't worried.

"Forty-two fucking percent," Terry said. "And fuck the rest of them."

Terry and the judge rubbed their big unshaved faces against each other, both of them slick with tears, Terry running his hands all over the judge's head.

Soon the party spilled out of campaign HQ into the Place Dumas, everyone coming out to drink and dance and enjoy the warm night, like Carnival in December. In anticipation of victory, Johel had used campaign funds to buy fuel for the civic generators on the rue Abbé Hué, and the streetlights came on all over town, lighting up a dark night.

No one was happier than Terry. He'd had a fight with Kay just a few days back, the two of them shouting at each other over Skype.

She said, "Terry, what I just want to know is why you're still doing all this."

"I want to build a road," he said.

"Give me a fucking break," she said. "Just for once in your life, give me a break."

But Terry thought the road would be solid. And one solid thing might be enough for a lifetime. For Terry, it's *always* been about the road.

That's what he said to the judge at the end of the night. Terry wrapped his arm around the judge, pulled him so tight he could smell his after-shave. He looked him in the eyes and said, "Thank you, brother."

The judge understood. "I was just hired labor," he said.

"Cheers," Terry said.

They knocked their glasses together.

"Promise me something. Look me in the eye."

"Anything," the judge said.

"I want you to promise me, whatever happens to me, you'll finish our road."

"You know it."

"What I'm saying is, that road, the day they get it done, I'm not there, whatever happens—you just drive down that road and think about what we did here together."

The victory had been Nadia's as much as the judge's, and when the results were announced, she had let out an exhilarated cry. But quickly, exhaustion took her and her face went slack. Soon Nadia asked Terry if he could drive her home.

Terry had not been alone with Nadia since they buried Toussaint. They drove up the hill in silence, a few stray dogs following the car and baying. Out in front of the low brick wall, Nadia closed her eyes. Terry put his hand on her dress, at the place where the hem met her thigh. She squirmed backward into her seat.

"I'm scared," she said.

"He's not coming back for hours."

"Every day, I'm so scared."

"It's almost over," he said.

But his voice was clouded by irritation. He didn't want to talk about her fears. His body was tense with desire. He leaned over to kiss her, and she turned her head away.

"I miss the thing we had," he said.

"What thing?"

"Our thing."

"When are you going home?"

"I'm not tired."

"No, I mean when you go home to—"

She gestured upward with her eyebrows, to his home across the waters.

"I don't know if I'm ever going home," he said. "I don't know if I have anything waiting there for me."

Terry had never said a thing like that to Nadia. He felt her drawing closer to him. Nadia looked at him for a long time. She was breathing in the air he was breathing out, and in that shared breath, he felt as if she were weighing, measuring, judging him.

"I'm pregnant," she said.

"Does Johel know?" he finally asked.

She shook her head.

Terry's face moved faster than his thoughts. Terry wanted his face to tell one story, but it was telling another—and just who was telling the truer story, his face or his thoughts: that was something Terry would wonder about for a long, long time.

Terry was thinking that this thing had to happen like this, sooner or later. The notion of a pregnancy had never crossed his conscious mind, but he wasn't surprised: he had seen the glow of life in her skin. Terry wanted his face—his dark, expressive eyes, the kindly cast of his mouth—to tell Nadia of the love he felt for her and all the fragile creatures who struggled alone in this hard world.

But Terry's face had another agenda altogether. Terry raced after his face as it told Nadia that it was over between them. Terry's face, shrewd and unsentimental, knew that there was no other way to understand this baby that wasn't his. Terry's face was thinking about Nadia and the judge, the judge rolling around on Nadia, her face and his face, and Terry's face, jealous of their pleasure, knew that all the love he had felt for Nadia had been like pouring water on hot sand, soaked up and leaving nothing behind. And then, just for a moment, no more than a passing instant, Terry's face was angry.

Nadia saw his face, and she knew she was alone. How foolish she had been to entrust her safety to a *blan*. She climbed out of the car.

"Wait," Terry shouted.

But Nadia had already closed the gate of the cement house behind her.

The judge called Terry the next morning.

"Too much last night?" Terry said. "You sound like death."

"Come on over," the judge said.

Half an hour later, Terry was up at the judge's house. The judge was pouring sweat: he was wearing his own campaign T-shirt, the red one, soaked through.

"You feeling okay?" Terry said, thinking heart attack.

"I've been better."

"Maybe we'll get you to a doctor."

There was a morning flight to Port-au-Prince—they had ninety minutes or so.

Terry followed the judge into the kitchen. Something wasn't right with the way he was walking, his stride stumbling, shambling, off-balance. In the kitchen, the judge poured himself a tumbler of *clairin*, the smell of ginger and alcohol so strong that Terry could smell it across the room. He'd never seen the judge drink in the morning, never seen the judge out of control.

"Want one?" the judge asked.

"It's too early for me," Terry said. "Maybe it's too early for you too."

"I'm still celebrating."

"Maybe we should stop the celebrating and get to work."

"You know who wrote me this morning?"

"Who?" Terry said, keeping an eye now on the judge's hands, an old instinct.

"You'll never guess."

Terry didn't talk. She must have stayed up late following the election results as they were published online. He imagined Kay sitting at the kitchen counter with a bottle of white wine, clicking and refreshing, clicking and refreshing all night long. Everyone was celebrating without her—she was alone, after all the work she had done. Maybe she was waiting for someone to call her and say thank you. Then she hit the send button.

"Oh," Terry said. Then, "Brother—"

"I'm not your brother."

"Johel—"

"She was my life," the judge said.

"Where is she?"

"She's gone."

"Is she—"

"They always ask me, 'How can you trust the *blan*?' And I always say, 'Terry? Like my brother, what we've been through. Man would throw himself on a hand grenade for me.'"

"It's true, Johel," Terry said. "I would."

"Throw yourself on my fucking wife."

"Where is she?"

"She doesn't want you. That's what she told me. She told me to stay away from you. She said you smelled like a pig. Had to take a bath every time she rode in the car with you."

Terry said, "Johel, I need to know from you, right now, where Nadia is."

That's the training talking, the two decades of experience, Terry thinking of the judge's big hands on her slender neck; the judge with a knife; the judge holding a pillow on her face. These things happen every day. Ordinary men snap. One man in a thousand will do something only one in a thousand will do.

"She's in the mountains. She's in Port-au-Prince. She's on the fucking moon. I told her to get out of my house, and she left."

The way he said it, Terry knew (twenty years of experience in interrogations teaches a man something) that the judge was telling the truth.

The judge started to talk, stopped. He walked over to the sink, let the water run. He washed his face, his big head. He came up from the sink looking like a lawyer who charges four hundred dollars an hour for his time.

"Brother, we've got problems, you and I, but we no longer have the same problems."

"Let me talk to her," Terry said.

"Let me tell you about your problem. As your lawyer, I'd advise you to get out of town, because if you're here in an hour, you'll be sitting in the penitentiary. They'll put you in the prison and leave you there until you rot."

"You can't do that."

"I can do whatever I want," the judge said. "I won."

———

Nadia went to her cousin's hut. She didn't know how long she would be allowed to stay: that hut was all mouths and no food, and she was bringing herself and a big belly too. In the mornings Nadia walked to the river with the girls to wash clothes and fetch water. Once, she saw Johel standing behind a tree. By the time she realized that it was only a shadow, the bucket of water she had carried up the hill had tumbled to the ground.

She was drowning when he woke her up. Before that she was on the *Trois Rivières*, where the men were eating chicken, ripping the bird apart. It was still alive. The judge's goatee was covered in grease. Terry was gnawing at a fluttering wing. The Sénateur was sucking from a bone. Ti Pierre was laughing, his face coated in feathers. The bird was gone, the men were still hungry, and Nadia knew that they would eat her next. So she jumped into the water. She felt the water pulling her down, and when she opened her eyes, her clothes were piled high across her chest: the dresses, skirts, and blouses pulled out of the wardrobe, thrown haphazardly across her. They weighed more than she expected.

She said, "What are you doing?"

Johel didn't speak. His face was rigid, as soaked from sweat as if he had stepped out of the shower. She waited for him to look at her, but he continued to throw her things on the bed with the mechanical gestures of a man seized by the *Loa*. She asked him again what he was doing, and he ignored her. His breathing was heavy.

When Johel picked up the ceramic figurine Nadia had bought for herself many years ago when Erzulie L'Amour played Boston, Nadia cried out. It was the only possession she had managed to maintain in her years of traveling. She had come to love the doll's pretty painted face and strange costume. Then he threw the doll at a spot on the wall just above her head. The doll smashed into a thousand pieces, and Nadia felt the fragments fall across her face and shoulders. She screamed, knowing that no one could hear her. Johel left the room.

Nadia lay in bed, panting heavily. Terry had installed bars on the windows, and Johel stood between her and the front door. The Fear was in the room with her: she could see the Fear's black shadow in the open armoire, smell the Fear's rotten breath, hear the Fear's ragged exhalations. Her figurine's tiny face, with its brightly painted lips and sad eyes, stared up at her from the bed.

Then Johel was back in the room. There was a look in his eyes of endless melancholy. Nadia pulled herself out of the bed and dropped to her knees. She held on to his massive bulk with all her strength. She was weeping. She knew that if he would only listen, then he would understand. But he pushed her aside. "Please," she said. "Please." He had a roll of hundred-dollar bills in his hands, and he started flipping cash on the bed. The money fluttered down on her dresses and skirts until the bed was covered in a thin layer of money. "Never tell them I didn't pay you," he said. "Everything that you deserve."

She waited for him to hit her, but the blow never came. This, in a way, was the worst thing: Nadia knew how to fight. She knew that if he came at her, she could scratch at his eyes, kick between his legs. They would fight until they were exhausted. Then he would put ice on her bruises, and she would tend his cuts. But he only stared at her. She had never seen in a man's eyes such a combination of cold contempt and profound sorrow. Nadia's mother used to say that a man who didn't have the courage to beat his woman was the man who had the courage to slit her throat.

Johel left the room, and the house was silent. Nadia waited—one minute, five, ten. Then she packed up her clothes and the money in her old suitcase. She put on a pair of jeans and laced up her sneakers. Her head was light, as if she were going to faint. But the darkness didn't come. Carrying her suitcase, she wandered through the house, through the living room to the kitchen. Johel was sitting on the terrace. She opened the door and spoke to him a minute, waiting for him to call her back. But he didn't.

Up in the village, Nadia dreamed every night about the *Trois Rivières*, about the men coming for her, about the black waters. The money Johel had given her was enough for six months, a year, maybe. She would have to live in Port-au-Prince—where would she have the baby? She imagined herself and the baby in a rented room, the rats and the mosquitoes, the open latrines. But she didn't know if she would even make it to the city. Her cousins were already asking her for money, and she couldn't say no. That was how the village worked. She felt like the cow that the *hougan* slaughtered to please the *Loa*, every eye on her waiting for the feast, the knives sharpening.

She had been in the village about a week when, just as the waters began to take her under, she heard a voice: *It's easy to swim*. It was a woman's voice. Erzulie La Sirene! Her heroine! Greatest of all the *Loa*! Mistress of men, but slave of none: a free woman, beautiful and proud. Nadia had always admired and served Erzulie for her beauty and her grace, enveloped inevitably in a cloud of perfume. She had a hint of blue in her skin from the sea; her long hair billowed in the warm waters.

Nadia reached out for Erzulie's blue hand, and just as soon as she found it, Nadia could swim too. She pushed against the water, first tentatively and then with greater confidence. Water didn't pull you down; it held you up. Nadia shed her clothes. Her lithe body planed against the water. She dove under and rose up. She arced out of the water like a flying fish and slid back in. She could stay under without breathing for as long as she needed, and when she came back to the surface, the air was clean and fresh. When she tired, when she began to sink back down into the water, she had only to reach for Erzulie and she could swim again.

Nadia followed Erzulie along the ocean bottom until they came to a ridge. It was easy to descend, and somehow, although it was very dark under the water, she could see. There, glinting ahead, balanced on a rock, swaying in the watery breezes, was the golden watch. Nadia seized it and began to swim toward the surface.

7 Micheline, the woman who cooked and cleaned for us, had heard from the judge's gardener that he had taken ill and hadn't left the house in days. Micheline was a kindly woman, who in addition to giving her vote to the judge had bestowed on him her highest epithet: "Good people." So she spent a morning preparing a plate of *poulet creole*, rice with black beans, deep-fried plantains, and a pitcher of fresh grapefruit juice. Then she assembled a hamper and asked me to take it up.

It will sound strange to say of a man of Johel's size that he looked haggard, but that was the word that came to mind when I saw him. I had never seen him, whether he was casual or formal, less than carefully dressed. Now he was wearing an old T-shirt stained by age and sweat from black to gray. He was unshaven, and his dark eyes, ordinarily so alert and splendid with intelligence, were dull and streaked with red. His smell, like ammonia, congealed sweat, and fear, made me queasy; I didn't want to shake his hand. He stumbled as he walked, caught himself, moved with effort. My first thought was that he was in the midst of a severe bout of food poisoning.

He surprised me, however, by eating all the food Micheline had prepared. He sat at the kitchen table and took huge, sloppy mouthfuls, shoveling the food in first with a fork and then with his hands, crunching on the chicken bones and sucking the marrow, mopping up the grease with plantains. He ate like a man who hadn't eaten in days, who had forgotten that there was such a thing as food. Sweat poured from his brow as he ate, and dark rings sprouted under his arms. He didn't talk, but occasionally grunted. He doctored the grapefruit juice with huge splashes of clear rum.

He sat at the kitchen table when the food was gone, as if stunned by a blow. He was breathing heavily, his pink tongue lolling over his lips. I was truly at a loss for words: no secrets to keep, no messages to pass, no stories to tell.

We might have sat in silence for five minutes or more when Johel said, "I should have stayed home."

I might have followed him down the path of self-recrimination and regret, but just then, from beyond his concrete wall, I heard two cats begin to fight in the garden. Their wailings sounded like women and children crying, and I remembered Madame Legrand in the morgue.

"Are you still going to build the road?" I asked.

That it was even in doubt—that after all the suffering and blood and work, I could even wonder about such a thing—will tell you how beaten a man he seemed.

"Road?" he said, and I knew that since Nadia walked out the door, he had not thought once of anything but Nadia, that his desire to win a seat in the Haitian Sénat was entirely extinguished, that it was a matter of indifference to him now how the citizens of the Grand'Anse transported themselves to their capital.

He poured himself another shot of rum. He had never been much of a drinker, and the liquor seemed to take him badly. He offered me a glass, but the rank smell of the raw alcohol dissuaded me.

"It feels like my head is going to explode. It just won't leave me alone," he said.

It didn't matter what I said. The judge wasn't listening to me.

"First time I saw her, I knew. Never had a feeling like that before or since. Not one person wanted to see me with her, not one. But that just made her sweeter for me."

I wanted him to be another man right then. I thought of the tens of thousands of peasants who had trudged out into the firing line to give him their vote. It was a terrible thing to see him so diminished.

"Maybe it was all destiny," I said.

I thought that word, which so many times seemed to quicken his speech and stiffen his resolve, might work a similar magic now. But he said only, "No such thing as destiny."

"What do you mean?" I protested. "Of course there's such a thing as destiny. It's what brought you back to Haiti, it's what . . ."

I struggled to think of the next item in the list. The judge's faith in his own destiny had been so superlative for so long that I had come to take it for granted. How many times in how many conversations had I told strangers about that road! It had become my purpose in Haiti also, to watch the judge fulfill his.

"Things happen," Johel said. "And then other things happen."

"Will she come back?" I asked.

That, I thought, was the only thing that could save the road.

Johel took another sip of that foul rum. His hand was trembling.

"She doesn't love me."

"Maybe she does," I said. "Women make mistakes—"

"No. She never loved me. She came back here with me because she didn't have a choice. But she didn't love me. This was just her cage."

The thing that bothered him most, he told me, was what she called him when she walked out the door. She called him *blan*.

New Year's came and went, and we waited for the judge. He didn't leave his house. Micheline was not the only woman who sent up a plate of food, but his security guard refused the plates. I tried to call him. For a few days his phone rang unanswered; then it was turned off. Nobody I knew had set eyes on the man. A rumor spread that the Sénateur had employed black magic to curse the judge. His students began to wonder if he would ever come down to campaign headquarters again, whether he would even contest the second round of the election. The Sénateur had begun his own ambitious campaign: advertisements sprang from every radio, and new posters went up. Somebody spray-painted, "Judge Blan— Judge Faggot" on the wall opposite HQ. I suspect the culprit was some- one as severely disappointed in the judge as we all were.

The only person I knew who hadn't given up hope in the judge, strange to say, was Terry. The day after the election, the Mission sent Terry to Port-au-Prince. I understand that he had no choice in the matter if he wished to remain outside the *pénitencier*. From Port-au-Prince he called me daily, wanting to know if I had heard from either Nadia or the judge. I told him I had no news from either one.

"Big Guy is taking this pretty hard," he said, as if "this" had nothing to do with him.

The tone in his voice angered me. "You broke his heart."

"He'll bounce back. What you got to understand is that this guy's got balls of steel."

Terry called me every day, and each passing day made his confidence in the judge's capacity for recuperation seem ever more fantastical. A rumor spread that the judge's security guard had found him passed out and bruised on the back terrace. Someone heard that someone had seen him wandering through town in the night, half dressed. Still Terry insisted on the judge's balls of steel.

I had all but lost hope when one of the judge's students called me: the judge had come into the office. I found him there half an hour later, dressed in his cream suit with the pink tie, a sheen of sweat on his forehead. By now there were two dozen students assembled and others were showing up every minute. He had lost weight, he was tired; his skin was an ashen gray.

But it was wonderful to hear him talk about the road. He told us that the road—a highway!—leading right out of Jérémie to Port-au-Prince would be no dirt track, but a solid tarmacked expressway, two lanes, signposted, metal barriers on the curves. It would be a broad-backed python of a road, creeping around the mountain bends before descending graciously down into the broad plains of the Département de Sud. Two hours, more or less: that's all the trucks would need to get from Jérémie to Les Cayes, then two hours more to reach Port-au-Prince. On this road would be trucks filled with mangoes, bananas, breadfruit, pineapple, avocados, and fish. That's what they were building together.

The judge stood up. I had never liked the man more or been more proud of him. Every eye was on him. He said, "Fish! In Santo Domingo . . ." Then he wobbled slightly, rolled his eyes, and vomited the contents of his breakfast across his desk, a big, ugly spray of fried spaghetti, coffee, and orange juice. The orange juice still reeked of raw rum. Then he fell over backward and collapsed on the floor.

You could tell just from his eyes, black and unreflecting, like pools of mud, that his situation was serious. The doctor at the hospital attached him to a saline line. His breathing was irregular and sharp. He was still dressed in his good shirt and cream trousers, both soaked in sweat; his face was covered in beads of sweat, and he was hot to the touch. The only doctor on service at the hospital that morning was fresh out of medical school. I took him aside to ask for details, and he told me that the judge was suffering from a combination of malaria, dengue, and exhaustion. He wasn't very sure in his diagnosis. Perhaps it was a heart attack. Or perhaps, the young doctor said, it was swine flu. Whatever the disease, there was no possibility of treatment in Jérémie, and the doctor recommended immediately transporting the judge to Port-au-Prince.

But he was in no condition to travel. The nurses set up a fan to blow over him. He floated in and out of lucidity. Once he said "Nadia."

"She's coming," I said, although I had already tried twice to call her and had no answer.

He tried to sit up, and his force failed him. He collapsed onto his back, groaning.

Out in front of the hospital, a small crowd was swelling, informed by rumor that the judge was inside and in the grip of serious illness. The crowd began to sing, "Sweet Jesus, Savior of Our Souls." Big birds circled high in the sky. In the sickroom there were at least two dozen of us.

He had lain there from morning to night when Nadia arrived at the hospital. It was well after dark. When she saw Johel, she cried out, swayed on her feet, and was caught by the bystanders. Then she sat in a chair by Johel's side, holding his hand and mopping his forehead with a damp washcloth. She spoke softly into his ear. Now his breathing was irregular and ragged. She sat by his side and massaged his arms and shoulders as he shuddered quietly. She fed him water with a spoon.

By midnight, a vast crowd had spontaneously assembled on the Place

Dumas and in the cathedral, where the faithful sat on pews and prayed. They had come on foot from every corner of the Grand'Anse, marching down the mountainsides from as far away as Gommier, Roseaux, Beaumont, Corail, Pestel, Anse-d'Hainault, even Dame Marie. Some had walked as long as a day and a night to reach Jérémie. They waited all through the night for news, telling each other stories of the time they had met the judge, the time he had settled their argument, the way he had put money in their pocket when the little one was sick. They lit candles, and no one slept except the children. Some of the men sipped *clairin*, and some of the women cried, but softly, as if the sound might carry and disturb the sick man.

Just after dawn, the cathedral bells began to toll and the town began to swell with light and a lady in a red dress sat up straight and swore she saw the Merciful Angel of the Lord.

PART EIGHT

PART EIGHT

On January 12, 2010, at 4:53 in the afternoon, Terry White was riding a desk at the Villa Privé, UNPOL HQ, two hundred meters from the Hotel Christopher. They were sending him home, but these things take time. Of all strange things, what they were after him for—after everything that happened—was the Toto Dorsemilus dossier. That felt as if it had happened to another man, it happened so long ago. That was the judge's farewell present to him, a request via the minister of justice that the dossier be reopened. So they gave him a desk at the Villa Privé and told him to sit there, and that's what he did.

Terry had called Nadia what must have been twenty times a day for a week. Sometimes the phone would ring, sometimes the phone was off. What you have to understand is that he didn't want anything from her, he never did—he just wanted to hear her voice. He knew that if she listened to him, he could make her laugh again, and if she laughed, she'd see him; and if she saw him, she'd let him hold her; and if he held her, he'd be all right.

The world had come apart so fast.

No mule had ever kicked a man harder than the judge's death kicked Terry. The way they say it knocked the wind right out of you? In his case no exaggeration at all: gripping the side of his plastic-and-felt office chair, moaning, trying to find oxygen. Eyes bulging, hand going up to his throat, heart beating two hundred times a minute trying to shuttle around the oxygen that wasn't going down the pipe. Enough time to think that he was going to have a heart attack and die too.

When he got his breath back, he wanted to go to Jérémie for the funeral: pay his respects and see Nadia. But he was scared, plain and simple. What do you call them, he wondered, those dreams you have in the daytime, as vivid as a nightmare, but eyes open. He didn't have a good word for it, but three times in two days, in the run-up to the funeral, he'd had a vision of Nadia turning to him in the cathedral, raising up this bony finger in his face, and the whole church of mourners turning on him, ripping him apart limb by limb. He couldn't chase away the fear, couldn't fight it, couldn't beat it down until the funeral had come and gone.

The day of the judge's funeral, he called Kay.

"They're burying Johel today," he said.

"I bet you feel just lousy."

"I do," he said, thinking maybe she'd talk to him, just talk.

"And you want me to tell you it's not your fault."

"Kay—"

"You want me to tell you that you had nothing to do with breaking him—"

He said, "It was a heart attack or something. Just one of those things that happen."

She said, "What do you want from me?"

"How did it all get like this?"

"You tell me, Terry. You tell me."

"I had my reasons, Kay."

"Funny thing is, I used to care."

The worst of it was that there was no one to talk to, no one who would understand. Only reason he got up in the morning and went to the office was to see faces: he couldn't take another minute alone in that hotel room. Now he was in a room with twenty other guys, each of them manning a desk, staring into space, waiting out their last few days in-country before being sent back home; and if one guy, just one, had walked over to Terry and said, *Tell me what's got you looking so troubled, my brother*, what a tale he would have told! He had seen it so many times, of course, from the other side of the desk. That desk wasn't six square feet of wood; it was like some vast abyss that separated a hopeful heart from a guilty one. Just to get across that abyss, men used to say the words to him that would put them in a cage for life. Men used to tell him their stories and then break down in tears of gratitude that he'd listened.

A week without sleep makes the dead walk: the judge kept strolling right into the Villa Privé, sitting himself right down next to Terry, looking him in the eye. Man looked terrible, but of course he was dead.

Nadia's phone was ringing, but she didn't want to talk to him. There was nothing more he could do for her. Phone was ringing all that day she was walking up into the mountains, the day Johel had put her out. Phone kept ringing all week long.

At the funeral, she saw Johel's body in the coffin, and she wanted to be buried with him. No man had ever loved her as he had. She threw herself right into the coffin to hold him one last time. He was dead, but he still smelled like Johel; his cologne was in the fabric of his dark blue suit. She felt his cold, fat flesh. She felt hands pulling at her waist, pulling her away from him, then other hands at her feet. Still she held on tight. They would never have taken her off him if she hadn't felt the baby move inside her.

The doyen of the Tribunal of Jérémie came to her in the house she had shared with Johel, just three days after she buried her husband, and sat beside her on the fauteuil and grasped her trembling hand.

"Beloved widow of my beloved friend," said the doyen, his Creole so intermingled with French that Nadia could barely understand him. "My most profound condolences."

The doyen folded his hands into fists, as if in prayer.

"But I am here this evening not to comfort your sorrows, but to add to your burdens. I address you now not as a suffering widow, but as a citizen. His sacrifice must not have been in vain."

All through that evening and the next, the doyen's plea was seconded by the requests of well-wishers and acquaintances: were the judge's place on the ballot to remain blank, the Sénateur would win by default. The road would never be built.

Nadia listened to them from some place deep inside, some place where sound arrives slowly and sight is blurry. She thought about how many lives she'd led already, and she remembered the feel of Ti Pierre's hand on her cheek, the weight of the judge's body, the smell of Terry's breath. She felt the baby kick. She wondered what choice she had but to listen to the men.

The next morning, Nadia flew to Port-au-Prince. The doyen had arranged for a lawyer to accompany her to CEH headquarters and get her on the ballot, employing whatever means were necessary. She spoke to Andrés Richard, who promised to offer her whatever resources she required. Père Samedi called to offer his condolences. He would support her candidacy also.

Nadia had a car and driver waiting for her at the airport in Port-au-Prince. The driver was a stocky, bull-necked creature with red eyes. He asked if she would mind stopping at the Caribbean Market on Delmas on the way to her hotel. His wife had just had a baby, and they needed diapers. Nadia didn't mind at all. Since Johel's death, her baby had wanted ginger. She had brewed cup after cup of spicy ginger tea, and still the baby's thirst wasn't satisfied. So she went into the supermarket to buy a can of ginger ale. That where she was on January 12, 2010, at 4:53 in the afternoon.

The Sénateur would meet that evening with the president at the Presidential Palace in Port-au-Prince, but before the meeting, the Sénateur decided to eat on the terrace of the Hotel Montana. He accompanied his steak with a good Burgundy. He ate and drank alone: he needed to think. The president was going to ask him to withdraw from the second round of the election. The foreign donors, you see—with the suspicions hanging over the Sénateur, with the disorder that had convulsed the country—here was a last sacrifice the Sénateur would make for the Haitian people. The president would protect him, see that he was not deported to the Cold Land. He would never see the inside of the Pénitencier National. A dignified retirement awaited him.

But the Sénateur was not convinced. He had lost the first round of the election, but narrowly, so very narrowly. Now that the bloated judge's strumpet widow was proposing to stand in her husband's place, the Sénateur was sure that he would win, and he was not prepared to sacrifice the accomplishments of a lifetime on the altar of the foreign donors.

The Sénateur stood up from his meal. His bladder was not what it had once been. He walked past the pool where the *blan* swam laps like deranged penguins. He wandered past the deck chairs where they bathed themselves in his people's sunshine.

A thought intruded on the Sénateur's newly resolute mind. The truth, he thought, was that he had been lucky to leave Jérémie alive. He attempted to suppress the thought, but by the time he arrived in the bathroom and unzipped his fly, the thought had returned with greater vigor: only the PNH, only the Mission had saved him. For the first time, he had seen hatred on the faces of his people. He had tried to attend, as a gesture of respect, his rival's funeral, and they had turned on him with scorn and rocks.

It was strange. His bladder had been so full, the need so pressing, but standing at the urinal, it was hard to coax out the stream. A few drops, a few more. An unaccustomed sense of weariness oppressed him. His bladder relaxed.

But hatred never bothered the Sénateur: he had suffered the hatred of his enemies before. Any man who stands for dignity will endure hatred. No, the worst was the laughter. The Mission had flown him out on the propeller plane, and behind the chain-link fence of the airport, his children had been laughing. He had served them faithfully for so many years, and now they were laughing at him. One man who not so long before had come to the Sénateur's terrace and promised him his love, kindness, and obedience shouted in a clear, carrying voice, *"Bon voyage, Sénateur!"*

Terry heard, before he felt, the rolling wave of earth moving slower than sound: bombs exploding, huge stones grinding, big trucks roaring, bulldozers digging, dump trucks smashing, cars colliding, jackhammers ripping, drums pounding, massively amplified static.

Then the first wave arrived, and the red and green and blue plastic Bics on his desk began to dance and chatter and the old serious desktop computer leaped giddily to the floor, and Terry felt a tepid wetness in his lap as a cup of cold coffee threw itself downward. Through the window he saw the solid horizon of parked vehicles and offices and palms sway at an angle.

But, Terry thought, *horizons do not sway.*

He went toward the office door. They were on the first floor. A long corridor led out to the open air. The bombs were dropping faster now, and coming closer. Terry, unbalanced and dizzy, reached for the wall, and the wall was gone. He could see through the sheared concrete the cement rods bending, twisting, deforming. He heard but did not see pieces of concrete tumbling to the ground and exploding.

The hallway was crowded with men and women sprinting toward the closed door. Terry's office was adjacent to the door; he was closest. The door swung open inward, into the hallway. He could step through the doorway and out into the parking lot or step backward into the collapsing building. If he stepped outward, the door would close behind him: the people on the inside would be trapped. Terry didn't hesitate. He swung the door open and stepped backward and out of the way, pressing himself against the corridor wall.

The walls began to roll, the floor buckled. The Sénateur held on to the ceramic urinal and clung to it with all his might. He wrestled with the writhing urinal for what felt to him like a day and a night. He felt a puddle of hotness spill out of the urinal onto his trousers. The urinal pitched left and back and forth, and then the urinal won: the Sénateur was on his back. Then the sound of an immense building collapsing just above his head, and he was in darkness, his leg crushed under something heavy from which he could not extricate himself. The Sénateur strained with his great force, but could not pull away the massive concrete pillar that pinned him to the rolling earth.

He had never feared Death, whom he saw as a fellow traveler, a companion and deliverer. His oldest friend was Baron Samedi, lord of the underworld. How many times had Baron Samedi come down the *poteau-*

mitan to inhabit his own soul. But the Sénateur had suffered a lifelong revulsion at the idea of imprisonment. Even as a child, dark and enclosed spaces had terrified him; even in the coldest winter night of exile, he had slept with the window ajar. In his will, he had commanded Dr. Philistin, the executor of his estate, to cremate his body and disperse the ashes to the hills of the Grand'Anse: no coffin for him, no concrete tomb, no marble sepulcher. He wished to be delivered into eternity on the winds of the *Gros Nord*, blowing down from the Atlantic in the north, crossing over Port-au-Prince, swirling and eddying in the gorges of his country. He would be forever like a great bird, mounting and soaring in the glens and hills, always in sight of the sea.

He felt the rising tide of panic. This was how his story was to end: trapped like a rat in glue. The dread swept up from his viscera. He was an old man. He had never been old before. He could not feel his foot or his leg, and his groin was wet with urine: the earthquake had struck midstream. How nasty to think that they would find him this way, soiled like a child. When he was young he would have simply risen up, no matter what lay across his legs, tossed the obstacle aside, and with a roar announced to Death, *This is how you come for me? Try again, old man! Try better! I am the one who shouts "Fire," not you! And I am not ready!*

Or perhaps *this* was the afterlife. Perhaps Baron Samedi had found him after all, and his old companion had deceived him. Here in the darkness was the place where zombies wandered. Had he been separated from his soul? Or was he a soul away from body? He had never been able to forget the sight, as a young man coming home from an evening of love in the mountains, of a string of zombies shuffling down a mountain path, led by a hooded *condeur*. These men had been separated from their souls: they were just animated bodies. Their souls had collapsed and been encaged in ceramic jars. Had the *boko* taken his soul also and enclosed it in a *canari*, to sell in the market, to infiltrate into the body of a cow, to make him a slave?

The panic was now total: it had him by the balls. Thank the good sweet Lord they were still attached, pulling downward toward the uncertain earth. But even the feel of his manhood in his hand was not enough to stifle his nausea. He felt himself drifting into darkness.

There was a voice crying in the darkness, the voice of a child.

On January 12, 2010, at 4:53 in the afternoon, the cereal boxes at the Caribbean Market fell down. They didn't fall one by one, but the supermarket tilted on its side and they all fell: the Special K, the All-Bran, the Wheaties, the Raisin Bran, the Chex. Then the supermarket tilted to the other side, and Nadia heard glass breaking as shelves of olive oil smashed at her feet. Then the supermarket tilted again, and the wall of sodas fell; and then the supermarket seesawed again and the massive refrigerators toppled over. Nadia began to pray. Her prayer came from the deepest recesses of her spirit, as spontaneous as a child's smile. *Lord, give me victory, give me victory. Jesus, give me victory.* She heard the sounds of the collapsing building and was aware that she was in darkness, buffeted from side to side as the reinforced concrete walls of the market buckled and gave way. Knowing that she would soon fall, she sat down, and then to protect herself from the hard-edged or sharp things flying down invisibly upon her, she huddled into a fetal position. She breathed in a cloud of dust and began to choke, but still she managed wordlessly to pray.

Only later would they comment on his heroism, the men and women Terry saved that day. They moved past him, not noticing him, not thinking in which direction the hinge of their fate had swing. Terry pressed himself up against the wall of the convulsing building. He held the door open and encouraged the people leaving to move quickly, waving at them with his free hand, knowing that to let go of the door would be to condemn others. When Rose-Marie Dessault, who worked as a secretary, stumbled at Terry's feet, he scooped her up, not gently, and pushed her through the open door.

Here were some of the people who rushed past Terry White out of the Villa Privé and into the open air: Ludmilla Voskoboynikova, from Ukraine, mother of three, on her third day on Mission, who had brought binoculars with her because she liked to watch birds; Lucner Antoine, Haitian, electrician, at the Villa Privé to replace a failing fuse box, who seduced the female members of his gospel choir; Alain Chirac, Canadian, who believed until the day of the earthquake that he was immortal; Li Chin-Yai, from China, who thought Michael Jackson understood better than any other man the intricacies of her heart; Serge Thibaut, French, who in the evenings composed his memoirs of life as a street cop in the roughest quarters of Marseilles; Michelle Rosamond, Haitian, a maid, who ran from the collapsing building still holding her mop and thinking of her six-week-old baby daughter, whom she did not know was now dead.

Terry held the door open for everyone who ran past, and for his sister also. It did not seem strange to him that Jackie was in the building, returned to her youth and beauty. Her red hair cascaded across her shoulders. When she saw Terry, she smiled at him: he was her hero. She meandered down the hallway, oblivious to the collapsing building—so typical of Jackie, who would not run to catch a plane if she was late at the airport, who had lived her whole life according to some private calendar of her own devising, arriving late and leaving all too early.

Terry was the last to leave the convulsing building. He could smell his sister's cleanliness as she pulled him into the light.

The Sénateur heard the child cry *"Maman!"* and he knew that he was alive.

"My child," the Sénateur said.

There had been a boy in the bathroom also. Now the Sénateur remembered. His mother had been waiting for him outside the door. She had said, "Are you sure you can go alone?" The boy had said, "But I'm big now, *maman!*" The boy had been sitting on the toilet when the earth attacked them.

"Come to me, child," the Sénateur said.

"But I can't see you," the boy said.

"Follow my voice."

Soon the boy was at his side. He told the boy to touch his face, and he could feel small hands wandering across his broad, bony skull. He could smell the child's hair. He could feel his heart beating. The Sénateur began to laugh. His story had not ended. His people needed him.

Life needed him. Old Baron Samedi had come for him, and he, the Sénateur, had been too tough.

Only when Nadia began to hear a woman's screams, "Jesus save me! Jesus save me!" did she realize that the thing was done. She began to crawl in the darkness, slipping and gliding through the oozing lake of oil. Something grabbed at her ankle—it was a hand attached to a body trapped under a slab of concrete—then slid off her greased limbs. She saw a distant light, wavering in the powdery clouds of dust. Past the olive oil there were pickles, which she knew by their vinegary smell. She moved steadily on her hands and feet in the direction of the light, which grew ever brighter and more distinct the closer she came to the hole in the supermarket wall. She slid over bodies and across exploded sacks of flour, found her forward progress stopped by an overturned shopping cart, a pair of hands still attached to the handle, the remainder of the body under collapsed refrigerators, writhing slightly.

Nadia slid through the hole in the wall and into the supermarket's parking lot. She blinked at the sharpness of the light. She stood up and saw that her hands and legs were red with blood, scintillating with shards of glass. The pain arrived from a distance. The others who had survived were coming out of the supermarket also. Nadia looked with a vague curiosity at their hysterical, frightened faces. She felt her baby kick and was comforted.

Nadia stood in the parking lot, breathing heavily. Her heart was leaping, bounding at her chest. Her lungs were raw. She could hear rising from every corner of the destroyed city an assortment of human voices: screams, groans, shouts, and cries. She looked at herself in the mirror of a car and began to laugh. Her face was white with flour, attached to her oily skin. She felt a greatness in her soul, a mastery such as she had never before experienced: She had lived. She had triumphed. She was not afraid.

For three days and three nights the Sénateur kept the boy alive. For three days and three nights the Sénateur never stopped talking, except when the boy slept, his small, warm body pressed close to the Sénateur's. Stories, poems, and doggerel—jokes, verse, and song—came forth from the Sénateur's tired, ragged consciousness like water from a spring. He told the boy stories of Bouki and Ti Malice.

"Krik," the Sénateur said.

"Krak," the boy said.

"He is taller when he sits than when he stands."

"I don't know."

"Think, child."

The boy began to whimper.

"A dog!"

The boy giggled as the Sénateur began to sniff like a beagle at the boy's dark curly hair. The boy giggled and relaxed.

Then the Sénateur confided in the child. He talked about politics, and a man's duty to protect his children. The Sénateur told the boy stories from his childhood, the sweetness of his first kiss, the rapture of love. He told him of everything that awaited him in manhood. He tried to teach the boy everything he knew, everything he felt was important: how to treat a woman, how to steer the *voilier* into the wind, how to compose a line of living verse.

They had no water and no food. The room was stiflingly hot and close. The Sénateur felt Baron Samedi approaching, circling, prowling, and he kept him at bay. The Baron had been working hard, but was not tired from his exertions. When the boy slept, the Baron told the Sénateur of the legions of freshly dead he had shepherded into his domain. And still the Sénateur told Death, "I'm not ready yet! Not ready! I won't cry fire!"

The boy was tiring. Now he whimpered and cried for thirst. The Sénateur told him to close his eyes and imagine a tall glass of Coca-Cola, the glass condensing. He told the boy to drink that glass of Coca-Cola and feel it filling up his empty tummy.

Later the boy would insist to his rescuers that there had been a Coca-Cola in the bathroom of the collapsed hotel. That he had drunk Coca-Cola.

And now the Sénateur could last no longer. He had kept the implacable Baron at bay so many hours, so many days. The firing squad was ready. The army had yielded: they would allow the priest to order his own execution. But they would wait only so long. There was work to be done, so many others to shoot. The Baron's patience was finite. All that the soldiers awaited was the word, and when the Sénateur—finally, after so much work and suffering, so much love and sorrow—could hear the voices of rescuers chipping at the walls of the bathroom, he cried, in a voice of command and resolution and hope, "Gentlemen, you may fire!"

PART NINE

PART NINE

I saw Terry again three years after the earthquake.

It had taken a few years longer than I expected, but I finally completed the novel I had begun in Jérémie. The work had been interrupted by the earthquake: that was too much Life and Death, too present and too intense, for me to retreat into my room and spend my days imagining. Serving no end and motivated by nothing, an earthquake is everything that fiction is not.

It was only when my wife found a new job, far from Haiti, that I was finally able to get back to work. Now my publishers were sending me on a publicity tour: twelve cities in twenty-four days, to an average audience numbering about twenty-five, average age about sixty, most of them there for the other writer on the program. But I saw cities I had never seen before, slept every night in comfortable hotel beds, and in every audience there was someone who told me that the black marks I had made on the page had helped them pass a long night or reminded them of times past or made them laugh. That's all that a writer can ask for, really.

When I posted my tour schedule on Facebook, both Kay and Terry, the one in Atlanta, the other in Miami, had promised to stop by and see me. But I was surprised that Terry, not Kay, had made the effort. I didn't notice him during the reading, but when I looked up from the table where I was signing books, there he was, an almost nervous look on his face.

I stood up and walked around the table. "Terry Fucking White," I said, and I hugged him. The last time I had seen him was on the night Johel Célestin won the first round of the senatorial election, and he had taken one hell of a bruising since then: his hair had gone gray and he was walking with a cane. A ton of concrete on your leg will do that to you. They took three days just to dig him out of the rubble—at one point the *Watsonville County Herald* reported him presumed dead. It took a week before he was medevaced out of Haiti, and the first doctor who touched him, in Santo Domingo, botched the operation. There had been some doubt whether he was going to keep the leg at all. He was in and out of hospitals for a year after the earthquake. That thing Terry always had, the almost animal quality, athletic and feral, that hinted at physical menace—that was all gone now. He suggested fragility, like you could take him in a fight. That's what made me feel such tenderness toward him, that and the memory of all the places we'd seen together and the people we'd known. And I must have reminded him of something also, because he hugged me longer and harder than I expected, the two of us standing in the Coral Gables Barnes & Noble, book buyers watching us and wondering.

Terry waited for me while I signed a couple of dozen books and shook hands and made small talk. Then we went to the Starbucks together. He got a black coffee and I ordered a double latte; then Terry pointed at a slice of chocolate cake and said, "I guess I can break the rules and get one of those too." We had a little tussle over who was going to pay, which he wouldn't let me win. But I had to carry the tray to the table while he limped on ahead.

Any two people who were in Haiti on January 12, 2010, at 4:53 in the afternoon—that's what they'll talk about first, that earthquake.

"I didn't feel it," I said.

"What the fuck do you mean, you didn't feel it?"

"I was with my wife, the two of us swimming at Anse d'Azur. Pretty big waves that day. Just didn't feel a thing. Afterward, everyone just looked at us like we were crazy when we asked what happened."

"Believe me, you didn't miss a thing," Terry said.

Jérémie suffered almost no damage in that earthquake, but we had plenty of drama nevertheless. The town was totally cut off from Port-au-Prince and the rest of the world for a while, and then the refugees arrived, tens of thousands of people made homeless in the capital. Soon my wife was transferred to the capital, where the needs were far more urgent, and we were living full-time in a city where half a million people were living in tents. That year I thought about nothing but the earthquake. I wandered through the ruined streets and asked everyone who wanted to talk to me to tell me their story. It amazed me how quickly Haitians turned this most random, most inexplicable of events into a story. It was always the same: grievance led to anger led to death. The only difference in this story was that that aggrieved party was God. But nobody could tell me what made Him so angry. I suppose I'll never get a good answer to that one.

Then Terry told me his earthquake story.

"I was dead," he said. "What you got to understand is that there are forces in this universe, and I felt them that day. People talk about God, but I just say 'forces.' Things more powerful than you."

It was strange to sit in that Barnes & Noble drinking Starbucks coffee, hearing Terry talk about his soul leaving his body and going toward the light. At the next table someone was on the phone scheduling dental surgery, and a couple of teenagers were giggling. Terry told me that he'd seen his sister walking down the hall of the collapsing building, then felt his soul rising up through the concrete. He wasn't alone: he'd been surrounded by the vast hordes of the newly dead.

"Were you scared?" I asked.

"The part of you that feels scared gets left behind. The part that feels happy too."

"But you're here now."

"I didn't want to come back. But it was like the Light was getting farther away, not closer, and then I was just lying there in the dark, my friggin' leg hurting like hell."

I asked him how the experience had changed him.

"Before, I used to believe in God, you know? I'd talk to the Old Man before bed, think He was looking out for me. But all those people who died, they weren't talking to Him? Those kids that died—their parents weren't asking Him to keep them safe? I guess what that experience taught me is that He's got his plan, and what we want doesn't count for shit in it. We're just along on His ride."

What got Terry through the year after the quake, he told me, was Kay. She was by his side the whole year he was in and out of the hospital. He'd had seven surgeries, and after each and every one, she'd been the first face he'd seen on waking up. Then, a year after the earthquake, when Terry was finally able to walk and take care of himself, she told him that she was moving to Atlanta alone. There was no rancor, no anger, no meanness on either side. "She gave me more than she owed me," Terry said. "You can't ask for anything more than that."

By now Terry and I had been sitting for the better part of an hour. We didn't have much more to talk about. Had Terry asked, I might have told him about life in the Sahel, or about the book that sat on the table between us. I had yet to sign it; I doubted he would ever read it. The conversation began to flag, and Terry revived it, telling me about his job (he was a consultant to a company that did security at twenty-three Florida malls) and trying to talk politics, both American and Haitian. He asked if I wanted another cup of coffee. I was starting to wonder just why he had come to the mall that afternoon, whether he had simply been lonely.

I was just about to excuse myself—I had a flight out early the next morning—when he asked if I had any news about Nadia.

The look on Terry's face made me understand why he had hobbled out to the Barnes & Noble to see me.

I had followed Nadia's career after the earthquake, but at a distance. She was four months pregnant when the earthquake hit, and that spring she gave birth. The second round of the senatorial election had been, of course, postponed: it took almost a year before the state and the international community could organize the event. When the election was finally held, Nadia rarely said more than a few words on the campaign trail, just waved to the crowds or sang. Her campaign slogan was, "Let's build his dream." Haitian electoral law allowed the Sénateur's political party to replace him with another candidate, but the result was a foregone conclusion: Nadia won her seat easily.

I only saw her once more. It was in Port-au-Prince, at the Boucan Grégoire. She had been in office three months or so. She was seated at a table with Madame Mireille, the onetime presidential candidate, and a number of other important members of the Haitian political elite. I couldn't hear what they were talking about, but the conversation at one point grew animated: the men were waving their arms, and Madame Mireille was shaking her head furiously. Then Nadia said something. Whatever she said captured the attention of the whole table. I spent an hour watching her, the way you watch anyone who has a natural talent for something. But just watching her was enough for me. I didn't say hello, and I don't know if she noticed me.

I told Terry that little story. I didn't think it would really satisfy him. Then he told me that he had gone to see her just a couple of months ago.

Terry first heard the rumors when he was in the hospital in Miami. This was about six months after the earthquake, his third time under the knife. A time of terrible pain for Terry: not just the leg and pelvis (which felt like it was crushed between black iron pincers) but searing soul pain. Not a day passed when he didn't think of the judge, when he didn't miss Nadia, when he didn't think about rising to the Light and being cast out again into the world of things and regret. He'd made two promises in his life—one to Kay and another to Johel—and had broken both of them. He wondered if he'd been sent back just to feel the pain.

After the surgery Terry went into physical therapy. His PT was a Haitian immigrant, body in Florida but soul still down in the old country—not that different from Terry, really. The PT was good, moving Terry's body, all the while following the train of Terry's thought where naturally it led: to the judge, to Nadia, to the situation on the island. Like a lot of Haitian expats, the PT followed the situation back home closely. There were dozens of Creole chat rooms where obsessives could toss around the latest rumors, gossip, and innuendo, everyone churning themselves up into a political frenzy. All the major Haitian newspapers were published online. And if that wasn't enough, Twitter had caught on big in Haiti. So the PT, who hadn't been home in years, knew the situation almost as well as Terry did.

That was the first time Terry heard the story about Nadia and Johel. He said, "It's not true." His whole body stiffened under the PT's hands, as if the therapist had twisted a nerve: the PT had to take a break and let Terry sweat the pain off. But Terry remembered what the PT said, the old Creole proverb: "There's no such thing as a natural death in Haiti."

After that, Terry started haunting the chat rooms himself.

The real inside dirt was all in Creole, but the written language was hard to understand, and Terry would spend hours sitting at his laptop, puzzling out what people were saying. He started following Nadia's career obsessively. He followed her election, her rise to prominence in the *sénat*, her alliance with the new president, himself a former musician. Terry read that several months after the installation of the new government, the long-delayed Memorandum of Understanding with the government of Canada allowing for the construction of a new road had been approved. Nadia was present at the signing. None of that exactly surprised him: she'd always given the judge shrewd counsel, and he'd known she was no fool. But if Terry was honest with himself, he never really imagined anything like that happening. And wherever he went on the Internet, there was always the same story.

When Kay moved up to Atlanta, she told Terry that Haiti was finished for her. And one reason she was leaving him was the way Terry was obsessing over the Internet. She knew it was never going to be finished for him. But Terry knew that wasn't exactly right. He knew that Haiti would be finished for him when he knew the truth.

Terry went down to Haiti unannounced. That was something he knew from two decades' experience in law enforcement: you want to talk to the suspect at the time and place of your own choosing. So he flew down on American Airlines, Miami to Port-au-Prince, with the missionaries and the aid workers and the diaspora coming home, then took a taxi over to the domestic airport, where he bought himself a ticket on the afternoon flight to Jérémie.

The next morning, Terry sat outside the judge's house in Calasse with the regular folk who came to see Sénateur Célestin and ask her for favors. The women wore clean, neatly pressed dresses, and the men were in good dark suits. A mason had filled in the bullet holes that had pockmarked the cement wall, but the fresh yellow paint, not bleached by sun or rain, showed where the damage had been done.

There were half a dozen plastic chairs in front of the house. They were all full, but a young man noticed Terry's cane and saw the beads of sweat on his face and bounded to his feet. Then Terry sat with the sun on his face, thinking of an afternoon he'd spent here a few months after he'd started working with the judge. Johel had an old football in the closet, and he and Terry had started tossing it around in the courtyard, right where Terry was sitting now. He was surprised what a clean, tight spiral the judge could put on the ball. Then Nadia showed up, and the three of them had started horsing around together. Because the courtyard of the house was narrow, they'd gone out onto the dirt road to have a little more space, and as will happen in Haiti, there were soon a dozen neighborhood kids playing with them. At first it was the adults against the kids; then Nadia, not so long out of girlhood herself, drifted away from Terry and the judge's squad. Terry and the judge tried to explain to her and the kids the complicated rules of American football, but the only thing anyone really understood was throw the ball, catch the ball, and run with the ball—but that was enough for a good time . . .

Then Nadia's bodyguard said *"Blan."* Terry stood up gingerly. He could feel shimmering ripples of pain running through his leg. He was glad for the feeling, distracting him from his nervous stomach.

The house was just the way Johel had left it, right down to the portrait of the judge in his judicial robes on the living room wall. The judge's family stared somberly from their silver frames; the judge's books filled the judge's bookshelves. Nadia was standing at the window, speaking on the phone. He saw the familiar back and muscled shoulders, but the straight shoulder-length hair was from another woman. Then she turned, and Terry fell, as if diving cleanly from a great height, into her sea-green eyes.

Neither of them spoke for a minute. Terry had thought that by presenting himself unannounced, he would have the advantage of surprise. But he had not counted on his own emotions. Nadia stumbled backward when she saw him, as if an invisible hand had pressed lightly on her shoulders. Then her face—unlined, unchanged—broke into a smile, and she ran to Terry, throwing herself—warm, fragrant, soft, alive—into his arms. Nadia was light, but the weight of her arms on his shoulders was enough to make him grunt with pain.

She said, "It's you."

"It's just me," Terry said. "It's just me."

Never let her go, Terry thought. *The past is under the rubble and bricks.* Terry felt her breathing and her heartbeat, and he thought, *This is all that's real, the past is like the dead—who wants to dig up those rotting bones?*

"They told me you were dead," she finally said.

She must have asked someone to look Terry up on the Internet and then stopped after the first link. Terry thought about those first weeks after the earthquake, when to see a familiar face was to see someone who had come back from the dead, when everyone was a presumed ghost.

"Not dead," he said. "Just in Florida."

Nadia stepped back.

"Then why you never call?" she asked. "I needed you."

Now it was Terry's turn to lie. "Johel told me to leave you alone. He comes to me in my dreams. And he told me to stay away."

Nadia sat on the couch. She invited Terry to sit beside her, but the high cushions were too painful for his back, so he took the judge's armchair. That's where Johel used to sit and watch football, and even now the imprint of the big man's body was in the cushions. Sitting in his chair felt like wearing the dead man's clothes. Nadia smiled, but it was no longer that first smile of pure joy. Now she has started to wonder why Terry has come back from the dead to visit her. People came to her all day and wanted something. The poor came and wanted enough to eat. The rich came and wanted to be richer. There was only one person on the planet who wanted to see Nadia because of the thing she is. She kept Johel's son in Port-au-Prince, in a house surrounded by a high wall, topped with barbed wire, and protected by a man with a shotgun.

But Terry knew about this secret place, this region of vulnerability. He asked about little Johel.

"He looks like his daddy," Terry said, thumbing through the pictures on Nadia's phone. There is no doubt—none at all—about who this chubby, round-faced child's father is.

"He's smart like his daddy," Nadia said. "He can almost read."

Terry said, "He used to worry about you, you know. I always said, 'Don't worry about Nadia. She can take care of herself.' But he made me promise to take care of you, come what may."

When Terry had walked into the room and felt her skin against his own, he had wavered. Truth never loved Terry, never slept on his chest; he never wanted Truth with every fiber of his being. Truth never took Terry's hand under the tablecloth and squeezed it. Truth never looked over her shoulder at Terry. But when Nadia broke off her embrace, Terry knew, come what may, that he was frightened of Truth. Twenty years of experience and interrogation had taught Terry that Truth was a lady who wouldn't take no for an answer.

"Do you ever dream about him?" Terry asked.

Nadia shook her head. Sometimes she dreamed of the men throwing the golden watch on the *Trois Rivières*, and sometimes she dreamed of the Caribbean Market, wandering through the collapsed corridors in blackness. On those nights, if she was in Port-au-Prince, she pulled her baby out of his crib where he was sleeping and put him in bed with her. But she never dreamed about Johel.

Terry said, "I talk to him sometimes in my dreams, just like I'm talking to you. And he's been telling me now to keep his boy safe."

Now Terry's training and experience have taken over. The Reid technique is a scientific procedure. It has been tested in tens of thousands of interrogations. Terry knew to keep his eyes focused on hers, and he knew how to let the silence talk for him. He kept his body as still as a statue.

If Nadia wanted Terry to leave, she only had to say so. She had two strong men on the other side of the door. If Terry resisted, they would throw him into the street. But the idea never crossed her mind. She was thinking of the boy: she knew what it was to be helpless, to be beaten, to be hungry.

"Nadia, Johel wants to keep that boy safe. And I want to keep that boy safe too. That means keeping you safe. But I can only keep you safe if I know the truth. And I know that you killed him."

Nadia opened her mouth. She wanted to tell him that it wasn't true. That was what the suspect always tries to say.

But Terry said, "Let me talk now. You can talk later. But I know for a fact what happened."

Now anything could happen. Nadia's phone could ring, the guard could knock at the door, and the moment would be lost. Then Terry would never know the truth. But nothing happened. Sometimes Terry will tell a suspect that they were captured on a surveillance camera. Sometimes he'll talk about a witness, or endotriglyceride levels. Today he talked about his dreams.

The café at which Terry and I sat in the Coral Gables Barnes & Noble was directly adjacent to the fiction department, in whose aisles a few dedicated members of my tribe sat cross-legged on the floor or stood balanced on one leg like fragile birds. By now afternoon had passed to evening. Darkness had fallen and the plate glass windows reflected only the bookstore's light. The air was thick with stories. At other tables, people read stories or told stories on their phones or sat at their laptops and typed out stories of their own.

It is nonsense, of course, that stories make us live: that is the precinct of a sufficient number of calories, of protein, of vaccinations and antibiotics, of clean air, safe water, solid shelter, and, as Johel Célestin understood, of good roads; for life you need money. But I learned in Haiti that stories, if not a necessity, are not a luxury either. Only the rich and the lucky can afford to live without stories, for without stories, as every Haitian peasant knows, life is all just things that happen to you, and you are just something that happens in the lives of others. The highbrows may snoot, as they will, but by my lights, a good story is the greatest of all literary inventions, the only realm in our existence where for every "Why?" there exists a commensurate "Because . . ." Those two words, "why?" and "because," might be the best thing our species has going for it.

And so we follow that trail, leaping across the terrifying abyss and landing on those strong stones until, just beyond the last "because," there is, as every Haitian knows, something sublime—so close that you can touch it, so near that you can smell it, so hot that it can burn you.

Not even Terry knows which story is true.

The first story Terry tells Nadia is the story he has read in the chat rooms, the story Nadia's enemies are whispering. It is the story of an ambitious man and an even more ambitious woman. Terry talks about a man who loved a woman with a rare love, who gave up everything he had for her: another woman, his home, his career. When did she first poison him? When he fell in love with her? When did she realize that she was smarter than the man? When did it occur to her that the crown was within her reach? Did she lie in bed and imagine herself dressed in a widow's weeds, the mournful crowd hushed, every tear a thousand votes?

How easy it was for such a woman to find the *boko*. How easy it was for such a woman to wait for the right moment: after the first round of the election, before the second. How easy it was for such a woman to slip the *coup poud'* in the judge's drink. How easy it was for this woman to cry.

But there are two stories; there are always two stories. The only difference between the stories is that we can live with one story and not the other. Innocence is never an option.

So Terry tells the other story. It is the story of a woman who had no choices, a woman who had no passport and no visa. This was a story of a woman just trying to get by—and the good Lord knows, getting by isn't a sin. This was the story of a woman who had never lived free a moment in her life, passed from man to man like a donkey or chattel, until she finally found herself in a cage with only one key, a terrible key. There were *loup-garou* in that cage with her. She didn't want to turn that key. She turned to Terry first to keep her safe in the cage; he couldn't. She begged, she pleaded with him to give her a visa; he wouldn't. Then she discovered something to live for, something more important than herself. And still she wouldn't turn the key until she had no choice, none at all.

Maybe she had prepared, just in case, visiting the *boko* when Johel wouldn't listen to her. Maybe she had what she needed tucked in a corner of her valise. Maybe that terrible morning when Johel hardened his heart to her, when he wouldn't listen to her story . . . A woman like that—who can blame her? Who can blame her for defending herself, her baby? Who can blame her for wanting freedom, for wanting what every man, woman, and child is owed by the good Lord? Who can blame her for wanting to live?

Not even Johel could blame her, says Terry. You have time to think in the Other Land across the Sea, time to reflect on your sins. Johel understood now that she had no choice. Johel understood his sins.

Now Terry waits. He knows the moment is ripe. He can see that Nadia wants to tell him the truth. He knows that she understands the gravity of her crime, that she has thought of nothing else since the moment she acted. He knows that human beings, sinful as they are, strive for goodness. He knows that human beings want to confess. They want to tell the truth and be forgiven.

And so, when Nadia looks at him, and says, "I want only to be free," he says what he always says.

He says, "I understand."

AUTHOR'S NOTE

ACKNOWLEDGMENTS

AUTHOR'S NOTE

I have taken liberties with the details of recent Haitian history. Attentive readers will know, for example, that there were no elections in the weeks preceding the earthquake. I am not I, you are not you, and my Mission is certainly not MINUSTAH, the Mission des Nations Unies pour la stabilisation en Haïti. Nothing that I have written here should be taken as true in the journalistic sense of the word: the characters, scandals, and successes depicted in these pages are all products of my imagination.

There are other scandals associated with MINUSTAH that I have not written about. Certainly the gravest is the introduction of the bacterium *Vibrio cholerae* by Nepalese peacekeepers into the Meille River. The resultant cholera epidemic has killed at least ten thousand Haitians. The crystal waterways of the Grand'Anse, when I knew them, were so clean that villagers drank river water without undue concern. I remember bathing happily in the Roseaux River. No one would dare do such a thing nowadays.

My spelling of Haitian Creole is unorthodox. I have decided to spell Haitian Creole as I have both because the currently accepted spelling of Creole is so ugly on the page, and to allow Francophone readers a firmer toehold into this wonderful but inaccessible language.

I have translated Avocat Noé Fourcand's speech from the words of the historical Noé Fourcand, quoted in Arthur Rouzier's *Les belles figures de l'intelligentsia jérémienne du temps passé—et du présent*. This is the finest introduction to the lost poets of Jérémie.

ACKNOWLEDGMENTS

This book could not have been written without the generous assistance of the Mrs. Giles Whiting Foundation and the American Academy of Arts and Letters.